The Pastoral $

C000005252

The Pastoral Symphony

By Tess Alps

To Indra & Charlie,
Love Tess.

YOUCAXTON
PUBLICATIONS

Copyright © Tess Alps 2021

The Author asserts the moral right to
be identified as the author of this work.

ISBN 978-1-914424-09-0
Published by YouCaxton Publications 2021
YCBN: 01

All rights reserved. No part of this publication may be reproduced,
stored in a retrieval system, or transmitted in any form or by any
means, electronic, mechanical, photocopying, recording or otherwise,
without the prior permission of the author.

This book is sold subject to the condition that it shall not, by way of
trade or otherwise, be lent, resold, hired out or otherwise circulated
without the author's prior consent in any form of binding or cover
other than that in which it is published and without a similar condition
including this condition being imposed on the subsequent purchaser.

YouCaxton Publications
www.youcaxton.co.uk

For Tim, Tom and Joanna.
And in memory of my mum, Kay.

Acknowledgements

The final part of the Beethoven trilogy ends the journey that began with a lucky encounter with the wonderful Kate and Greg Mosse who encouraged me to believe I could write. They introduced me to the late revered literary agent, Felicity Bryan, who gave me so much valuable advice. I thank all three from the bottom of my heart; without them I would never have had the confidence to start and hope that I have now served my writing apprenticeship.

I also would like to thank Bob Hellon, my English teacher at high school who inspired me to study literature and introduced me to many writers who sustain me still. Thank you to Bob Fowke, my tolerant and generous editor and publisher, who has held my hand through this fascinating but challenging process. I must also thank the friends and family who read it in its less polished state and shared their thoughts, particularly my Irish relatives who did their best to prevent too many howlers. Finally, I am indebted to my husband, Tim, who has not only supported and encouraged me as I have written the trilogy but has been my indispensable advisor on all musical matters.

I read widely as background to the story but I would like to acknowledge the debt I owe to a few books in particular:

Modern Ireland 1600-1972

R.F. Foster (Penguin)

Founded on Fear
Peter Tyrell edited by Diarmuid Whelan (Transworld Ireland)

Survivor: a true story of survival
R.F. Heeney (CreateSpace,
Independent Publishing Platform)

Ada English; Patriot and Psychiatrist
Brendan Kelly (Irish Academic Press)

The Collected Poems of WB Yeats
WB Yeats (Wordsworth Poetry Library)

What Happened First

The Pastoral Symphony is the final volume of a trilogy.

The Harp Quartet - Book One of the Beethoven trilogy
This covers the years 1916-1920 where we are introduced to the talented violinist, Hannah McDermott, her sister Stasia and her Rowanbridge family. We follow her to the Maple Academy in Dalkey, where she finds friends and lovers, eventually marrying John Fitzgerald. After many pregnancy difficulties, the book ends with the birth of their first child, Cathy.

The Moonlight Sonata - Book Two of the Beethoven trilogy
This covers the years 1924 – 1951. We see the world through Cathy Fitzgerald's eyes; she enjoys an idyllic childhood despite the Depression until tragedy changes her life forever. We follow her to Dalkey and then to England where she joins the war effort as a nurse. After a twelve-year banishment, she is eventually invited back to Rowanbridge by her mother, Hannah, where she reconnects with her three siblings and learns the secrets that have shaped her family so profoundly.

What readers have said:

About *The Harp Quartet*

'…it wears its historical, musical and literary research lightly and is an engaging, immersive and authentic romantic novel…'

'…I have thoroughly enjoyed reading this book which is beautifully written. The storyline and the settings kept me entranced…'

'A gorgeous read, full of finely drawn characters, love, family, friendship, music, and Irish history, and a feisty heroine whom you root for from her first moment of rebellion.'

'Warm-hearted, wise and highly entertaining The Harp Quartet is a fantastic holiday read which will leave you desperate to get your hands on the next two novels in the trilogy.'

About *The Moonlight Sonata*

'Despite their very human flaws, you cannot help but love Alps's finely drawn characters and the stories of their lives, all of it framed in Irish history and culture…'

'It's entertaining, engrossing and a real page-turner. I couldn't put it down. It's got family drama, love, passion, feuds and friendships with a backdrop of music and poetry…'

'She writes with great fluency and eloquence and one is quickly swept up into her world…'

'…there are some unexpected cards revealed in Cathy's game of life and we become absorbed as she manoeuvres herself through triumph and disaster…'

Chapter 1 – July 1951

Cathy remembered the kiss like it was yesterday. Cheese and onion. A delicious first kiss from Sam McCarthy after he had shared his sandwich with her; she was just thirteen and Sam a year older. And he had taught her to ride a bike. What an all-round lovely fella he was, though, to be fair, it had hurt a little to see him kissing Marion Magee the summer after. Now he was kissing her sister Rose, celebrating their engagement, their families gathered around them in the house where Cathy and Rose had been born and raised, and their mother before them.

The last time they had all been together, three weeks ago, had been a very different occasion. They had been saying goodbye to Hannah, mother of Cathy, Rose, Fergus and Bridie, after her death from breast cancer.

'Everyone, please raise your glasses to toast the engagement of my sister, the beautiful Rambling Rose Fitzgerald, to Sam the Man McCarthy.' Fergus was addressing the room with a confidence that belied his mere twenty years' existence. 'To Rose and Sam.' Everyone stood, cheered and took a swig.

Cathy looked around. Here were all her relations, the biological ones at least. Her Aunt Stasia seemed composed but subdued, sitting next to Uncle Edmund, surrounded by the Apostles, as Aggie had dubbed Stasia's four sons. After a lifetime of squabbling and needling her sister, Stasia looked emptily bereft.

They had all been hit hard by Hannah's death, but she had insisted from her deathbed that Rose and Sam must get on with their life and announce their engagement without delay. Even from beyond the grave, Hannah was not someone easily disobeyed. Cathy smiled watching Fergus wrap his strong, generous arm around their half-sister Bridie's shoulders, the pair looking for all the world like twins with their dark, unruly curls.

There was a secret that explained their striking similarity; unknown to Fergus, Bridie was actually his full sister. Cathy had only found out when her mother confessed on her deathbed, along with other long-hidden secrets, but Auntie Stasia had known since before Bridie was born and had conspired in its cover-up. Cathy had barely come to terms with this revelation; it challenged so much of what she had believed and done since Fergus's birth. Most of all, it tormented her that her and Rose's beloved Daddy had also known that Fergus had not been fathered by him – that his wife had been unfaithful – and it was impossible not to conclude that this had contributed to his depression and subsequent suicide. Certainly, Hannah had been convinced that her infidelity had driven John to take his life; her guilt had grown into a monstrous burden that no number of penitent prayers had lightened. Cathy's childhood had been blissful until that dreadful day when her father was brought home dead. Then everything had changed.

But now was not the time to dwell on past betrayals and tragedies. This was a happy occasion. Rose and Sam deserved a lifetime of happiness, full of hugs and kisses and babies - *and* cheese and onion sandwiches. Sam would treasure Rose and Rose would cherish Sam. Cathy wished she could have experienced a long and contented marriage herself but a cornered Nazi sniper had put paid to that, snatching away her husband, Joe, at the fag end of the war.

'Mama, can I have some more lemonade?'

Cathy turned to her golden-haired son, Johnny, holding up his empty glass. She and Joe had shared no more than fifty nights in the same bed during the war but they had still miraculously created this precious child together. Cathy stroked Johnny's silky hair, so like her own and her father's.

'Of course, my love, but just half a glass. Aggie will pour you some. Go on, don't be shy.'

Johnny walked hesitantly over to where Aggie, the family's faithful housemaid for the last forty years, was standing guard over all the drinks. Johnny had only just met all these people, his family, yesterday when he and his Mama had been driven down to Rowanbridge from Dublin in his Great-great-aunt Lily's car. One day, he resolved, he would have a car as luxurious and leathery as Lily's but he would drive it much faster than Slattery.

'Now then, young man. What can I do for you? Would you like some Guinness, or a drop of whiskey maybe?' Johnny wasn't sure whether Aggie was joking or not.

'Could I please have some more lemonade. Just half a glass, Mama says.'

'Oh, stuff and nonsense. Don't listen to your mother. You can have as much as you can pour down your throat. It's not every day that you get to meet your long-lost family, is it?' Aggie knelt down beside the young boy. 'We've waited seven long years to meet you, Johnny, so I think we can break all the rules today.'

Johnny took a sip from his brimming glass. He wrinkled his nose.

'The bubbles make me want to sneeze.'

Aggie laughed and ruffled his hair. "Oh, little man, you have no idea what joy you would have brought to your poor dead granny and grandpa if only they could have met you. You know that you're named after your Grandpa John, don't you?'

'Yes. Mama told me. I've got another granny you know, who's not dead. I haven't met her either, but she writes to me and sends me presents. And so does my Auntie Shirley.'

'Yes, your Granny Ashfield in England. I know about all these things.'

'This granny, the one who lived here, never wrote to me or sent me anything.'

'Oh, Johnny love. You must wonder why, I'm sure, but it's a long story. Grown-ups can be very daft you know. Very stubborn. One day you'll understand. But you knew your great-granny very well, didn't you?'

'Yes, we came to live with her. In her school. And she taught me to play the piano. But she died too.'

'Mrs Fitzgerald. I only met her the once, Johnny, on a very sad occasion, but I heard a lot about her. She was a very clever lady, I was told, like her son, your wonderful Grandpa.' Aggie searched Johnny's face hoping to find strong evidence of his Irish ancestry. His grandfather John was unmistakably there in his fair hair and blue eyes but where was his Grandma Hannah? And maybe that straight nose came from his English Daddy? Aggie had saved all the rejected photos that Cathy sent to her mother over their long years apart and Joe Ashfield was in quite a few.

'Here's your Uncle Fergus now.'

'Now then, Johnny, would you like to come with me to see some baby chicks,' offered Fergus. 'And tomorrow I'll take you to see the calves. They're over at the big farm.'

Johnny handed Aggie his empty glass and took Fergus's proffered hand.

Cathy watched the pair leave the room and smiled. It wouldn't take Johnny long to get to know his relatives. Children were amazingly adaptable. But she wasn't sure whether her own fractured heart, after twelve years' enforced absence from the family home, would ever heal.

Cathy looked around the familiar drawing room. Little had changed: the piano, which she had been taught to play by her Daddy, still stood in the corner and there was the tapestry fireguard, which Cathy had heartlessly allowed toddler Bridie to fall into when she should have been looking after her. Bridie still bore the small scar on her temple and it gave Cathy a stab of guilt every time she saw it. Why had she been so mean to an innocent little child? The reason was standing over in the corner: Tricky Byrne, her mother's second husband.

Cathy had spent her childhood in fear of Tricky. She had thought him a dirty, shifty, sinister tramp, lurking in the fields by Cromwell's Tower doing disgusting things, when he was actually the elder son of the richest family in Rowanbridge, albeit one who declined to live up to the role. Her mother and Tricky had been strange allies from their teens; he was silently devoted to her and she was protective of him. When Hannah had announced to Cathy that she was going to marry Tricky, soon after her father committed suicide, Cathy had been repulsed at the idea. And her revulsion had increased when her mother immediately became pregnant. The combination of grief and fear had twisted themselves into a fantasy that Tricky had murdered her poor father in order to climb into her mother's bed.

These feelings had poisoned Cathy's perception of baby Bridie – how could she love the offspring of the man who had killed her father and taken his place? But her dying mother had finally nailed that delusion. Tricky had only married Hannah to save her reputation and he had never shared her bed. Hannah was pregnant by a different man altogether, one who could never marry Hannah or publicly admit paternity of his two children, Bridie and Fergus. And that man was in the room too, chatting with Great-aunt Lily, glass of whiskey in hand. He was Father Stephen, Rowanbridge's priest.

'Cathy, I was just telling Father Stephen what a wonderful job you've made of updating and expanding the Maple Academy.' Lily was beckoning Cathy to come over and join them. 'She has a very sound business head on her you know, Stephen, just like her mother, who rescued all the businesses here after John's death. He had allowed them to go to rack

'Was this your bedroom when you were little?'

'No, I had the room I'm in tonight and Rose was next door. This is Fergus's bedroom. See his hurleys in the corner. We were a long way from our parents' bedroom, the other side of the drawing room. They got peace and we got freedom to lark about.'

'Why do they have their drawing room upstairs, Mama?'

'There's a big pub on the ground floor so there's a lot of space in the house above it. When I was little, my Daddy would wake me up by putting a record on the old gramophone in there. Much nicer than an alarm clock. Then I knew I could go into their bedroom. And sometimes we would all dance about like loons until Aggie shouted up to stop the herd of elephants cracking the ceiling.'

'I like hearing all the stories about when you were little and about my granny and grandad, and all my relatives. Uncle Fergus says he'll take me to the big farm tomorrow to ride on a tractor.'

'That'll be fun, my love. He's a great farmer, Fergus, like my Grandad James. Rose says he's a natural. Not like your Grandpa John who hated working on the land.'

'Would *my* Daddy have been a good farmer?'

'Well, your Daddy was very strong and hard-working but he didn't live in the countryside so I don't know whether he would have liked being a farmer. His family were all miners and went under the ground to dig coal. He joined the army to make sure he didn't have to do that himself. Maybe he would have loved being a farmer if he'd had the chance.'

Johnny snuggled down in the bed holding Tiny Ted tightly to him. 'Can I go and meet my Granny Ashfield one day? And Auntie Shirley? She made Tiny Ted for me, didn't she, and I love him.'

'She did, precious. Night night now. I promise you we'll go to England as soon as I can find the time, and when I've bought a car. Give me a kiss.' But Johnny was already asleep. Cathy kissed her son's pale cheek and smoothed the sheets before taking away the oil lamp, leaving the door ajar so that a sliver of electric light would cast a little comfort in the unfamiliar house.

Aggie and Rose were already on Cathy's bed. Rose held out a glass for her. 'It's gin and lime, madam. The best we culchies can offer you sophisticates.'

'That'll do nicely.'

'It's a tart's drink, you know. Give me a glass of Tullamore Dew any day.' Aggie, cradling a very full glass, kicked off her shoes and stretched out. 'Aah, that's good.'

'Well, on our wedding day, I won't let you do a thing, Aggie. You'll be the guest of honour and be waited on and we'll call you "Agnes".'

'Jeezus no. That's what Stasia always called me when she was eating the head off me.'

'When do you and Sam have in mind, Rosie?' asked Cathy.

'We thought next Easter.'

'Too feckin' cold,' objected Aggie. 'Make it May or June when the flowers are out.'

'I don't want to wait any longer than I have to. Sam is thirty-three and I'll be twenty-four next February. Practically an old maid and I've never made love to anyone. I can't imagine how exciting it'll be being in the same bed as Sam.'

'I wish you both happiness and a long marriage sharing a bed with someone you love.' Cathy clinked glasses with Rose. 'Neither Aggie nor I managed it.'

'And we've managed fine.'

'You maybe, Aggie. But I'd love to have someone to share a bed with. Not that I'm exactly lonely in Dalkey – how could I be when the school's packed with students? Ellen and Aoife are there and Seamus calls in most days and Johnny's at my side every other minute. But it's not the same.'

'So, it's just the sex you're after? I've told you, you can have as much as you like without needing to tie yourself down. You just have to go and look for it. I could still get myself laid, even at my age, just by going into the bar any night and chatting to the ugly ones. They're grateful for anything they can get. Though maybe even I will struggle soon. I'll be sixty-three next birthday, you know.'

'Just keep the lights off, Aggie.' Cathy dodged the pillow hurled at her. 'It's not *just* the sex. It's being so close to someone you know what they're thinking, so close that you can utterly rely on them to look after you whatever happens. Someone you can share the good things with, and the bad.'

'Anyone in mind, Cathy?' Rose leaned forward to look her sister in the eye.

Cathy laughed. 'No, not at all.' Cathy was being less than honest. 'I shall have to add some extra criteria when I'm next interviewing for teachers. Enough about me and my non-existent love life. Have Fergus and Bridie started dating yet?'

'Nothing serious,' said Rose. 'Fergus would be spoiled for choice; everyone loves him and he loves everyone back. Bridie has had a couple of fellas hanging around, just dances and the pictures. She's set her sights on bigger things. Not like me; I'm more than happy to stay in Rowanbridge, marry a local boyo and stay in the family home. But Bridie wants to go to university and become a lawyer.'

'And she's clever enough. Tricky has obviously got bigger brains than you'd credit,' Aggie threw Cathy a look. Both of them knew full well that Tricky's genes had nothing to do with Bridie's intellect.

'Aggie, I'm not stupid and neither is Cathy. Mammy has gone now, so can we just be honest.' Rose stood up to face them. 'It's obvious that Father Stephen is Bridie's father, and Fergus's too, probably. I know you know the truth, Aggie. It's time to share. We can take it, can't we Cathy?'

Cathy stood up and hugged her sister. 'You're right, Rose. But I already know it to be true because I got it from Mammy's own mouth just before she died.'

'And you didn't tell me?'

'I would have done in time, Rosie, honest. Mammy made me promise not to tell Fergus and Bridie, for Tricky and Stephen's sake as much as anything, but she didn't ask me not to tell you. But I had to go straight back to Dublin after the funeral so there was no chance – not something I fancied sharing over the phone.'

'How long have you known, Aggie?'

The housemaid shifted uncomfortably on the bed and took a long swig of whiskey. 'Since soon after your Daddy died. I'd had my suspicions before, mind – I'm not stupid either. When your mother got pregnant, she told me everything. I wanted her to get rid of it. There's a woman in Thomastown but she wanted to get it done in Dublin by a posh doctor. That's when she told Stasia, because she needed cash, but Stasia came up with the plan for her to marry Tricky and pass off the baby as his. Tricky was more than obliging and Hannah agreed. The timing was a bit bloody tight though.'

'Auntie Stasia knows? Christ almighty, how many people are in on this?'

'More than is wise, Rosie. By my reckoning, it's now at least seven: you and me, Aggie, Tricky, Auntie Stasia and Uncle Edmund plus Father Stephen himself obviously. And, who knows, maybe plenty of others have guessed. I'm sure you'll tell Sam. I can remember all the village gossip when Bridie was born, how she must have been a honeymoon baby and born *so* prematurely, but I thought they were just trying to imply that Mammy and Tricky had been carrying on before they married. Fergus and Bridie looking like twins might have made them conclude that they are more than half-siblings but I don't know whether they'd have linked them to Father Stephen... '

'Never.' Aggie drained her glass. 'I'd have heard whispers by now. I get all the gossip in this village.'

'And people think all priests are saints and some of them get away with murder, quite literally on occasions,' Cathy said.

'A priest has literally murdered someone?' Rose was open-mouthed. 'Has it been in the news? We would have read about it.'

'We don't read about it, Rose, because it's always all covered up. You remember that terrible school in Letterfrack where Daddy worked for a while before he married Mammy? Well, one of the young boys from there, Liam, was sheltered by Daddy's in-laws and he tells stories about boys beaten and starved to death by the Christian Brothers and then buried in the grounds of the school with not even a stone to mark them. He can't prove it and he can't get the Garda to take it seriously. But I believe him.'

'Wicked. Imagine anyone hurting an innocent young lad, like Johnny maybe.'

'It's unbearable. I'm convinced that their sadism and Father Stephen's adultery all come from the same root: celibacy. Get rid of that and you'd get rid of a lot of perversion and misery all over Ireland.'

'Dead right, Cathy. That's why I have always believed in the healing power of a good jagging. And, on that thought, I shall take myself off.' Aggie stood up slowly. 'Someone has to cook breakfast for everyone.'

'Here we are again, Cathy, my darling. Just the two of us, back in your bedroom. Maybe you could brush my hair and read me a fairy story, like when I was little.' The women laughed lying side by side on the bed.

'If only we could go back to when everything was perfect and Mammy and Daddy didn't argue and there was music all over the house. Maybe if we could go back and change something they'd both still be alive now. I don't know what though...'

'Those are your memories, Cathy. I never knew them like that. Remember, I was only three when Daddy died; you were eleven. You saw their marriage in the best of times. I only saw them being miserable with each other and Fergus saw nothing of their marriage. What was he? Three months old when Daddy took his life?'

'I forget how young you were. Fergus wasn't much more than a new-born. The Depression put a terrible strain on their relationship, with Mammy trying to keep the businesses afloat and Daddy trying to feed the village.'

'To be honest, I remember our Daddy mainly from the stories you told me after he'd gone. Tricky's been much more of a father to me. Don't make that face, Cathy. I know you hated him but he's fine. He was always kind to us kids even though he didn't say much.'

'I know, I know. I'd even go so far as to say he's a good man who loved Mammy and who did his best to protect her.'

'And got himself an heir into the bargain. I think he's quite happy with the deal.'

'What'll he do now with Mammy gone? He looks like a lost soul.'

'Him and Father Stephen. Well, I've told Daddy - Tricky - that he would be more than welcome to stay living here, even after Sam and I get married. It's been his home for the last eighteen years after all, though Bridie will be gone off to university by then. I'm guessing that Fergus will stay living here too, even though it might be easier for him to go and live at the Byrnes' farmhouse, and if Fergus stays so will Tricky. They're as thick as thieves. Tricky has shown him everything he knows.'

'That's good. I'm happy for them both. Fergus got himself a father and Tricky a son.' Cathy looked over at her pretty sister; it hadn't escaped Cathy's notice that Rose called Tricky 'Daddy'. That might have enraged her once upon a time, but Cathy was more philosophical about what being a parent meant these days. 'We all find ourselves mothers and fathers wherever we can, don't we?'

'I suppose so. That means we can have as many as we like I guess.' Rose swung her legs off the bed and stood up. 'Right. I'll be off. Sleep tight and don't let the bed bugs bite. I love you Cathy and I've missed you so very much.' She bent down to kiss her sister.

'Love you to bits, Rosie. I'm sorry I wasn't here for you for so many years.'

'Stop it. You're here now and that's all that matters.'

Undressing by the light of an oil lamp in the bedroom, Cathy was filled with a deep ache for her Mammy and Daddy. They would have approved of Rose marrying Sam, no doubt about it. But what would they think of her life now, running the Academy and bringing up Johnny as a single parent? They would have wanted her to find happiness with someone who would love her as much as they had. Was there such a person? Cathy thought back to last summer in Cleggan. Maybe. Just maybe.

Chapter 2 – July 31st 1951

Breakfast was a blur of rashers and toast and endless pots of tea, Aggie presiding over the frying pan and Rose the kettle. Fergus arrived back after milking and proceeded to stuff down half a loaf of bread and a heap of eggs and bacon, all the while teasing his sisters about their leisurely rising. Bridie was still in her dressing gown.

'Just as well the men in this family know how to do a decent day's work so that you women can swan about like geishas.' Aggie made to whack him on the hand with her spatula.

'Some of us were up a good hour before you, young fella. And give me that shirt for the wash. You stink.'

Johnny was cracking his second boiled egg. Cathy had missed out on this bustling family life when, just fourteen, she had chosen to live with her grandmother to escape the man at the head of the table. Tricky was sitting, silently stirring sugar into his third cup of tea, looking calmly at the mayhem, a perfectly benign figure. What had she seen thirty years ago that had so disturbed her, wondered Cathy. Was it his squint maybe that made him look scary? Cathy was embarrassed to think she might have demonised this strange but decent man just because of the way he looked.

'I'm walking over to see Auntie Stasia. Anyone coming with me?'

'Sorry, Cathy. I have to do a stint in the shop as Teresa has to go to the dentist.' Rose's future mother-in-law had been working in the shop for the last twenty years and had been another vital support to Hannah as she had gone about restoring the family businesses after John's suicide. Teresa McCarthy was a regular diamond.

'I need to wash my hair,' Bridie popped the last corner of toast into her mouth, 'and, frankly, we see quite enough of Auntie Stasia, thanks very much. Now Mammy's gone, she'd like to start bossing us about as well as her own boys.'

'And Johnny and I are off to see the calves at the big farm.'

'And the tractor.'

'Oh yes, that yoke too, for sure. Are you ready?'

When the house had quietened down, the washing up was done and Aggie was settled out on the backyard bench, enjoying a fag and a copy of the *Kilkenny People*, Cathy put on her walking shoes and ventured over to Aunt Stasia's villa. Somehow, Main Street seemed shorter, the houses smaller, the pavement narrower than in her childhood. Cathy waved to Paddy in the Post Office who waved back; he probably had no idea who she was. She peeked through the window into their shop. Teresa was still on duty, awaiting relief from Rose, serving a young woman with a baby and two small children. Good God, it was Marion Magee. Cathy put her head down and walked on briskly. Well, Marion hadn't managed to bag Sam McCarthy for keeps at least; he was now Rose's prize.

Cathy turned and walked past the school playground where she had spent some happy years playing with Marion and their best friend, Bernie. Cathy wondered what had happened to Bernie and the O'Rourke family over in America. She hoped they had found their pot of gold. Past the presbytery – she spied Father Stephen at his desk – and the church. No, she told herself, don't go into the graveyard now, plenty of time to do that before she left for Dalkey. Cathy dreaded seeing her mother's grave under the heaps of earth.

Cathy gazed at the church door, thinking of times spent inside: sad occasions like the funerals of her parents and her grandfather, but also happy moments like her siblings' and cousins' christenings, and significant ones making her first confession and taking her first Holy Communion. If only she could offload her sins now. One sin in particular was weighing heavily but she had lost her faith in her teens, well before nursing dying soldiers had closed that door for good.

Stasia spotted Cathy walking up the lane and came to the front door to greet her.

'Come in, Cathy. Just leave your shoes on the mat.' They walked into the drawing room which overlooked the river and village beyond.

'Is Aunt Lily not up yet?'

'We leave her be after we've taken her a tray of tea. She likes to stay up in her bedroom until midday, reading or writing letters. Then she does her bathing and dressing and she appears in all her splendour in time for lunch.' Lily's skill in making an entrance, learned from her years in the theatre, had never left her. 'Stay and take a bite with us, then you'll see her.'

'I need to collect Johnny at eleven. Fergus has been showing him around the baby animals, though I think Johnny is more interested in the machines, to be honest.'

'Like Andrew. Hah, boys! I love my four sons, of course, but I so envied Hannah her beautiful daughters. Every time I got pregnant, I crossed my fingers that this time it would be a girl. But no, it just wasn't to be. Even my baby who died in childbirth was a boy.'

'James.'

'Yes. James.' Stasia took out her handkerchief and squeezed it hard. 'It was only when I lost James that I understood what your mother had gone through with all her lost babies. I wish I had been a little kinder. I miss your mother very much, Cathy. I know we used to spark off each other but it was just our way. I regret some of things I said and did over the years but she knew I loved her. I think I showed her that very much before the end.'

'I'm sure you did, Auntie Stasia. Aggie said you came every day when she took to her bed and you always brought her flowers from the garden...'

'Yes, I hope it was enough.' Stasia sat down and patted the sofa inviting Cathy to join her. 'I wanted to have a little special talk to you, just the two of us. You've always been so dear to me, Cathy. We have a special bond, you know, with you being born on my wedding day. I want you to think of me in place of your mother, if there's ever anything you need. I wish I had some lovely daughters like you and Rose and Bridie. But we must be grateful for what the good Lord gives us. Johnny must be a great comfort to you.'

'Of course. He's my life. Thank you, Auntie Stasia, for that kind offer. I can't imagine I will need any practical help. I've been making my own way in life for a long time now, but I can do with all the love you have to spare. And I'm sure Rose, Fergus and Bridie will be grateful for you keeping an eye on them now that Mammy's gone and me away up in Dublin. But – and please don't take this the wrong way - I'd wait until they ask for your help. They're a wonderful support to each other, and now Sam is there too for Rose.'

'Maybe. But you'll remember that I know what it's like to lose a mother when still in my teens. Hannah and I would have benefitted from some kind woman in the family taking us under her wing but Lily was too far away up in Dublin. That's why I thought I needed to protect Hannah and try and be a sort of mother to her – but she never saw it like that.'

'No, Mammy hated anyone telling her what she could or couldn't do.'

Stasia nodded. 'It used to drive me crazy, but I'd give anything to have her back right here with us, probably arguing.' Stasia laughed. She took Cathy's hand and stroked it. 'I have something for you, my dear.'

Stasia reached into her cardigan pocket and took out a small box, opening it to reveal a handsome emerald ring. 'It was our mother's. I took this diamond one...' Stasia held out her left hand '...and Hannah took this one. But then, after she married, she needed to sell it to raise some cash and I bought if off her. I'm so ashamed that I didn't just give her the money she needed at the time.' Stasia blinked hard. 'But the ring was hers by rights and should now pass to you.'

Cathy was on the verge of protesting, but she could see that her aunt's gesture was an important act of contrition. She let Stasia put the ring on her right hand. 'It's beautiful, Auntie Stasia. I shall treasure it. Thank you so much.'

'No thanks necessary. It's where it belongs now and I shall rest easier knowing Hannah's daughter is wearing it.'

Cathy bade her aunt good-bye and walked up the lane towards the Byrnes' farmhouse. As she walked into the courtyard behind the elegant house, she could hear Johnny squealing and Fergus laughing loudly. She followed the noise into the barn where Fergus was throwing Johnny up onto straw bales so he could slide down them.

'Thank Christ, here's your mother now.' Fergus gave Cathy sweaty hug. 'I'm wrecked. He's had me at this malarkey for the last quarter of an hour. I thought I was fit but clearly not enough for a seven-year-old.'

'Ha! It's good for you, and for him. He doesn't get this sort of fun in Dalkey surrounded by middle-aged teachers.'

'You'll have to send him down to us every holiday. He'll be able to do something useful around the place soon enough.'

'Mama, Mama, watch me.'

Johnny had climbed onto the tallest pile of bales and lifted his arms. Cathy, seized with terror, raised her hand to stop him but too late. When he landed, he ran over to his mother, straw sticking out of his hair, socks and jumper.

'You gave me a fright, my love,' Cathy picked out the straw from Johnny's hair, 'and now you look like a scarecrow.'

'Give over with all the molly-coddling. No-one stopped us when we were kids. We did what we wanted.'

'I might have done if I'd been here.'

'But you weren't, and we survived just fine.'

'Mama, Fergus let me drive the tractor in the field for a bit.'

'Don't tell your mother, Johnny. She'll be telling me off. I only let him steer for a few minutes, Cathy. I was fully in control the whole time, don't fret. And we saw the new-born calves too and fed the pigs, didn't we.'

'And I sat in the combine harvester. It's so big, as big as the house.' Johnny stretched his arms wide.

'Great. Say thank you to your Uncle Fergus. We need to leave him to do his proper work. Farmers don't have time to play about, you know.'

'Thank you. Uncle Fergus.'

'You're more than welcome, Johnny. Seven years of fun all in one go. Next time you come, I'll get you to do some proper work, shifting bales maybe. Get some muscles on those scrawny arms of yours.'

'Come on, Johnny. See you tonight, bro. Go and have a rest on the tractor.'

Supper that evening in the Main Street house was a jolly enough affair though most people around the table could sense the ghosts present. Aggie had set up the table in the dining room rather than in the kitchen because Lily was joining them before the Dublin crowd departed the next morning. They had rarely eaten in the dining room when Cathy was little but Aggie told her that she used to have to set it every night when Stasia and Hannah were teenagers, living here with just Grandad James. What a lot of fuss that must have been. Why hadn't they just sat in front of the comfy range in the kitchen with Aggie? Tonight, Rose and Bridie were doing more serving than the housemaid, though Aggie had cooked everything and she now had the most challenging task of the evening: making conversation with Tricky.

Sam had the opposite challenge, not to talk but to listen politely to Great-aunt Lily's accounts of her trips to Dublin's theatres and concerts. Lily told Sam about the terrible fire at the Abbey Theatre recently but that she had been lucky to visit only a week before to see the revival of O'Casey's *The Plough and the Stars* there. 'Do you know the play, Sam? It deals with the 1916 uprising which is unfinished business for Ireland. I hope you support the cause of a united country which has been so botched up by politicians.' Sam nodded but Lily had already moved on to wondering where the Abbey company would find a home now and how the theatre would raise the fortune needed to rebuild it. 'I will be the first to make a donation, of course. What else am I going to do with all my money?' Sam thought that he and Rose could make very good use of a bit of extra cash to rewire this old house, install some plumbing and modernise the bar.

As soon as the main course was cleared away, Lily rose to leave. 'No, please don't let me break up the gathering. But I need to get a good night's sleep before our long journey and Slattery is out in the car waiting for me. Let me kiss you all goodbye now.'

As soon as the front door closed behind Lily, Aggie brought in a massive blackberry crumble. 'You know why Lily has gone back to Stasia's early, don't you? She refuses to piss in our outdoor jacks. That woman has never, ever been down the yard and now her bladder won't last out like it used to.'

'To be fair, it's a bit of a shock to me too after so many years away,' laughed Cathy.

'You with your Dublin airs and graces.' Rose put her arm around her sister. 'But I promise that next time you come home we will have all mod cons installed, won't we, Sam. No excuse for you not to visit us often.'

After much drinking and reminiscing, Cathy was lying in her old bed when there was a gentle knock at her door; Rose walked in and sat down.

'Darling Cathy. I shall never get enough time with you. These three days have gone by so fast.'

'I know. Still so much left to talk about. But I can't tell you how thrilled I am for you and Sam. He's a lovely fella and from a lovely family too.'

'Yes, we do marry the family too, I guess. But you never see Joe's family, do you?'

'No, but I am going to remedy that as soon as I can and not just for Johnny's sake. Mam Ashfield was always so kind to me when I lived with her and Shirley. She was the one who held my hand while I screamed my way through childbirth, not my own mother.'

Rose paused and twisted the engagement ring on her finger. 'Now, don't say no, Cathy, but I've left Daddy's cello in the hall for you to take back and give to Johnny when he's big enough to play it.'

'That's very sweet of you, Rose. I'm delighted to have it and Johnny will make good use of it in time.'

'Not just the cello. I've left Mammy's violin there too. Please take it back with you. None of us is ever going to play it.'

'But neither will I, Rose. I can only play the piano.'

'But you're the musical one. The three of us haven't a musical bone in our bodies.'

'Only because you were never given the chance.'

'Maybe, but I'd like you to have it. You saw Mammy playing it more than any of us ever did. It's a bit of her you can keep to remember her by, seeing as how you missed out on so many years. And you might have another child one day...'

'Ha-ha. Stop it now. You and Sam will be the ones rocking a cradle soon enough. But I will take it, Rose. It has a heap of memories for me and Grandad James spent a lot of money on it, so I'll look after it carefully for whoever in the family shows the first sign of inheriting her musical genius. Thanks for making me its guardian.'

Chapter 3 – August 1951

It was gone eleven. Cathy was still up, trotting around the Academy, packing for tomorrow's journey out to Connemara for their summer holidays. She was looking forward to a break from the school routine and all the high emotion that the last month had brought. She yearned to feel the wind blow through her hair out on the wild, Atlantic way and to sit snugly inside the little cottage in Cleggan in front of the peat fire. The trip meant a lot to her. But she was also rather anxious.

First of all, she would be driving them all there for the first time in her new car. 'You can't go wrong with a Ford,' Seamus had said while driving her around to car showrooms in his enormous Jaguar. What on earth would Cathy do without Uncle Seamus by her side whenever there was an important decision to be made.

And then there was the prospect of seeing Liam again. Cathy had been thinking about him most days since their trip last summer to Cleggan, and not just when she received one of his weekly letters in which he chronicled his determined and often hilarious quest for a girlfriend, following Cathy's strict instructions. She wrote a reply every Sunday afternoon, with more dating advice and encouragement, but, secretly, Liam's lack of long-term romantic success made her think there might be another future for him. For them both.

Cathy, with loud support from Ellen and Aoife, had done her best to persuade Seamus to accompany them out to Connemara this summer, but he had politely declined. 'No, no. I'm a man for the city, you know. I rarely ventured onto Killiney beach even when I was at the Academy. I like a solid pavement beneath my feet and a good orchestra to listen to, not all those rocky cliffs and awful céilí bands.'

Seamus, Ellen and Aoife had supported and protected Cathy for years, unofficial godparents all three. None of them had children of their own but they had been drawn to Cathy because of their attachment to one or other of her parents.

Seamus's unrequited love for Hannah had been woven from the threads of their music-making together at the Maple Academy. Seamus had played his viola alongside Hannah as generously and self-effacingly as he lived the rest of his life. Realising Hannah was lost to him, he then became engaged to Ellen, her mother's best friend at the Academy, before he went off to fight in the trenches of the First World War. After many years officially tied to each other, he and Ellen had eventually conceded that, although they undoubtedly loved each other, it wasn't 'like that' and certainly not enough to sustain a marriage.

Ellen had returned to the Academy as a teacher in 1933 and, over the next decade and a half, had become indispensable to Mrs Fitzgerald, Cathy's grandmother, eventually taking over as the Academy's principal. Ellen and Cathy made a great partnership, the older woman happy to leave all financial and administrative matters to the younger one, allowing Ellen to devote her time to the students. The daunting Mrs Fitzgerald, now deceased a full two years, had been an impressive and inspiring headmistress to all her pupils but she had been a soft and indulgent grandmother. Ellen was nothing like Cathy's grandmother in most ways: she was short and plump with a pronounced limp from contracting polio as a child. Ellen was always sunny, with a wicked and rather vulgar wit, and yet she followed Mrs Fitzgerald's footsteps perfectly in her devotion to the Academy, to Cathy and to the teaching of dead languages.

Aoife, Cathy's third guardian angel, was in many ways the most mysterious. The younger sister of John Fitzgerald's first wife, she had lived out in Connemara into her fifties, working in the little local school, until Cathy had persuaded her, a fluent Gaelic speaker, to come to the Academy three years ago to start teaching Irish to the students. Aoife was a genuine relative of Cathy's, the sister of Ailsa, her Daddy's first wife. Aoife was a strong link to her father and to Máire, the child born to John and Ailsa so Cathy's half-sister. Aoife had dedicated herself to the invalid Máire after Ailsa's death until the little girl too had died in her father's arms. When Cathy watched the tall, elegant woman, with her still dark hair and green eyes, her full mouth and her translucent skin, go about her life with such calm modesty, Cathy could imagine what her father might have looked like in his youth, arm in arm with Ailsa.

John Fitzgerald had taken Cathy out to Connemara when she was ten, an adventure for just the two of them, and there she had met Aoife and her parents for the first time, staying in the cottage by the sea, collecting shells and hearing the traditional Irish songs and myths that had utterly entranced her. And there too she had met Liam.

Although Cleggan was a liberating place for her father, full of love and happiness, it was also a place where he had experienced great pain. Ailsa and Máire had both died in the cottage. There was also the deadening guilt that John Fitzgerald endured from the time he had worked at the hateful Letterfrack School – and Liam was part of that.

When he was just six, Liam Molloy's widowed mother had sent him from their miserable home in Cork to St Joseph's industrial School in Letterfrack, run by the Christian Brothers. She thought she was saving him from destitution and that the Christian Brothers would give her son a good start in life. Instead, Liam had entered a different world of pain. For nine years he had witnessed the shocking abuse that went on in that place of fear: boys beaten, starved and abused. He had suffered abuse himself, both physical and sexual, until he had run away and been rescued by the de Bhailis family in Cleggan. There, he met John Fitzgerald for the first time – and Cathy.

John had recognised in Liam all the damage that St Joseph's could inflict, the scant education, the stunted growth and the silent terror. John had tried to get justice for the boy and to expose the school, but when it resulted in Liam being forced back into Letterfrack school by the Garda at the behest of his mother, John had blamed himself. Eventually, Liam was old enough to be offered a proper job by Ruari de Bhailis and the peaceful, loving Cleggan cottage became the first true home he had ever known. But, by then, John had been dead three years. Taught to fish by Ruari, to read by Aoife, and fed properly by Shawna, Liam had grown into a strong, hard-working man, full of gratitude and love for his rescuers.

When Aoife joined the Academy after losing both parents, she had left the Cleggan cottage in Liam's care. She hoped he might find himself a wife, but he lived there alone still, working as ferociously as if he still had the Christian Brothers at his back, beating industry into him. Liam grafted and grafted and, with his saved money, had started to buy bits of land to keep sheep on so that he wasn't totally dependent on the sea.

This was the grown-up Liam that Cathy had discovered last summer on her first visit to Cleggan for twenty years. It was a shock to see that such a straight-backed, good-looking man had emerged from the shadow of the terrorised boy she had known. A shock, but a very pleasant one.

Cathy was about to close her case, but she remembered to pack one last thing: her swimming costume. Last summer, Liam had promised he would teach her to swim.

******

'Everyone back in the car. I want to get to Cleggan before tea-time.' The holiday party had stopped off at a café for lunch and some urgent visits to the lavatory.

'Johnny, go and have another wee before we set off?'

'I don't need one, Mama.'

Ellen stood up from the table. 'You and I should go, Aoife. At our age, we should never pass up an opportunity to empty our bladders.' Ellen linked her arm with Aoife's and they set off for the bathroom. Cathy watched them stroll off and marvelled that they had found love in each other's arms late in their lives. It gave her hope that it was never too late to find a soulmate.

'Mama, if you drive a bit faster, we'll get to Cleggan sooner. I've been checking and you never go faster than fifty miles an hour.'

'And I've no intention of going any faster, my darling, at least not with Aoife in the back. I don't think she's totally relaxed with me driving. I keep hearing her make little gasping noises when I overtake or go around a bend.'

It was gone five o'clock when they turned into the lane leading to Cleggan. Ellen had been asleep, snoring softly for the last hour, but Aoife had kept her clenched hand on the back of the driver's seat and Johnny had been fidgeting endlessly in the front seat so it was a relief for Cathy to see the familiar cottage come into view. Or maybe not so familiar.

'Here we are. But … what's happened?' Cathy was shocked to see the cottage now considerably wider than last summer.

'It's a surprise. Liam has been busy on it all year.' Aoife sprang out of the car the instant Cathy applied the hand-brake. 'Just look. Isn't it exciting?'

The small cottage had grown an extra wing and to the left of the narrow front door were two new windows, one up and one down. Liam stepped out of the front door, his tanned arms already open wide to dispense hugs to his favourite people.

Aoife got first dibs, then Ellen. The two then walked into the cottage without invitation.

'Hello Liam. Do you like our car?' Liam lifted Johnny into the air and spun him round before popping him back onto the ground.

'It's grand. Is your mother a good driver?'

'She's OK. A bit slow though.' Then Johnny was off, running behind the cottage to visit the pony.

Liam walked slowly over to Cathy, fixing her with a soft stare and a wide smile. He enfolded her in a warm and generous embrace.

'I've missed these, Cathy Ashfield. You give great hugs.'

'You too, Liam.'

'Well, I had a good teacher,' he whispered in her ear. Liam let Cathy go and started to walk around the Prefect. 'But look at you, driving around in your fancy new car. You aren't the only one who's learned to drive, you know. I have my own van now. It's a bit knackered but it's a godsend for doing the fish deliveries and I've given it a lot of punishment, carting all my building supplies around.'

'You've done the building work yourself? That's fantastic.'

'I've had some help the last couple of months from Brendan. I wanted to get it finished before you all arrived.'

'Who's Brendan?'

'Just a lad I've taken on from St Joseph's. I reckoned I could afford some help, so where else would I go? He's only sixteen and mad as a ditch but he makes me laugh a lot. It's a miracle he's kept his sense of humour with the Christian Brothers beating the life out of anyone with a spark of humour. He says it's what kept him going and cheered up the other lads. But he's a real grafter. Come inside and look.'

Cathy walked out of the bright sunlight into the dim interior and waited for her eyes to adjust. The big downstairs room, which was both kitchen and sitting room, looked much the same as last summer apart from the addition of an electric stove. Aoife had already made herself at home and put the kettle on, while Ellen had settled herself in the big carver chair at the head of the table and put her bad leg up onto a chair beside her.

'We waited for you to show us round, Liam.' Aoife gestured to the wall behind Cathy.

Cathy turned to see a new door in the side wall; Liam had his hand resting on the latch ready to reveal all. He opened the door and waved the women into the newly built extension.

Aoife gasped and clapped her hands before walking around, stroking the new stone walls appreciatively. 'It's wonderful, Liam. What a grand job you've done. Come in and see properly, Cathy.'

Liam had created an extra sitting room, with an open fire and sheepskin rugs on the wooden floor. There were two plump armchairs by the hearth. 'I'll get more furniture when I can afford it, but we can come in here of an evening after supper, to get away from the cooking smells. And maybe, Cathy, we could persuade you to play something for us.' Liam nodded towards the corner behind Cathy. She turned to find an upright piano in the corner.

'What? Liam! You've bought a piano. How wonderful. But why? Do you mean to take lessons?'

'Ha! I don't think me and my big coarse hands would get far trying to play a piano. But I thought you'd like it, Cathy. Aoife's always telling me about your lovely playing and you write to me about the new pieces you've been learning. But I've never actually heard you play and I'm mad to hear you. Only if you're willing, mind.'

Cathy walked over to piano and ran her hand along the mahogany lid, surprisingly dust-free, then opened it to reveal the inviting keys.

'Course I'll play for you, Liam, though I have no music with me and I don't know much off by heart.' She pulled out the piano stool and sat herself down. 'There's always this…' The first few bars of Beethoven's *Moonlight Sonata* crept out tentatively, 'Though that's a bit sad for this sunny day.' Cathy shut the lid and stood up.

'Well, I don't mind. It's beautiful. Will you play me the rest this evening? Please.'

'If you like, but I'll try and think of some jollier tunes. It's a lovely thing you did though, Liam. Thank you.'

'It was free. They were getting rid of it from one of the hotels I supply, so I grabbed it. Just had to borrow a truck and Brendan and I moved it in last week as soon as the room was finished. It nearly killed us, but the only cost was getting a piano tuner in.'

'Apart from the cost of building a whole new room to house it.' Ellen dropped herself into one of the new armchairs. 'Ooh, lovely. I assume these chairs are for me and Aoife. I shall certainly not be moving from here for a while. Bring on the scald!'

While the women enjoyed their fresh brew, Liam transported all their baggage from the car up to their bedrooms with some enthusiastic if not very effective help from Johnny.

'Come and see, Mama. I have my own bedroom now.' Johnny dragged Cathy upstairs, Liam following behind. Above the new sitting room, Liam had built a small bedroom and next door to it a new bathroom and toilet.

'Oh, this is amazing, Liam.'

'All mod cons now. I thought Johnny was getting to an age when he needs his own room.' Liam discreetly placed his hand on the small of Cathy's back; a small electrical shock ran through her.

'Yes, that's great. Aren't you lucky, Johnny?' She turned to Liam. 'So, am I in my usual room, opposite yours?'

'Where else?'

Cathy had always slept in the back bedroom, where her father had lodged when he first joined the de Bhailis household. Cathy had also slept in Liam's bed for several memorable nights last summer but she had run the risk of Johnny discovering her night-time absences; that was now solved.

Johnny ran past them down the stairs. 'Can we go to the sea now?' Cathy heard Aoife shushing Johnny so as not to wake Ellen, who was having a snooze. The door opened and closed and the house fell silent.

'I was very sorry to hear about your mother, Cathy. But at least you got to see her before she passed.'

'I did, and I'm very grateful for that. But it hurts to think of all the years she kept me from her side. And I found out a lot of her secrets too. I'll tell you some time maybe. Anyway, I don't want to be sad here in Cleggan, Liam. This is my happy place. Come on, let's go to the beach.' Cathy ran down the stairs and straight out to the breezy sunshine, leaving Ellen happily asleep.

******

Liam had made a lamb stew for supper. 'I know every blade of grass that animal ate. Did it taste OK?'

Ellen gave a little belch. 'It was divine, Liam. You're an even better cook than Aoife.'

'She taught me everything I know, so you should thank her too.'

Ellen took Aoife's hand and squeezed it. 'Oh, I'm very thankful for Aoife.'

'And Mrs Gallagher, five doors down, has made an apple pie. She's always baking things for me.' Liam took the pie from the larder shelf with a jug of thick yellow cream. 'She's given Brendan a bed too, while you're all here. He's been in your room, Aoife, just while the new bedroom was being built, but now he'll go in there. I hope that was OK.'

'Oh, you mustn't think of it as my room, Liam. I don't think I have a claim over any room here any longer.'

'But the cottage still belongs to you, doesn't it, Aoife?' Cathy asked.

'On paper, I suppose. But after all the work Liam has done, he has the best claim to it. And I'm not likely to want to come back and live in Cleggan, am I? And who else would I leave it to when I die but Liam? I have no other relations and I doubt Ellen would want to come and live in Connemara on her own.'

'Jeezus, Aoife. That's a very cheerful topic of conversation on our holidays.'

'I'm just being practical, Ellen. I'll get Seamus to make out a proper will. You never know when death might come knocking. Look at poor Hannah. No age at all. How old was she, Cathy?'

'Just fifty-one.'

'Same age as me, you daft mot. We were at school together, weren't we.'

'Yes, of course, taken too soon. But she is at peace now and in the arms of your father again. Take comfort from that, Cathy.' If only she could.

'I wish I could have met my granny from Rowanbridge,' said Johnny. 'But Mama has promised to take me to England to meet Granny Ashfield. She'd better not die before I get there.' The grown-ups smiled at Johnny's serious face.

'Right then. It's time for Cathy to show us what she can do on the old ivories.' Liam took Cathy's hand and led her to the piano.

'Okay. I've been racking my brain and I think I can remember a couple of things.' Cathy began to play *The Last Rose of Summer* followed by *O Danny Boy*, fudging some of the harmonies at times, but with Aoife and Ellen singing along which covered up any gaffes.

'And I can play this.' Not wishing to be left out, Johnny pushed himself in front of his mother's legs and treated them to *Chopsticks* three times over.

'That's enough now, sweetheart.' Cathy gently took Johnny's hands from the keyboard and closed the lid. 'Johnny's real instrument is the cello, you know, Liam, just like my father. I have brought Daddy's cello back from Rowanbridge but it'll be a few more years before he's big enough to play it.'

'I'm big enough now, Mama.'

'Nearly, my sweet.' Cathy looked at her son and her heart ached. Time did go very fast. It would be no time before Johnny was tall enough for the full-sized cello, and then he would be a teenager and then he would be gone. You couldn't mess around with time; it was relentless.

'Who's up for an evening stroll? Best take advantage of the fine weather while we have it.'

'I'm whacked, Liam. Tomorrow maybe.' Ellen stood up and stretched. 'I'm off to my bed.'

'I'll put Johnny to bed, macushla,' offered Aoife. I miss it now we're not living in the Academy. You go off and take the air.'

Cathy was happy to obey Aoife who was probably match-making, but Cathy didn't give a damn. They were on the same side.

As they walked towards Cleggan harbour in the dusk, Liam took Cathy's hand easily. No words seemed necessary. Just holding Liam's big, warm, rough hand gave Cathy comfort after several stressful weeks. They walked down to the beach and sat on the dunes.

'I wonder whether I can still skim a stone.'

'It's like playing the piano or driving a car. Once you can do it, you never lose the knack completely.' Liam put his arm around Cathy's shoulders. 'That piece you started, will you play it properly for me tomorrow?'

'I will. It's called the *Moonlight Sonata* and it's by Beethoven. I've been playing that first movement since I was about eight. Not very well, mind.'

'Good enough for me, Cathy.' He leant over and kissed her softly. 'Will you come and see me tonight? I want to prove that I've been doing my homework.'

Cathy laughed. Last year, she had been shocked to discover that Liam had reached the great age of thirty-two without even kissing a woman, let alone making love to one. The sexual abuse he had endured at Letterfrack School had left deep scars but with Cathy's kind and patient attentions over that week in August, Liam had begun his slow progress towards the intimacy he craved. Cathy had left him with strict instructions to carry on the good work and his weekly letters recounting his amorous escapades always made her chuckle.

'I thought you'd never ask.' Cathy lay back on the sand and waited for a long-anticipated proper kiss.

Chapter 4 – August 1951

'**M**ama, wake up. Your porridge is ready and even Auntie Ellen is up.'

'Wha…? Oh gracious. Look at the time.' Cathy sat up and rubbed her eyes.

'It's nearly half past nine and I want to go to the beach, Mama.' Johnny ran off, leaving Cathy to drag herself from bed and use the splendid new bathroom. She could smell Liam on herself which was arousing but she gave herself a shallow bath and came downstairs smelling of rosewater instead. Cathy was a bit sore after making love twice last night, rather vigorously. Of the pair, she was now the one out of practice, but she would soon catch up. Liam had progressed into a skilful and tender lover and, miraculously, he had acquired condoms via a drinking pal in the Clifden pub he frequented. All was set fair for a pleasurable week ahead.

Ellen was deep in a game of snakes and ladders at the kitchen table with an equally competitive Johnny. Aoife was standing stirring at the stove and gave Cathy a wide smile. 'Good morning, macushla. You needed that sleep I bet after driving for so long yesterday.' Yes, that must be why she was so tired, thought Cathy, and not at all because she'd been up half the night having sex.

'Yes, I went out like a light. Where's Liam?'

'Oh, he went off about seven, a bit later than usual. He needs to tend to the lobster pots first thing and then deliver the catch to his customers around Clifden. Lobsters are his biggest money-spinner these days. There's a lot more money in shellfish than mackerel.'

After breakfast, they took themselves off to the beach with a couple of buckets and spades provided by Liam. Cathy enjoyed building sandcastles as much as her son. While Ellen and Aoife sat reading, Cathy grabbed handfuls of wet sand, digging out moats and shaping bridges to complement the walls of the castle Johnny was building. Cathy smeared a thin layer of sand over her palm. What an incredible substance. You could make out all the different coloured grains when you looked carefully and yet it formed a cohesive mass. Amazing to think it had started out as hard shells which, under the sea's relentless pressure, had turned into this soft and mouldable substance.

A morning of doing nothing very much went by. As they sat eating bread and cheese in the cottage, Liam walked in carrying two live lobsters which he put straight into two buckets of water.

'Oh, how exciting.' Ellen clapped her hands together. 'Are they for us? I love lobster but it's been years since I've had any. In fact, I think it was at your Aunt Lily's, Cathy, during the war. How on earth did she always manage to get her hands on those things? Connections, I suppose – and money.'

'I thought we all deserved a treat tonight. But the price, Cathy Ashfield, is you have to play me that Moonlight piece after supper.'

'It's a deal, and a small price to pay.'

After supper was cleared away, the household gathered in the new sitting room, Ellen and Aoife enthroned in the armchairs with cups of tea and Johnny at their feet doing a jigsaw. Cathy sat herself at the piano while Liam came over to study her face and hands closely.

'Here we go then. I hope I can do this justice from memory. Even though I've been playing it since I was eight, I can't promise there won't be some hiccups. It's known as *The Moonlight Sonata* but Beethoven didn't call it that; he described it as *Sonata quasi una fantasia,* so a 'fantasy' or a 'dream' if you like. More than anything, I think it's full of melancholy, a soulful yearning for something lost maybe? Very beautiful but very sad.'

Cathy began, her right hand playing the pianissimo rippling triplets and her left hand anchoring them with dark octaves sinking deep into the keyboard. It was mesmerising. Even Johnny looked up and listened to his mother. When she finished, there was silence for a moment until Johnny ran up to the piano.

'Can I learn to play that too, Mama?'

'Of course, my love. Next year maybe, when you're eight, like I was when I tried it first. Your hands need to be big enough to stretch across an octave. See?' Cathy demonstrated and then took Johnny's hand. 'Nearly there. Keep eating your cabbage.' She stood up. 'Thank you so much, Liam, for organising the piano. It was so thoughtful, but next time I'll bring lots of happy music with me.'

'No, thank *you*. I loved that.'

There was an urgent knocking at the door. Liam went out to answer it and sounds of a lively conversation drifted through.

'Come in quick and say hello,' said Liam and ran upstairs. A flash of bright red hair poked itself around the doorway followed by a stocky body. 'Missus, missus.' The young man nodded to Ellen and then to Aoife. 'Oh, and hello to you too, missus.'

Cathy went over and shook the lad's hand. 'You must be Brendan.'

'That's me, that's me right enough. Sorry to disturb you an' all but I've just found a feckin' ewe fallen down a crevice and she's too heavy for me to lift her out by meself – awkward place – I need Liam to come too while there's still a shred of light left. Sheep, they're all complete spanners you know, missus.' And Brendan shuffled backwards as he heard Liam come downstairs, now changed into his rough clothes. 'Good evenin' to you all then,' and Brendan followed Liam out of the door.

Liam wasn't back by the time they went to bed. Cathy sat reading until she dropped off to sleep. Around two o'clock, she woke up with a stiff neck, fully dressed, lying on top of the bedclothes, her book fallen to the floor. She went to the bathroom, washed, changed into her nightdress and went to Liam's bedroom. Putting her ear to the door, she could hear nothing but there was a needle of light peeping out. She opened the door gently to find Liam in deep sleep, also lying on top of the sheets, but undressed down to his underpants. He had been waiting for her, no doubt about it. Cathy walked up to Liam's side of the bed, appreciating the long muscular body, pied with strips of tanned flesh on his arms, legs and neck, the rest of his skin as pallid as a pearl, bathed in soft light from the bedside lamp. His face and chest were covered in a rusty scruff. She longed to stroke them and feel them on her own skin but she took pity on the man who had been up since dawn after little sleep and a night making energetic love to her, who had done a day's hard work and then had to rescue a daft sheep until gone midnight. She looked at his gentle and generous face; the kindest thing she could do for him would be to let him sleep until the morning. She took a blanket from the floor, carefully laid it over him, switched off the lamp and went back to her own bed.

Everyone was up bright and early the next morning. Liam was already out by the time Cathy and Johnny came downstairs at half past eight to be served scrambled eggs with mushrooms cooked by Ellen.

'Liam says he is taking an afternoon off so we need to be here when he gets back,' Aoife announced as she cleared the table.

The morning was spent mooching around the fields near the cottage, feeding the pony, counting the sheep and digging up potatoes. Cathy picked some hedgerow flowers – montbretia, fuchsia and honeysuckle – and popped them into a jam jar. She sniffed the posy. How many little bouquets of honeysuckle had she picked for her mother over the years when she was a young girl? Some had been treasured and taken to her Mammy's desk, others had been ignored and allowed to wilt on the drainer.

Liam arrived home in time to eat a speedy ham sandwich. 'So, Cathy, I thought we should take advantage of this lovely weather to get you swimming. I promised to teach you last summer, do you remember?'

'I do, and I packed my swimming costume with that in mind.'

'I don't think it'd be wise to take Johnny with us though. We'll be too preoccupied to keep a proper eye on him.'

Aoife stepped forward. 'That's no problem at all. Ellen and I will take him to the beach and he'll be as happy as a sandboy there. He can paddle. I could even take him swimming if I had a costume. I used to swim all the time when I lived here, didn't I, Liam?'

'Right then, all sorted. Get your clobber together, Cathy, and let's get off.'

Once they were out in the boat on the open sea, bouncing along the waves, Cathy soon stopped feeling guilty about leaving Johnny behind. 'Where are you taking us?' she turned to Liam, shouting above the noise of the little engine.

Liam grinned. 'To the Caribbean,' he yelled.

As soon as they rounded the next headland, he cut the engine and they sat swaying gently in the middle of shallow turquoise water. 'See. We could be in some tropical lagoon.'

'Slight difference in temperature, I'm guessing.'

'Well, you'll find out soon enough.' Liam shuffled along the boat and came to sit next to Cathy. He put his arms around her. 'I'm sorry to have dragged you away like that, but I was desperate to be alone with you. I hope it wasn't too obvious. You should have woken me last night. I knew you'd been in my room because I woke up covered in a blanket.'

'I didn't have the heart to wake you but I wanted to, very much.' Cathy kissed him. 'This is such a lovely place, a healing place. I feel like I've been turned inside out the last few weeks, Liam, seeing my mother after twelve years apart, hearing all her secrets and then watching her die after having so little time with her. It's cut me up something terrible. But I think I can find some peace here.'

Liam took her hands and kissed them. 'Do you want to tell me about her? You don't have to but I'd like to hear.'

Cathy looked him straight in the face and burst into loud sobs. He held her close until her heaving body calmed, then she drew away and faced into the oncoming breeze, speaking hesitantly.

'My mother wanted to confess to me before she died, and God knows there was a lot to confess. She ... she told me that she had been having an affair ... with our priest can you believe ... since before my father killed himself. In fact, that's probably why he killed himself. Not money worries at all, nor guilt about you. It turns out my brother Fergus is only a half-brother and my half-sister, Bridie, has the same father as him: Father Stephen. My mother's second marriage was just a sham to cover up her pregnancy. I thought Tricky was a monster who had murdered my father but it turns out he was my mother's saviour and he has posed as Bridie's father all these years. It was my Auntie Stasia's idea, so she has known all this time too. And Aggie, our housemaid, has known all along and my sister Rose has guessed. It wouldn't surprise me if the whole village knew and that I was the last to find out.'

'I have no difficulty believing what priests can get up to.' Liam put his arm around Cathy again and she took his hand.

'But there's more. I have to tell someone.' Cathy looked up into the bright blue sky. 'I killed her, Liam. I killed my own Mammy.' Cathy began to sob again.

'Cathy, Cathy, there, there.' Liam took out a crumpled handkerchief and handed it to her. 'I don't know what you mean but I'm sure you didn't hurt her in any way.'

'But I did. I did. I meant to kill her. I filled a syringe with a load of morphine and injected it into her sad, thin arm, knowing it would kill her.'

'You were just showing her some mercy, taking her pain away. You couldn't do anything that isn't kind, Cathy. You're kindness itself.'

'No, you're wrong, Liam. I'm not my father. *He* was nothing but goodness. I know I'm a lot like him but there's a nasty, sharp streak of cruelty in me that I got from her.'

'But it *was* the right thing to do. You took her pain away.'

'Yes, it was the right thing, I don't doubt that. It's what was in my heart that makes me hate myself. It was an act of mercy but also an act of revenge for... oh, so many things.'

They sat hugging each other for several minutes until Cathy's sobs had subsided completely and then they sat, hand in hand, silently watching the gulls circle and dive into the water.

'Look, Cathy. Look out to the horizon.' Liam pointed out to sea. 'Dolphins, a couple of bottle-noses, I reckon.'

Cathy could see the dark shapes in the distance forming elegant curves as they darted in and out of the water. Such a dance of freedom. Such simple joy.

'How graceful are they. Come on, Liam. That should be the pair of us. Teach me to swim.'

After a half hour of serious tuition, during which Cathy barely let go of Liam's strong hands, they stumbled out of the chilly water and fell onto their towels on the white sand, laughing.

'Oh God. Why did I never learn when I was a child? Johnny took to it in ten minutes flat, like a baby dolphin. I'm like a great floundering jellyfish. And I'm freezing.' The breeze was raising goose-pimples on Cathy's wet skin.

'Here, let me warm you up.' Liam took his towel and wrapped it around Cathy, giving her back a brisk rub. 'You need to take off this wet thing if you want to get properly dry. May I?' He slipped the straps of Cathy's bathing suit down her arms and peeled the whole thing off. He knelt and looked at her naked body shivering on the sand before drying it roughly.

'There you go. That better?' Cathy lay back on her towel under Liam's gaze. 'Just look at you, Cathy: a mermaid is what you're like with your long hair and blue eyes.' He bent over her and licked each hard nipple in turn.

'Oh, that's warmed them up a bit.'

'The sea works wonders for your beautiful breasts but it's bad news for my cock.'

Cathy laughed and pulled down Liam's dripping shorts. 'Mmm, let me see what I can do to help.'

They enjoyed some leisurely foreplay, exploring each other's bodies, unable to distinguish between the saltiness of the sea and the taste of themselves, before Liam knelt behind Cathy and penetrated her, rubbing her with one hand until she shuddered in climax. He then withdrew and took her hand to his erection so that he ejaculated over the sand. They both lay back in exhausted contentment.

'You didn't need to do that, you know. Finish outside me, I mean.'

'I forgot to bring a condom.'

'But I know my cycle, like a good nurse. The Pope would be proud of me. I can't get pregnant right now.'

'Ah well. I shall bear that in mind later today.' Liam folded Cathy into his long arms and kissed her deeply.

'Thanks for doing it doggy style though. That way I didn't get even more sand ground up my arse.'

'My pleasure. It's one of the little techniques I've been working on this last year.'

******

'Ah, there you are,' said Aoife when Cathy and Liam walked back into the cottage. 'You've been a while. I was starting to get a little worried. I'll make you some fresh tea and look what Brendan has brought for us.' She gestured to the big sponge cake sitting on the table, a large chunk already missing, most of which was currently disappearing down Brendan's throat.

'Don't you worry, Liam, I'll be back out to the fields in two shakes when I've just finished this. Mrs G sent you the cake for your visitors and the missus here offered me a slice and I couldn't say no, now could I?' Brendan stuffed the last morsel into his mouth and took a big swig of tea.

'Rest easy, man. No rush or you'll get indigestion. The work will still be there.'

'Brendan has been telling us all about how he prepares the lobster pots, and all about his room and all about Mrs Gallagher's daughter, Dearbhla, and all about...well... everything.' Ellen winked at Cathy.

'I have plenty more tales to tell, missus. Maybe when young Johnny is in bed. I wouldn't want him to be hearing about St Joseph's or he'd cack himself and be up with the nightmares.'

'I'm not scared of stories,' Johnny was indignant at Brendan's concerns. 'I'm reading *The Lion, The Witch and the Wardrobe* and the White Witch doesn't frighten me at all.'

'Brendan, some time I *would* like you to tell me about your time at St Joseph's.' Cathy sat down next to the young lad. 'My father worked there, you see, and he was horrified at what he saw. He tried to get the Garda to do something but no-one wanted to hear.'

'Yes, missus, whenever you want. You won't believe it though.'

'I will, sadly. But don't let me keep you now. Brendan, if you have work to do.'

'Oh yes indeed, I must be off. The feckin' sheep have completely banjaxed a bit of fence, so I'll be away now or I'll be late for me supper.' And Brendan waved good-bye to them all from the door.

'He's a very friendly soul," said Aoife, collecting up the plates and cups.

'Bit too friendly maybe?' ventured Ellen.

'He's a good lad but he doesn't know when to stop jabbering.' Liam sat at the table. 'I just ignore him when we're in the boat and he doesn't seem to mind. Maybe working on the sea isn't the best job for him. It's a bit solitary. But the Brothers told me he was good with animals and he seemed a cheerful fella so I gave him the job.'

'I thought you said they starved the boys at St Joseph's. Brendan doesn't look like he's gone without food for more than an hour or two,' quipped Ellen.

Liam laughed. 'You should have seen him three months ago when I picked him up, not exactly a skeleton but not much flesh. He's barely stopped eating since then. I don't think he can believe that someone isn't going to come in and take the food off him. And Mrs Gallagher is always taking pity on the two of us and bringing us things she's baked.'

'I'm happy to think of him having his fill for once. And I'm pleased Mrs Gallagher's looking after you in my place.' Aoife set down a fresh pot of tea for Cathy and Liam.

'I fear he'll never have his fill, however much he eats, after what he's been through.' Cathy poured the tea. 'Abuse like that leaves a big emptiness.'

Hours later, as Cathy lay in Liam's arms after more energetic love-making, he stroked her right arm, then picked up her hand and placed it on his chest, his hand over hers. 'You know what you said about Brendan – him never being able to recover from St Joseph's – is that true for me too?'

Cathy paused before answering, choosing her words carefully. 'These traumatic experiences go very deep – we learn to cope but they're always there. I'll never get over learning that my Daddy killed himself, but I've managed to put it into a box in the corner of my heart and I try to keep it locked up. I think you are doing an amazing job recovering from what you suffered but, yes, I think you will always carry the scars. And you shouldn't be ashamed if they overwhelm you sometimes. I know I have times when I just wake up in the middle of the night and howl about my Daddy, and now about my Mammy too. I have no advice to give anyone about how to cope, but I think the more people you can find to love, who will love you back, definitely helps.'

They kissed softly and fell asleep wrapped around each other.

Chapter 5 – August 1951

The holiday party spent as much time by the waves as they could while the sun shone. Liam took one more afternoon off to take Johnny swimming and to give Cathy another lesson. The next day he returned from delivering the fish around Clifden with a football and a ball and bat. Brendan couldn't wait to play with Johnny after work, before supper.

'It's lovely to see the pair of them, isn't it, without a care in the world?' said Aoife to Cathy, as they both sat on the sand, supposedly reading, but drawn to the sight of the two lads kicking the ball around, laughing freely.

'Brendan isn't much older than a child himself, is he, and has a lot of childhood to make up for.'

When they woke up on Saturday, you could barely see twenty yards ahead. There was a slight, insistent drizzle smudging all the colours, throwing a veil over the landscape.

'Ah well, we've done better than expected I suppose,' said Ellen, eating toast. 'And, quite frankly, I'll be just as happy sitting in that comfy armchair reading my book as on the beach getting sand in my pants.'

Johnny was disappointed. 'I could still go in the sea, Mama, because I'll be getting wet anyway, won't I.'

'Not really, my love. The sea will be rougher than you're used to and none of us wants to stand around getting soaked to the skin watching you.'

Johnny was soon distracted. Tutored by Aoife, he started doing some drawings of the shells, seaweed and driftwood that he had collected over the week. At just gone eleven, there was a brisk knock and the door opened to reveal a very damp though still smiley Brendan, holding a wicker crate.

'It's a soft old day out here, missus,' he said as Cathy went to take the catch off him. 'Liam gave me this to give to you for your tea tonight.' Cathy looked inside to find a load of prawns, oysters and a very big fish.

'That's a sea trout there, you lucky devils. We never get to keep them; they always go off to be sold. But you're quite the VIPs.'

Aoife showed Cathy how to gut and prepare the fish and they cooked and shelled the prawns.

'I'll leave Liam to open the oysters. It's a bit tricky and I've lost the knack. And you want to eat them straight away once they're opened.'

'Well, it'll be an experience. I've eaten most things, thanks to Aunt Lily, but never those.'

When Liam got home, everything was ready to cook for supper; the beans growing on the sunny side of the cottage had been picked and spuds dug and washed.

'We shall have a banquet tonight,' said Liam, 'and, afterwards, I wondered whether you'd all fancy coming along to the céilí at Doyle's hotel. I've just seen the poster when I delivered their order.'

'Not me, thank you, Liam. Dancing is not exactly my forte.' Ellen gave her bad leg a whack with her stick.

'We'll stay here and look after, Johnny. But you and Cathy should go.' Aoife put her arms around Johnny. 'We'll play draughts, won't we?'

'Why can't I go too, Mama? I can dance.' Johnny pulled free of Aoife and twirled Cathy around. 'See.'

'You're a smashing dancer, son, but it'll be too grown-up for you. There'll be a lot of drinking and smoking. In a few years' time it'll be OK.'

Johnny bore the disappointment stoically, shrugged his shoulders and ran up to his bedroom.

'Wear some comfy shoes, Cathy,' said Liam. 'I mean to have you dance your legs off.'

As it was raining and there were just the two of them, Liam offered Brendan a lift into Clifden, which he jumped at, and asked to bring Dearbhla Gallagher too. Doyle's Hotel was in the centre of Clifden. It boasted a large bar with padded benches, considerably smarter than Cathy's family pub but the sounds and smells were familiar to her. The noise levels were already raised and the band hadn't even started to play. This was the sound of working people out for a good time at the end of a long week, spending their hard-earned money on plenty of alcohol.

The party of four found themselves a table and Liam went off with Brendan to buy drinks. Cathy tried to chat to Dearbhla but it was hard to be heard above the hubbub. Dearbhla was a shy fifteen-year-old, with black hair and blue eyes and a pleasing roundness to her face and body. She flashed a broad smile at Brendan when he and Liam returned carrying their drinks, Guinness for the men, a half-pint of shandy for Dearbhla and a vodka and tonic for Cathy.

'Sláinte, everyone,' said Brendan and they all raised their glasses.

Cathy watched the band set up on the little raised stage, with a fiddle, an accordion, a flute and a bodhran to keep the beat. After a few numbers, Liam dragged her up to join Dearbhla and Brendan in an eightsome reel, shouting the instructions into her ear. It was simple enough to learn, even though Cathy did not think of herself as any sort of dancer. The first night she had met Joe in Colchester, she had refused to dance almost the whole evening, but, when Joe finally persuaded her to risk the floor, she had found dancing in his arms totally instinctive. Dancing was just music made physical.

They returned to their seats, sweaty and exhausted. Liam went to buy more drinks.

'It's great craic. You did well, missus, learning the steps from scratch. Dearbhla here has been teaching me at home and we usually go to the céilí in Moyard of a Saturday night, don't we.'

Cathy let Brendan talk on while her thoughts drifted. She looked over to the bar where Liam was chatting to the handsome, buxom young woman with ruby red hair serving him. Not naturally red hair, she thought. Did Liam know her perhaps? They certainly seemed deep in conversation until another punter needed to be served and Liam brought over the drinks.

'Here you go. You'll need some rehydrating before we start dancing again.'

By ten o'clock, everyone had jigged and reeled their fill and people sat back to listen properly to some songs, a few in Irish but mostly in English. Cathy knew some, like *The Wild Rover*, well enough to join in. Brendan stood on his chair for *Molly Malone*, bawling as loudly as he could, which amused everyone around them.

'Sorry about that, missus, but I'm a Dublin boy meself and I can remember my poor dead Mammy singing that to me when I was just a chiseler.'

'How old were you when you were sent away to St Joseph's?'

'Not until I was twelve, missus, when my mother died and I got into some wicked company. So, I only had to endure the Brothers for four years, not like some of the other lads who'd been there since they were five or six. They were broken-down poor creatures.'

At just gone eleven, the four left the bar and outside the rain was lashing down. They ran to the car and piled in, dripping all over the leather seats.

'It's only God's good rain, missus. It won't hurt us but I hope it won't spoil your fine car, us sitting in our wet clothes.'

'Don't worry, Brendan. I honestly don't care.'

Cathy drove Dearbhla and Brendan right up to Mrs Gallagher's front door and the two dashed inside. Then she reversed and parked outside the cottage. The rain was drumming hard onto the car. When she turned off the windscreen wipers, it felt like they were sheltering underneath a waterfall.

'This is exciting. I love a good storm.'

'Fine when you're tucked up inside a car, not so good when I'm out on the boat. Though getting wet is no bother. I can see right through your dress, by the way.' Liam put his hand onto Cathy's breast and kissed her. She pushed him away.

'Nope. I'm not having sex in a car. I want to get out of these wet clothes.'

'That's good because I want you to get out of those wet clothes too.'

An hour later, they lay back, satisfied, on Liam's bed. The rain had stopped and they watched the last clouds pass over the nearly full moon through the un-curtained window. Liam turned on his side and ran his hand down Cathy's body.

'You look even more like a mermaid tonight, Cathy, with this silvery light on your skin.'

'More scaly, you mean?' They laughed and then kissed.

'Liam, who was that woman at the bar you were talking to? The one with the red hair?'

'Sheenagh? I told you about her in my letters. We walked out together for about two months in the spring. I deliver fish to Doyle's three times a week and I couldn't help noticing her in the bar. She's a good-looking woman but I'll have you know she came on to me. I would never have dared ask her out. She looks too much to handle, if you know what I mean, but I didn't need to.'

'Why did you stop seeing her then?'

'She started seeing someone else, and, to be honest, I thought she was way above my league. But tonight she said she missed me and that she'd been a fool to dump me.'

Cathy hardly dared ask but she felt compelled. 'What do you think about that?'

Liam looked hard at Cathy. 'Well, I'm not sure. I'd like to find someone to settle down with sooner or later. I'm thirty-three. I'm OK on my own but it would be better if I could find a wife to share my life with. I must have met all the girls in Moyard and Clifden. Maybe I should get more serious with Sheenagh – if she'd have me.'

'If she'd have you? Anyone would be lucky to have you, Liam.'

'Aww, Cathy. You're very kind, but I know I'm not much of a catch. Anyway, we should get some sleep now.' He kissed her cheek and pulled up the sheets over the pair of them but Cathy sat up and swung her legs out of the bed.

'I think I'll let you get a peaceful night on your own, Liam. See you in the morning.'

******

After a fretful night, Cathy came downstairs early the next morning to find Aoife putting on her jacket and hat.

'Cathy! What are you doing up? I'm just off to early mass and I thought I could creep out without anyone hearing. Did you have a good time at the céilí?'

'It was fun. Brendan sings as loudly as he talks, you won't be surprised to hear.'

'Well, if he's at mass, I'll soon find out.'

'Aoife, let me run you in the car. I want to go over to Omey Island anyway and I can wait until mass is finished and then bring you home.'

'I was looking forward to the walk, like the old days, but the sky is a bit threatening so, okay. Thank you, macushla.'

Dark clouds filled the sky but there was no rain as the two women got into the car for the short drive to Our Lady Star of the Sea, the little church at Claddaghduff.

'We're a godless lot, aren't we, Aoife? I'm sorry you have no-one to keep you company at mass.'

'That doesn't make you godless at all, Cathy. I see God shining out of you all: Liam and Johnny and my beloved Ellen - despite her foul mouth at times. I'm a Catholic because that's how I was brought up, but I don't for one minute think there's only one way to find God.'

'You're the most god-like person I know, Aoife.' Cathy squeezed the older woman's hand. 'You and my Daddy.'

'Aww, go on with you.'

After she'd dropped Aoife off, Cathy drove down the track to the wide strand linking Omey Island to the mainland. The tide was still going out but, to save time, she decided to risk following the markers and drove through the shallow water – she only had an hour before mass ended. Once she had parked the car on the other side of the strand, she walked to the graveyard where Máire and her mother, Ailsa, were buried. She wasn't surprised to see the graves clean and moss-free and on Máire's grave a neat collection of cockle shells and polished white pebbles. That was thanks to Liam. Ever since the young Cathy had made him promise to maintain her decoration, Liam had kept his word.

The meticulous display of shells and stones made Cathy weep silently. After all that Liam had suffered, he truly deserved to be happy and if this Sheenagh woman could do that, Cathy knew she shouldn't stand in his way. He had never said anything to her approaching a declaration of love, despite all their physical intimacy, neither in his letters nor in person. He was clearly just grateful for the sex that Cathy had offered last year. She'd positioned it as therapy after all and Liam had taken it as such and nothing more. She looked at the neat graves. What a hard, short life both Ailsa and Máire had had compared to hers. Yes, she had lost Joe in the war, but she had a very comfortable existence; a rewarding job in her own business, loved by her family and her guardian angels and, above all, she had the gift of Johnny. If she never found romantic love again, she would still have so much to be thankful for and so much to devote her energies to. But did this Sheenagh woman deserve Liam?

When Cathy and Aoife got back, they found Ellen cooking breakfast for Liam and Johnny. 'Get your coats off quick. There's fresh tea in the pot and bread cut. You'd better make the most of this as I have no intention of cooking again.'

'It looks lovely, my dear,' said Aoife as she contemplated the heap of greasy food in front of her. 'And then I'll get the chicken in to roast. Could you pick the beans please, Liam.'

'Sure, and then we've promised Brendan a kick around on the beach. Will you come and watch us, Cathy?'

'Maybe. But I'd really like to finish my book before the holiday is over. I'll never do it once we're back – always too tired during term.' But Cathy had something other than reading planned.

The Clifden church bells tolled eleven. Cathy locked her car, parked neatly outside Doyle's Hotel and walked into its front lounge, taking a seat with a view of the reception desk. A waitress came and took Cathy's order. She wasn't sure why she'd come to the hotel but she hadn't been able to stop herself, slipping out of the house while the others were on the beach.

The coffee arrived in a silver pot on a silver tray with three neatly arranged triangles of shortbread on a doilied plate. This could almost be the Shelbourne, thought Cathy.

'Is Sheenagh in today?'

'Sheenagh Lynch?' Cathy nodded. 'She's in the back office. Do you want me to get her for you?'

'Oh, no. I was just curious. Thank you. Please don't tell her I asked after her.'

'I won't. I try and stay out of her way as much as possible to be honest.' The girl rolled her eyes and walked off.

Cathy stirred hot milk into the coffee, took out her book and tried to read, but, at the slightest noise or movement, she lifted her eyes, searching for Sheenagh's red hair. Guests came and went, the porter shunted luggage in and out and a few punters ordered pre-lunch drinks. Ten minutes later, her coffee was all drunk, just crumbs on the doily. This was hopeless. Sheenagh was clearly not going to show herself today and Cathy needed to get back to help prepare lunch.

It was gone midday when Cathy got back into her car; she sat looking up at the hotel, searching for… she wasn't sure what. Then, in the passageway that ran alongside it, two figures appeared, a wiry middle-aged man and a woman with a shock of red hair tumbling around her shoulders. Cathy froze. The man pushed Sheenagh against the wall of the passageway and kissed her roughly, running his hand up her skirt exposing the tops of her stockings and suspenders. She, in turn, grabbed his crotch and the pair writhed around for a few minutes until Sheenagh pulled down her skirt and threw the man's hand off her breasts. She took out a pack of cigarettes, stuck one in her mouth and offered them to the man, which he took and struck a match. They stood chatting, dragging on their fags until they were finished, threw down the stubs and ground them into the paving, then they emerged from the passage and walked in opposite directions without a wave or a word.

Cathy studied Sheenagh's receding figure, tottering on heels too high to work in and squeezed into a skirt a couple of sizes too small. Should she follow her? What more could she hope to learn? She had seen enough. Cathy tried to imagine Liam married to this woman. He must be attracted to her if he was thinking of proposing, yet Sheenagh looked nothing like herself. That explained why Liam had never said anything to suggest that he would want to marry Cathy. She had to accept that reality and she felt the dull weight of lost hope in her gut. But that didn't mean she shouldn't save Liam from a woman she felt unworthy of him, even if she herself wouldn't be the beneficiary. But why was Sheenagh unworthy? Wasn't Cathy being a big snob, disliking the high heels and dyed hair? Maybe Liam liked that sort of look – Sheenagh certainly had a magnificent bosom. And, as for messing about with a fella in broad daylight, Cathy could hardly talk – hadn't she and Liam had full sex in the open air on the beach only the other day.

The clouds were parting, allowing peeks of bright blue sky to show through when Cathy arrived back in Cleggan. There was a valedictory feel about the cottage, their last day here on holiday, time to pack and load the car ready for the off first thing. The afternoon continued to brighten up so they all embarked on a long walk around the headland, even Ellen, though they slowed the pace down to suit her which meant that an impatient Johnny kept running ahead and doubling back to rejoin them.

As they strolled along, Liam pointed out fields that he had his eye on, one with a large ramshackle farmhouse in the distance. 'That's where Jack Brodie lives but he doesn't seem to farm any longer. I'd love to get my hands on the land.'

'Well, he must be over sixty, and his children have moved away,' said Aoife. 'It might come up for sale in a couple of years.'

'And I mean to buy it when it does. I'm working hard and saving hard. No-one seems to want to farm properly around here anymore so I don't think the land will go for too high a price even though it's decent grazing. It's a damn sight better than the craggy fields I have the sheep on. I'd like to put beef cattle on it.'

'Well, can you make sure you get a donkey too, so that I can be carried around next summer like an oriental empress.' Ellen's leg had had enough. 'I shall head back to the cottage, if you'll excuse me, but don't let me stop you lot continuing your walk.' But Aoife wouldn't hear of Ellen returning alone. The two women linked arms and headed back to the village, watched by Cathy and a smiling Liam.

'It's grand that they've found each other, isn't it? Never too late to find love.'

Cathy said nothing, just turned and continued towards the sea.

******

'Have you enjoyed your holiday, my darling?' Cathy was tucking Johnny and Tiny Ted into bed. She had spent the afternoon packing cases and carefully collecting up the various items that Johnny had created over the week, the drawings, paintings and models made out of driftwood and shells. 'Leave me one of the paintings, would you, Johnny, to remind me of you all?' Liam had asked and Johnny had solemnly chosen a crayon sketch of the boat with full nets and lobster pots inside.

'Yes, very much. I love the sea, Mama. And I think Brendan is kind and funny. But I've missed some things too; I've missed the trams and playing my cello.'

'Gracious, I didn't expect you to say that, my love. You always moan when I tell you to do your practice.'

'I know. I'm surprised too.'

Cathy kissed her son and leaned over him to switch off his bedside lamp.

'Mama, if Liam gets Ellen a donkey, can I have one too, do you think?'

Cathy laughed. 'I think Ellen was joking, darling.'

Johnny considered this for a moment. 'But a donkey would be fun, and maybe we can get Ellen a new leg.'

Cathy went downstairs. Ellen and Aoife were installed in the plush armchairs, glasses of whiskey in hand. Liam was sitting on the rug, his back to the door, talking quietly to them.

'He was called Bernard. He can only have been four or five. I remember his little freckly face. One day he was lying ill in his bed and the next morning he'd disappeared. No-one said a thing. But then I found a pile of freshly dug earth behind the school and I reckon that's where they buried him. No name, no cross, nothing to mark that there had once been a life. Me and a couple of the older boys would make little crosses out of twigs but they always got pulled out. Eventually the soil sank and the grass grew and covered over the grave but I never forgot where it was.'

Cathy sat down quietly on the piano stool. So Máire's grave was not the first Liam had been custodian of. What a decent man he was, far too good for that Sheenagh Lynch.

'It's a feckin' scandal. Christian Brothers? Huh, the irony,' fumed Ellen. 'That's why I simply cannot understand why you can keep on with the church stuff, Aoife, playing along with all this nonsense.'

Aoife said nothing. She was used to being challenged by Ellen on the subject of religion but she always kept her quiet dignity and refused to be riled.

'Has Johnny gone off now, Cathy?'

'Yes, out like a light. So much running and fresh air.'

Liam stood and came over to Cathy. 'Would you maybe play us that Moonlight piece then once more. Before you go and the piano falls silent for another year. Please, Cathy.'

'I think it might wake him though. His room is right above our heads. And it's far too sad for our last night.'

'But it *is* sad that you're going. Sad is exactly how I'm feeling. Aoife, will you sing us a song then please. What's the one about the shy farmer?'

Aoife smiled at Liam. 'You mean *Ar Éirinn ní neosfainn cé hí?* All right then, as it's you, but only very softly so as not to wake the boy. And Cathy, I sang this to your mother and father when they came here on their honeymoon. Can you believe that'll be over thirty years ago now, but I remember it like yesterday.' And Aoife began to sing in her pure, silvery voice.

'Aréir is mé ag téarnamh um neoin
ar an taobh thall den teora ina mbím'
Cathy understood only the odd word but it still captivated her.
'Do léimeas fá dhéin dul 'na comhair
is ar Éirinn ní neosfainn cé hí.'
There were two more verses and, by the end, even Ellen had been sucked into the mesmerising melody.

'That is so beautiful, Aoife. Thank you. And to think my Mammy and Daddy heard it in this very place all that time ago. I recognise some words but what does it all mean?'

'The title means *For all Ireland, I'd not tell her name.* It's about a farmer who sees a beautiful young girl on his land. He's captivated not just by her beauty but also by the kindness and generosity that shines out of her face. He wants to talk to her and look after her and place her in his heart, but he won't tell her name to anyone, not for all of Ireland.'

'Right. I'm definitely going to get you to teach me some more Irish when we get back, along with the students. I'm not proud. We were taught so little at school in Rowanbridge.'

'Your father will be so pleased to hear you say that. That's why he came out to Connemara after all.'

'Such a waste of time and effort. Aoife knows my opinion on the topic. It's fine for singing old songs like that but we should just let it die out naturally, though I suppose it's no less important than Latin or Greek, so I should just shut my mouth and get myself off to bed. Long journey tomorrow.

Come on, Aoife. Good night to you both, and make sure you get plenty of sleep, Cathy, before risking our lives in that car.'

Once they were alone, Cathy went over and sat in one of the armchairs. 'I'm just sneaking a go in one of these. I haven't had a look in all week. They are very comfy indeed.' Liam came over and sat in its twin. He took Cathy's hand and lifted it to his lips.

'Next time you're here, there will be more chairs and somewhere more fitting to place your lovely arse than the floor or a kitchen chair. Will you come and see me tonight? One last lesson before you push me back out to fend for myself?'

Cathy avoided answering and took her hand away. 'Tell me more about Sheenagh. You said you thought you two might get back together soon.'

'Well, she seemed keen last night.'

Cathy took a deep breath. 'Liam, I don't think she's right for you.'

'Not right for me? No-one's right for me. I'm damaged goods. But how on earth would you know, Cathy? You haven't even met her.'

'Don't be angry, but I went to Doyle's Hotel this morning and I waited to see if I could catch sight of her.'

'You did what?'

'I know, I know. It sounds dreadful but I just wanted to make sure she's good enough for you. I didn't see her in the hotel in the end but I watched out for her from the car. She came outside eventually, along the side passageway, on her way home I think, and she was with a man. And she kissed him … and touched him and stuff. She's very good-looking and everything but I don't think you can trust her.'

Liam stood up and walked to the door in silence. He stood facing it for some moments before turning back to Cathy, his jaw tense with contained anger.

'How could you, Cathy. Spying on someone I care about. You might have meant well but you're not my keeper. You have to stop trying to fix everything and everyone.' He glared at her. 'I don't want to say anything else or I might regret it, so I'll bid you goodnight.' He left the room and closed the door behind himself very firmly, leaving Cathy sitting in the armchair wondering how she could have messed up so badly.

Chapter 6 – Easter 1952

Cathy sat at her desk as she did most Sunday afternoons, catching up on paperwork. It was eerily quiet. Term had just ended and the students had left. Johnny was out with his Uncle Seamus, watching him play golf.

Seamus seemed to think it was his responsibility to get Johnny interested in sport. In February, he had taken the boy to two games at Lansdowne Road in the Five Nations rugby championships. Johnny had been thrilled when Ireland beat Scotland but mightily disappointed when they were thrashed by Wales a fortnight later. Johnny was always happy to be driven anywhere in Uncle Seamus's Jaguar and to spend time with the tall, cheerful solicitor who took such great care of his mother and himself. Uncle Seamus played the viola and sometimes he would put it between his knees and play it like a cello to make Johnny laugh. When his Mama accompanied him on the piano for his exam pieces, Seamus would often add impressive embellishments over the top on his viola for fun.

Cathy looked at her watch, nearly six o'clock. They would be back soon and then Ellen and Aoife would arrive for supper and their weekly bridge session. Cathy took out the pile of opened letters at the back of her desk, undid the ribbon round them and read the top one. It was the last letter Liam had written to her before their holiday to Cleggan last summer, all about the weather and how much he was looking forward to them coming but saying nothing about the new building work, the piano or even about Brendan.

Cathy returned it to the pile and took out the letter half-way down, the one from spring last year, where Liam had casually talked about having a few dates with a girl who worked at Doyle's Hotel. He hadn't named her Sheenagh but

Cathy knew it was her. She realised now that Liam hadn't always shared everything in his weekly missives, but she still missed them. Oh well, it was probably for the best. He needed to get on with his life in his own way and, for that, he needed to break old habits.

But what about her life? She was only thirty-one but her only social life was with her soon-to-appear middle-aged guardian angels. She loved all three dearly but it was like spending your life with your parents.

Cathy heard the car on the gravel and then the front door open and close and in ran Johnny to give her a hug.

'Mama, Uncle Seamus says that if I grow another inch I can be his caddy and he'll give me a shilling every time.' Seamus followed in at a more relaxed pace and gave Cathy a wink. 'He drove a hard bargain but that's the going rate for first-class caddies these days. And he has learned negotiation skills from his mother of course.'

When Ellen and Aoife arrived they all enjoyed Cathy's signature toad-in-the-hole, accompanied by a classy bottle of claret that Seamus had brought along. 'It was left over from the case I took to Rowanbridge at Christmas. Surprising that there was anything left really, when you think how much Father Stephen put away.'

Last Christmas, for the first time ever, Cathy had persuaded Seamus, Ellen and Aoife to join her, Johnny and Aunt Lily in the trip to the family Christmas. There were enough bedrooms in Main Street with Fergus and Bridie moved out to the Byrne farmhouse and Aunt Lily at Stasia's. But Sam and Rose had been busy and the old house now had electric lights upstairs and, most importantly, two indoor lavatories and a bathroom in the little boxroom where Tricky used to sleep. Tricky had taken over Hannah's old bedroom.

Johnny said it was the best Christmas ever and who could argue with him, surrounded by doting and indulgent aunts and uncles of all types, all ready to give him a game of ludo, play charades or go for a walk along the River Nore.

'Drink will be the death of that man, mark my words,' pronounced Ellen. 'I watched my uncle in Limerick drink himself into the ground and that priest is well on the way.'

'Rose said that he nearly fell down the pulpit steps at Midnight Mass and the whole congregation gasped,' related Cathy.

'I was there,' said Aoife. 'Yes, he stumbled but he managed to save himself. But I wonder what the drinking is all about.' Aoife had no idea that Hannah's ghost was Father Stephen's torment and Cathy had no intention of telling any of the three of them.

'Well, it was delightful to be part of your family for a few days. God knows there are enough of you when you get together.' Much as he had loved seeing all of Hannah's offspring so clearly happy and thriving, Seamus, who lived alone, had found spending three days in such noisy and exuberant company rather exhausting.

'It must put Stasia's nose out of joint to have Lily there playing the great matriarch,' Ellen chuckled. 'But lovely for the little chap to find so many relations all desperate to entertain him. It's going to be a bit different over in England. Just the two women.'

At the end of the week, Cathy was venturing over to England on the ferry to introduce Johnny to his Granny Ashfield and Auntie Shirley at long last. The boy had been reminding her at least once a week since last summer, that she had promised to take him, and she had finally organised the trip.

'I wonder what Johnny will make of it all,' said Cathy. 'If he thinks England is some grand and aristocratic place, teeming with kings and duchesses and the like, Ollerton is going to give him an almighty shock.'

******

Their crossing from Dún Laoghaire to Holyhead went smoothly enough, but a gruelling five-hour cross-country drive followed. Cathy and Johnny didn't draw up outside the semi until nearly six o'clock, but Mam Ashfield was nevertheless waiting at the window and she waved excitedly when she saw Cathy get out of the car. How long has she been sitting there? wondered Cathy, realising how much this visit meant to her, not just to Johnny.

It felt much longer than six years since Cathy had last walked out of that front door, babe in arms, to go back to Ireland to live with her grandmother at the Academy. It had certainly been the right thing to do but Number 27 held some happy memories: her wedding night with Joe, eating the best scones she had ever tasted, giving birth to Johnny as she squeezed Mam Ashfield's hand, seeing her baby with his father on Joe's few visits home before he had been killed. Mrs Ashfield and Shirley were both admirable, hard-working women who had warmly welcomed Joe's pregnant wife and had done their best to make her feel at home in a foreign land. Despite all they had done for her, Cathy had never truly thought of them as her family, although they were certainly Johnny's.

'Mam, how are you? And Shirley? It's good to see you both looking well.'

'You too, duck. So … this is our Johnny.' Mam Ashfield beamed at her grandson, who was hanging back behind his mother on the garden path. Cathy took his hand and brought him to the doorstep. 'Yes, this is Johnny. Give your Granny and Auntie a kiss.'

'No, leave the lad until he's ready. Come on in then. Shirley's put the kettle on. You must be exhausted.'

After tea and a couple of Mam's miraculous scones, Johnny relaxed. He asked about all the photographs of Joe in frames arranged around the cramped sitting room: as a toddler posing on Shirley's lap for a professional portrait; in short trousers at school; standing in front of a tree brandishing a bow and arrow; as a teenager playing cricket; in his army uniform; newly married with his Mama outside Mansfield Register Office. A precious life summed up in six black and white rectangles. Johnny asked the two women lots of questions about the father he had never known.

'Was my Daddy a good cricketer?'

'He was good enough to play for the county juniors when he was at school,' answered Shirley, 'but that all stopped when he joined the army. I think his cricket bat is still upstairs somewhere.'

'It's in the glory hole, Shirley. You can take it home with you if you like, Johnny. Can you play?'

'No. We play hurling in Ireland.'

'There are plenty of cricket teams in Ireland, Johnny,' said Cathy, 'but I think it's seen very much as an English sport these days, so less popular than it was.'

'I love cricket. Maybe next time you come, Johnny, I'll take you to Trent Bridge to watch Notts County play. We had a terrible season last year and were nearly bottom of the table. We need some decent bowlers. Maybe you could be one in the future. You're a Nottinghamshire lad after all.'

'Am I, Mama?'

'You are, I suppose. Born in this house. I've never thought of it like that, I confess, but you have every right to an English passport as well as an Irish one. You'll have choices, my love. What do you want to be, do you reckon?'

Johnny blushed and squirmed at the question. Did his Mama really want him to choose between being his mother's or his father's son?

'Leave the lad be.' Shirley stood up. 'Come on, duck. Come and see your bedroom, Johnny. You'll have to share it with your mother but there's someone up there waiting for you.' Johnny looked mystified and followed Shirley upstairs. Five minutes later and he rushed back into the room holding a large soft toy.

'Look, Mama, it's Big Ted, Tiny Ted's Daddy.'

'Oh, aren't you the lucky one, Johnny! Have you said thank you to your Auntie Shirley?'

Johnny turned to Shirley who had come downstairs rather more sedately than the boy. 'Thank you for Big Ted,' he mumbled shyly.

'You're very welcome, big chap. I thought you should have a proper sized bear instead of that midget. You just couldn't get the fur fabric during the war, could you, Mam?'

'No, nor much of anything else. Shirley had to use the fur collar of one of my coats to make Tiny Ted, you know.'

After supper and a few games of rummy, Cathy took Johnny up to bed and read him some stories.

'How are Tiny Ted and Big Ted getting on?' Cathy put both toy bears under the covers with her son.

'OK. But, Mama, I think I'm too old to have a new teddy, don't you?'

'You're never too old to have a new teddy bear. Anyway, your Auntie Shirley made him especially for you.'

'I'll look after him, don't worry. But I'll always love Tiny Ted the best.'

Cathy could hear someone coughing persistently as she came back downstairs. Shirley was offering a glass of water to her mother who was holding a handkerchief tightly to her mouth and barking into it. Eventually the coughing abated.

'Sorry about that, duck, I just got something caught in my throat.'

Shirley looked at Cathy and shook her head. 'Mam's cough's been getting worse these last two years and it doesn't help living in this mucky place. Dust everywhere and everyone with their coal fires burning away. I wish I could persuade her to move but she won't hear of it, will you.' Shirley put her arm on her mother's back.'

'Don't be daft. I'm fine. Anyway, can I get you a cup of something, Cathy? And I've made some ginger cake too. You always loved that.'

The next day, after breakfast, Shirley suggested that they take a trip to nearby Sherwood Forest to see the giant oak tree that Robin Hood and his Merry Men had supposedly lived around and hidden inside.

'Who's Robin Hood?' asked Johnny.

'You don't know who Robin Hood is? What's your mother been teaching you?' Shirley picked up the photograph of Joe holding a bow and arrow. 'This is your Daddy dressed as Robin Hood. He lived in the Middle Ages – not sure exactly when – and he was a hero who took money from the corrupt, rich people to give to the poor.'

'Isn't that stealing?'

'It's not stealing when those people got their money unfairly by oppressing the peasants and those poor people could barely survive; it's justice. Robin Hood was making things a bit fairer. Even today, the people who are lords and ladies, dukes and what have you in their big houses on their big estates are living on the money and land they took off poor people centuries ago. Robin Hood was a posh bloke himself to start with but he could see that things needed to change, so he set himself against the evil Sherriff of Nottingham and King John himself. Robin Hood is our local hero and your Dad wanted to be like him. And he was a crack shot with a bow and arrow.'

'Can we go to see Robin Hood's tree, Mama?'

'Of course, darling. I'm sorry I haven't told you about him. I don't know why not, especially as me and my schoolfriends used to pretend to be Robin Hood and Little John and Maid Marion all the time.'

Mam Ashfield declined to join the outing the next day. Cathy drove past Edwinstowe and on to the forest entrance where Shirley led them along a well-trodden path, lined with dense woodland and ferns, to find themselves eventually in the presence of the magisterial oak tree.

Johnny was dumbstruck for a while and walked around it slowly, gazing up into its leafy canopy. 'There's a hole in it, Mama! Can I go inside?' Cathy nodded. Johnny tentatively stepped into the hollow tree and stroked the inside walls.

'Did my Daddy come in here, Auntie Shirley?'

'Of course. This is where the photograph was taken.' Shirley turned to Cathy and whispered, 'Shame we don't have a camera with us.'

'You're right. I'm an idiot not to have brought it. I'll bring him again before we go back and take a shot like the one of Joe. I need to get him a bow and arrows somewhere.'

The two women sat on the grass, watching Johnny run around, in and out of the tree and through the ferny undergrowth nearby.

'If it was the weekend, there'd be loads of people around but it's quiet enough today. Nice to come in a car for a change, instead of the bus and Shanks's pony. Joe would be so proud to see his son turn out so handsome and clever, you know.'

'You and Mam must miss Joe terribly.'

'And so must you, surely.' Shirley fixed Cathy with a hard stare.

'Yes, of course. I try to keep his memory alive for Johnny's sake too.'

'Mam and I expected you to be remarried by now. We hoped you would. Joe would want that too because Johnny needs a Dad.'

'Well, it hasn't happened. It's not easy meeting men when you have a child to look after and I'm busy all week with the Academy. Did you never want to marry, Shirley?'

'I could never leave Mam. But I do have a gentleman friend that Mam doesn't know about. I've never brought him home and I only see him at work. He's the caretaker at the factory. He's Polish – and he's married.'

'Oh dear. That's not easy.'

'It is what it is. He's Catholic, so he's never going to divorce his wife. And he's got a couple of kids so I live with it. It's better than nothing. And there's more to life than men.'

Cathy wanted to ask more about Shirley's lover – how and when they had found each other, where they went to be alone at the factory - but decided that she would wait for Shirley to tell her if she wanted to.

'One thing I do regret is not having kids. I look at you with Johnny and … ,' Shirley turned her face away, ' …and I can see how special that bond is. I'm too old now anyway. But at least Joe lives on in that lad there.'

Cathy took Shirley's hand and they sat together watching Johnny whoop and jump through the greenery.

On Easter Sunday, Johnny was presented with an enormous chocolate egg. Cathy didn't try to prevent him eating it all, Johnny's own stomach told him he needed to stop after wolfing a mere quarter. He offered some broken chocolate shell to the three women.

'No, duck, it's for you. Save it for your journey home.'

Two days later, Cathy was packing up the car again ready to drive back to the Holyhead ferry. Johnny came out of the house carrying the prized cricket bat.

'Granny says I can take this home with me. I'd like to play with it. Will Uncle Seamus teach me cricket, do you think?'

'I'm sure he'll do his best, my love. It can't be that different from golf, I reckon.'

'Golf's easy, Mama. You only have to hit the ball when it's still. But I'll need a team to play cricket properly.'

In addition to the bat, the back seat was full of other gifts; Big Ted sat alongside his 'son', next to them a bag containing sandwiches, apples and drinks, a tin of scones, a ginger cake wrapped in greaseproof paper, assorted jars of homemade jam and two plant pots of white dicentra that Cathy had admired and Shirley had promptly dug up and split for her. On the back shelf was also the toy bow, with a quiver of arrows with rubber stickers on the ends that Shirley had found triumphantly in a shop in Ollerton, enabling Cathy to recreate the photograph of Joe at the Major Oak.

Mam and Shirley came out to wave them off. 'I want to take a last shot of you all on the doorstep, and I'll send you copies.' Cathy organised the two Ashfield women with Johnny standing in front of them, before taking several shots just to be sure. 'Thank you for looking after us, Mam, but will you promise to look after yourself and get that cough checked out for me? There's no excuse now you've got that marvellous National Health Service I've been reading about. I wish we had something like that in Ireland.'

'Bye-bye, Cathy. Me and Shirley have loved having you here. Please come back soon.' The old lady started to cry as she embraced her daughter-in-law. 'And Johnny, I love you very much, duck. I can see your Daddy in you. That nose. This was his home and it's yours too, whenever you want to come.'

'Bye, Granny. Thank you for all my presents, and you, Auntie Shirley. I promise to come back soon.' Johnny turned to his mother. 'We will, won't we?'

'We will, my love.'

Chapter 7 – May 1952

'*Unforgettable. That's what you are...*' Nat King Cole was on the radio and Aggie was singing. With her, around the kitchen table, were Bridie, Fergus and Rose, whose nails Bridie was painting with pink varnish. Fergus had his curly head down, checking through tomorrow's speech while Cathy ironed her dress for Rose and Sam's wedding. Aggie looked with pride at Hannah McDermott's four children, now all so grown-up and handsome, as she sipped tea between verses. *'That's why, darling, it's incredible, that someone so unforgettable, thinks that I am unforgettable too...'*

'Isn't it a bit weird, having the bride's brother as your best man?' asked Cathy.

'Why not? I like being a bit weird.' Fergus looked up. 'It's better than being boring and doing what everyone else does.'

'Sam has no male relatives, Cathy,' said Rose. 'Not any more anyway. His little brother died, didn't he Aggie? I don't remember him but you might. Sam says that Kevin would be the same age as me if he'd lived.'

'What happened?' asked Bridie.

'He caught the measles and then he fell to pneumonia.' Aggie put down her cup and leaned over to switch off the radio. 'We were in the midst of the Depression – 1931 - and Ned and Teresa couldn't afford to call out a doctor. Little Kevin wasn't the only child who died for want of medicine in those dark times.'

'Most healthy children can cope with measles.' Cathy hung up her dress on the door and came to sit with them. 'But it's dangerous if they're already in a poor state of health as I guess little Kevin would have been because of the poverty through the Depression. And no magic penicillin either then. Ireland needs a proper health service like they have in England now. Mam Ashfield has been having her emphysema seen to, and all for free.'

'We tried back in 1948, didn't we?' asked Bridie.

'We did. Something else sensible that the Church opposed,' said Aggie collecting up the dirty crockery. 'God knows why. Maybe they want to fill up heaven as soon as possible. Now, I need to do a bit of work on the cake before bed - and you lot shouldn't be too late. Big day tomorrow.'

'For you too, Madame Carroll...' Fergus stood and picked up Aggie, cradling her like a baby; she was not a small woman but Fergus's size and strength made her look as light as a bird. '... because you will be there in place of our Mammy, as honorary mother of the bride, whatever plans Auntie Stasia or Great-aunt Lily might have to nab that spot.'

'Well, I'll be wearing one of your mother's hats for the occasion so, from the back, someone might mistake me for her – apart from my fat arse of course.'

Fergus carefully put Aggie back on her feet and turned her round. 'I'm no expert on arses but it looks okay to me.' Bridie slapped her brother's backside. 'No, you're not an expert on arses, you just are one.' Fergus chased his sister around the table before throwing her over his shoulder. 'Stop it, you eejit. Put me down now.' Bridie banged on his back with her fists, laughing hysterically all the while. 'Fergus, you big bully. Just 'cos you're strong enough to pick us up, I take great exception to you imposing your strength on us women without our consent.'

Fergus put her down. 'There speaks the budding lawyer.'

Rose came over and kissed Aggie. 'Well, I couldn't ask for a better substitute for our Mammy, Aggie, and your arse is just perfect.'

'Jeezus, stop it now.' Aggie looked round at the four of them with great pride and not a little emotion, before taking the iced wedding cake out of the pantry in order to add a few final flourishes.

'How are you finding uni, Bridie?' asked Cathy, putting on the kettle.

'Aww, it's grand. It makes a change being able to have intelligent conversations about stuff – politics, art and the like – instead of having to listen to chat about the slurry run-off in the milking parlour or the clapped-out tractors – or how much the bar needs some new seats.'

'I'm sorry we're so boring but those are the things that are paying for your fancy degree, you know.' said Rose gently and she gave her shiny nails a final blow.

'Oh God, I didn't mean you lot are boring. Just that it's exciting to meet new people and learn new things. I've joined the Literary and Debating Society committee.'

'That must be ideal for someone who wants to be a lawyer,' said Cathy. 'Did you know that the Kilkenny TD, Thomas Derrig, went to Galway Uni too? Our Daddy did an awful lot to help that man win his seat here back in the day.'

'He's still our TD, and now he's the Minister for Lands, whatever that means.' Rose started to make cocoa for everyone.

'Daddy tried to get Derrig to do something about the industrial schools like Letterfrack but nothing came of it even though Derrig became Education Minister,' said Cathy, her thoughts turning to the man still living with the terrifying memories from that school. Unforgettable.

'It's not all serious debate and politics though. Galway is a beautiful city. You should come and visit me now you have a car. But the best thing is: no more bloody nuns.' Bridie picked up two cups of cocoa and headed for the hall. 'I'll just take up a drink for Daddy.' Tricky had taken himself off to his bedroom soon after Johnny had gone to bed. 'Night night everyone.'

'And I'd better get on that bike.' Fergus drained his cup. He kissed his sisters and Aggie before folding up his speech and putting it in his shirt breast pocket. 'I mustn't lose this. I'm nervous as hell but also very excited about tomorrow. Seeing Rose marry the man she loves would have made our Mammy so happy. I intend to be happy all day long for her sake as well as mine. See y'all in the morning.'

'Rose, get yourself off to bed, love. Aggie and I will clear up here.'

'I'm not sure I'll be able to sleep, Cathy. This is the biggest thing I'll ever do. This is for the rest of my life, you know.'

'I hope so, Rosie. You deserve it.'

******

Teresa McCarthy looked at her son in the front pew with a bursting heart. Sam had always been a tall lad by McCarthy standards, but Fergus, sitting at his side, made him look rather ordinary. She took her husband's hand and Ned gave her a kiss on the cheek. 'You look smashing in your fancy hat.' Aggie and Teresa had raided Hannah's wardrobe and the pair of them had taken ribbons and feathers from different ones to make some original creations. Teresa had assembled a navy felt beret with a little netting over the eyes and a few nodding ostrich feathers at the back. Aggie, across the aisle, had chosen a straw boater with a lavender ribbon and white silk flowers stuffed in at the bow. Both women felt fabulous.

Cathy was wearing a green straw Juliet cap. 'I've never seen you wear a hat in the summer before, Mama. You look very pretty.'

'Thank you, my darling. But shush now. I think Rose has arrived.'

The organist started playing the Mendelssohn *Wedding March* and Rose, holding Tricky's arm, began her short walk down the nave. Cathy wished it was their own father walking his daughter towards the altar but the sight of Tricky taking his place did not enrage or disturb her in the slightest. Rose looked exquisite, her long fair hair in a stylish chignon that Cathy had constructed just an hour ago and with the beautiful veil that had been in the family for decades over her face. Sam and Fergus came out of their pew to greet her, smiles cracking their faces open. Bridie had put her foot down and absolutely refused to wear pink - an unmistakable flash of Hannah - and wore a frothy pale blue dress with a navy sash instead.

Father Stephen had shaved and washed his curls for the occasion, so his good looks were more evident than usual as he stood at the altar waiting to receive the bride and groom. Cathy had liked the priest very much when she was a child; he was a great story-teller and always kind to her; he had been an ally. But she could never have guessed at Stephen's secret life as her mother's lover. How strange it must be for both Tricky and Stephen to be playing these roles, knowing that a fair number of people in the congregation knew the truth, though neither was aware that Rose had guessed their secret.

Rose and Sam gazed at each other, hypnotised by love, as they recited their marriage vows. Cathy recalled the freezing day in January 1942 when she and Joe had done the same. But when she had promised to take Joe 'for better, for worse, for richer, for poorer, in sickness and in health, to love and to cherish, till death us do part', she hadn't expected that death would part them a mere two years later, leaving her with a babe-in-arms.

******

The rain held off but a strong breeze was making the sides of the marquee on Stasia's lawn billow and flap as if friendly ghosts were trying to get inside. Aggie refused to sit on the top table but Seamus was up there, between Rose and Bridie, in place of Tricky who was on the other side of his daughter.

Tricky had been happy enough to walk Rose down the aisle but had baulked at any speech-giving whereas Seamus had leapt at the opportunity to fulfil that duty.

'Ladies and gentlemen, it is wonderful to see you all here on Rose and Sam's wedding day. On behalf of both families, I welcome you most warmly. It is such a privilege to be standing here, making the father-of-the-bride speech, but I know that we would all be so much happier if Rose's own father, John, could have been here to do the honours. And her mother, Hannah, also left us too soon, only last summer. They would both be thrilled to see their beautiful daughter marry the love of her life. I watched Hannah and John fall in love back in 1918 and I hope that Rose and Sam are blessed with as passionate, strong and fruitful a marriage as Hannah's and John's, though let's all pray for a longer one. Please join me in a toast to the bride and groom.'

Everyone stood and raised their glasses. Cathy's eyebrows had risen at Seamus's description of her parents' marriage: passionate… yes; strong… debatable. Seamus had no idea that Hannah had betrayed John and that Fergus and Bridie were the priest's progeny. If he had known, he would wonder why Hannah had turned from John to Stephen and not to himself. Cathy studied Tricky - silent and impassive, whose life as Hannah's second husband Seamus had chosen to ignore - and Father Stephen, who at least had the decency to look at his feet while Seamus spoke. The priest emptied his glass in one at the toast.

Johnny had been extremely well-behaved throughout the service and the meal, but he had been still for quite long enough. Before Cathy could stop him, he slipped out of his chair to go and talk to his Uncle Fergus, whom he now idolised. Fergus lifted Johnny onto his knee and put a finger to his lips – it was Sam's turn to speak.

'It's grand to see everyone here on our special day and on behalf of my wife and myself...' Loud cheers, clapping and some stamping greeted this. Sam laughed '... you'll get used to it, like me... on behalf of Rose and myself, thank you for coming today, some of you from a fair old distance: Dublin and Belfast, and my mum's cousins all the way from Liverpool. I've known Rose since she was just six and I was about fifteen. It's fair to say that I ignored her for the next ten years. But every day she was becoming sweeter and kinder and more lovely until, one day, I looked up and there was this beautiful young woman asking me to help her shift the barn door. I thought I'd show her how strong and manly I was but I couldn't shift the feckin' thing either. Then round the corner marched Fergus and it moved for him like it was on oiled wheels. I was mightily embarrassed to be shown up by such a young fella, admittedly one who eats whole cows for breakfast, but I thought Rose would now always think of me as a puny weakling compared to her little brother.' Rose blushed, laughing at Sam's story, and took his hand. 'Thankfully, a couple of years ago I let my Mammy know what I felt about Rose, but I said how could I ever ask her out, working for her parents as I did as just a lowly farmhand and barman. But you know how Mammies get talking to each other and somehow Mrs Byrne got to find out that I was sweet on her daughter and she whispered something to Rose and things started to look up from then on. I shall be forever grateful to Hannah Byrne for shifting this great lump of a barn door into action. I know how much Rose is missing having her Mammy here with her today, but, Rose, you are now part of the McCarthy family and my Mammy and Daddy are so delighted to have you join us as their daughter-in-law. If our marriage is half as happy as theirs, we will be blessed indeed. You will always have a home with them. And you, my beautiful girl, will always have your home in my heart. Ladies and gentlemen, to the bride.'

'What a smashing fella he is,' whispered Aggie to Cathy as they stood and raised their glasses. 'I just hope he doesn't want to clear me out of his house.'

'Don't be daft, Aggie. If I thought it was worth it, I'd fight Rose to get you.' Cathy caught Johnny's eye and gestured for him to come back to her because Fergus was gearing up to make the best man's speech. Fergus took a big glug of beer, folded away the speech he'd been studying and stood up.

'Now, settle down everyone. The moment has come for the best man's speech and who else could possibly be delivering it but me, the best man, as I'm sure you will agree.' Fergus held out his arms and spun around as if to display himself for inspection. Everyone laughed. 'I'm sorry that Rose isn't marrying the best man but, you know, marrying your own brother is still not legal in Ireland though, like so many other things in our beautiful country, that doesn't necessarily mean it doesn't go on.' And he tapped the side of his nose. Oh God, thought Cathy, he's speaking off the cuff.

'I had a list of all the things a best man should speak about. First, I'm supposed to compliment the bridesmaids and say how lovely they look, but there's only one, and it's Bridie. There's absolutely no way I'm saying she looks pretty even though she does, because I would just get a boot in the backside for it later. So, you'll have to make up your own minds on that score.'

'I'm also supposed to thank all the people who have laid on this lavish reception. The spread has been fantastic. I've gone easy on the drink so far but I mean to have my fill of scoops when this malarkey is over and so should you. I'm sure that Rose and Sam would especially like to thank Auntie Stasia and Uncle Edmund for hosting this do in their garden. When you think that Auntie Stasia hates anyone even walking over her precious lawn, she must really love Rose to be letting us mad crowds trample over it today. Sorry to drop you in it, coz, but I saw cousin Andrew fall into her tulips earlier.'

'Then, I must remember to mention Father Stephen who did the deed itself. I know that Rose and Sam would like to thank him for a beautiful service and all of us Fitzgerald and Byrne children have a lot to thank him for over recent years. When our Mammy got sick, he was always there for her, visiting every day, praying with her and at her side near the end and he was always there for us too, with words of advice and comfort. Thank you, Father.'

'Apologies, that was a bit serious. But don't fret; my last duty is to dish the dirt on Sam McCarthy. Now, this seems a bit daft to me. Surely, if I was going to drop him in the shite I should have done it while Rose still had a chance to back out? But it's too late now, sister, so it just means you'll be starting your honeymoon with some bitter regrets. Only codding you. I have asked just about everyone in Rowanbridge for their embarrassing stories about Sam McCarthy. I have chatted up the old ladies of the village and bought more fellas pints than I have ever drunk myself to get the gossip. Hopeless. The best I've managed is Father Stephen says it took Sam nearly six months to learn when to ring the bells for communion when he was an altar boy and then he gave it up soon after. Teresa, his Mammy, says that he has dreadful smelly farts – worse than Ned's - after he's eaten beans, but so do we all, don't we? Just lay off the stuff is my advice.'

Everyone in the room laughed loudly. Everyone, except Lily and Stasia who exchanged glances of weary disapproval.

'Sam McCarthy came to work for our mother and father when I was just three so I've grown up with him always around. And I've always looked up to him – at least, until I grew so much that I had no choice but to look down on him. But only in the physical sense. Across all these years, I have never seen him do anything but work like a Trojan, never complaining, always ready to take on the jobs no-one else wanted to do, like cleaning out the jacks in the yard every year when he was a younger lad. As time has gone on and he has taken on more responsibilities and he's become the perfect landlord, ready with a listening ear and a ready smile for all the punters. I'm now the one who has to shovel the shit out but Sam has promised that his first job as a married man is installing some inside lavs. He also knows how to pour a decent pint of the black stuff which is more than Rose can do. It's amazing how blind you can be. I had no idea they had eyes for each other until last year, although I do know he has always had a taste for a Fitzgerald girl, isn't that right, Cathy?'

Everyone turned to look at Cathy who smiled at her cheeky brother and raised her glass towards Sam.

'He was never anything but kind and patient with me as I grew up, always under his feet, asking questions, poking my nose and fingers into things that didn't concern me. I get a taste of what that must have been like for Sam when young Johnny comes to stay. Knackering, but at least Johnny goes home eventually. I was there, being a complete pest day after day and he never lost his temper once. So, even though he's clearly only the second-best man, I can honestly say that my gorgeous sister, Rambling Rose, is the luckiest woman alive to be marrying Sam McCarthy and vice versa because Rose is a genuine earth-angel. Our Mammy was always very busy with the businesses and Rose was the most perfect little mother Bridie and I could have hoped for. She would read to us before bed and would invent games for us to stop us tearing pieces out of each other. Rose, along with our Aggie, made our childhood a happy and safe one. I'm so grateful that Rose and Sam will still be living in Rowanbridge in our house so that I'll get to see them every day. That is, until I'm forced out because they've filled it with loads of their own babbies, which we all dearly wish for them. Would you all please be on your feet and join me in a very loud cheer for Rose and Sam.'

******

'Let's hope so. Anyway, it's been a wonderful day and I think Rose and Sam will have a marvellous life together. He's a bit older than her but they're just right for each other.'

'I'm not a big believer in all that lovey-dovey nonsense, as you know, but I do think they make a fine couple. I never felt the need for a husband but Rose definitely does. What about you, Cathy? Are you happy to be on your own still?'

'Aww, don't ask Aggie. I'm just not sure. I'll be thirty-two next week, you know. Isn't that a bit old to be looking for true love?'

'Don't ask me about romance. Not my area of expertise. But if there's something you want it's worth giving it a shot, whatever it is. Never too late; never too late to try at least. Time is a funny old thing. I can remember the day you were born like it was yesterday but not what we had for supper two days ago. But, listen to me - don't let time run out on you.'

'If you say so.' Cathy pushed herself out of the armchair to give Aggie a goodnight hug. 'Thank you, Aggie. Thank you for everything. For always being here for Mammy and for us kids when Daddy died and when Mammy was too busy. And for being here for Rose and Fergus and Bridie when I went away. I owe you so much and I love you.'

Chapter 8 - June 1952

The applause was generous after the Dublin Orchestral Players' performance of Grieg's *Holberg Suite* and more bows were demanded than usual. Seamus was quietly pleased with himself; all the practice he and Colm had put into the section for solo first violin and viola had paid off nicely. When he and Colm came out to the foyer, they received many compliments and slaps on the back.

'Cathy!' Seamus hailed his honorary god-daughter. 'Thanks for coming and bringing Lily and Ellen. But why no Johnny? He would have enjoyed it.'

'I know, but it's school tomorrow.'

'Well, you absolutely must bring him to our next concert. It's a Saturday-night one and the Haydn *Cello Concerto* is in the programme.'

'I definitely will. The Haydn was the piece that made my Daddy want to take up the cello, so it's rather special.'

'I wouldn't be able to trust any of my little scamps to sit still through a concert,' said Colm. 'Can I get you another glass of wine, Ellen?'

'Thank you, Colm.' Colm O'Brian had attempted to court Ellen in the 1930s after her engagement to Seamus had ended, but he had quickly taken the hint and was now a contented father of four, living in Bray.

'The *Holberg* is an agreeable piece,' said Lily, dressed in an elegant purple satin two-piece with a fine cashmere shawl to match. 'I'm very partial to a spot of neo-classicism, though I'd take Stravinsky over Grieg any day. The Radio Orchestra gave a fine *Pulcinella* only last year. You're very lucky to have a conductor as distinguished as Brian Boydell.'

'We consider ourselves to be the equal of any chamber orchestra in Ireland and maybe England too, Mrs Murphy,' said Colm, rather offended. 'There's fierce competition to get into the Dublin Orchestral Players, you know.'

'I'm trying to keep one step ahead of Johnny learning the rules of cricket, Cathy,' laughed Seamus. 'I'm not sure I'm up to it at all.'

'He just wants to use his father's old cricket bat. I'm sure it'll be a short-lived obsession.'

'I'm happy enough to throw him a tennis ball on the lawn any time, as long as he does all the fielding as well as the batting, but it's hardly a game. He needs a club. I'll have a hunt. Merrion Cricket Club has a good reputation and I think it might have a youth section. Leave it with me.'

'I'm happier with him playing cricket than rugby, though I suppose he could still get his hands smashed by those balls and never play the cello again. Am I a terrible over-protective mother, Uncle Seamus? Fergus says so.'

'Well, it's only natural. Johnny is a precious child, to all of us, but maybe you need to let him go where his fancy takes him.'

The stragglers were eventually shooed out of the hall. Cathy brought the car up to the door for Lily and Ellen, waved goodnight to Seamus and Colm and headed home. While Cathy helped Lily up the front steps and saw her safely inside, Ellen moved into the vacated front seat.

'You're a fine driver these days, Cathy. Even Aoife would be relaxed.'

'Ha-ha! Don't tempt fate, Ellen.'

'And you can bet the boy will be nagging you to let him drive just as soon as he hits sixteen. It makes me roar the way he sits in the parked car and pretends to be racing it.'

'He'll soon be too self-conscious to do it. He made me put Tiny Ted away in his wardrobe last week though I found him in bed yesterday morning cuddling him still.'

'Nearly eight years old. Time must be speeding up.'

Cathy drew up outside the little house in Nerano Road that Ellen and Aoife shared.

'Thanks for taking us tonight, Cathy.'

'I loved it, and always happy to support Uncle Seamus.'

'Now, listen, before I go I need to say something. Don't be giving out at me. Aoife and I have talked about this and she agrees that I must speak up.' Ellen took an audible breath in. 'We know that you have feelings for Liam, and him for you.'

'You're mistaken, Ellen. Liam is intending to get engaged – might already be engaged - to a younger woman who works in a Clifden hotel. He told me so himself last summer.'

'That's absolute crap. I know you've stopped sending letters to each other but he and Aoife still write regularly. He dumped that red-haired bint last autumn. There's been no-one since.'

Cathy felt her heart start racing.

'You might think that I've got a bloody cheek lecturing you on your love life when I spent far too long not realising what would make me happy. When Aoife appeared, it took me an age to admit to myself that she was the one. We might still be tiptoeing around each other if I hadn't decided to throw caution to the winds and tell her what I felt. She has transformed my life. Aoife and I can see that you and Liam are stuck, like we were.' Cathy was silent.

'We know you have been in his bed, and why ever not? you're a grown woman. We're not judging you. I'm sure Liam couldn't believe his luck, but he will never, ever ask you to marry him. He wouldn't presume; you'll have to do it. Your mother would have done it by now, no question. You have to find the bit of Hannah inside you. She believed in not giving up, in letting your heart lead you and, my God, she always got her way in the end.'

'Did it make her happy though?'

'Of course, it did. Happier than if she had done nothing. Life's not plain sailing, you know. Don't wait until you're fifty like us before you grab your chance. There I've said it now. If I've said anything that makes any sense you should get yourself to Cleggan the moment you can and Johnny can stay with us. Please think about it, Cathy. You are too dear to us to watch you live your life with regrets over what might have been. Goodnight, love.' Ellen kissed Cathy on the cheek and opened the car door to get out. Cathy put her hand on Ellen's arm.

'Thank you, Ellen, and to Aoife too. It's good to be so loved and I promise to think hard about it.'

******

The speedometer dropped from fifty-five miles an hour to fifty and then, ten minutes later, to just over forty-five. Cathy was desperate to reach Cleggan but also terrified of arriving and what might happen next. She had wasted no time taking Ellen's advice and had set off for Connemara the following weekend, leaving Johnny at Nerano Road. He was curious as to why he couldn't come with his mother.

'I'm going to Galway to see your Auntie Bridie and we need to do some very boring grown-up things.'

'OK... but come back soon, Mama.'

Cathy had, in the end, spent the Saturday night in a Galway hotel, so that she could arrive in Cleggan in good time on the Sunday, the only day off that Liam allowed himself. She'd thought about getting in touch with Bridie to spend time with her but realised she would be too distracted to be good company.

Cathy drove through the breath-taking landscape of lakes and hills, barely noticing it. Eventually, she arrived in Clifden and found herself driving past Doyle's Hotel; she stopped herself looking at it in case she saw something she didn't like. She turned off towards Cleggan. Sheep were grazing on the open green expanses and she wondered whether they belonged to Liam. One field had a couple of donkeys in it. She smiled remembering Ellen's request for such a steed - Johnny too. No, even Liam, considerate as he was, would not have acquired the beasts after a throwaway comment.

As the outskirts of Cleggan came into view, Cathy feared she might actually pass out, her heart was beating so fast and her breath so short. She stopped the car. The nurse in her knew it was just a panic attack and she needed to breathe more shallowly. Still, it was unnerving to feel her body so out of control.

When her breathing settled down, Cathy set off again and soon drew up to the cottage. She sat looking at the blue sky filled with a host of clouds scurrying across the horizon. Is this where she would live soon? It was beautiful in June but what about November, or February, with lashing rain and bitter winds off the Atlantic? But Cathy knew she didn't give a fig about anything except Liam, not the weather, the shops, Dublin society, the Academy, or even her guardian angels. Johnny was the only other thing she treasured and he had always loved it here too.

Cathy walked up to the cottage door. She had never had to knock on it before but that was appropriate today. She gave three loud knocks and waited. No answer. It was gone ten o'clock and surely Liam would be up by now. She knocked again. After a couple more minutes the door was opened a crack by a young lad with a pinched face and messy brown hair that had obviously just been lifted off a pillow.

'Hello.'

'Morning. I've come to see Liam.'

'Sorry, he's out.'

Cathy wondered whether Liam was sleeping in some woman's bed. 'Is Brendan in then? I'm a good friend of Liam's and we came to stay here last summer so Brendan knows me. Can you tell him Cathy is here. Please.'

'OK.' And the young lad made to close the door but Cathy held out her hand to stop him. 'Can I come in. Liam will be fine with it, I promise.'

The door was opened wider and Cathy saw that the lad was still in his pyjamas. She walked in and shut the door as he went up the stairs, presumably to wake Brendan.

Cathy looked around. The kitchen was as neat and tidy as always. The discipline of the Christian Brothers wasn't easily shaken off. She filled the kettle, took the big teapot down and counted in four teaspoons of tea. There was a lot of clattering going on upstairs, doors opening and shutting and several exclamations. Ten minutes later, Brendan charged down the stairs, his red hair wet and stuck to his forehead after a hasty wash, followed quietly by the young lad.

'Missus. How are you? Good to see you. You've given me an almighty shock though. Liam didn't say we should expect you, so you've caught us still in our beds. You'll have to forgive us – Sunday's the only day we get to sleep beyond dawn.'

'Don't apologise, Brendan; it's fine. Liam isn't expecting me. I was just in Galway overnight seeing my sister, she's at University College there, so I thought I'd pop over and say hello.'

'That's a helluva pop, missus, all the way from Galway.'

'Yes, well. When you have a car... anyway, would you introduce me to your friend here.' Cathy offered her hand which the young man took tentatively.

'Sorry, I'm a complete eejit. This is Mikey. Mikey, this is Missus Cathy. Mikey came to us from St Joseph's last January, didn't you, Mikey? He's a bit younger than me but we were good pals at Letterfrack and I knew he was coming up to sixteen and he was the best lad with the sheep and Liam had been talking about getting another pair of hands with all the extra land he's taken on so I told him about Mikey and ... bingo.'

'That's lovely. I hope you're happy here, Mikey.' The lad mumbled something inaudible. 'Anyway, do you know where Liam is and whether he'll be back soon?'

'Well, I'm not sure, but last night he was talking about the van having a puncture so maybe he's gone to try and get it sorted, though the Clifden garage will be shut today of course, but he has a mate from the pub who's a mechanic and he used to work at the garage so I reckon that's probably where he's gone.' Brendan took a breath.

'OK. Maybe he won't be too long then. I've made some tea. Can I pour you both a cup?'

Cathy sat for the next half-hour listening to Brendan's description of life in the cottage: how Mikey was the best cook of the three, played the tin whistle like an angel and could get any lamb out of a ewe in labour with his slim hands. And how Mrs Gallagher was still baking them bread and cakes and pies but there were three of them now so Brendan got a bit less than before but that was alright because he'd had to buy some bigger trousers and enough was enough but Mikey was glad of the cast-off trousers anyway. Brendan managed to talk continuously while buttering thick wedges of soda bread and devouring them. Mikey ate a little too.

The door opened and Liam walked in.

'Jesus. Cathy. I saw the car but I couldn't believe it was you.'

'Hello Liam.' Cathy rose and went over to give him a hug. 'It's good to see you. I've missed you. Can I pour you some tea?'

Liam struggled to find anything to say. 'You've met Mikey then.'

'Yes, and Brendan has been telling me what you've all been up to.'

'Right then.' Liam walked back to the door and gestured to Brendan to come outside with him. Soon Brendan reappeared. 'Come on, Mikey. Liam has given us a few quid to go into Clifden for some scoops. We'll see you later, missus.' Mikey stood up, nodded at Cathy and followed Brendan out.

'And don't come back 'til late. Okay?' Cathy heard Liam's whispered parting words and then he walked back inside and shut the door behind him.

'Well, Cathy. This is a big surprise – a very nice surprise. What's brought you all the way to Cleggan?'

'I came to visit Bridie at Galway uni … and I thought I would just drive over to see you this morning, you know. Would you like tea?' Liam nodded. 'I haven't heard from you for a while and, though Aoife would give me any big news, I've really missed hearing from you myself.'

'Me too. I don't know why I stopped writing.'

'I do. It was because I had done an unforgivable thing and tried to get between you and a woman you cared about. I should have kept my big nose out of it and my big trap shut.'

'Cathy, I never cared about Sheenagh or any of the others. And I shouldn't have taken offence the way I did because I know you were just looking out for me. And it turned out you were dead right. She wasn't to be trusted at all.'

Cathy reached over the table and took Liam's hand. 'It's true that I was looking out for you…' Cathy took a deep breath and focussed on their linked hands, '… but the real reason was that I was just heaving with jealousy. I wanted you to be just mine… because… because I love you, Liam. I have loved you for a while now, but I only realised it properly last summer. And I want to spend the rest of my life with you … if you'll have me.' She looked up. Liam's eyes were smiling. They stood up together and moved into a silent embrace that lasted for several minutes.

'So ... will you have me?' Cathy searched in Liam's face for the answer. He put his hands on her shoulders and spoke slowly.

'Cathy, macushla, I...love...you. I have worshipped you for more years than you could possibly guess. How could I not? But listen, it's because I love you that I couldn't let you marry me. I'm damaged goods, not fit to marry someone as perfect as you. You were generous enough to help me - with my problem with women - but I'm still not totally right. And I'm rough and uneducated whereas you're clever and sophisticated. How could you come and live here? Or how could I live in Dublin? No, I couldn't let you do it to yourself. But hearing you say you love me ... well, I think my heart might just explode and if I were to die right now it would be as the happiest man on earth.' He kissed her softly.

'Liam, listen to me. I lied to you that first time I came into your bed. I pretended I was just being kind and helping you get over your problem but the truth is I had a raging desire to kiss you and make love to you. I've lied again just now. I didn't come to see Bridie at all; I came all the way here just to see you and to tell you the truth of what I feel for you. I'm sorry. I promise I will never lie to you ever again, never.'

Liam took her hand and led her upstairs to his bedroom where they undressed each other hesitantly. The next two hours were spent saying all that was in their hearts as much through actions as in words. Then they slept, Liam curled around Cathy. When Cathy woke, she turned to watch Liam sleeping on top of the sheets, his breathing calm and regular. She studied the body that she hoped would become part of her life, with its defined muscles, the fuzz of auburn hair on his chest and between his thighs and all the tanned patches

people, do anything else you want, but for me, be *only* my wife.' And he bent his head to look Cathy squarely in the eyes.

'I understand. That's what I want too.'

'So, what I ask is that you go back to Dublin and wait a month and think really hard about what that would mean: where we'd live, what you would do with your time, what Johnny would think of it all. At the end of that month, if you still feel the same about me then you can do with me whatever you like.'

'It's a deal.'

'I won't even write to you or phone you.'

'Okay.'

Liam stood up and held out his hand to pull Cathy to her feet and they held each other tightly before getting back in the boat for the return trip, as the sun kissed the horizon.

Back in the cottage, they shared some bread and cheese, followed by a slice of Mrs Gallagher's fruitcake, before Cathy went upstairs and ran a bath. Liam followed her up.

'I can scrub your back for you maybe.'

'You can get in with me if you like.' Liam's shocked face betrayed that such an idea had never crossed his mind but he was eager to experience all these new intimacies.

'Careful! don't make the water spill over the edge,' advised Cathy as Liam lowered himself into the water opposite her. 'You won't get quite as good a soak as if you were on your own - but you'll save water.'

They were in bed together by nine o'clock, tenderly exploring each other's freshly washed bodies, learning how to please each other best.

'You smell of my rose soap.'

'Is that a problem? Should men not smell of flowers?'

'Not a problem for me, not one tiny bit.'

They fell into such a deep and satisfying sleep that even the return of Brendan and Mikey, stumbling up the stairs at gone ten o'clock, couldn't raise an eyelid.

Chapter 9 – July 1952

Cathy was at her desk, sorting out the insurance renewals for the Academy. She glanced at the pile of old letters tied with ribbon that Liam had sent her a year and more ago. He had kept his word and not been in communication since she'd returned to Dalkey after last weekend. She was tempted to stop work and re-read one or two but she felt that would be breaking the spirit of their promise.

She had been thinking, as Liam had instructed. There was no denying there would be complications: where would Johnny go to school and who would run the administration of the Academy if she decamped to Cleggan? But, equally, how on earth could Liam come to live in Dalkey? Anyway, she wanted to be in Cleggan for many reasons. She opened the second drawer in her desk and took out the envelope which held the lock of Máire's hair. The cream wool was yellower these days but the hair itself, as golden as butter, hadn't faded at all. If she had lived, Máire would be over forty now and no doubt her hair would be duller than the lock in her hand.

Cathy heard the front door open and shut and familiar running feet. The door to her sitting room burst open and Johnny stood triumphantly, holding his cricket bat aloft, Seamus behind him, smiling indulgently.

'Mama, I hit a four and twelve runs in total before my turn ended.'

'He has the knack, sure enough.' Seamus had taken Johnny to his first under-tens cricket session. 'He's much taller than most of the other boys his age, so that must help.'

'And his Daddy was an excellent cricketer, according to Shirley, so it's in the genes.'

'And I did some bowling too, just with a soft ball, though we threw the hard ball to each other in a circle, to get used to how heavy it is.'

'Very exciting. Say thank you to your Uncle Seamus for taking you.'

'Thank you, Uncle Seamus. Can we go again next week please?'

'You'll be going every week across the summer season, if you want to.'

'Yippee!'

'Go and wash your hands ready for supper. Auntie Aoife and Auntie Ellen will be here soon to watch you. Uncle Seamus and I are off to the ballet with Aunt Lily.'

Cathy and Seamus left at six to pick up Lily for a performance of *The Sleeping Princess* at the Gaiety. Almost the instant Cathy knocked on the Pembroke Street front door Lily opened it herself, dressed in a kingfisher blue gown with a paisley stole draped casually over her shoulders.

'You're ten minutes late, Cathy. I hate to be in a rush, as you know. But I'm pleased to see you have taken some effort tonight with your dress, and a little lipstick suits you.'

The three were soon settled into their prime seats. 'I rarely frequent here,' said Lily. 'It's all a bit frivolous for me, Gilbert and Sullivan and what have you. But there are fewer new productions from the Abbey and I don't think it's just because they are camping out at the Queen's. Where are the playwrights to match Synge or O'Casey, eh? The fire has gone out of Ireland's dramatic belly it seems.'

'Do you remember, Lily, when Hannah and I played Mozart's *Sinfonia Concertante* here at the Gaiety in 1917. You'd organised it all with Felix Brennan. It was one of the most terrifying and exciting days of my life.'

'I'm not senile, Seamus; of course, I remember. That was when we all thought Hannah would go on to be a soloist instead of spending her life in drudgery in Rowanbridge. Such a criminal waste.'

'I don't think Mammy wasted her life. She was very happy with my Daddy and having her children. She worked hard but it wasn't drudgery. There were some difficult times after Daddy died but she beat them. It's the cancer that came out of the blue that got her and that could have happened even if she'd been playing her violin on some stage around the world.'

'Hmmph. Well, I couldn't have done what she did. Will we be seeing Felix Brennan leading the orchestra tonight?' asked Lily, swiftly changing the subject.

'Gracious, no. Felix has been retired five years now, but he's well enough. I pop in to see him from time to time so he can put me straight on my fingering.'

'Retired? The man can have been no age at all.'

'He's well over seventy, Lily.' Seamus and Cathy exchanged a smile over Lily's neatly coiffured brunette head.

After the performance, the three strolled to where Seamus had parked the car, Lily humming Tchaikovsky's famous waltz theme. 'Well, I hold with my opinion that ballet is a lot of silly, fluffy nonsense but I do concede that the music is magnificent. I know opera can have plots that test credibility sometimes but, seriously, who can believe that a princess could be dead to the world for a hundred years, wake up looking as fresh as a daisy and be able to dance a pas de deux? Her muscles would be totally atrophied. And she has to be woken by a prince's kiss and she has to be a princess to be the heroine. You'd think ordinary people never fell in love.'

'It's just a fairy story, Aunt Lily.'

'I know, and I did enjoy it, Cathy. But these sorts of stories weaken our moral fibre insidiously over time and idealise the aristocracy. But thank you, Seamus, for inviting us.'

'My pleasure, Lily. We'll do it again. I shall see if there's a ballet all about the struggle of the workers against the evils of capitalism next time. Surely one will come out of the USSR soon.'

'Keep up, Seamus. It's already happened. Shostakovich has written three ballets featuring factory-workers, young communists and a football team. I concede they might not go down too well in Dublin.'

With Lily safely back at Pembroke Street, Seamus and Cathy set off for Dalkey, chatting about the performance and Lily's reaction to it.

'I shouldn't laugh because, frankly, she's amazing for her age,' said Seamus. 'She knows everything. Fancy knowing about some obscure Russian ballets.'

'She knows everything because she reads every newspaper every day. And she can do that because she has nothing else to do. She's always had the money to hire people to run around after her so she can concentrate on being the best-informed society hostess in Dublin. Normal people, who have to work for a living, are just as clever as Lily but will never be as well-informed.'

'She clearly loves you best of all her nieces and nephews, even when you don't wear as much make-up as she'd like.'

'Maybe. I'm closer to her world than my sisters and brother, but she doesn't love me as much as she loved my Mammy.'

'Ah well, we all loved your Mammy.'

Seamus swung into the Academy's drive to find a shabby black van parked under the trees.

'Who on earth can that be at this time?' said Seamus. 'Some workman? Maybe they've had to call out an electrician or a plumber.' But Cathy knew exactly whose van it was and her heart was pounding as she followed Seamus into the drawing room.

'Cathy, look who's here.' said Aoife standing up. 'Seamus, come and meet Liam, my adopted son… sort of.'

Liam stood up and shook Seamus's hand but with his eyes fixed on Cathy the whole time.

'Well, it's grand to meet you finally, Liam. Heaven knows I've heard enough about you, but I'm not the man to brave the wild west. What brings you to Dalkey?'

'Come along, Seamus, will you drop us home now please. It's getting late.' Ellen stood up, tapping her stick, and she and Aoife walked out to the hall.

'No chance of a quick nightcap then?'

'No!' said the older women in unison and they dragged Seamus out of the front door.

Cathy and Liam stood staring at each other for an age before Cathy walked over to Liam, put her arms around him and kissed him tentatively.

'What happened to the month then? I haven't had enough time to consider fully all the consequences of spending the rest of my life with you,' teased Cathy.

'Exactly. I wanted to get here before you made your final decision in case it's one I don't want to hear. I am terrified that you'll see sense and dump me if I give you any longer to think about it.'

Liam reached into his trouser pocket and took out a ring and put it on Cathy's right hand. It was formed of two golden hands holding a heart made of a green stone surrounded by tiny seed pearls. 'This is a Claddagh ring. It's a traditional ring from Galway. The hands mean friendship and the heart means love. Sometimes there's a crown on top too meaning loyalty but I thought you wouldn't like one like that given your republican tendencies.' Cathy smiled at him. 'I spent the whole morning going into every jeweller in Galway trying to find the right one. I chose this one because it has something of the land - the Connemara marble - and something of the sea – the pearls.'

'It's beautiful.'

'What this ring means is that whatever decision you make in the end, Cathy, you and I will always have our friendship and love. Nothing can destroy that even if you come to your senses and decide you shouldn't marry me. So, I wanted you to know that. You won't lose me totally, even if you take the sensible decision. It's not an engagement ring …'

Cathy took off the ring, handed it back to Liam and kissed him.

'Now, put it back on where it belongs.'

******

Johnny opened his mother's bedroom door the next morning to find her fast asleep in Liam's arms. It was only just gone seven o'clock but Johnny had been excited by Liam's arrival the evening before and wanted to know why he had come all the way to Dalkey. He backed out of the room and closed the door quietly. By the time Cathy ventured downstairs, Johnny was dressed and eating breakfast in the big dining room along with a few of the students.

'Good morning everyone.'

'Morning, Mrs Ashfield. Good morning. Morning.' The students' greetings ranged from bright and perky to gravelly and grumpy.

'Thanks for getting Johnny his breakfast. It looks like we're going to have a fine day ahead. Johnny, when you've finished your sausage would you come into my sitting room please.'

No sooner had Cathy sat down at her desk than Johnny ran into her room and launched himself into her arms.

'How are you, my darling? Did you have a fun evening with your aunties?'

'Mama. Liam came last night and I know he slept in your bed. Are you in love?'

'Ha-ha! Yes, we are in love. Is that OK with you?'

'Yes, it's great. It means you're happy.'

'I'm very happy, darling boy, but I want you to be happy too. Liam and I will be getting married at some point and then you and I and Liam will all live together.'

'Hurray. It'll be great because Uncle Seamus is a bit slow getting the ball back when we play cricket. Liam will be a better bowler, I'm sure. But what will happen to all of Liam's animals?'

'Well, we'll have to wait and see. But I think it's likely that we'll go and live in Cleggan rather than Liam come to live in Dalkey. You love it there, don't you?'

'Yes. It's a holiday place. Where *is* Liam now, Mama?'

'He's up in my bedroom but I'll go and wake him. Let's take him a bacon sandwich and a cup of tea, shall we?'

When Cathy and Johnny walked into the bedroom, Liam was sitting up in his bed, reading the book of Yeats's poetry that was always on Cathy's bedside table. Liam started at the sight of Johnny and scrabbled on the floor for his shirt.

'How are you, young fella? And is that for me? Thank you very much.'

Johnny leapt up onto the bed. 'Will you come and play cricket with me on the beach, Liam. When you've had your breakfast. Please.'

'Woah there, Johnny. Just let Liam sort himself out, have a drink or two, get dressed and then we can decide what to do with the morning. Liam has to drive back home this afternoon, you see.'

'I know nothing about cricket, Johnny, but if you show me how, I'd be happy to give it a go.'

The phone rang downstairs and Cathy left the pair of them to go and answer it. It was Ellen.

'So? What's happening?'

'Well, Liam is just having his breakfast and then we're going to the beach to play cricket and I expect we'll find ourselves something to eat and then he has to drive back and I need to get on with the paperwork … and then we'll be getting married at some date in the future.'

The squeals on the other end of the phone nearly deafened Cathy and she could hear Aoife's excited remarks too before she took the phone from Ellen and spoke directly to Cathy.

'My precious girl. We're so happy for you. Can you imagine my joy knowing that John's daughter is to be married to my boy.' And then she dissolved into sobs putting Ellen back on the phone.

'Don't worry about her. They're just happy tears. That's such great news, Cathy. Just what the doctor ordered. Do you all want to come and have lunch here with us? We have a big old piece of beef and Aoife will do her special roast spuds. I'll make sure she's stopped crying by then. I mean to invite Seamus too. The dear man has barely exchanged a word with the fella his adored Cathy has chosen to marry and I think he might appreciate a bit of a chinwag. Is that okay with you?'

Five hours later, after Cathy had kissed Liam good-bye and waved him off in his old van, she went and sat alone for a while in her sitting room. Was it that easy being happy? Could you just decide to be happy, and make everyone else happy too? Liam had indulged Johnny for nearly an hour on Killiney beach, bowling a tennis ball at him, and then the three of them had gone swimming before walking around to Ellen and Aoife's where Seamus was already sitting with the glass of whiskey he had been deprived of the evening before. He and Liam got on famously of course, because they both loved Cathy. She picked up the phone to give the news to Rose who was so excited she ran off to bring Aggie and Sam to the phone too. So many questions but also so much laughter; Cathy couldn't remember a time when she had made this many people so utterly delighted and all on the same day. Then she remembered and picked up her phonebook, time to ring Auntie Stasia and Great-aunt Lily, both of whom would probably be a little less thrilled to hear that Cathy was intending to marry a fisherman.

Chapter 10 – August 1952

The Cleggan cottage felt so different this August. Brendan and Mikey had gone to lodge with Mrs Gallagher so Cathy was still staying in her normal bedroom at the back or, more accurately, her clothes were. Most nights she slept in Liam's bed. She felt no need to pretend to the grown-ups that this wasn't the state of affairs but, strangely, she didn't want to flaunt it to Johnny until she and Liam were married.

'Mama, when you marry Liam, will you be called Mrs Molloy?

'Yes, my love.'

''Will I still be Johnny Ashfield?'

'Yes, of course.'

'So, I'll be the only person called Ashfield.'

'Your Granny and Auntie Shirley are Ashfields.'

'Yes, but I mean here, in Ireland?'

'Well, there must be other people called Ashfield somewhere in Ireland.'

'But not my relatives. And should I call Liam "Daddy"?'

'Not unless you want to. You have your own Daddy, even though you don't remember him. If you were a baby we might have thought about changing your name, but I don't think you'd want us to do that. Just call him Liam.'

There were many other decisions, small and large, to be made. After making love each night, Cathy and Liam would whisper their thoughts and plans to each other as they lay relaxing in bed. They had quickly concluded that Cleggan would be their home. Seamus had offered to take over Cathy's duties at the Academy and sell his partnership at his law practice. He would also move in so that there was always a senior member of staff on the premises. That left Cathy free to go where her heart took her and that was most definitely to Connemara.

Liam laughed when Cathy imitated her Great-Aunt Lily on hearing the news. 'I was very unhappy when my sister decided to leave Dublin to marry your grandfather, but at least James was a landed farmer and businessman. Subsequently, I was disappointed when your mother abandoned her musical career to marry a teacher and took herself back to Rowanbridge. But I cannot pretend that I am not horrified, Cathy - *horrified* - that you have decided to become a fishwife in the wilds of Connemara.'

Liam chuckled and lay back, his arm behind his head on the pillow. 'Let's face it, macushla, she does have a point.'

Seamus had brokered a fair deal whereby Cathy sold the business of the Academy to Ellen and himself but she retained ownership of the property and hence would receive quarterly rental income from them. With the proceeds of the sale, Cathy and Liam had agreed to buy the cottage from Aoife.

'I'm so spoiled, and so are my sisters and brother,' said Cathy. 'We've all inherited money or land or businesses, whereas you've just had to work your fingers to the bone to get anything at all, and those poor old fingers tell the tale.' Cathy kissed Liam's rough hands. 'But I love them all the same.'

Cathy couldn't help making plans for some changes to the cottage. 'I'll need somewhere for my clothes and I think a new bed is fairly urgent. Not only did Ruari and Shawna sleep in this one for years, they both died in it.' A bed was ordered, a double wardrobe and a sofa for the sitting room. 'And I'll really miss the refrigerator we had at the Academy; is it okay to buy one?' Liam said yes to everything Cathy wanted.

Then there was the issue of Johnny's schooling. There was the local National School of course, where Aoife had been a teacher, but it wouldn't be long before Johnny would need secondary education and the only option in Clifden was run by Franciscan monks. 'Not as bad as a Christian Brothers school, but I can't let you send Johnny there,' Liam had said. There was no secular option like The Maple Academy within easy reach so Cathy deferred the decision.

Johnny's cello lessons were more easily solved with an ancient lady cellist in Clifden. Seamus had bought the boy a new three-quarter size cello only last year but Johnny was impatient to get his hands on his grandfather's full-size instrument, stored at the Academy. He was growing fast. Last month, he had demonstrated that his hands could span an octave on the piano so, as promised, Cathy started to teach him the first movement of *The Moonlight Sonata*.

The many arrangements that needed to be discussed and agreed could not dent the mounting joy Cathy felt at her imminent marriage. It was going to be a very simple affair at Clifden Register Office with just Ellen and Aoife as witnesses, but then there would be a Dublin reception – a party in reality – for family and friends. Thinking of Rose's wedding, Cathy was relieved that she didn't have to worry about who would give her away, or what the bridesmaids would wear, or who would make the speeches. But a few modest preparations were made: Liam had a haircut, bought his first ever suit and a gold ring for his bride. Cathy bought three bottles of champagne, a new dress and some matching lipstick.

The night before the wedding, Cathy told Liam that she wanted to sleep in the back bedroom, away from him. 'It's silly really – just a superstition – but it'll make our wedding night feel extra special.' Liam smiled at her and stroked her cheek. 'Whatever makes you happy, macushla.'

Cathy woke early and looked out at blue skies and wispy clouds floating over the sea. 'Perfect.' The ceremony was not until three-thirty so there was time to fill. Brendan and Mikey had undertaken all the fishing duties that morning and when they arrived with the catch Liam drove off to deliver it to his customers. But they were all free by half eleven so the three men took Johnny off to the beach to play cricket. Brendan was no athlete but he could bowl a fair ball at Johnny's feet. Mikey, however, was a lithe and speedy fielder and becoming better at batting too, whenever they could persuade Johnny to yield the precious bat.

After getting everything ready, Cathy and Aoife took a stroll along the lanes towards Selerna beach. Compared to the lanes around Rowanbridge, the hedgerows were scrubbier and thinner but Cathy managed to find blue scabious, purple knapweed and even a little honeysuckle to put on the kitchen table.

At half-past two, the five cottage residents were ready to leave for Clifden. Ellen was in charge of Cathy's camera, Johnny was clutching a bag of rose petals that Dearbla had gathered and Aoife was carrying her prayer book. As she was about to get into the front seat, Cathy ran back into the house and took the honeysuckle from the jug, stuck one stalk in Liam's buttonhole and held the rest, breathing in memories.

******

Liam picked up Cathy and carried her into the cottage, kissing her long and hard before setting her back on her feet. 'You romantic fool.'

'That's the only old marital custom I intend to observe, Mrs Molloy. And now I can't wait to get out of this,' said Liam, pulling his tie loose and taking off his jacket.

'That must be the first time you've worn a tie and it's probably the last, but at least I've captured the moment for posterity,' said Ellen, patting the camera before handing it back to Cathy.

'You'll have to wear it when we have the reception but, after that, you're welcome to use it to mend your nets.'

Aoife took a hand each from Cathy and Liam and placed them on her breast. 'I can't say much because my heart is too full. So, I'll put the kettle on.'

Johnny was still outside, playing in the driver's seat of the car, but he came in when Cathy called him. 'Johnny, my love, could you please run along to Mrs Gallagher and ask her to cook the lobsters whenever she's ready.'

They enjoyed a delicious supper accompanied by the champagne. 'Thank God for the refrigerator but a few wine glasses wouldn't go amiss next time.' The champagne, and lemonade for Johnny, was being drunk out of three beer glasses and two teacups.

'Next time, Cathy? Do you have plans to dump me and get a better model some time then?'

'Ha-ha. No, but we might have other reasons to celebrate. Who knows?' Cathy clinked her tea-cup against Liam's tumbler and winked at him.

Aoife was clearing the table when there was a sharp knock on the door. It opened to reveal Brendan, carrying a very large chocolate cake, Mikey following behind, his tin whistle in hand.

'Congratulations from me and Mikey, and Mrs Gallagher and Dearbhla send theirs too. Mrs G asked me what sort of cake you might like - should it be a fruit cake or a vanilla sponge - but I said that I thought you couldn't go wrong with a chocolate cake and I know young Johnny's partial to a spot of chocolate at least. So, I'll just put it down here for now, shall I?'

'Wow, that's looks amazing, Mama!' Johnny went over and sniffed the cake. 'Can I cut it?'

'It's the custom for the bride and groom to cut a wedding cake together, but, as we weren't expecting one, I don't see why you shouldn't do the honours, my love.'

'So, there's the cake - oh jeezus, that looks good, doesn't it now, Mikey – but the two of us have also prepared a little treat for you to celebrate this grand day. Better than a cake, I'd say. Here's a song about the sea, *The Ballad of Ó Bruadair*, who's a devilish pirate captain with a fierce eye for the ladies. Please join in when you can.'

Mikey put the whistle to his lips and out poured a stream of liquid silver, and Brendan drummed a beat on the kitchen table and eventually began to sing in his lusty baritone voice, encouraging everyone to join in the rollicking chorus. Soon everyone was shouting the refrain: 'Rollin' glory on the ocean' and Johnny danced around the kitchen with his Mama.

'Thank you, friends. That was a hoot.' Liam stood and shook Brendan's and Mikey's hands. 'Will you stay for a slice of cake and a glass of something? We have champagne here or you can have a nip of whiskey if you prefer.'

'I think a finger or two of whiskey would suit us best. The champagne is more a ladies' drink, I'm thinking.'

'That was an unusual choice of song, Brendan. If I understood right, wasn't it all about pirates having to turn their backs on women in order to go to sea? Wasn't there a line *I shut my eyes on women, forgot their sturdy hips*' which is a strange choice for a wedding night, isn't it?' Ellen couldn't resist teasing Brendan.

'No, no, no, missus. You had to listen to the end where he wants to go back home to his girl; Brendan sang again:

'Although those Spanish beauties are dark and not so dear,
I'd rather taste in Mayo, with April on the air,
One bracing tender female so swing your canvas here.

'So that's me, is it, a tender, bracing female?' Cathy laughed and held Liam's hand.

'I think you got it about right, Brendan,' Liam said. 'Mostly tender but definitely bracing when needs be.'

'Well, I'd rather be described as bracing than one with sturdy hips.'

'Nothing wrong with sturdy hips, I'll have you know.' And Ellen stood up, turned around, wiggled her backside at the party and gave it a slap.

'How much have you drunk, Ellen? Go easy now,' whispered Aoife.

'I think we should all get some sleep, so drink up, boys,' said Liam. 'Maybe Aoife can sing us something peaceful before we go up to our beds.'

'Aoife, will you sing that song about the shy famer,' Johnny asked.

'You mean *Ar Éirinn ní neosfainn cé hí?* Of course, I will. Try and remember how to say the words.' Aoife held out her hand to Johnny and he walked over and sat on her knee as she began to sing. After the first verse, Mikey started to accompany her on the whistle. Even Brendan sat still, absorbed by the haunting music.

'Thank you, Aoife, and Mikey. Fancy you being able to pick up the tune just like that. It was beautiful.' Liam wiped the tears from his wife's cheek with his shirt sleeve.

'What do all the words mean though?' asked Johnny. 'I know that *Éirinn* means Ireland.'

'When your Irish is better you'll understand it all,' said Aoife. 'These are some of the lines in English, just for you:

If only this maiden would listen to me, what I'd tell her would be true. I would devote myself to her and see to her welfare. I would tell her my story and I long to take her to my heart where I'd give her pride of place. Generosity and kindness shine in her face along with her great beauty. Her hair reaches to the ground, sparkling like yellow gold. Her cheeks blush like the rose but for all Ireland I'd not tell her name.'

'Mama's hair does look like gold but it doesn't reach the ground.'

Chapter 11 – September 1952

'Ingram and Pollock batted great, but Shearer was the best fielder and Kenny was the best bowler - and he's a new player.' Johnny recounted the day's play between the Irish cricket team and the MCC at College Park that Seamus had taken him to.

'Have you thanked your Uncle Seamus for such a big treat?' asked Cathy.

'Yes, of course.' Johnny rolled his eyes. 'I know my manners, Mama.'

'It was my pleasure. Never thought I would develop such an interest in the game. It's better to watch than golf – but I'm never going to be a cricketer myself, unlike Johnny here.'

'Who can afford to spend three days watching or playing a sport? It's definitely one for the privileged classes,' said Liam sitting over by the window reading the newspaper.

'Are you not interested in playing hurling, my love? Your Uncle Fergus is a crack player and he'd love you to play it too.'

'Maybe.' Johnny ran off to his bedroom.

'So, this will be your little sitting room from next week, Seamus. I've cleared out everything I can and all the papers to do with the Academy are sorted properly. The room needs a coat of paint, mind – I've been meaning to get rid of my grandma's dark crimson walls ever since she died.'

'Yes, well, there are some aspects of my student life here I shall be happy to retain, but I think a calm pale blue would suit me better.'

Cathy had assumed that Seamus would move into her bedroom when she finally moved out of the room that her father had once occupied on the second floor of the Academy. But Seamus had declined, saying that he didn't fancy scaling two flights as he got older and had chosen instead to take Ellen and Aoife's old rooms in the converted stables. He didn't tell Cathy that witnessing Hannah go in and out of John Fitzgerald's bedroom in their student days was still a painful memory.

'Is there anything I can do, Seamus?' Liam came over to the desk. 'Anything you need shifting or sorting? I'm not sure what to do with myself, to be honest, just sitting around.'

'Why don't you take Johnny for a quick walk to the beach, darling, before all the ladies arrive.'

'Right. Will you come, Seamus?'

'Thank you, but no thank you. I've done enough walking today.'

Cathy was nervous about dinner that night: Lily was coming, along with Ellen and Aoife, and it would be the first time that her great-aunt had clapped eyes on Liam.

Seamus poured himself a whiskey, made Cathy a vodka and tonic and settled down to read the paper. He looked perfectly at home in the chair, sitting by the window of the school that had been such a big part of his life, and, very soon, he would be literally at home in that chair.

At twenty-to-seven, Ellen and Aoife arrived.

'Where are Liam and Johnny?' asked Aoife.

'On the beach. They should've been back by now. Liam needs to change into his suit for one thing.'

Fifteen minutes later, Cathy heard the front door open and she rushed out to chivvy Liam and Johnny only to find Liam standing in the hall next to her Great-aunt Lily. There were pronounced sweat patches on Liam's shirt, his coppery hair was plastered to his head and his trouser legs were wet up to the knee.

'Hello Aunt Lily. You're a little bit early but it's lovely to see you. You've met Liam then.'

'We introduced ourselves outside, Cathy.'

'Sorry we're a bit late,' mumbled Liam. 'We lost the ball in the sea and Johnny wouldn't come back without it so we've had to run back … and I'm a bit warm now.'

'Clearly, a man who can't keep away from the sea.'

'Never mind. Aunt Lily, come into the drawing room and I'll get the others through. Liam, maybe you could take Johnny up with you to wash and change.' Cathy made frustrated gestures behind Lily's back, following her into the drawing room.

Ten minutes later, Liam crept into the drawing room, looking rather more respectable in his suit and tie, to hear Lily addressing the room.

'I was delighted to see Fianna Fáil win back Waterford but, sadly, it was at the expense of another woman TD. And we also lost the great Helena Concannon this year, perhaps our greatest female republican politician ever. We need more women in politics to bring their special empathy to what can be a tawdry business, don't you all think? If only we could have voted for a woman President this last year, but I suppose better to have O'Kelly back than the other lot. If I were thirty years younger, I'd think of standing myself. I hope I get to see a female Taoiseach or President before I die. Cathy, would you ever think of getting into politics yourself?'

'Gracious, Aunt Lily, I'd be useless. Now, my mother certainly could have done it and I reckon Bridie might make a decent fist of it too. But I'm going to be off in the west, looking after my husband and son.'

'I'd vote for you in a heartbeat, Cathy,' said Ellen. 'If you ran the country the way you've run this Academy we'd do brilliantly.'

'Ellen will undoubtedly let me know when I fail to live up to your standards, Cathy,' laughed Seamus. 'But Liam, come in properly, man, get yourself a drink and have a seat.'

Lily twisted around and beckoned to Liam to join her on the sofa. 'Come and sit here next to me, Liam. There are so many questions I want to ask you.'

Cathy tried not to laugh seeing the trepidation on Liam's face but he recovered and manfully took up his designated place. 'What is it you'd like to know, Mrs Murphy?'

'No, no, call me Lily. Aunt Lily if you must, but I prefer to be just plain Lily. I'd love to hear what your plans are for your seafood business. Cathy has told us that you've expanded into lobsters, crayfish and oysters, all of them favourites of mine, and found new customers further afield.'

Lily insisted Liam sit next to her at dinner too, and questioned him about the cottage: who did his house-keeping, his family in Cork and his traumatic experiences at Letterfrack School. For a man who normally talked little and listened a lot, it was an exhausting two hours. Eventually, Liam managed to ask Lily a few questions himself: what had she been to see recently at the theatre, what had she been reading and those were enough to start Lily off on extended monologues, allowing him to finish his food.

'Well, I must get back into Dublin. Slattery is outside waiting and tomorrow is a big day. Pembroke Street is all set for your reception, Cathy. I hope you'll be pleased. You too, Liam.'

Lily had done her best to outdo Stasia's hospitality for Rose's wedding with extravagant flower arrangements and choice food and wine. There would be no dancing but Lily said she had arranged a little 'entertainment'. Cathy walked her great-aunt to the door.

'We'll all be there at three on the dot, I promise.'

'Make sure you do now. Your man's time-keeping seems no better than yours. But...' Lily leaned in and whispered in Cathy's ear, '... he's quite handsome, and charming. I think he'll do.'

******

Cathy was excited at the prospect of seeing all of her relatives that day and showing off her new husband. Stasia and Edmund were staying overnight with Lily but Rose and Sam, Fergus, Bridie and Aggie were coming back to the Academy to sleep, the first time they had all seen the place that had figured so largely in their parents' lives. They were as curious about the school as they were about Liam. The Apostles and their families were driving to Dublin for the day and straight back. Tricky had chosen not to come, which Cathy understood but she felt rather guilty about it. She had never given Tricky any reason to think she didn't despise him and she resolved to do something about that before too long. But, right now, she had her new husband to take care of and he was looking extremely anxious about the next few hours.

'Don't leave me, okay, macushla. Not even for a minute. Not even to go to the jacks. Take me with you if you need to go. Just stay with me. I'm still recovering from Lily's interrogations – are all of your family so nosey?'

'But you passed the test; she said you were quite handsome and very charming.'

'Only *quite* handsome?'

Cathy embraced Liam and put her hands on his buttocks, giving them an affectionate squeeze. 'If she had seen these of course ...'

'Ahem.' Lily had entered the room. 'Good afternoon, Cathy and Liam. Are you well today? I hope you like what I've done with the house.' The Pembroke Street townhouse was looking very sleek and polished, not unlike Lily herself. The air was full of the scent of Mrs Murphy's signature lilies in the abundant flower displays.

'I know you don't want anything formal, but I hope you'll forgive me if I say a word or two later on. I think people will expect it and I think the speeches are the best part of a wedding. Now, let me get you both a drink. We may as well start as we mean to go on.' Lily clicked her fingers and, seemingly out of thin air, a waiter appeared with glasses of champagne on a silver tray.

'Everything looks perfect, Aunt Lily. We're very grateful indeed, aren't we Liam?'

'Very. Mrs Murphy, do you think I could just have a glass of water for now.'

There was an explosion of chatter and squeals at the arrival of Cathy's siblings. Rose was the first to run in and give Cathy a hug followed by Bridie. Fergus appeared at the drawing room's double doorway, with his outstretched arms practically filling its width.

'C'mere and give me a kiss, Mrs Molloy,' and he ran towards Cathy.

"No. No, Fergus, don't you dare pick me up. You'll mess up my hair.' Too late, Fergus lifted her over his shoulder and carried her over to Liam where he shook his brother-in-law's hand. 'Good man. Congratulations and thanks for making a respectable woman out of my old sister.' Liam was rather taken aback. He laughed along with everyone else but put his arm protectively around Cathy's shoulders the instant Fergus had deposited her back on her feet.

'It's great that you're going to be in Connemara. I'll be able to come and see you for weekends when I'm back at uni.' Bridie sounded genuinely excited at the prospect.

'Where's Aggie? You did bring her, didn't you?' Cathy ran out to the hallway, leaving Liam alone. Aggie was hesitantly giving her coat and hat to a maid. Cathy kissed her, took her arm and brought her into the drawing room. 'Darling Aggie. You have to come and meet Liam. I've told him all about you and that you'll be the most important person here. I know you'll get on just great.'

Liam was relieved to see his wife return to his side. 'How do you do, Aggie. I've heard an awful lot about you.'

'And all of it awful, no doubt.'

'Very much the opposite. Cathy says they wouldn't have made it as a family without you.'

Aggie shook her head. 'Cathy and Rose never gave me a moment's trouble, unlike that great lump over there.' Fergus was already stuffing canapés into his mouth. 'But they've all faced a lot of turmoil in their short lives. You too, I've heard.'

'Ah well. That's all behind me and now I have a beautiful wife to fill my life.'

'Yes, she is beautiful, inside and out. I'm sure you deserve each other. Now, I need something to drink and not that champagne shite. Find me whiskey, Cathy.'

Not long after, the Hughes contingent arrived and there was another assault of names and faces for Liam to contend with. Stasia shook his hand very formally and introduced Edmund and her four sons, two with partners of their own.

'Edmund and I wish you and Cathy as long and happy a marriage as we've been blessed with. Cathy's very dear to me, Liam – did you know she was born on our wedding day? If you need any advice about farming or keeping livestock as you expand, Edmund and Peter would be only too happy to share their knowledge.'

Cathy was especially delighted to see her cousin Matthew, the only apostle who had escaped working on the Hughes's farm. 'Liam, this is my cousin Mattie, Auntie Stasia's third son and his wife Lucy and son Fintan. He's a doctor now in Carlow. Oh Mattie, we had so little time to talk at Rose and Sam's wedding but it's wonderful to see you with your lovely family.'

'Aren't they just. I thought I might be the only Hughes boy to get hitched so it's exciting to see Peter finally find someone special in Maureen. Maybe there's hope still for Andrew and Paul. We must swap our gruesome hospital stories some time, Cathy, though I've never been at a war front like you and seen those sorts of horrors. Auntie Hannah was so proud of you risking your life to save others, and so sad that you lost your first husband like that, though Johnny must be a consolation. Where is he? He's a bit older than Fintan but they might play together.'

Yes, where *is* Johnny thought Cathy. Seamus was bringing him, along with Ellen and Aoife, so that he could enjoy a ride in the Jaguar but they should have been here at least fifteen minutes ago. She heard the door knocker – that was them now, thank god.

Lily herded everyone towards her dining room. She had organised an additional table so that all twenty-one of them could sit down for a meal. She had even devised a seating plan, complete with name-cards in her own copperplate hand, with an obvious class system at work – Aggie had been placed as far away from Lily as possible. The hostess had seated herself between the groom and Seamus while Aggie was placed between Mattie and Paul, the two most junior apostles. Cathy, sitting between Liam and Fergus, whispered into her brother's ear and he immediately got out of his seat and walked down the room towards Aggie. 'Mattie, change places with me would you fella, so that you and Cathy can talk blood and bones without making the rest of us vomit.' Aggie beamed as Fergus sat down next to her.

Everyone was enjoying cheese, port and relaxed chat when Lily got to her feet and tapped her Waterford crystal glass.

'One moment, everyone. It has been such a pleasure for me to be able to welcome the whole family here today to celebrate Cathy and Liam's marriage which, as you know, took place a couple of weeks ago in the back of beyond. We all so enjoyed Rose and Sam's lovely wedding this spring but that sort of celebration wasn't what Cathy wanted apparently and we must respect that. I'm sure I speak for you all when I say that we've all been wishing for Cathy to find happiness after losing her first husband so tragically at the end of the war. For such a lovely, kind young woman she's been through an extraordinary amount of loss and pain in her life; thankfully, she managed to be reconciled to her mother before Hannah sadly passed away last year. So, although I would be lying if I said that Stasia and I had not raised an eyebrow on hearing that Cathy had chosen a man brought up in an industrial school out in the wilds of Connemara and now a fisherman, having met Liam, it's clear that he is a very decent man and Cathy loves him to bits. Liam will be a perfectly good husband and a kind father to Johnny and for that we must be thankful. So please join me in a toast to Cathy and Liam.'

Everyone rose, raised their glasses and sat down again. The chatter resumed instantly. Talk about damning with faint praise, thought Cathy.

There was a faint tinging which was ignored, but then louder ringing and finally Ellen shushed everyone and clapped her hands: Aoife was on her feet.

'I hope you'll forgive me for following Lily's words with a few of my own. I had no plans to speak today and I apologise to you both, Cathy and Liam; I know that you didn't want any speeches.' Aoife took a deep breath. 'Liam is my son. Not in any conventional sense but in all the ways that matter, and I couldn't be prouder of him. To see him marry Cathy, whom I have loved for twenty odd years, not just because she's the daughter of my dear brother-in-law, John, God rest his soul, but because she's a complete angel, well… *tá no chroí ag canadh le háthas*, which means "my heart is singing with joy" for those of you who need to brush up your Irish. If you knew what Liam went through at that dreadful school, what he has battled and put behind him, how hard he has worked and will keep working to create his business from nothing, you would feel as humbled as I do. What I ask of you all, as we celebrate the start of this most auspicious marriage, is that everyone here does what they can to stop that evil school and the others like it. Shut them all down!' Aoife banged her hand on the table. 'Some of you here have money and influence and contacts in high places.' She threw a glance over to Lily. 'Please use them. Liam has been saved but not all those poor boys are so lucky. Anyway, I've said enough. Sláinte, beannacht Dé leat!

Aoife sat down, her face flushed with exertion and embarrassment. Cathy started the applause but was quickly joined by everyone, even Lily. It went on for quite a while and only stopped when Cathy herself stood up.

'We're not doing very well on the 'no speeches' rule are we? But as it seems to be a day for the women to get on their feet, I just want to say a couple of things. Firstly, thank you, Aunt Lily, for this splendid and generous reception. You're such a strong link to my mother and you've always looked after me, as have so many other women in the room: Auntie Stasia, Aoife, Ellen, Rose and Bridie and, last but certainly not least, the incomparable Aggie. Thank you from the bottom of my heart. But I have also had the protection of some incredible men: my Daddy of course, but, when I lost him, Uncle Seamus rode to the rescue and has been looking after me ever since. And Fergus has given me so much love, even when he was a tiny baby, then a toddler and now a man mountain. If I ever need a wardrobe moved, I know I can depend on him. But now I'm putting myself into the hands of my Liam, who I love so much and am blessed to say he loves me in return. I know he'll protect Johnny and me with his life and I'll do my best to make him the happiest man on earth which is the least he deserves. So, here's to my husband, to our future together and to you all.'

Cathy's speech was greeted with some laughter, sighs, nods and a few tears from Aoife and Aggie. Everyone then stood, cheered, toasted and hooted in appreciation. Lily's dining room had never seen such a rowdy rabble.

Seamus spoke up. 'No, good people, don't worry, no speech from me. But when you've finished your coffees and teas would you be good enough to join Johnny and me in the drawing room – we've prepared a little nonsense for you all.'

Everyone gathered in the drawing room, glasses in hand. Two music stands were set up and Johnny was sitting with his cello, Seamus by his side, viola in hand.

'Cathy and Liam, Johnny and I wanted to mark your marriage with something musical that would relate to your future life in Cleggan, a place I don't know and have no intention of visiting – no offence intended. I asked Johnny what Cleggan means to him and he said 'fish'. He did also say the sea and boats but it was mainly all about the fish. So, we've been preparing my version of Schubert's *Trout Quintet*, just the last movement. Please forgive the scrappiness but we've been forced to rehearse in secret after Johnny's Saturday cricket club sessions.'

Seamus checked that Johnny was ready and they began to play. The first time through, Seamus had the melody on his viola with Johnny adding a very basic bass line on the cello but, on the repeat, Johnny took the melody with Seamus adding some elaborate ripples over the top. Everyone applauded wildly but Seamus raised his hand to stop them.

'No, we haven't finished torturing you yet, have we?' Johnny shook his head, a beaming smile on his face, and put down his cello carefully. He and Seamus walked over to the grand piano.

'Last year, Cathy took Johnny to see Disney's *Alice in Wonderland* which he loved. He could remember there was a song where the Walrus and the Carpenter eat all the oysters - but I couldn't find the music so we're not doing that.' Everyone laughed. 'But I did find this.' Seamus waved some sheet music in the air. 'It's *The Lobster Quadrille*, which you will all remember is the song that the Mock Turtle sings. Please

join in when you've memorised the very complicated chorus.'
Seamus began playing the introduction, then he and Johnny
started singing:

Will you walk a little faster? said a whiting to a snail
There's a porpoise close behind us, and he's treading on my tail
Don't you see how eagerly the turtles and the lobsters all advance
They are waiting on the shingle, won't you come and join the dance?

As the chorus began, Johnny skipped over to his mother,
linked arms with her and spun her round, and then he did the
same with Liam.

Will you, won't you, will you, won't you, will you join the dance?
Will you, won't you, will you, won't you, won't you join the dance?

People soon got the hang of it, joining in the chorus and
improvising their own little dances until everyone had spun
around with everyone else and was totally out of breath.

Will you, won't you, will you, won't you, won't you join the dance?

******

Johnny wanted his mother to sit and chat for a while before
the light went out. He was too excited to even think of sleep.
Seeing all his Rowanbridge relatives again was such a treat
and they had all told him what a clever fella he was to play and
sing for the newly-weds.

'I knew you'd love *The Lobster Quadrille*, Mama.'

'I did love it, my darling. So funny. And *The Trout*. You
played that beautifully.'

'Uncle Seamus helped me. And we had to do it all in secret.
I couldn't even practise in my room in case you heard.'

'Well, it was a brilliant surprise and a perfect treat for us all.'

Johnny turned over in bed and pulled Tiny Ted close to his chest. 'I'm pleased Tiny Ted can come to Cleggan with us, but I wish we could take Uncle Seamus too.'

Cathy returned to her bedroom to find Liam waiting for her, sitting up in bed, reading Yeats again.

'Come to bed, macushla, while you've still got a grand mahogany bed to get into. You know, seeing you here at the Academy, seeing the life you are used to, amid all your well-educated and moneyed relations, your Aunt Lily's amazing house, it's made me even more worried about the squalor I'm taking you and Johnny back to in Cleggan.'

'Squalor? Rubbish. Simplicity is what I want. And, anyway, none of that matters besides being with you. But, while we still have the chance, why don't you make love to me in this very large and luxurious bed so we can make some comparisons when we're home.'

'You're a very demanding woman, Cathleen Molloy, but I'm not likely to get a better offer anywhere in Dalkey tonight, am I?' whispered Liam into Cathy's ear as he unbuttoned her best dress.

Chapter 12 – November 1952

Cathy was woken up in her simple pine bed with Johnny shaking her. 'Mama, wake up. It's Mikey again.' Johnny ran out to the landing, Cathy stumbling after him in the dark. She switched on the light and sent Johnny back to bed. There were groans and sharp cries coming from the back bedroom and the sound of the wooden headboard being struck. Mikey's nightmares – night terrors in reality - were a regular occurrence and Cathy had learned how to respond, how to sit and wait until the terror had passed and how to make sure Mikey wasn't at risk of hurting himself as he thrashed around on his bed. She would comfort Mikey if he woke but, often, he would simply return to deep sleep without waking at all.

Cathy opened the bedroom door. Brendan was already sitting on Mikey's bed. He had put pillows against the wall for protection and was holding Mikey's hand. 'It's okay, Missus Cathy; I'm here,' whispered Brendan. 'Get yourself back to bed.'

'Thanks, Brendan, see you in the morning.' Cathy first checked that Johnny had gone safely back to sleep and then slid into her own bed without waking Liam.

She lay awake wondering what to do for the best for Mikey; she could only guess at what monsters were filling his sleep. Occasionally, Mikey would also wet the bed during these terrors, and then it was a toss-up whether to wake him to change the bedding or to let him sleep until the morning in his own urine. Mikey was always crushed with shame when this occurred. The first time it happened after Cathy had moved in, Mikey had crept downstairs at dawn with his soiled sheets and tried to wash them himself at the sink. After the men had gone off to work, Cathy followed a mysterious trail of drips and found the sopping wet sheets draped from the curtain rail in Mikey's room, the mattress bearing witness to that night's trauma and previous ones too. She had turned the mattress before they got back from work and replaced the wet sheets with dry ones, but she had hung them from the curtain poles in the hope that Mikey wouldn't realise she had intervened.

Six weeks later, it happened again. Cathy came downstairs early to find Mikey doing his best to squeeze as much water out of the heavy linen. He mumbled embarrassed apologies unable to look her in the eye. She gently put her arm around Mikey's shoulder and told him not to worry one little bit, she would sort it all out. There are only two sides to any mattress, so Cathy had bought a waterproof sheet and ordered a new mattress.

Later that evening, when she and Liam were relaxing in the sitting room, there was a knock on the door and Brendan walked in.

'Sorry to disturb you both but can I just come in for a moment or two. I won't be long I promise 'cos I need to get to my bed soon - those lobster pots won't bait themselves tomorrow morning - but Mikey has asked me to speak to you about his problem with the bed-wetting which he is totally mortified about as you can imagine but sure, the poor lad cannot help himself.'

'Of course, he can't. I've told him he mustn't worry,' said Cathy. 'Please will you tell him it doesn't matter at all. We seem to have a sort of solution for now – as far as the laundry is concerned anyway.'

'You see, he was only little, just six, when he arrived at St Joseph's and he'd never had any trouble with the bed-wetting before but the first time he was given a beating by the Brothers for some little thing – he thinks he had spilled some food on the floor – that very same night he wet the bed for the first time, and then of course he got a beating in the morning for wetting the bed and not only that they made him take the wet sheet off the bed and out into the yard in front of all the other boys and he was made to run around holding the sheet above his head to dry it off and him just a wee chiseler too, and of course everyone was laughing at him as he ran and the air was full of mist that day so the sheet was never going to dry in that weather but eventually he was allowed to take the sheet back to the dormitory and put it back on his bed. He says the bed-wetting got even worse for a while but by the time I got to St Joseph's – I was twelve so Mikey would have been eleven – it wasn't too bad, maybe once a week say, and I tried to help him by making him go to the jacks last thing before getting into bed and told him not to drink too much at his tea and that helped a bit, but he was always so terrified to go to sleep in case he might wet the bed and get another beating.'

'Good God, Brendan. That's savage. No wonder the poor lad has nightmares.'

'I saw endless dreadful things like that at St Joseph's.' Liam stood up. 'Some boys cope but many were destroyed by it. It used to sicken me that a boy who was a particular target of the Brothers' cruelty would then also be bullied by other boys. They smell blood. Human nature can be an ugly thing. But let me go up and speak to him, Brendan. He needs to know that I've been through it too. We understand and we will always protect him. It's nothing to be ashamed of.'

'Yes, that might help, Liam sir, but the thing is it's been so much better since he's been here in Cleggan. How often has the bed-wetting happened recently? Not more than once a month, I'd say, or even less. But he just can't crack it completely.' Brendan shook his head, looking solemn which the cheery lad rarely did.

'Sheets and mattresses can be washed or replaced but a boy's mind is not so easily sorted,' said Cathy. 'Forget about the bed-wetting; it's the nightmares that worry me and they are happening just as frequently as ever. If we could help him banish those, maybe the bed-wetting would stop too. Liam, please tell Mikey that he can talk to us all about St Joseph's any time, though I guess he'll probably find it easier to talk to one of you two rather than me.'

'Talking isn't always a cure, you know,' Liam said. Since their wedding, Cathy had been encouraging him to talk to her about what he had lived through at St Joseph's, but he would just kiss her softly and say it was better to leave such memories buried beneath his present happiness. Why dig up skeletons if they were safely underground? Better to pile on more and more joy. Cathy didn't have an answer for that.

It was true that they were doing their best to have as many good times as they could. Cathy had taken over the administration of Liam's business which freed up some of his time so they could have more fun as a family: swimming, boating or pony-riding. Johnny seemed reasonably settled in the local school and had made a couple of friends his own age who would often join Liam, Brendan and Mikey to play beach cricket at the end of the working day. Maybe these happy times would eventually help Mikey banish his terrors.

The morning after Mikey's latest night-time disturbance, Cathy woke to find Liam and the boys already gone off to the boat and Johnny sitting quietly in the bed next to her reading her old book of *Irish Fairy Tales*.

'Morning, my love. What's that you're reading? Ah, I used to love that book; I'm pleased you do too.'

'It's okay. I've read it lots of times before but I'm trying to really remember all the stories. I need to make myself more Irish, you see, Mama.'

'More Irish? What on earth do you mean?'

'My friends at school keep asking whether I'm English, because of my name. And I can't understand them much when they speak in Irish which is most of the time and I don't know

lots of the Irish myths and legends, so I need to try harder.'
Cathy pulled Johnny close to her and kissed the top of his
head. 'You don't need to try to be anyone you're not, Johnny.
The Irish words will come to you soon enough just by hearing
them all the time. Just be yourself.'

After Johnny left for school, Cathy tidied away the breakfast
things, wrapped up warmly and took her cup of tea out to the
beachside of the cottage to sit on the dunes. She hoped Johnny
was happy. Cathy herself thought her life was *almost* perfect.
She couldn't get enough of the wide Connemara skies; she
could feel her brain expanding when she sat contemplating
waves and clouds.

But she found managing the cottage more stressful than she
had anticipated. It wasn't the hard work - she had no problem
with that - but being the person first in line for cooking and
cleaning was a novelty. Cathy realised that never in her entire
life had she lived without some sort of help or housekeeper,
whether Aggie, nursing orderlies, Mam Ashfield or, latterly,
the whole domestic infrastructure at the Academy. She was
determined to rise to the challenge and had buckled down.
However, she thought it was stupid not to make full use of
all that modern technology could offer. The refrigerator was
soon joined by an electric washing tub with a built-in mangle
which meant they stopped sending their weekly laundry off to
Mrs Gallagher. Getting their laundry clean wasn't the biggest
challenge; getting it to dry in the changeable Cleggan climate
was a Promethean task, especially as autumn approached. She
would run in and out all day long trying to catch the gaps in
the rain.

The other technology Cathy decided she couldn't live
without was a telephone. One was installed soon after she
moved in which caused a flurry of excitement. It was only the
second one in the village. The phone allowed her to keep in
weekly touch with Ellen, Aoife and Seamus to hear about how

the Academy was coping without her. Johnny would spend just as long chatting to the three of them as she would.

Cathy also loved to phone Rose every Sunday afternoon, to hear all the news from Rowanbridge. Most of it was reassuring: Rose and Sam had refurbished the bar and were getting good custom as a result; Fergus's hurling team were at the top of the league; Mattie and Lucy's second baby had been born safely. 'Auntie Stasia's just over the moon to have a baby-girl after so many boys,' said Rose.

'And I'm guessing she's delighted she's been christened Elizabeth, after the new queen in England,' added Cathy wryly. But some of Rose's news was concerning. Father Stephen had been admitted to Kilkenny hospital for a few days after he had vomited blood. 'The man's lost so much weight and he's as yellow as a buttercup.'

'That'll be cirrhosis, I'm afraid. Let's be honest, Rose, he's been kicking hell out of his liver for years.'

'Even more since Mammy died. He slurs his words at mass and has to hold onto the lectern to stay upright. A couple of times his housekeeper has found him still asleep in his chair when she's arrived in the morning, empty bottles at his feet, Aggie heard.'

'Oh God, poor man. Not much you can do about it, Rose.'

'Maybe you could talk to him about it next time you come home. You're a nurse and you two have always been close, haven't you.'

'I suppose so, Rosie. Let's see.'

Cathy finished her tea and walked back inside to find two envelopes on the mat. She recognised Bridie's handwriting on the first and eagerly tore open the letter. Bridie was asking to come for the following Sunday with a friend who would drive her to and from Galway. Cathy needed to get her positive reply in the post fast. She turned over the second letter, which was intriguing: American airmail stamps and postmark, typewritten but the old Rowanbridge address crossed through and replaced by the Cleggan address, hand-written by Rose. Cathy sat down at the kitchen table and took out the sheets of fine onionskin paper.

At the top was a New York address and a date two weeks past.

'Hiya Cathy,

I hope this letter reaches you, but I guess, if you're reading it, it must have. I've sent it to your old home, hoping that your mother will forward it to you if you don't live in Rowanbridge any longer.

It's me, your schoolfriend Bernie, writing to you from the Big Apple! I hope you remember me. I've never forgotten you and your family and neither has anyone in our family. I moved into a new apartment last month and, when I was packing up, I found the copy of 'Little Women' that you gave me just before we all sailed to the States back in 1931. Do you remember? I loved that book so much. I must have read it at least ten times over the years and I think it played a big part in me wanting to become a writer myself, like Jo March. But it reminded me what a great friend you were to me.

Twenty-one years! I can hardly believe we've been gone that long but the O'Rourke family has done bloody well for itself over here in the 'land of the free'. My father got a job almost immediately in the New York fire service through an Irish mate. Three of my brothers are also firemen now and one is a police officer but Sean decided to go a completely different route and he's a tailor in the Bronx. Very useful for getting some overcoats and suits made!

As for my sisters, Gerry and Harry are married with kids out in the suburbs. They both married Irishmen, naturally, but Bobby and Jo have their own little businesses: Bobby has a shoe shop and Jo has a hairdressing and beauty salon. So, between them all, there's no excuse for an O'Rourke not to be turned out well!

I went a different route. After high school I went to a journalism college and studied hard. In the early days I did my time sitting in court rooms or knocking on doors to follow some grisly story. But then I discovered there was a whole different word of journalism – magazines! People are so much more attractive in magazine-land. I got my first break on Life magazine as a junior dogsbody but I proved myself and moved onto McCall's (that's a big one over here) as a features writer. Two years ago, I was considering a job offer I'd had from Harper's Bazaar when I met the editor of Charm magazine at a cocktail party. Charm is not so famous as Harper's but I really like its mission. It's 'a magazine for working women'. At least, that's the claim – and yes, I know that all women are working women. But we have no recipes, no food ads and no feckin' knitting patterns! Anyway, I decided to accept the deputy editor's position there and that's what keeps me busy still. No husband by choice, though I have a smokin' hot boyfriend who doesn't want to tie me to a kitchen sink or a cradle and that suits me just fine.

What are you up to? You were always the cleverest one at school so I'm expecting to hear you're a brain surgeon or even a TD. Something where you can use your intelligence to take care of other people. I know you won't have wasted your life anyway. It's only looking back now that I realise how much you tried to do for me, giving me bread and jam every night, packets of tea and eggs to take home – and even your best winter coat! Thanks a million.

Moving to the States has been such a liberation for my family. If we had stayed in Rowanbridge, my Pa would still be cutting the Byrnes' hayfield and Bobby would still be serving in your little shop, weighing out rashers. But losing you and your friendship was the downside. Maybe we can pick up where we left off, now we're both sophisticated grown-ups? If you ever come to New York there's a room here waiting for you. I'd love to show you the sights.

Please, please write back to me; I'd LOVE to hear from you! Do you have telephones yet in Ireland? If you do, there's a number for my apartment at the top there.

Bye for now and say a Hail Mary for this shameless sinner,

Your old friend, Bernie.

Cathy laughed out loud. What a wonderful surprise. She could hear Bernie's voice saying all those words. She would definitely write back, or maybe even phone.

******

Johnny heard the sports car roaring from a distance before it flashed past the cottage and disappeared. Five minutes later the noise returned and stopped outside the cottage.

'Whose car is that Mama? It sounds amazing.' A brisk knock followed and Cathy opened the door to Bridie who threw herself into Cathy's arms, then pulled off her headscarf.

'Hey sis, great to see you. Is this really where you live?'

'Come in, come in. Did you come in that car? Whose is it?'

'It's mine, ma'am.' A handsome black man appeared in the doorway, took Cathy's hand and bowed over it. 'William Kenny Junior at your service.'

'This is Bill. He's on my law course and he's one of the only students with a car so I asked him to bring me over.'

Liam came over to shake his hand. 'How do you do, Bill. That's a hell of a car you have there.' Bill took him and Johnny outside to admire the sportscar.

'Just leave them to their car nonsense, Bridie. Come inside and let me get you a drink. Tea or something stronger?'

'What do you think, Cathy. I'll have gin if you've got any and Bill drinks whiskey.'

'Not too much, I hope, when he has you in the car with him.'

'Oh, don't fuss! He's very sensible. So where are your two lodgers? I want Bill to hear from their own mouths what Letterfrack School is like. His father is a Congressman in Georgia, but he knows some Irish judges because he went to Trinity with them. He used to be a law professor and I thought he might help us get some ball rolling somewhere up high in Dublin like Aoife suggested.'

'His father is in Congress? A black Congressman?'

'His father is as white as you or me, and he's Irish too. He only went over to the States to teach law at Chicago university where he met Bill's mother. She was a PhD student, though not in law, in German philology, whatever the feck that is. She's the black parent, obviously.'

The men walked back inside and Cathy handed Bill the glass of whiskey. 'Thank you kindly, Ma'am.'

'Just call me Cathy.'

'I shall. Thank you for letting me come to visit you in your home.'

'Bill said he wanted to see how the Irish peasantry live.' Bridie laughed throatily while Bill looked a little uncomfortable.

'I said I'd like to see how real Irish people live. We don't get a proper idea in our ivory towers at university. But my own father lived on the west coast when he was a child. Further south, in County Kerry, but a similar fishing community.'

'It's such a co-incidence, you being American, because only this week I got a letter from an old school friend who emigrated to the States with her family before you were even born, Bridie. There were ten O'Rourke children in all and they've all done really well for themselves in New York. It seems that America really is the land of opportunity.'

'It sure is … if you're white.'

'Was your father a black Irishman then?' Johnny asked earnestly.

'No, young man. My father's white and as Irish as you are.'

'But I'm half English. My Daddy was English. He was a soldier and he was killed in the war.'

'Well, I am sorry to hear that. When people look at me, they just see my black mother, and I guess when people hear you, they can't hear your English father. But we know who we really are, don't we, Johnny? I chose to come to university here to explore my Irish heritage. It's invisible but it's there inside me.'

Johnny nodded solemnly.

After lunch Cathy took Bridie and Bill for a blustery walk, Johnny running alongside them, bouncing a tennis ball. Bill was fascinated by the picturesque harbour and how small most of the fishing boats were moored along the pier.

'I wouldn't fancy risking my neck in one of those tiny things in this weather,' exclaimed Bill.

'Lucky for you that your father escaped into the law, saving you from a life among the fish,' answered Bridie.

They sauntered out of the village along the lanes to go and admire Liam's expanding flocks. 'That sheep is definitely giving me the evil eye,' remarked Bridie. 'It probably knows I've just eaten its cousin.'

'Did you know that our mammy and my father came here on their honeymoon, Bridie? Next time you come, when the weather is a bit kinder, I'll take you out to Omey Island where Daddy's first wife Ailsa, Aoife's sister, is buried along with my half-sister, Máire. It's a beautiful spot but today we'd all just get blown into the sea. I've learned to respect the weather a lot more living here.'

'Yes, I'll be honest, ladies, I am *freezing* to death. I'm still not used to the Irish climate.'

'You big sap.' Bridie slapped Bill across the back. 'Come on then. Let's get back and get you a cup of something hot, and then we ought to set off back to Galway, Cathy.'

'Well, it's been a treat to see you out here. Maybe you can come again soon?'

'I'd love to, if Bill doesn't mind driving me, though I suppose I could get the bus to Clifden. And next time, make sure I get to meet your two lads who were at Letterfrack.'

'I'm always happy to play the big, black chauffeur, Bridie.'

'But you should come to Galway too, Cathy, and then I can show you around.'

'And when you come back will you play cricket with me, please Bill?'

Chapter 13 – Christmas 1952

'Mama, look what Granny and Auntie Shirley have sent me.' Johnny's hands were full, balancing four boxes, each containing a Scalex toy car. 'There's an MG and an Aston Martin. And this one's a Maserati and this is a Ferrari.'

'Heavens. How wonderful, you're such a lucky boy.'

'I know. Can I phone them to say thank you and wish them a Happy Christmas?'

'They don't have a telephone yet, sorry love. But I shall take a photo of you with the cars next to the Christmas tree and send it with your thank-you letter. Is that okay?'

Johnny nodded and took the cars over to Liam and Sam, who he hoped would show a little more interest in the gifts. It was only just gone eight o'clock on Christmas morning but they hadn't been able to make Johnny wait any longer to open some of the tantalisingly shaped parcels under the Christmas tree up in the Rowanbridge drawing room. Fergus, Bridie and Bill were over in the Byrnes' farmhouse, Bridie and Bill almost certainly still fast asleep.

Bridie had asked if she could bring Bill for Christmas because he wasn't flying home that holiday. 'Why not,' said Fergus. 'What's one more person? There's plenty of room over with Nicholas and Louisa.'

'Is he her boyfriend then?' asked Aggie. No-one had a clue.

Liam read out the instructions for the clockwork cars and Johnny immediately set off the MG racing towards the women. 'Watch out, Aggie. Catch it! Don't let it crash.' Cathy caught the little car. 'I think you should put some cushions around to protect the cars and the furniture.'

'I'm out of here before I trip over the bloody things,' said Aggie. 'I have a turkey calling me.'

'We'll be down in a minute.' Rose shouted after her.

'Come on, then. Let's leave the boys to their car chases,' said Cathy. As they walked along the landing, Rose put her hand on Cathy's arm. 'While I have you alone, can I tell you our news – I'm pregnant.' The sisters threw themselves into a tight hug.

'How wonderful, Rosie, darling. There's no Christmas present that's going to match that. How far gone are you?'

'About four months. I could've told you on the phone last week but I thought I'd wait. I wouldn't have got that hug down a wire.'

'Who knows – apart from Sam?'

'Just Teresa and Ned. And Aggie of course. I plan on telling everyone else at Auntie Stasia's today.'

'I know it's silly but it means so much to have our Mammy and Daddy live on through the next generations. When I look at Johnny, I love him for himself but also for all the people whose blood is in him somewhere: Joe and his Mam, our Granny Fitzgerald and Grandad James, plus all the people I never knew.'

'What about you? Do you think you and Liam will try?'

'Ah, go on with you. We've only been married two minutes. We haven't talked about it, or even thought about it.' Cathy was not being strictly honest with Rose yet again. She and Liam had not talked about it but she had certainly been thinking about the possibility ever since their wedding day when Cathy had stopped Liam using condoms saying she would use her natural cycles. In fact, Cathy had stopped calculating whether it was a fertile week or not and they had been making love freely without any pregnancy following on. She was a bit worried about that, but she would be thirty-three in the spring and knew that fertility declined after thirty. Maybe it wasn't to be, or they'd need to try harder. But she should talk to Liam about it rather than let it just happen; that wouldn't be fair.

Christmas lunch was a noisy, chaotic affair, with fourteen of them around the table.

'I'm afraid the crockery and cutlery doesn't all match like at Aunt Lily's,' said Rose.

'At least you have proper glasses. We had to drink champagne out of beer glasses and tea-cups when we got married. Mind you, thanks to Auntie Stasia's wedding gift, I can now give eight people a respectable glass of wine in lovely crystal.'

Bill was sitting between Louisa and Fergus who was plying him with every dish on the table.

'Here, try this. Bread sauce. I can't get enough of it.' Fergus slopped a big spoonful onto Bill's plate.'

'What's in it?' Bill sniffed.

'I've no idea. Aggie, how do you make the bread sauce?' Fergus shouted across the table.

'Have you not had any stuffing either yet?' Louisa spooned on a helping for Bill. 'I thought you Americans ate turkey all the time.'

'For Thanksgiving yes, but we don't have these accompaniments. We have cranberry sauce and baked squash. Are all of these made from bread?'

'Wait until you taste the Christmas pudding, Bill. That's not made from bread and it's just delicious; it's full of fruit and booze, and with Aggie's measures of brandy too.' Fergus kissed his fingers.

Aggie tutted. 'And what do you know about making Christmas pudding, you big eejit? All you've ever done is stir in some sixpenny bits and licked out the bowl. I'll have you know that all good Christmas puds contain a decent heap of breadcrumbs.'

After lunch, while the older relatives sat chatting, Nicholas passing around cigars to Ned, Tricky, and Sam, Johnny dragged Bridie, Bill and Fergus upstairs to the drawing room where he had arranged cushions and rugs around a clear space for his new cars to be raced safely.

'Oh god, Johnny,' Fergus groaned as he knelt on the floor. 'I'm too full to be messing around on the carpet you know. Just as well it's you. You get to choose first which car you want. I reckon the Ferrari is the flashiest.' Johnny considered the choice carefully. 'I like them all, but I think I'll take the Aston Martin. It's a classic English sports car, you know.'

Cathy crept into the drawing room with her camera to capture the four of them sprawled on the floor, revving up their chosen vehicles.

'Well, I didn't think I'd be chasing an MG, Ferrari and Aston Martin in a Maserati when I came to Ireland,' said Bill.

'Ready, steady go!' Johnny didn't notice that the other three set down their cars just a fraction later than he did. It was Christmas Day after all.

Rose and Sam's announcement at tea-time at Auntie Stasia's was greeted with many congratulations and a few knowing nudges from Fergus. 'Good man, Sam. All the plumbing's in good working order then.' Rose gave her little brother a slap on the backside.

'I hope you get a good sleeper, not like our two,' said Mattie, wandering over. 'It's a relief to come home here to be honest and let Mother take over for a few days.' Stasia had hardly let baby Elizabeth out of her arms the whole afternoon.

'Many blessings on you both and the babe to come.' Father Stephen had been sitting quietly in the corner but had stirred himself to come and talk to Rose and Sam. 'I hope you have an easy time of it, Rose, not like your mother.' Cathy overheard his remark. 'I think Rose will be like me, Father, and I had no trouble at all with Johnny. She shouldn't be anxious.'

'Sorry, Rose. I shouldn't let what's in my head just pop out of my mouth.'

Cathy walked Stephen back to his chair and sat down next to him. 'You look tired, Father. Christmas services are a big burden I suppose.'

'Perhaps. But what other point is there to me? If I can't turn up and make a decent fist out of Easter and Christmas I should throw the towel in. But I can relax now and enjoy a dram or two.' He held up a full glass of whiskey before knocking half back.

'Take care, Father. You shouldn't hammer your liver like that. Sorry, that's the nurse in me talking. It's none of my business, is it.'

'No, no. I suppose I should take it a bit easy.' Stephen settled back in his chair to drink the rest.

Later that evening, Liam smiled indulgently from under the sheets as he watched Cathy get into her nightie and fuss around packing a small bag for him. He was driving back to Cleggan in the morning leaving Cathy and Johnny to spend a few more days in Rowanbridge before going on to Dalkey by train. They were going to see the pantomime at the Gaiety with the three guardian angels, a long-standing tradition they all loved.

'Well, I have survived my first Rowanbridge Christmas without any major mishaps. I love your sisters and brother, and Sam seems a very decent, normal bloke. My sort of man. Even your Auntie Stasia is not as scary as your Great-aunt Lily.' Cathy got into bed beside him. 'She's changed – she's softened. I don't know whether it was her losing my mother or becoming a granny but she's not at all the same driven, unbending woman she was when I lived here. She never seemed to take much pleasure in her own kids but my god she loves Mattie's two.'

'Watching you there with the baby, you looked like a natural.'

'Ah well, you never forget how to hold a baby.'

'I'd be terrified to touch one in case their head dropped off.'

Cathy laughed and rubbed her cold feet up and down Liam's warm legs. 'Don't be silly. You pick up new-born lambs all the time but I noticed you kept well away from baby Elizabeth.'

'I suppose when Rose has hers I won't be able to avoid picking one up.'

'I'm so thrilled for them. They'll be lovely parents.' Cathy paused. 'And you would be too.'

'Me? I'm not fit to be a father.'

'I think the exact opposite, precisely because of what you went through as a child at St Joseph's; no-one could be more aware of how much love and protection children need. You'd probably spoil one to death.'

Liam stroked Cathy's face. 'Does this mean you're after having a baby yourself maybe?' He kissed her.

'Am I so obvious?'

'Well, you promised never to lie to me again, so I'll take that as a 'yes'. And I promised to give you anything you wanted … if I could.'

Chapter 14 – May 1953

Soon after New Year, Cathy sent a handful of photographs over to Mam Ashfield and Shirley, not just ones of Johnny proudly holding his Scalex cars but others featuring every member of the family, annotating the backs with names. What a lot of relatives there were. Johnny wrote a long thank-you letter, politely asking how their Christmas had been and whether they had liked the little gifts he and Cathy had sent over. Shirley wrote back almost immediately to say that Mam had loved the soap and talcum powder and her own earrings were perfect, thanks, and how handsome Fergus was and what a lovely, kind face Liam had. She and Mam had enjoyed the Christmas break, thank you for asking: they had been invited out on Boxing Day to a neighbour's for tea which had been nice. As Cathy read Shirley's letter, she realised how different their Christmases had been and how blessed she was to have a big, noisy family. Having been banished from Rowanbridge for twelve long years, Cathy vowed never, ever to take them for granted.

All through spring, Johnny had asked Cathy when they could revisit Ollerton. It hadn't been possible at Easter because Aoife and Ellen had come over to Cleggan but now, in early May, mother and son were on the deck of the ferry over to Holyhead, enjoying the bracing surge of the boat as it sliced through the waves of the Irish Sea.

'How deep do you think the sea is right here, Mama?'

'I've no idea, my love. Sorry. We'll look it up in the encyclopaedia when we get back home.'

'I don't understand how the sea can be soft, just water, but so strong at the same time.'

'And dangerous. I get scared sometimes when Liam goes out in the boat and the waves are higher than him.'

'And waves wear away the cliffs and turn the shells into sand, but you can't even pick them up.'

Johnny let himself be hugged by his granny and auntie when they finally arrived. Tea was ready, complete with scones and gingerbread.

'You've grown so much in the last year, Johnny, so eat up, duck.' Mam Ashfield beamed at her grandson who was now not much shorter than her.

'Living by the sea must help, not like the filthy air around here we have to breathe. You both look really well, and happy.' Shirley filled up their teacups.

'Thank you for all the photographs you sent from Christmas,' Mam said. 'You'll have to talk me through who everyone is again. But Shirley and I were so pleased to get a sight of Liam. What a smashing chap he looks. Joe must be happy that his wife and son have someone so kind looking after them. He'll have blessed your union from heaven.'

Cathy shuffled awkwardly in her chair. 'Thanks, Mam. We're lucky to have found each other and Liam is a great Daddy to Johnny.'

'He's not my Daddy though. He's just Liam.'

'Yes, of course, my love. I just meant that he cares for you like a father.'

Shirley started packing up the tea-things. 'You finished, Johnny? We've got a surprise next door.' When Johnny walked into the front room, it took him a while to notice what Shirley had meant but eventually, he spotted the wood-panelled box in the corner with its small, green, glass screen. 'What's that?' he asked.

'Have you never seen a television, Johnny? Let me switch it on for you.' Shirley twiddled a knob at the front and a small dot appeared in the middle of the glass. 'We have to let it warm up.'

Mam followed them in and sat down in her chair. 'We'd been talking about splashing out on a television in time for the Coronation but when we heard you were coming we thought we'd get it right away. It's wonderful. So many things to watch, things we know nothing about and things we'd never get to see otherwise. Shirley watched a test match last week.'

'Yes, the Australians are over and I watched them play Worcestershire ...' Shirley was interrupted by the television bursting into life with a bunch of cowboys firing guns, raiding a covered wagon amid circling cattle. The driver of the wagon was shot and slumped forward. 'Oh no!' shouted Johnny and he ran over to the television set and sat on the floor cross-legged, as close to the screen as he could get.

'It's a Tex Ritter film,' whispered Shirley, 'not something we thought we'd like but we watch all the cowboy films now, don't we, Mam?'

'I even watch all the children's programmes, like *Bill and Ben, the Flowerpot Men*. "Flobadob" – that's how they talk.' The three women laughed. Johnny turned around and shushed them.

'We'll have to go back out if we want to chat. Come on. Let's leave him to it.'

Shirley and Cathy left the room, leaving Mam to watch with Johnny, and started the washing up together.

'Do you think you'll give Liam a child of his own?'

Cathy sighed. 'Liam cares for Johnny as if he were his son. And I'm getting on a bit. Probably wouldn't happen even if we wanted it to. How's your gentleman friend?'

'His wife died in February – heart attack - and he's asked me to marry him and come and live with him and his kids in Mansfield. But I couldn't leave Mam, now, could I? But it does mean Kazik and I feel a lot less guilty than we used to.'

'Does Mam know about him?'

Shirley nodded.

'Could she not go with you?' asked Cathy.

'I wouldn't uproot her. Don't know how long she's got left. Her chest is still very bad, despite the medicine they give her. Anyway, I'm not sure I'd want to live with a man all the time, him seeing me in my curlers and stuff, and I definitely don't fancy being housekeeper to him and his kids as well as holding down a job. This way, we keep the excitement and mystery.' Shirley gave Cathy a hefty nudge and laughed.

In the front room, the film credits were rolling. 'We have to switch it off now, Johnny, but we'll put it back on later. Mam and I always watch the news at eight.' Shirley turned the knob and the image contracted to a small dot of light. 'Kids would never go to bed if the programmes didn't stop at six o'clock.'

They filled their time with card games before the television was switched back on for the news. Then they watched a programme about some bell-ringers getting ready for the Coronation, and a variety programme with a troupe of long-limbed dancers followed.

'I wish I could dance like that still,' said Mam. 'I used to be a good dancer, like Joe.' Cathy fondly recalled Joe introducing her to the foxtrot. The discussion programme up next enabled Cathy to drag Johnny away from the screen and up to bed, though he would have happily sat through it.

'Can we have a television when we get home, please Mama?'

'There's no TV in Ireland, my love. Well, I think a few people in Dublin can get a signal from the BBC across the water, but there's no Irish television company yet. One day there will be, but I fear Cleggan will be one of the last places it'll reach.'

'Ireland doesn't have lots of things that England has.'

'Maybe – but we also have lots of things that England doesn't have.'

'Like what, Mama?'

Cathy had to think fast. 'We have the best lobsters, and the cleanest air, and the greenest grass, and the best fairy tales and myths and the kindest people in the world.'

'The Christian Brothers aren't very kind, Brendan says.'

'Sleep tight now, my love.' Cathy smiled at her beautiful boy cuddling Tiny Ted. She kissed his cheek and watched his eyes flicker and close.

Shirley had a pot of tea ready when Cathy came back downstairs. A programme was starting about the music that Bach and Handel had written for royal patrons and their coronations. There was clearly a great deal of excitement round for the imminent Coronation. Cathy knew that her Aunt Stasia too would be reading everything she could get her hands on about the lovely young queen and her family.

'You can't beat a bit of Handel, can you,' said Mam. 'When I still had lungs to speak of, I loved to sing in *The Messiah* every year.'

'And I adore Bach,' said Cathy. 'I try to play something of his every day, just to keep my hand in. He keeps me sane.'

'So, you've got a piano out in Cleggan, then?' remarked Shirley.

'Yes, Liam bought it for me as a surprise before there was any talk of marriage. That moment probably clinched it for me.'

'Such a shame we've never heard you play. And we'd love to hear Johnny play his cello. Maybe next time you come over you'll bring it, so we can hear him'.

'I'll definitely do that, Mam. It's a promise.'

The next morning was spent pleasantly enough, walking in the park, reading, playing cards and, in the afternoon, Mam watched some racing on the television while Cathy and Johnny helped Shirley weed the garden, until just before four o'clock they came inside.

'Now then Johnny. There's some cricket on the television soon which you can watch but I've got an even better treat.' Shirley took an envelope from the mantelpiece. 'I've got tickets for you and me to go to Trent Bridge to watch Nottinghamshire play Kent tomorrow. What do you think about that?'

Johnny was beside himself with excitement, so much so that he had to go into the garden again, run along the garden path several times and jump up and down on the lawn. He came in to watch the cricket eventually but kept asking Shirley all about the Nottinghamshire cricket team, the names of the players and their form so far this year all the way through the broadcast.

Mam got up early the next day to make packed lunches for Shirley and Johnny. Cathy offered to drive them to Trent Bridge and then they could make their own way back on the bus. Cathy thought she might take the opportunity to wander around Nottingham itself, see what had changed, if anything, since she had last been there in 1946.

Shirley directed Cathy through Nottingham's streets, quiet enough on a Sunday, until they approached West Bridgford. 'Just drop us off here, Cathy, would you. We can walk over the bridge; the ground is just the other side and it's fun to see the river.' Johnny was so excited he almost forgot to kiss his mother good-bye. Cathy sat in the car, watching him hop and skip over the bridge by Shirley's side, overwhelmed with love. It was important that he capture a little of his own father's life, the people and places that had mattered most to Joe. Cathy wondered what her life would be like now if Joe had survived the war. Dark, dashing, self-confident Joe, so different from Liam.

Cathy made her way through the city streets to the base of Castle Rock. She had always meant to visit Nottingham Castle when she lived near but had never managed it, what with the war and a young baby to look after. All those years playing Robin Hood games with Bernie but she had never visited the Sherriff of Nottingham's home. She parked in a side street and climbed up the steep paths through the park towards the castle, now a museum. It was a disappointment when she arrived. The Sherriff could never have lived in this castle; the architecture was clearly from later centuries. She looked around at the view from the summit and her eye was drawn to a red telephone box below. She practically ran back down Castle Rock to where it stood. She checked her purse; did she have enough money? She spoke to the operator and waited to be connected. The phone rang and rang. She was just about to abandon the attempt when she heard his voice. 'Hello. This is Liam Molloy. How can I help you?' Cathy fumbled with the shilling coin but managed to push it into the slot.

'Oh, my darling, how wonderful to hear you. It's me. It's Cathy.'

'Cathy, macushla. Are you OK? Is everything all right?'

'Yes, everything's fine now. I was desperate to hear your voice.' Beeping started and Cathy pushed another coin into the slot. 'I miss you so much. I have such a fierce ache for you to hold me.'

'I miss you too. The bed feels awfully empty.'

'I don't want to do this again, go away without you.'

'Is Johnny OK?'

'God, yes. He's in heaven at the cricket with Shirley at Trent Bridge. They're the best of friends. And they've bought a televis...' More beeping and one last coin.

'Listen, I don't have any more change. I love you with all my heart, darling.'

'I'm just off to Mrs Gallagher's for Sunday lunch with the boys but I would rather starve if I could sit here talking to you all day. I adore you, macushla. Give Johnny a hug and come home to me soon.'

'I will. Here take these kisses to bed with you tonight...' but before Cathy could send any air kisses down the line, the damned beeping started again and she had to concede defeat. Still, she had heard his velvety voice; she closed her eyes and imagined being back in his arms. Just two more days.

Chapter 15 – June 1953

Cathy and Bernie had exchanged five letters each since that first hopeful missive. With each one, they carefully reconstructed their early friendship, becoming more relaxed and intimate, helping themselves rediscover exactly what they had always liked about each other. In Cathy's first letter, she had told Bernie of her mother's death and explained how, because Rose had married Sam McCarthy last year and they were living in the old Main Street House, her letter had still managed to reach her. Bernie expressed polite surprise that Tricky Byrne had become Hannah's second husband and that a baby had ensued. Had it been a face-to-face conversation, Cathy suspected that Bernie's response would have been a little less polite.

Reassuringly, they found that they shared similar views and values: the British Coronation provided an excellent pretext to ridicule the concept of hereditary monarchies. The same things made them laugh: Charlie Chaplin, PG Wodehouse, The Marx Brothers and Stella Gibbons. They gave each other plenty of book recommendations. Bernie encouraged Cathy to try some American male writers: Salinger, Steinbeck and Hemingway. Cathy, in return and with a slight sense of inadequacy, recommended some women writers she enjoyed: du Maurier, Bowen, Pym and even Christie. By the time Cathy wrote her fifth reply to Bernie, she felt able to admit that she was really enjoying Johnny's Narnia books and that, like a complete eejit, she had ordered Samuel Beckett's novel, *Molloy*, on account of a shared name, only to find it was written in French. There was no escaping the fact that Bernie was better read than Cathy, but Cathy was confident that her brain was as good as her friend's; it just needed to be fed. In her last letter, Cathy had tentatively suggested that they try out a telephone conversation, despite the eye-watering costs of transatlantic calls. Bernie had agreed eagerly and a Sunday date, when charges were lower, had been settled on.

Cathy was in the sitting room waiting for Bernie's call to come through. There were patches of blue through the window and the house was empty. All the boys were on the beach playing cricket and football. She jumped when the phone rang and took a deep breath before picking it up.

'Hello? Cathy speaking.'

'Hiya Cathy. Great to hear you. How are you?' Bernie's voice was disturbingly loud considering it was coming from three thousand miles away, but she still had a discernible Irish accent.

'I'm fine. Lovely to speak to you in person, Bernie. I'm surprised and delighted that you sound as Irish as ever.'

'Well, I still see a lot of my family and they all sound like they never left. I can turn it on and off a bit, depending on the company. I can also do a reasonable Jewish accent. My man, Harry, is an Ashkenazi Jew so I've developed a taste for salt beef on rye.'

'Does that make it difficult with your families, having different religions?'

'Christ no, Cathy. We're both atheists and think all religion is a load of rubbish. Just a bit of tradition that we play along with when it suits us. Harry is very fond of a rasher or two, though he doesn't tell his mother.'

Cathy asked after all the O'Rourkes, and Bernie wanted to know all about Cathy's siblings and the Hughes cousins.

'So, you're living out in the wilds of Connemara with your new man. Thanks for the photo of Liam and Johnny by the way. He looks like a lovely fella and Johnny is the spit of you and your Daddy.'

'I know. Johnny also plays the cello like his grandfather.'

'What about you and your piano-playing?'

'Yes, I have a piano here and it's a great comfort to me. I get enough time to practise. There's not much else to while away the long winter nights. Liam reads the paper while I play to him. In the summer we stay outside until late and I do the garden while he does little repair jobs. We have a couple of lads who help with some of the upkeep jobs, but Liam likes them to have the evening off and they go to the pub in…'

'Jesus Christ, Cathy, stop. You'll go mad. This is all very well when you're newly married, when washing your man's socks feels like sex, but that won't last. What on earth will you do with that big brain?'

'I do all the accounts now for the business…'

'Stop. I can't bear to hear this. Promise me that you'll find something better to do than hang out sheets, grow spuds and add up pounds, shillings and pence. You could become a nurse again - or teach music. Or teach anything, frankly.'

'There's a house here to be looked after.'

'Do you love cleaning and cooking then?'

'No, I hate it to be honest. Doesn't everyone?'

'See? Get someone else to do it. There must be some biddy in the village who would do a better job for a few shillings. Wait, is it because you're expecting to get pregnant maybe? Not that it's any of my business of course…'

'No. That's not why. Though I suppose a baby might come along but that's looking increasingly unlikely. I don't know why I haven't found anything else to do.'

'I'm going to send you some articles from the magazine about how to start a career in your thirties, and how to organise the household. Get those lazy feckers to do their bit.'

'None of them are lazy in the slightest, Bernie. They work their fingers to the bone actually. I couldn't expect them to do anything more than they already do.'

'How did they manage before you arrived?'

It was a fair question and it tumbled around Cathy's head long after she and Bernie had said their fond farewells, conscious of the telephone bill that was racking up but with an agreement that they would try to talk once a month. It would be Cathy's turn to foot the bill next.

******

Bill and Bridie were in Cleggan for the weekend. Brendan and Mikey had been happy to move out to stay overnight with Mrs Gallagher so that the two students could have separate bedrooms in the cottage. Cathy wasn't sure this was absolutely necessary, assuming they were courting, but thought it wise to provide the option.

Brendan and Mikey had agreed to spend some time talking to Bill and Bridie about their traumatic experiences at St Joseph's which Bridie was going to write up as proper testimonies which Bill would then send over to his Congressman father, who would in turn pass them on to the TDs and judges he still knew in Ireland. Generating pressure from every possible quarter was a worthy mission, even if it yielded few immediate results.

'We need to keep making the case, Cathy. Pile it on, that's what we must do. Build up a huge bank of evidence that can't be ignored.' Cathy loved Bridie's youthful optimism, her belief that the world could be changed for the better if enough good people combined their efforts and refused to give up. She hoped Bridie was right because if relentless energy and determination were the key, Bridie would succeed.

They started with just an hour on the Saturday afternoon, the five of them sitting around the kitchen table. Brendan had asked for Cathy to be present, so Liam had taken Johnny to his cello lesson in Clifden. Cathy knew Liam would not wish to take part; he hated talking about St Joseph's. Cathy told Bridie that the interviews shouldn't last too long. They would be very distressing and, anyway, it was Brendan and Mikey's time off work.

'So, where would you like to start?' Bridie asked the lads. 'Mikey, how about you? seeing as you arrived before Brendan and were one of the youngest.'

'Begging your pardon, missus, I think it will be better if I go first because, you're right an all, that Mikey had longer in St Joseph's and started before me, but I'm sure it'll take a while before he'll feel comfortable enough to talk, whereas me, you won't be able to shut me up once I get started.' Brendan laughed.

Brendan recounted all the regular goings-on at Letterfrack School. He told his personal story and he tried to tell Mikey's, seeking his agreement as he went along. Mikey would nod or quietly say, 'That's right,' if Bridie or Bill checked anything with him. Details were shared and names were named. None of the Christian Brothers Brendan described was precisely a monster; many of them could be kind at times and even the worst of them could display a grim sense of humour. But it was a never-ending catalogue of normalised deprivation - physical and emotional - a total lack of empathy, institutionalised punishment and occasional savage sadism. The aspect that both lads agreed was hardest to live with was the unpredictability. They never knew when or from whom the next assault might come; they lived in constant fear.

In the end, the conversation only lasted forty minutes. There was only so much telling of and listening to stories of systemic failings, casual cruelties and heartless abuse they could all stomach. When they'd had enough, Cathy made tea and put a fruit cake on the table and they were all glad to have some sweetness and warmth inside their bodies.

Liam and Johnny arrived back not long afterwards and made a beeline for Mrs Gallagher's barmbrack. Then the men took Johnny took off to the beach to mess about with ball and bat, leaving the sisters alone.

'Bloody hell, Cathy. It's a shocker. I'm so angry, I can't tell you. And this is what Liam went through too?'

'Yes, and worse, though he hates to talk about it.'

'He should, though, for the sake of the boys still in these schools.'

'He knows that and he's made statements to the Garda in the past but I don't think he's told anyone the half of it yet.'

'Better out than in, or it'll eat away at him.'

'I'm sure you're right. I wish I knew more about how to treat the after-effects of childhood abuse. I'd like to help him. Help all of them.'

'You must. You should train to be a psychologist or a psychiatrist or whatever it is you need to be.'

'It looks like the law might be one way to help them. It's so good of Bill's father to agree to do what he can.'

'I think being married to a black woman has made him very aware of how many injustices there are in the world. It's all too easy to be ignorant. We never knew that these things went on when we were growing up.'

'I did, because Daddy had taught at St Joseph's and he told me something about it. It was one of his dearest wishes to see it closed down and the Brothers responsible held to account.'

'And we'll make that happen. Justice *will* win in the end.'

'Bless you, Bridie. Bill is such a love too. Fancy giving up your weekends to come and pursue this story.'

'Well, it's fun to come and see you all and get out of Galway for a change of scene.'

'He's a smashing fella. Are you serious about each other?'

'Me and Bill? Serious? He's not even my boyfriend, Cathy.'

'Oh. I'm sorry. I just assumed…'

'I'm "not his type" apparently. At least, that's what he said after I threw myself at him in Freshers' Week. What I've since learned is that I'm not his type because I don't have a cock, if you get my drift. But we're great buddies and I love spending time with him, not just because he has a car, and he seems to like me a lot. Maybe I'm a good alibi. I'm not sure how tolerant some of the rugby crowd at uni would be if they knew. I don't think he's been sexually active at Galway yet but then, neither have I.'

'Well, I would never have guessed!'

'No, a six-foot athletic black law student and basketball player isn't exactly the conventional Irish image of a queer guy, is it? We think they have to be wafting around on a stage holding a flower - like Oscar Wilde or Micheál Mac Liammóir. He calls himself "gay" by the way.'

'Gay? I've never heard that one before.'

'It's rather lovely isn't it.'

The telephone rang in the sitting room next door. Cathy ran through and picked up the handset.

'Hi Sam, how are you? Lovely to hear from you. What's the news ...oh... oh, hurray! Oh, how wonderful. How are they both? How big? Wow. Aww, that's so great. Congratulations to you all. Sam, Bridie is here with me so have a quick word.' Cathy beckoned to Bridie to come over to the phone. 'Give her all our love and big kisses for them both. Congratulations to you too. Tell her we'll speak to her when she's feeling more herself and we'll see her soon.' Cathy passed the receiver to Bridie before returning to the kitchen to get out some glasses and the gin and whiskey. They needed to toast the birth of the new-born Kevin McCarthy.

******

That evening, Brendan persuaded Bridie and Bill to come out with him and Mikey to the céilí in Moyard. 'Mr Bill, if you're really interested in finding out more about your Irish heritage and stuff then you surely have to come and see a proper céilí in full flow with all the singing and dancing, and the drinking, and me and Mikey will be doing a few songs together and they seem to go down very well with the punters but you see for yourself.'

Cathy declined, saying she needed to stay home with Johnny, and Liam had excused himself on the grounds of a long, hard week just past, but, secretly, he was simply looking forward to spending a quiet evening in with his wife. They were together on the sofa in the sitting room, Liam's arm around Cathy and her holding Liam's hand, stroking the length of each finger delicately.

'Are you checking out my hands, you devil? I am putting the cream on them day and night, I promise. I don't think they look too bad.'

Cathy laughed. 'No, I'm not checking up on you. I just love touching your hands: the wrinkles around the knuckles and the veins on the back and the shape of your nails. They could be a bit cleaner, mind.'

Liam pulled Cathy closer to him and kissed the top of her head. 'It's grand to have a bit of peace, isn't it, Johnny reading in his room and the noisy crowd out of the way for once.'

'Well, you'd never know Mikey was around, and Bridie and Bill will be gone tomorrow. It's only Brendan who makes all the racket.'

'I'm seriously thinking of asking them to move out. I'll pay them a bit more and Mrs Gallagher would be glad of the income. I think Brendan is a bit sweet on Dearbhla too, you know.'

'I don't blame him. She's pretty and she's kind and happy to let him do all the talking. But would Mikey be alright? He could take his waterproof mattress cover with him I suppose, though he seems on the mend, the nightmares as well as the bed-wetting.'

'I told you: time is a great healer, macushla.' Liam stood up. 'Can I get you a glass of something, to celebrate becoming Auntie Cathy today.'

'Oh Jeezus. I'm not sure I want to be an auntie. I can only think of my own aunties, Lily and Stasia, and I don't want to be like either of them. Tell me I'm not. But I'm so thrilled for Rose and Sam. Vodka and tonic, thank you very much, my love.'

They sat sipping their drinks in front of the small peat fire, arms around each other, their own private thoughts about babies and births unspoken. Johnny came downstairs for some cocoa and the three of them toasted baby Kevin before Cathy took Johnny back up to bed. If this beautiful boy was to be her only child, so be it. She was eternally grateful for the priceless gift that Joe had given her but she regretted that Liam would not become a father himself.

'Will you play something for me, macushla?' asked Liam when Cathy came back downstairs. 'It needs to be something soft and gentle, and I can't promise I won't drop off to sleep.'

'You bloody dare.' Cathy thumbed through her volume of Beethoven sonatas. 'How about this one, then...' She started playing the first movement of the 30th sonata, Op 109, with its calm, singing lines and Liam watched her from the sofa, marvelling at the precision and dexterity of her pale hands scattering arpeggios up and down the keyboard. When it ended, she swung around on the piano stool to face him.

'What do reckon? I love it and that movement's not too hard either. When you think what Beethoven was struggling with - money worries, family troubles, loads of ailments and totally deaf – I'm amazed that he could find such serenity.'

'I hear raindrops or teardrops, but happy ones maybe. It's very beautiful.'

'I'm still working on the third movement which is amazing...'

The kitchen door crashed open followed by rowdy chatter.

'Oh, god, they're back.' Cathy opened the sitting room door to find Brendan trying to teach Irish dancing to Bill while Bridie was putting the kettle on. Mikey was propped up against the door.

'Cathy, Cathy, Cathy. Will you have a cup of tea if I make a pot?' Bridie walked unsteadily towards her sister and draped herself over Cathy. 'We might be just a teeny bit scuttered.'

'Surely not.' Cathy laughed.

'Did you know what an amazing singer Brendan is, and Mikey plays like he was born with that whistle in his hands.'

Bill didn't seem to be quite as drunk as the other three. 'I heard lots of great rebel songs tonight.' Bill started singing *'Come out ye Black and Tans, come out and fight me like a man'*. Brendan and Bridie joined in but Mikey stayed by the door, looking embarrassed. Their singing grew louder *'Tell her how the IRA made you run like hell away, from the green and lovely lanes of Killishandra.'*

'Those were the glory days of the IRA back in twenties I suppose,' said Bill. 'They're a bit of a spent force now, aren't they?'

Liam sauntered into the kitchen and sat at the table. 'The IRA did themselves no favours during the war, trying to make deals with the Germans. Sinn Féin is the more acceptable voice for nationalism now. I'd like to think the IRA is finished but some diseases just lie dormant in the body waiting for the right conditions to multiply.'

'For as long as De Valera is leading Fianna Fáil, surely Sinn Féin itself will struggle, let alone the IRA.' Compared to most nineteen-year-olds, Bridie had a good grasp of politics. 'But they definitely have the best songs, don't they Mikey?'

Mikey, blushing, nodded and opened the door behind him.

'Come on now, Brendan. Let these good people get to their beds.'

Chapter 16 – September 1953

'Dear parents and godparents, you have come here to present this child for baptism. By water and the Holy Spirit, he is to receive the gift of new life from God, who is love.'

Cathy was aghast watching Father Stephen conduct Kevin's baptism. His trembling hands were holding the baby at a precarious angle over the font; she hoped Fergus would be quick enough to catch the baby should anything unfortunate happen.

'On your part, you must make it your constant care to bring him up in the practice of the faith. See that the divine life which God gives him is kept safe from the poison of sin, to grow always stronger in his heart. If your faith makes you ready to accept this responsibility, renew now the vows of your own baptism. Reject sin, profess your faith in Christ Jesus.'

How could he say these words? thought Cathy. Such hypocrisy. Reject sin? Leaving aside the betrayals, the adultery, the broken vows and lies, the man's gluttony alone, albeit of a liquid variety, would surely condemn him to a fair stretch in Purgatory. But she could see that Father Stephen's punishment was happening in the here and now. His face was like an ancient vellum map with its sallow skin and tracery of red veins. He was struggling to catch enough breath to recite the service. Cathy was sorry to see him laid so low, a man who had been so kind to her in her childhood. Surely, he could have little time left before his liver claimed its victim, and you could hardly blame it given the abuse it got.

The physical contrast with Fergus, the priest's spiritual and biological son, couldn't be more dramatic. Fergus, with his muscular frame squeezed into a suit for his role as godfather and his vibrant good health radiating out of every pore, had taken the baby out of the priest's arms. Kevin was safe now.

At the modest baptism party in Main Street, Stasia caught up with Cathy. 'I confess that I shed a tear seeing Rose holding her first baby. Imagine how much joy it would have brought Hannah. She never got to see her grandchildren, not even Johnny. I'm blessed with mine and I hope for many more once Peter and Maureen marry. And I think there's hope for Paul too – Rose tells me she thinks he has a girlfriend from the pub. But Andrew will be with Edmund and me until we pass on - unless he marries a tractor.'

Father Stephen was sitting in the corner talking to Aggie, both cradling large glasses of whiskey. As Cathy approached them, Aggie stood up. 'Take my seat, Cathy. I need to go and make a few more sandwiches.'

Cathy smiled at the priest and she sat beside him.

'It's grand to see you back home, Cathy. Johnny's growing up so fast.'

'I know, Father. Time is speeding up, I reckon.'

'Wait until you get to my age. I've barely delivered one sermon when it's time to write the next.'

'You should take a rest, Father. Do priests get to retire? I hope you don't mind me saying, but you don't look very well. I think maybe you should try and ease up on the drink or your liver will rebel and kill you.'

He chuckled quietly. 'Dearest Cathy, you were never very good at speaking out unless it was to save someone else, were you? But you see, I don't want to be saved. The quicker I can leave this earth the happier I shall be, though I realise I face a long stretch of purification.'

Cathy put her hand on Father Stephen's arm and lowered her voice to a whisper. 'I know you miss my mother dreadfully, but are you not interested to see how Fergus and Bridie turn out?'

Stephen placed his hand over Cathy's. 'I can see already that they're beautiful souls; that's not going to change. What a privilege it's been to watch them grow, albeit from a distance.'

Lying in bed that night, listening to Kevin's whimpers and the sounds of his parents comforting the wee babe, Cathy contemplated the priest's words. The man was knowingly and steadily poisoning himself, willing his own death. It was every bit as much a suicide as her father's had been.

******

There was always a pang of regret whenever Cathy left Rowanbridge. She didn't want to live here but it was full of so many beloved people. At least, this time she was taking one of them along with her. Cathy had offered to take Bridie back to Galway; it would be good company, saved her sister a long train journey and was just a small diversion.

They made their affectionate farewells and set off. She had just reached the crossroads in the middle of the village and was about to turn right when Bridie shouted.

'No, turn left, turn left, Cathy. I need to say goodbye to Father... Father Stephen.'

'Yikes, OK.' Cathy switched her indicator without any traffic mishap and turned into the road leading to the church. She dropped Bridie off and drove on to the next junction to turn the car around. Cathy considered joining Bridie but something made her refrain. Instead, she and Johnny wandered off into the churchyard where she pointed out the graves of his grand-parents and great grand-parents.

As they walked back towards the car, the front door opened and Bridie and Father Stephen emerged. 'Bless you, my child,' said the priest and the pair hugged each other tightly before Bridie ran to the car just as Cathy and Johnny reached it. Stephen waved them off, until the car disappeared beyond the crossroads.

'You OK, Auntie Bridie?' Johnny could hear her sniffling and blowing her nose. The boy was sensitive enough to realise that she was weeping silently and he put his hand on her shoulder from the back seat.

'Thank you, Johnny, love, but I'm fine, honest. I just hate goodbyes, don't you?'

Bridie kept Johnny chatting for the first leg of the journey asking him all about how school and his cello lessons were going, who was doing best at beach cricket and whether Brendan and Mikey had taught him any more of their rebel songs. They stopped for a break, halfway through the journey, and got back on the road.

Not long afterwards, Bridie turned around to check on Johnny. As she suspected, he was fast asleep in the back.

'He's solid gone. Safe to talk now.'

'OK. What shall we talk about that Johnny shouldn't hear? How's your love life?'

Bridie paused. 'Father told me that you and Rose know too.'

'Know what?'

'Know that he's our real father.'

Cathy felt an icy blade in her guts.

'I had to tell him that me and Fergus have known for years now,' said Bridie, 'ever since Mammy got ill the first time, I guess it was. But we've told no-one else because we didn't realise other people knew. It was our secret. We just talked about it to each other. It's a huge relief that you and Rose know, and Father says Auntie Stasia and Aggie do too.'

'And Uncle Edmund, and Tricky of course. But I think that's it.'

'Daddy knows? Oh my god, poor man.'

'No, not poor man. He's always known. Did Stephen not say? Tricky came to Mammy's help by marrying her, knowing that Fergus and you were the priest's. He loved her enough to do that and he clearly loves you both like any father. He's a very good man and he's still your Daddy.'

'Fergus and me, we've kept it to just the two of us, but I had to go and see Father and tell him we know, because … I don't think I'll ever see him again?' A sob broke out of Bridie.

Cathy took her left hand off the steering wheel and took Bridie's, squeezing it warmly. 'No, I don't think you and I will get to see him again, Bridie; he can't have very long left at all. I'm so, so sorry but how wonderful of you to go and talk to him straight like that. I'm not sure I would have been bold enough. And now Stephen can talk to Fergus as a father too. That's such a blessing. Rose and I had talked about whether we had a duty to tell you both but Aggie was dead set against it.'

'Secrets. I hate them,' growled Bridie. 'We think we're protecting people but they're just a poison.' 'But sometimes people have no choice,' said Cathy. 'Look at Bill. He'd get locked up if he didn't keep his sexuality secret.'

'That's true. It's wicked to criminalise love, don't you think, Cathy?'

'I most certainly do.'

They arrived in Galway around three o'clock and Bridie took Cathy and Johnny straight to her room and made tea. 'I'll give you a tour when you've finished your drinks, and we can call in on Bill on our way. He should be back from the States.'

They walked through the campus heading for Bill's room, Bridie waving at people as they went, shouting 'Dia dhuit' or 'Cad es ainm duit?' or, less frequently, 'How are you?'.

'There's a lot more Irish spoken here than at home. Most students are quite happy to talk in English but a few are very militant about it and some professors too. There's only one in the law faculty, thank God. I've really had to brush up my Gaelic. I suppose I should thank the nuns for giving me a good grounding.'

Bill was not in his room so they carried on until they got to the beautiful quadrangle at the heart of the University. Johnny was in awe. 'It's just like a castle. Isn't it beautiful, Mama.'

'Yes, darling. It's very handsome. Must be an inspiring place to study, Bridie, not like the gloomy sheds at Our Lady's Convent.'

'It's not as old as it looks. It's based on an Oxford College but it was only built a century ago.'

'It's still very grand.'

'I find the legacy of all the people who have studied and taught here more inspiring. Some amazing women have come out of UCG, you know; Maureen O'Carroll, who has just won her seat in the Dáil for Labour. The very first woman to get an engineering degree in the whole of Ireland, Alice Perry, graduated from here before the First World War and there have been women professors here too; the first professor of German at Galway was a woman called Emily Anderson just after the first war. But the most famous woman is probably Ada English.'

'I've heard of Ada English. Wasn't she a TD for Sinn Féin before the war? I remember my daddy reading out something about her from the newspaper and saying he wished he was as brave and fearless as Ada English in her fight for a united Ireland.'

'Yes, that's what she's famous for. She spent time in Galway jail for owning nationalist books, and she sheltered De Valera - can you imagine? But way before that, she became the very first lecturer in mental illnesses here, just after the turn of the century I think, one of Ireland's very first female psychiatrists. She lived all her life near Galway, working at and running Ballinasloe Asylum. When I read about women like that I get very excited and hopeful that I'll be able to make as big a contribution.'

'Oh, you will, Bridie. I have no doubt about that whatsoever.' Cathy laughed. 'You have all the determination of our Mammy. I wish I had a bit more of your confidence and energy.'

'It's there inside you, Cathy. Just believe in yourself more. Rose and Fergus and I thought you were so amazing and brave when you left Rowanbridge when you were ... what ... just fourteen? And then you went to England and then off to the war.'

'Maybe. I think I lost all my bravery when I had Johnny. Being a parent makes you very risk-averse.'

After a stroll along the River Corrib, Cathy, Bridie and Johnny had early supper in a fish and chip café, Johnny's favourite treat, and then walked back to Bridie's residence. Bridie hugged Johnny good-bye and then her sister. Cathy stepped back and traced the barely visible small scar on Bridie's forehead with her finger. 'I've been meaning to apologise for your scar. It's my fault – I let you fall into the hearth when you could barely walk. But look...' Cathy lifted her fringe to reveal a similar silvery scar. '...snap. I got that when Mammy booted me down some steps after I was rude about you. So, I thoroughly deserve mine for being a proper bitch but you don't deserve yours one iota. I'm so sorry.'

'Don't be daft. I like that we have matching scars.'

Chapter 17 – October 1954

Cathy was standing nervously awaiting her first lecture at the start of term as a mature psychology student at University College, Galway. She couldn't quite believe she'd made it. The previous autumn, Bernie had sent a load of articles and books from New York about being a working woman or how to build a career after having a family. They lit a small fire in Cathy's guts. She had tentatively broached the prospect of her doing some sort of retraining with Liam, with a view to a new career, and he had been as enthusiastic and supportive as she had hoped.

'Macushla, if you want to go and get any sort of qualification or do any sort of training, you know my answer will always be yes. It be will yes to anything you want, always, and if I can help you in any way I will. I just want you to be happy. I only wish I could give you the baby you long for - I'm so sorry for that, my darling - but you're free to grab whatever else you want and make a different dream a reality.'

It was true; Cathy had resigned herself to the fact that a baby was not going to happen. She had started to investigate more seriously the possibility of doing some sort of university degree that might lead to a new career, but also one that she would enjoy, in and of itself. She kept returning to Ada English and her legacy, in part because her father had revered the woman but also because understanding human behaviour and emotion was something she aspired to do, and not just for the three damaged men in her own household.

Cathy found nothing about Ada English in Galway's public library and bookshops, but Bridie helped out by researching what UCG held on their alumna. Cathy consumed everything she could lay her hands on about Ada English and became increasingly inspired by her many humane reforms, the discipline of occupational therapy in particular, which she had introduced to the care of her patients at Ballinasloe District Lunatic Asylum, before being buried there herself in 1944.

Just before last Christmas, when she had finally made her decision, Cathy told Liam that she intended to study psychology at UCG, because it built on her nursing qualifications and was an emerging and fascinating discipline. Liam had raised an amused eyebrow and kissed her indulgently. 'That's just grand, macushla, as long as you don't come home and expect to practise all your voodoo on me.'

At Christmas time in Rowanbridge, Cathy told the whole family what she was planning and all but one of them was delighted to hear of her plans.

Auntie Stasia was concerned. 'Cathy, you'll become exhausted, looking after your family and the house while you try and study. You need to take care of yourself.'

But she was a lone voice.

'You're much too clever to be just a housewife, Cathy so why not? And I look forward to you analysing me and all the crazy nonsense that swirls around inside my head,' laughed Fergus.

Cathy was moved most by what Father Stephen, frail and suffering, whispered to her, taking her to one side at the Boxing Day lunch at the Hugheses. 'This might be the last time we see each other, Cathy. But I'm so happy you're planning to do this. You were born to make people's lives better. Your Mammy will be very proud of you indeed.'

Even Tricky offered Cathy a 'Good luck' with something that resembled a smile.

Later that evening, she witnessed something she had never believed possible: her three siblings, Aggie, Sam, and Liam, with Father Stephen and Tricky, chatting away in the Rowanbridge kitchen over cocoa, tea or whiskey, all knowing her mother's shameful secret and knowing that each of them knew it too. Bridie and Fergus addressed Tricky as Daddy and Stephen as Father with ease, each man loved and acknowledged as a parent in his own right. When Cathy called in to the presbytery alone the next morning to say a quick good-bye to Father Stephen before they started the drive back to Connemara, he insisted she come in for a quick cup of tea with him.

'It's wonderful to see you with your fine, fisherman husband. Have you saved him, do you think?'

'I hope so, Father. I think so.'

'And you'll be able to save other poor souls once you get your degree, though I know I won't be around to see it. But the last few months have been such a blessing to me, to be able to talk to my children as their father, for them to hold my hand and embrace me. It'll be hard to say good-bye to them but I'm ready to go. Thank you for all you've done for me, Cathy, and for your forgiveness. If I ever get to heaven, I'll do my best to watch over you all.'

In May, Cathy received final confirmation from UCG that she had a place to study psychology, starting in October. Two pieces of the jigsaw remained to be slotted into place: money and Johnny. Not only did Cathy need to find the finances for her tuition fees, they would need to pay for help in the house.

Liam dismissed Cathy's concerns. 'Look, I earn enough money to keep our bodies and souls together, so you can use the money you get from the Academy every month to fund your degree. I can wait to get a new boat.'

And Dearbhla Gallagher was delighted to be offered the position of domestic help, doing the laundry, the cleaning, some cooking and keeping an eye on Johnny after school. It got her away from her mother's beady eyes and brought her some independence. But then, before Dearbhla started the job, the need for her to look after Johnny disappeared.

Johnny was nearly ten, so the need to find him a new school was pressing. All the options near to Cleggan and Clifden involved priests or nuns. Liam rarely asserted his will on the household but on that matter he was insistent; he could not tolerate seeing Johnny go to a school run by the Catholic church. Cathy began the search for somewhere that would be acceptable to everyone and it didn't take long to realise that Galway Grammar School was the only viable option in the county. It was an Erasmus Foundation school which offered scholarships and it had a mere sixty students, both boys who could board and girls as day pupils.

But it was a Protestant School.

'What do you think about that, Johnny, having to attend Protestant services and say Protestant prayers and such.'

'I don't care Mama. It's all make-believe anyway, isn't it. I have to say Catholic prayers and sing Catholic hymns at school now. Anyway, I suppose my daddy was a Protestant, wasn't he? I'll check with Granny in my next letter.'

Cathy and Johnny went to visit the school. They were shown through the buildings and went up to inspect the dormitories. The dormitories looked clean and comfortable though Cathy worried that it was rather cold.

Johnny dismissed her concerns. 'I'll just wear an extra vest, Mama.'

All the pupils they bumped into looked healthy and happy enough. The school had a science lab, a library and a thriving orchestra. The matter was clinched when Johnny spotted photographs of the various sports teams along the corridor.

'Look, Mama, they have a cricket team.' he said excitedly.

And so, by June, everything was settled. Johnny would board at Galway Grammar School from Monday to Thursday, Cathy driving him there early on Monday mornings with a bag of clean clothes and a full tuck box, and he would come home with her each Friday afternoon. Cathy would spend all day on Mondays and Fridays studying within University College itself, in addition to attending any lectures or tutorials on other days. If she ever needed an overnight stay she would sleep on Bridie's floor. The rest of the time she would study at the desk Liam built for her in the back bedroom.

After his first week at Galway Grammar in September, Johnny pronounced himself 'really, really happy. It's brilliant. The food is yummy, the bed is comfy and we don't have to talk in Irish. The water is a bit cold to wash in, mind, but we played cricket on Thursday and I have two friends already.'

The smooth start to Johnny's new life meant that Cathy stopped worrying quite so much although she wasn't entirely comfortable with him not sleeping next door to her every night. 'Johnny, you must tell me if anything happens that you don't like. I want to know,' she impressed upon him.

Dearbhla began working for them in the mornings a couple of weeks before Cathy's course began so that she could be shown what to do and how Cathy liked things but, in a matter of days, Dearbhla had mastered the oven, the washing machine and the ironing board, not to mention washed out the refrigerator, dusted down all the walls and cleaned all the windows, inside and out. The cottage had never looked so shiny. When Liam remarked, at Sunday lunch the day before Cathy's term began, that she had never cooked such a delicious beef stew and treacle pudding, Cathy laughed, confessing they were all Dearbhla's work. She now had no qualms whatsoever about passing over the entire household to the young girl. All was in place for Cathy to start her degree with a clear conscience.

Finally, after a year of planning, here she was. She looked around at the other students gathering outside the lecture hall. She didn't think she looked too much older than them and when she spotted a man and a woman in the throng who seemed to be well into their forties or fifties, she told herself to relax. A huge yawn took her by surprise. It had been an early start that morning. She and Johnny had left the cottage at half-past six though Liam was already out in the boat. She would get used to it. Next Sunday, she would not let Liam start making love to her at gone eleven o'clock and instead get a decent night's sleep before her second week in this next phase of her life.

Chapter 18 - August 1955

'Sorry to interrupt, Cathy, but I've made up the spare beds and cleaned the bathroom and the downstairs jacks. And I've scrubbed the spuds and carrots and put the pork in to roast, so is it okay to go off now? Brendan has promised to take me into Clifden on his new motorbike.' Dearbhla was standing at the door to the sitting room, hopping excitedly from one foot to the other.

Cathy broke off playing the piano and waved to Johnny to put down his cello. 'Dearbhla love, of course it is. Thank you so much for coming in on a Saturday morning, but we have an extra special visitor arriving today.'

'No trouble. Brendan is working until midday anyway.'

'I hope you don't mind me asking, Dearbhla, but are you two … courting now?'

Dearbhla's face flooded with embarrassment. 'Heavens no, just friends, you know.'

'Well, have a fun time but tell him to drive very carefully with you on the back.'

'Oh, he takes great care of me. I know he's a bit of a joker but he's not daft. Not like Mikey.'

'Mikey drives his motorbike like he's Reg Armstrong in a Grand Prix race,' said Johnny. The boy was well-versed in all of Ireland's champion drivers of any sort of vehicle.

Liam had enjoyed a very profitable year with the sheep and had decided the previous month that he should give the lads a bonus. He had advised them both to open a savings account but at the first opportunity the pair had bowled into the garage in Clifden, returning to Cleggan each astride a second-hand Norton.

'Liam, I know you're probably thinking we're a pair of eejits but Cleggan's not an easy place to get to and from and Mikey and me, we're starting to get invites for our singing and playing from all over the county so really it's a sort of investment, you know.'

Brendan looked earnestly at Liam for approval but all he got was a shake of the head and a wry 'Well, it's your money, lads,' in return.

'That's sounding very good, Johnny. Shall we try it through just once more before Liam gets home?' encouraged Cathy. They were practising an arrangement of Bach's *Jesu, Joy of Man's Desiring* for piano, violin and cello that Seamus had sent them along with a Brahms trio. Johnny was disappointed to find the Brahms too tricky for him to manage all the way through but had declared the Bach 'dead easy'. They were missing the upper-string player. He would be arriving shortly in his Jaguar, chauffeuring Ellen and Aoife from Dalkey for their annual summer residency. Ellen's leg made the journey via train and bus too demanding these days so, finally, Seamus had been lured to Cleggan. He intended to stay only a few days and then return at the end of the women's three-week holiday to transport them back to the Academy but he had investigated what there was to do in Cleggan for an avowed gentleman of the city and discovered, to his delight, that there was a fine golf course near Clifden. His golf clubs took their place in the Jaguar's boot alongside his viola and their suitcases.

Seamus thought a little chamber music would be a lovely way to fill the Cleggan evenings but the repertoire for viola, cello and piano was depressingly limited. He suspected that the Brahms was probably an unrealistic choice. No matter. Give the boy a few more years and they would be playing it together. In the meantime, the Bach would be a start.

Cathy ran out when she heard the Jaguar drew up and gave her three special people massive hugs.

'I can't believe we've dragged you here finally, Seamus. I hope you've brought your swimming trunks.'

Seamus was about to protest.

'Only kidding!'

'Conas atá tú, an fear is fear liom?' said Aoife to Johnny, as he appeared at the doorway.

'An-mhaith go raibh maith agat. Is bréa an rud é tú a fheiceáil, a Aintin Aoife,' replied the boy which earned him a kiss and applause all round.

Liam appeared around the corner of the cottage and ran towards Aoife, wrapping his strong arms around the slender woman.

'Liam, my lovely boy.' Aoife stroked his cheek.

Liam and Johnny took all the bags to the bedrooms while Cathy made the tea. Aoife and Ellen were installed in the armchairs while Seamus stood by the piano looking over the music she and Johnny had been playing.

'I see you've been practising the Bach. Excellent. What do you think, Johnny? Shall we have a go tomorrow?'

'Why not tonight? It's really easy, Uncle Seamus. I tried the Brahms but that's too hard. But I'll keep practising and maybe next time…'

'You'll find the cottage very basic, Seamus, but comfortable enough, I hope – none of your Dublin luxuries I'm afraid,' said Cathy, handing him his tea.

'I've been coming here for nearly a decade, Seamus, and I'm not sure I've recovered from the shock yet,' said Ellen. 'But at least you won't have to shit in an earth privy like I had to at first.'

'Oh, we have all the modern conveniences now. I wouldn't have dared bring Cathy to live here without a proper bathroom. But then she demanded a refrigerator and a washing machine as well. There's no satisfying her,' said Liam, stroking his wife's back.

'I'm afraid your bedroom is a little cramped, Seamus, because that's where I study; there's a desk in there and a bookshelf for all my books.'

'How do you feel now that your first year is over? Did you make the right choice, Cathy?' Aoife asked.

'I think so. It's really interesting. Some of it, the biology of psychology, how brains are structured and so on, I did to some extent during my nursing training. But all the stuff about human development, how we learn and think, how personalities develop, is fascinating. I have no idea how I'm going to make a career out of it at the end mind you.'

'Oh, a little bit of psychology comes in jolly useful in any career, I'd say, whether you're a solicitor, a teacher or even a humble farming fisherman,' Liam said, smiling at Cathy. 'I wish I understood how to make Brendan talk less and Mikey a bit more.'

'Psychology is just about people, in the end,' said Aoife. 'Some people have an instinctive understanding and skill with others, but it's always better to understand why some things work and others don't.'

'Normal human behaviour is all very well, but eventually I'll be learning about pathologies, when our mind goes wrong and we end up with a mental illness. I want to learn how to help those people get better. If I can.'

Remarkably, Seamus was persuaded to stay in Cleggan for eight whole days in the end. He played golf three times, twice with Liam's bank manager whom Seamus was instructed to impress with Liam's industry, and he was seduced by the quality of the seafood he was presented with most evenings. And playing music with Hannah's daughter and grandson was a delight, even though the repertoire they had was fairly undemanding.

'Just because a piece of music is simple doesn't mean it isn't wonderful, you know, Johnny, like this Bach. I've missed having you accompany me, Cathy, and our bridge evenings have petered out - although Aoife thinks the new history teacher at the Academy might be game.'

On the following Saturday, Bridie and Bill arrived to spend the day in Cleggan, ostensibly to pick Seamus's brain about whether to pursue a career as a solicitor or a barrister. 'It's a matter of personality as much as anything else, Bridie, and only you two can make that decision for yourselves.'

'Sir, I think we both know what Bridie will be doing a few years from now: on her feet fighting for justice. And she might even be getting paid for it,' said Bill, smiling at his friend.

'Yes, I would happily put a few quid on that though I doubt any bookie would be daft enough to offer odds,' said Seamus.

'We need people like Bridie over in my homeland right now. It's been a scary place with all the fear Senator McCarthy has whipped up and the segregation of black folks is as bad as it ever was. I don't mind so much for myself but it makes my blood boil to see my mother treated like a second-class citizen. But my father says there is hope, even in Georgia, with black preachers speaking out against oppression. You can't stay silent. Silence only helps the oppressors.'

'But what's the best way of fighting for justice? Do you just talk and talk and write stuff or do you have to take up arms at some point?' Bridie looked earnestly into Seamus's and Bill's eyes.

In the afternoon, Liam took Bridie, Bill and Johnny for a trip to see the seals on Inishbofin Island. As they walked back from the pier, they bumped into Brendan and Mikey out on the roadside, polishing their motorbikes ready for their evening out.

'Good day to you all, pardon me not shaking hands with all the grease and polish on them because I like the bike to look its best when I take Dearbhla out on the back of it and we're out tonight at a gig, so why don't you all come, everyone, to hear me and Mikey doing our stuff at this new pub just outside Oughterard which a mate of mine in Clifden has introduced us to and they have a céilí every month and music every Saturday night and he says the Guinness is perfect there, not to mention the sausage rolls and the money is not at all bad either, is it Mikey?'

Mikey smiled and nodded.

'What do you reckon, Bill?' asked Bridie.

'Well, it's on our way back to Galway so I can't see why not. And now that I've learned how to dance a reel …'

'Ah, we'll have great craic, Mr Bill. So, what about you and the missus coming along with them, Liam?'

Liam smiled. 'I'll ask her. It's been a while since we danced together, and we do have three very reliable child-minders on the premises.'

Just after half past seven, Cathy got into the car beside Liam. 'Look at you, Mrs Molloy. Beautiful.' Cathy was excited to be out for the evening. She had put on her best dress with its matching lipstick and had tied her hair in a ponytail. 'Seriously, you look about eighteen.' Liam kissed his wife briefly, conscious that Bill was leaning against his car door waiting for Bridie to emerge. Liam was not one for public displays of affection.

'You never saw me when I was eighteen, so that's bullshit for a start,' but Cathy beamed all the same.

An hour later, the four walked into the fug of the Oughterard bar and found themselves a table. There was already a woman singing in Gaelic, playing a bodhran with a man accompanying her on the fiddle. They waved at the table in the opposite corner where Dearbhla and Mikey were chatting to each other, while Brendan was on his feet, waving a pint of Guinness in his hand and talking to a couple of rough-looking men.

Liam bought drinks and they listened to the elegiac traditional songs, happy to be in each other's company. The dance band came on next and Bill instantly got to his feet with Bridie. 'Come on, Bridie. I can do this. Line dancing is pretty much like a hoedown back home.' Cathy and Liam soon joined them and after two dances they swapped partners. Bill was an extremely elegant and impressive dancer and he was totally oblivious to the many stares he was attracting. A black man doing Irish jigs like he was born to it - whatever next?

Eventually, the dancing stopped and it was time for Brendan and Mikey to get on stage.

'Jesus Christ, it's nearly ten. We'll only be able to stay for half an hour or so, or I'll be sleeping on Bill's floor again,' exclaimed Bridie. 'I think my landlady was a nun in a previous life. She locks the door at eleven.'

'And we all know who will actually end up sleeping on the floor,' said Bill wryly.

'I love to see the pair of them at their music,' said Cathy. 'Mikey's never so happy as when he has that whistle in his mouth. I don't know how he gets those gorgeous sounds out of it.'

Dearbhla came over to join the four of them. 'Brendan and Mikey are so made up that you've come all this way to see them. Brendan wants me to buy you all a drink, so what can I get you? It's his money.' Dearbhla waved a five-pound note around.

Liam stood up 'You just sit, lovely, and you can sit down too, fella.' Liam put his hand on Bill's shoulder as he made for the bar. 'You're a student and Dearbhla's using money that I only paid Brendan this morning. So, what'll you all have?'

Brendan and Mikey started their collection of songs. Cathy knew some of them: *Ashtown Road and Foggy Dew* and others she had heard them perform before. *Come out Ye Black and*

Tans got the whole pub singing along and several other rowdy republican songs followed them. But the next song changed the mood completely. *Kevin Barry* was a melancholy song about a young medical student who had been hanged in Dublin in 1920 for being an IRA member. The atmosphere was hushed and reverential. The two rough men who had been talking to Brendan earlier starting walking between the tables, each with a bucket, asking for money, while Brendan and Mikey sang and played on. One came up to Bill holding out the bucket and the student threw in some coins.

When he was approached next, Liam looked up at the man and asked, 'What's this for?'

The collector seemed surprised to be asked. 'For the cause, man.'

'And what cause would that be?' challenged Liam.

'What every decent Irishman wants – a free and united Ireland.'

'No, thank you,'

The man glared back at him but Liam just picked up his pint and the man walked away resentfully.

As soon as Brendan and Mikey came off the stage, to wild applause, Bridie and Bill said their good-byes. Cathy and Liam decided to leave too, leaving Dearbhla seated between a triumphant Brendan and a smiling Mikey.

'Fine music, lads. You've earned your drinks. I'll see you on Monday.' Liam looked tense, almost angry.

Driving back along empty roads, with the moon shimmering over the landscape, Cathy rested her hand on Liam's thigh. 'What was the problem with the collection? You want a united Ireland, don't you?'

'Of course, I do. But what's the betting that money won't end up in the hands of the IRA, buying some bloody guns or explosives.'

'It might have just been to fund Sinn Féin.'

'Well, I don't support Sinn Féin either. Anyway, I like to know where my money is going.'

'Fair enough.'

They drove on in silence for half an hour, until the road crossed over a small expanse of water. Liam stopped the car and took Cathy's hand. 'I'm sorry. I didn't mean to spoil your evening, macushla. We don't get out much, do we, and I loved dancing with you.'

Cathy opened her door. 'Come on.' She took his hand and led him down to the water's edge, where she sat on a low stone. 'Sit with me a while.' Liam joined her on the stone.

'This is what I love about living here in Connemara, the peace. People have their own battles and causes but we can't be responsible for them all. If Brendan and Mikey want to help raise money for what they believe in, that's their business.'

'Yes, but I'm just not sure they understand what it all means.'

'Well, talk to them about it sometime, but not when anyone's been drinking.'

Liam laughed and kissed Cathy. 'Christ, you're a wise thing, aren't you. You were so, even when you were just ten years old.'

Cathy picked up a stone and tried to skim it across the lough but it sank without trace. 'Damn, I've lost the knack.'

'No, you just picked up a crap stone in the dark. Here, try this one.' Liam handed her a flattish stone which Cathy coaxed a couple of skips from.

'There you go.' Liam hugged Cathy and kissed her deeply. 'Will you lie with me here? I like making love to you in the open, beside the water.'

They lay down together on the grass, kissing and stroking each other with mounting desire. Liam lifted Cathy's skirt, removed her knickers and began to kiss between her legs. She moaned. 'Come on inside me, my love.' She undid his zip and he stretched himself out on top of her, thrusting himself against her. Cathy held on to his backside, still clothed in flannel trousers, urging him on. When his fly zip caught on her pubic hair, she couldn't help but cry out. 'Ouch. No, don't worry.' Liam tried to recover his stroke but in vain.

After a minute or so of increasingly desperate grinding, he rolled away. 'Nope. No good. I'm sorry, macushla.'

'Don't worry. You've had too much to drink. And it might be romantic by the water but it's not as comfortable as our lovely bed, is it?' Cathy chuckled and peeled a lump of moss off her left buttock before putting her knickers back on. 'Come on. Give me the keys, mister. I'm driving us home.'

Chapter 19 – December 1956

There were two people around the Rowanbridge Christmas table that Cathy had not expected to be there. Neither of them was in the best of health but they were at least alive. Rose and Sam's second baby, Thomas, had arrived the week before Christmas, a month early and needing constant care; and Father Stephen was sitting between Fergus and Bridie, shrivelled and yellow as a mouldering apple, but still breathing.

There had been a funeral in Rowanbridge that year, two in fact. In February, on the way back from a Fine Gael fund-raising dinner in Kilkenny, Nicholas Byrne had swerved to avoid a deer, skidded on ice and smashed into an oak tree. He and Louisa had died instantly. A dreadful accident compounded by alcohol without doubt. Nicholas and Louisa were buried with all due ceremony and were laid to rest beside Nicholas's parents in the smarter section of the churchyard.

Tricky Byrne thus became the sole owner of the entire Byrne estate, with its acres of prime farmland, the huge Georgian farmhouse and all its attendant outbuildings and machinery. It took Tricky a mere two months to organise for the estate to be made over to Fergus and Bridie in full, split equally and with immediate effect, an arrangement which had been agreed in principle between the Byrne brothers some years before. Tricky had then promptly moved out of the Main Street house and installed himself back into his childhood home. The only thing he took over to the big farmhouse, apart from his few clothes, was his bed. Hannah's bed. A few weeks later, Fergus moved in with him, and Mrs Nolan, a jolly matron in her forties, began her duties as their daily housekeeper.

Mrs Nolan would leave food prepared for Tricky and Fergus but, more often than not, Fergus would turn up at the Main

Street kitchen door for supper from Aggie, a hug from Rose and, over a pint next door in the bar, the day's gossip from Sam. But Tricky always came to Main Street for his Sunday lunch or would occasionally join the rest of the family at the Hughes's villa.

Tricky never talked about losing his brother in such a shocking accident but he was as fastidious about Nicholas's and Louisa's shared grave as he was about Hannah's. Both were kept clean and supplied with fresh flowers, which was surprising, given the man's own appearance was as grubby and shabby as ever.

Cathy wondered whether the openness with which Father Stephen was now acknowledged as the biological father of Fergus and Bridie within the family had made Tricky feel rejected, but there was no change in the way her two siblings treated Tricky and when Bridie came home for the holidays, she was as likely to go and stay in the Byrne farmhouse as in Main Street, particularly if Bill had come with her.

'Pass the sprouts, please Sam,' said Bridie. She turned to her other brother-in-law. 'So, what do you make of the shenanigans over the border, Liam?'

On December the 12th, the IRA had begun orchestrated raids on British government targets near the border using bombs and gunfire. Army barracks, police stations, a courthouse and a relay transmitter had all been attacked. The IRA had issued a statement to justify their actions: *Spearheaded by Ireland's freedom fighters, our people have carried the fight to the enemy... Out of this national liberation struggle a new Ireland will emerge, upright and free. In that new Ireland, we shall build a country fit for all our people to live in. That then is our aim: an independent, united, democratic Irish Republic. For this we shall fight until the invader is driven from our soil and victory is ours.'*

'You know very well what I think, Bridie. I'm horrified.'

'But don't you want a free and united Ireland?'

'You know I do. But not at any price.'

'The democratic process is so corrupted up there, what choice is there but to take direct action? It's not like they're attacking innocent people, is it?' Bridie was in her element.

'Would you say that to the mothers of anyone who gets murdered? You realise that is where the money goes that Brendan and Mikey help raise in pubs and bars. I've told them they're eejits and they at least have had the decency to look ashamed. The IRA are disgusting articles.'

'IRA members are now going to be interned without trial. Where's the justice in that, eh?'

'Sister, sister. Shut up with your big gob.' Fergus intervened. 'It's Jesus's birthday and we have young Johnny and Kevin here wanting a fun Christmas not a family fight.'

'The Catholic church has condemned the IRA's campaign, Bridie, even though most republicans are of the faith,' Father Stephen said quietly.

'Yes, Father, the Catholic church condemns them in public but gives IRA members blessings before they kill people and absolution after.' Liam was blazing. 'Exactly the sort of hypocrisy we expect from the church.' Liam threw his napkin down and marched out. Cathy followed him into the backyard.

'Liam love, I agree with you, but you mustn't let Bridie wind you up like that. She's a hot-headed young idealist and she has no concept of the suffering that violence brings.'

'I know. And I love her idealism, I do. I'm sorry, macushla. It's Christmas Day and here I am ruining it for everyone.' He pulled Cathy into his arms. 'I should know better by now and just ignore her. I just can't bear people hurting others, even if they deserve it.'

'Come back in then and have your pudding.'

'You go. I'll stay here and cool off with the hens.'

'Don't be long.'

Cathy returned to the family who were already playing charades, laughing and joking, drinking merrily, all arguments forgotten. It was so unlike Liam to lose his temper but Cathy had noticed him becoming more tense over recent months. Maybe it was money worries. He had borrowed the money to buy a second boat and had taken on a couple of new lads from St Josephs, filling up Mrs Gallagher's boarding house. Their love life had become intermittent and not always successful, which she could see distressed him greatly, however much she reassured him that all she wanted was to be in his arms. Since they had arrived in Rowanbridge, Cathy had noticed him gazing at her when she was holding baby Thomas. She recognised the hunger and loss in his eyes.

After tea, Fergus, Liam, Tricky, Aggie and Sam went into the closed bar for a private drinking session while Rose and Bridie stayed, sprawled on the floor, helping Johnny and Kevin make animal shapes from some plasticine before bedtime. Cathy was left to keep Father Stephen company and to cradle baby Thomas, which she was more than delighted to do.

'I'm sorry you missed Thomas's baptism, Cathy, but we thought it best to get on with it. He was very fragile at first but I think he's out of the woods now though.' The priest stroked the baby's hair. 'I only ever got to hold my own babies for the time it took to baptise them, but I shouldn't complain, should I? How many Catholic priests get to have children at all?'

'More than you think, would be my guess, Father. You could have moved to the Church of Ireland, I suppose.'

'Or leave the church altogether. That's what I really should have done, but I'm a terrible coward.'

Despite the sad absence of Nicholas and Louisa, the Boxing Day gathering over at Stasia's would be crowded with more people squeezed in than ever and the addition of several young children and babies. Cousin Paul was bringing his new girlfriend, Siobhan, barmaid at Sam and Rose's pub, to meet his parents for the first time and Fergus had asked whether he could invite his friend Hugo along, the half-forward from his hurling team, whose parents had retired to Bristol in the summer.

'Did Auntie Stasia really say, *'the more the merrier'*?' questioned Bridie as they stomped through the frosty air of Rowanbridge. 'It doesn't sound like her at all.'

'It's grandmotherhood,' said Fergus. 'It has magically transformed her into a cuddly, relaxed, devil-may-care old biddy.'

'I'll know that's true if she's put out the best china and crystal despite all the kids that'll be charging around,' said Cathy.

The Hughes's everyday crockery was set out on the dining room table.

'Not so relaxed after all then, eh, Fergus?' Bridie winked at her brother.

'You've laid on a tremendous spread for us as usual, Auntie Stasia. Thank you,' said Cathy.

'I'm used to having five hard-working men in the house and your Liam is a farmer too who must need his food. Then there's Fergus who would probably be better off with a trough rather than a plate. Bridie and Maureen eat well as does Siobhan, I see,' Stasia sniffed. 'But I wish Matthew's Lucy would eat more. She looks like a stick despite having two children.' Stasia looked squarely at Cathy. 'When can I expect to hear some good news from you on that front?'

'You're not supposed to ask that sort of thing, Auntie Stasia, but there's no prospect of it at all. We're not going to have a child which is partly why I'm doing this degree.'

'Are you enjoying it?'

'I love it. It's truly fascinating and it's made me much more aware of things I should and shouldn't do in our family, of why I am the way I am and how my childhood might have affected me. I realise now that losing my own Daddy and then Joe has made me anxious and over-protective of Johnny for instance.'

'I'm sure you look at us all and see what we should have done differently.'

'There's no 'should' about it, Auntie. I think you probably had the same reaction as me to losing a parent too young. You tried to protect Mammy and she fought it. We are all victims of our upbringing and circumstances in so many ways.'

'And none more so than your Liam, I suppose.'

Cathy looked over to her husband, deep in conversation with Peter about breeds of cattle, and sighed. 'You're right there.'

Hugo Moran arrived soon after everyone had started eating. Fergus introduced him to Stasia and Edmund first and then brought him over to meet his sisters.

'Hugo, this is my big sister Cathy, who lives out in Connemara with her husband, Liam, and son, Johnny. And this is my beautiful sister, Rambling Rose. She's married to Sam over there and that little lad on the floor, Kevin, is hers and she's just had this little chap, Thomas, too.' Fergus bent over and kissed the baby's head. 'Oh, I love that smell. And here, last but definitely not least, because there's no way she would allow it, is my little sister, Bridie. This is Hugo everyone.'

Hugo looked a little daunted but he smiled bravely and shook everyone's hand. 'Pleased to meet you all. Fergus has told me lots about you.'

'Yeah, sorry girls, I thought it was better to be honest from the get-go 'cos you'll be seeing a fair bit of Hugo around the place. He's a very average hurling player but he's a tip-top accountant and Daddy and I need some help on that score now that Uncle Nicholas is sadly departed. Hugo's gonna come and work in the farmhouse a couple of days a week on all the books, isn't that right, man.'

'I'm going to do my best.' Hugo, though reasonably tall and fit, with sandy hair falling over his tortoiseshell spectacles, was dwarfed by Fergus. Hugo looked around the room. 'The person I must meet is Aggie. Fergus talks about her most of all.'

Bridie laughed. 'That's because Fergus has always been her favourite. She would never admit it but she always let him get away with murder when we were kids. Still spoils him something wicked.'

'Sorry, Hugo, but you'll have to meet Aggie another time,' said Rose. 'We made her go to her cousin's for the day. If she'd been here, she'd just have spent the day running around after everyone.'

'Yes, she's like a precious antique artefact and we want her to go on for years and years, so we take good care of her,' added Fergus.

'She's only in her sixties, Fergus,' Cathy objected.

'Yeah well, after they get to about fifty, all women just look ancient to me.'

'Thank you very much for that, Fergus,' said Stasia, handing a glass of beer to Hugo.

Liam was in bed by ten, getting an early night before his drive back home the next day. Cathy came up soon after. 'What are you reading?'

'Oh, you'd love it, macushla. *Beef Farming: Theory and Practice.* Right up your street.' Cathy laughed, starting to undress. Liam closed his book to watch her.

'I love to see you peel off your stockings like that and then I wait to see your lovely breasts peek from beneath your bra.'

'Peek? Flop more like.' Cathy picked up her nightdress from the bedside chair.

'No, leave that,' said Liam. 'You won't be needing it. I intend to provide you with all the warmth you need tonight. Come here to me.'

Cathy wriggled into bed beside Liam to find he was as naked as her. He stroked her body from top to bottom, cheeks to ankles, pausing over her curved belly. He caressed and licked her breasts. 'Seeing Rose put baby Thomas to her breast fills me with such a fierce envy. I ache to see you do the same to a baby of our own.'

'I know. I see how you look at me when I hold him. I can see you wishing and hoping – but you must know that you and Johnny are all I need.' Cathy pulled Liam onto and into herself, willing her body to give Liam what he so desired.

Chapter 20 – March 1957

Cathy was trying to immerse herself in the Gestalt principles of perception but the play of sunlight dancing on the pages was distracting. The cottage was totally silent. Johnny was in Ollerton that Easter, being dropped off by Seamus at the start of the bachelor's tour of the great cathedrals of eastern England. Mam Ashfield had offered Seamus a bed but he had politely declined, booking himself into several fancy hotels instead. He had made up for any possible offence by delivering Johnny with his cello so the two women could finally hear their boy play.

Cathy was missing Johnny, but she needed to study hard this break before her final exams started. She was confident that she was a good student but she wanted to do as well as possible to prove to herself and everyone else that it had been a worthwhile undertaking. Johnny would be ridiculously indulged during his stay with lots of TV, cricket at Trent Bridge and Mam's scones, so any guilt Cathy felt was soon assuaged.

She looked out to the sea; for a late March morning it was sunny with just a few clouds. It looked quite warm, though experience told her the breeze would make it a different kettle of fish outside. A great day for drying laundry though; Cathy looked with some satisfaction at the sheets flipping and flapping out on the washing line.

Cathy closed the book. Why shouldn't she have a break? She wrapped up warmly and stepped out. It was chilly despite the sunshine, which was all the more reason to keep up a fast pace. She turned down the lanes, past their own fields, now dotted with ewes and their lambs. Her mind was focussed on all she had been studying about cognitive psychology that term, but her legs strode briskly forward. Without thinking, she found herself in Claddaghduff, at the edge of the strand which led over to Omey Island. She ought to go back really and pick up her books but the glittering beach was so seductive. She took off her shoes and socks and stepped onto the cold, virgin sand. She curled her toes to make the firm sand squeeze up between them, like she had as a child. With her lungs full of bracing sea air, she marched over to the other side of the strand and on up to the graveyard where Ailsa and Máire were buried.

It had been a while since she had made this trip. Máire's grave now boasted few shells and pebbles. Cathy told herself not to feel so guilty at the sight of grass growing through the gaps in the stone. Life was busy, exceptionally so now she was spending as much time as she could studying. She knew her father would forgive her neglect if he was watching, but of course he wasn't; there was no heaven, only the here and now. Maybe she could encourage Johnny to take on the task of tending the graves, but why should he bother either? He had never met these people and nor had she, for that matter. Aoife was the only person left who had known Ailsa and Máire in person. Tending graves was for the benefit of those left behind not for the departed. Cathy made a deal with herself: she would spruce up the graves when Aoife was due to visit but would leave them to the elements the rest of the time. The graves should fade away naturally and sink into the landscape.

She walked home. As she approached one of their own fields, she could hear the sound of Mikey's tin whistle. He was practising *Sheep May Safely Graze*. It was their little joke, but now he was actually playing it to a field full of ewes and lambs.

Cathy had been teaching Mikey how to read music since Christmas. He learned eagerly, practised assiduously and so progressed quickly. Music transformed him. When he was playing, all his anxieties seemed to melt away, his brow relaxed and he even stood differently. It seemed to be more effective than any drug or therapy Cathy was learning about in her degree course; it was magic medicine. Cathy slipped silently past the field and on home without making Mikey aware of her presence. Let him enjoy the peace and solitude too.

Back at her desk, she reopened her textbook but found it hard to concentrate. Her visit to Omey Island had awakened vivid memories of her daddy. Cathy went to her wardrobe and took out the wooden box where she kept small treasures: Johnny's first milk tooth, her grandmother's emerald ring, the lock of Máire's golden hair tied with cream wool and the goodbye note her daddy had written to her on the back of Yeats' *A Poem for my Daughter*. She used to read his farewell message regularly, often in tears, but she hadn't unfolded it once since she had moved to Cleggan. Reading it today, she found her Daddy's words no less painful but she knew they were long past.

'Please forgive me, Cathy. I am going because I know your lives will get better without me here. I have chosen this poem for you. You have brought me nothing but joy; you are beautiful, kind and learned and I hope you find a bridegroom one day who will cherish you. But don't think you have to 'root yourself in one perpetual place'; Yeats and I don't see eye to eye there. Please don't judge your mother. Whatever has happened is entirely my fault. Look after your sister and brother, and remember your other sister, who was born with the sound of the Atlantic in her ears. I love you so much, my darling Countess Cathleen. Goodbye, macushla, my beloved daughter. Your adoring Daddy.'

Well, she had certainly found a bridegroom who cherished her – two in fact – and she had not stayed rooted to one place. And she hadn't forgotten Máire, even though she didn't visit her grave often enough.

What her father hadn't known when he wrote it was that she would one day have another half-sister. Cathy was confident her Daddy would have loved Bridie, if he could have separated the essence of her from the adultery that had spawned her. John Fitzgerald would have loved Bridie for all the qualities she had inherited from her mother. Cathy also adored Bridie's feistiness, her self-confidence, her energy, her belief in a united Ireland and her pursuit of justice for the boys of Letterfrack. Cathy could do nothing for Máire but she could do lots for her living half-sister, and Bridie really needed her, especially now that she just lost her own father.

Last month, after a short stay in Kilkenny Hospital, the cirrhosis finally destroyed its host. Father Stephen died with two nuns at his bedside but neither of his children. His funeral had been conducted by the Bishop of Ossory in St Mary's Cathedral in Kilkenny and was a rather elaborate affair but he had requested he be buried in the little graveyard in Rowanbridge where he had served almost his entire life as priest. There were just five graves between him and his great love, Hannah McDermott.

'Did you see Father's brothers there and his cousins?' Bridie had asked after the funeral as she and Fergus sat with Cathy in the vast Byrne kitchen. 'They're our uncles, I suppose, Fergus, and they're all our relations.'

'Best let sleeping dogs lie though, sis. We don't want to mess up his memory, now do we? In my heart, I shall always know he was my father and so will you. That's enough for me and, God knows, we have plenty of other relations already.'

Fergus had put his arm around Cathy, seeing her tears. 'You okay, love?'

'Just a bit sad. Thinking about losing fathers. It's hard - but remember, I'm always here for you. I love you both very much.'

Cathy folded her own father's farewell letter and returned it to the box with the tiny tooth and the ring. But not the lock of hair. If Máire was alive today, Cathy guessed her hair would no longer be as yellow as the celandines in the hedgerows. She went downstairs clutching it and out to the beach where a strong crosswind was blowing. She undid the woollen bow and held her arm above her head, letting the strands of hair be carried to wherever the wind gods chose to take them.

Chapter 21– April 1957

Cathy was parked in front of Galway Grammar waiting for Johnny to appear. No sooner had he arrived back from Ollerton than she had lost him again to boarding school. But Cathy had a fun weekend ahead planned, with minimal studying: Bridie and Bill were coming. Cathy hoped that Mikey, Johnny and she would be able to perform *Sheep May Safely Graze* to everyone after a bit more practice.

Cathy had also bought, on impulse, two kites, one orange and one green. She'd seen them in a shop in Galway and wanted them instantly, as much for herself as for Johnny. Why had they never tried out kites before? The car door opened and Johnny threw himself inside, kissing his mother cursorily and throwing his bag into the back seat. 'I'm starving. What's for supper?'

'And hello to you too, my darling. Let's get you some chips.' Johnny was growing so fast at the moment. He was coming up to thirteen and his voice was treading a precarious line between treble and bass. No surprise that he needed a constant injection of food.

'Want one?' Johnny offered the bag of chips to his mother.

Normally Cathy would have been only too happy to snaffle a couple but today she had no appetite; she'd been feeling a little off colour for the last few days. 'No thanks, love. How's your week been?'

'Tolerable. Too much Latin. But we did some great experiments in chemistry, explosions and stuff. Nothing dangerous,' he added quickly, seeing his mother's concerned expression. 'There have been lots of strange men wandering around all week, coming into lessons and measuring walls. But we had a great game of hurling yesterday. Uncle Fergus will be pleased that I'm pretty good at it. Not as much as cricket obviously, and it's lethal.'

'Christ, I know I'm being a silly mother, but I'm terrified that you'll get badly hurt playing any of these sports. I'd hate for an injury to stop you playing your cello. I think you're tall enough to take over your grandfather's cello now, by the way. We must bring it back from Dalkey next time we get up there.'

'Great.'

'We need to do a bit more practice on the Bach before Bridie and Bill arrive tomorrow.'

Johnny groaned. 'Must I?'

'Yes, you must. Mikey has been practising hard. It'd mean the world to him and it's a beautiful piece.'

'Okay, okay. Can we play some Elvis Presley next time?' He started singing. *'You ain't nothin' but a hound dog, Cryin' all the time.'* Johnny's American accent was impressive. 'One of the lads in my dorm has a radio. And he can do all the moves too.'

'Radio signals in Galway must be a damn sight better than at home. We get more crackles than frying chips. But it doesn't bother Brendan; he has it on all the time while he's mending the pots. If you like that sort of music I'll see if I can get some Elvis Presley sheet music for the piano. Not sure it'd sound quite right on the cello.' They laughed. 'I'll probably have to send off to Dublin though.'

'Everything good's in Dublin.' Johnny screwed up the chip bag and threw it into the back seat. 'Before I forget, there's a letter for you in my bag.'

Bridie and Bill breezed into Cleggan late on Saturday morning, bringing chocolates and bundles of cheerful energy.

'None of us should be doing this, should we - taking time off?' said Bill. 'We should have our noses deep into our books all weekend.' He and Bridie were also facing their finals.

'It's good to have a break,'reassured Cathy. 'Too much stress is debilitating and can affect your concentration. At least that's what my lecturers say.'

'What are going to do after you graduate, Cathy? Are you going to become a fully-fledged psychiatrist?' asked Bridie.

'No. I think I've decided what I'd like to do.'

Last term, Cathy and a group of fellow students had visited Ballinasloe Asylum where Ada English had worked for forty years. The lecture detailed the many reforms she had introduced to the care of people with mental illnesses, from electro-convulsive treatments to all forms of occupational therapies and they had met several patients. They had even seen Ada's grave in the grounds. As Cathy listened to descriptions of the many therapeutic and humane activities now offered to patients - sports, drama, gardening, painting, even visits to the local cinema - she knew that this was the area of psychiatric care she wanted to devote her time to.

'I've decided I want to become an occupational therapist, if you know what that is. If I can. What about you Bridie? have you made up your mind?'

'Well, it was pretty obvious and Uncle Seamus agrees. I'd be a shite solicitor so I'm going to do my barrister-at-law degree at Kings Inns and then I'll do pupillage. Uncle Seamus has lots of contacts and he'll introduce me to some barristers, but I'm very picky. I only want to work for someone I can respect, someone who has defended people fighting for justice.'

'You mean the IRA?'

'They deserve justice, don't they? Look at all the IRA men Costello arrested after the Brookeborough attack; a total misuse of the *Offences Against the State* Act. It'll backfire on him, I swear, in the election. There's loads of support for reunification in the country and Sinn Féin will be the beneficiaries, just you see. But I don't just want to defend IRA members. There are other good people who need the protection of the law.'

'Don't let Liam hear you call the IRA 'good people'. He gets very wound up reading the paper. He finds it very depressing. Even I can't reconcile myself to their methods, much as I might agree with the ambition.'

'But you have to fight for what you believe in, Cathy.'

Bill put his hand on Bridie's arm. 'There seems to be another way back home. A lot's happening on the civil rights front. People are protesting against segregation and trying to get more black people the vote. I'm not saying there's been no violence but it's a fight that's been mainly waged through resistance and civil disobedience. Did you hear about a woman called Rosa Parks? In '55, she was on a bus and refused to give up her seat to a white man. That led to a complete bus boycott in Montgomery that lasted more than a year but last year they passed a law that ended segregation on buses. An amazing victory thanks to Rosa Parks and her peaceful protest.'

'That's inspiring, Bill. Will you go back home after you graduate to join the fight?' asked Cathy.

'I hope to, Cathy, even though I'll miss the friends I've made in Galway. There are several Democrats in the Congress and the Senate who might welcome a cheap assistant, especially someone of colour, and my father can introduce me to them.'

'That's naked nepotism!' protested Bridie.

'Excuse me, Miss Hypocrisy,' said Cathy. 'Did I not just hear you say that Uncle Seamus is going to introduce you to Dublin barristers? Ignore her, Bill. What you're planning sounds very worthwhile. We all need a mission.'

Johnny burst through the door and ran to hug his Auntie Bridie.

'Hey, big fella. Can you just stop growing! At this rate you'll overtake Fergus and he'll be extremely grumpy about that.'

All political talk was dropped when Liam arrived home. The chat switched to family news and the state of fishing. Johnny took Bridie and Bill to see the newest arrivals, three lambs born just yesterday, and then he took them to Mrs Gallagher's where they were going to take witness statements from the new lads from St Joseph's.

'It makes for some grim reading,' Bridie said before supper. 'Are you sure you won't add your account to it, Liam?'

'I think you have plenty there to convict the worst Brothers several times over, don't you? Where do you plan to send it all, Bridie?'

'Aunt Lily is going to give me the names of some Senators and Uncle Seamus has already tipped off some judges. All we can do is our best and keep going.'

There was a knock at the door; it was Dearbhla, Brendan and Mikey, holding his tin whistle ready to play the Bach.

'Evening to all you good people. I'll shut the door quick 'cos the wind is blowing up strong and Dearbhla has only a thin shawl on her, but I hope it's okay if her and me come in to listen to the music you've been getting ready and I know it'll be very different from the songs that Mikey and I play in the pubs but he says it's beautiful and we'd love to hear it, wouldn't we Dearbhla?'

The young girl nodded.

'Of course, you're very welcome,' said Cathy, holding the door to the sitting room open. 'Get yourself a glass of something and take a seat.'

The five spectators made a miniature audience but they were all charmed by the performance of *Sheep May Safely Graze*.

'Oh gracious, Missus Cathy, that is so beautiful and just how I imagine it must be like being up in heaven with lovely flutes and harps and suchlike, and all the angels dancing around,' said Brendan.

'Thank you. Brendan. I'm not sure what Bach would have made of his music being played on a tin whistle but if it works for you that's good. We had fun too, didn't we?' Mikey and Johnny nodded.

'I'm mightily pissed off that Fergus and I never got to learn any instruments like you and Rose,' complained Bridie. 'Why didn't Mammy send us to lessons, Cathy?'

'Come on now, Mikey. I'm sorry you good people, but we have to dash off now to our gig in Ballyconneely tonight and we get free food thrown in and we don't want to miss that, do we Mikey, because they have the best pies in Galway by all accounts. Have a grand evening yourselves now and if you feel like coming along for a jig or two you'd be most welcome as always.' Brendan marched off out the door, but Mikey waited for Dearbhla to pick up her shawl and they followed on. 'That was lovely, Mikey,' Cathy heard Dearbhla whisper to Mikey when they stepped out into the dusk and she saw the girl give him a kiss on the cheek before the door closed behind them.

Cathy and Liam took the opportunity for an early night, with Bridie and Bill instructed to lock up when they returned home from the céilí.

Liam lay back in bed, supposedly reading the paper, but in reality watching Cathy go around the bedroom, folding and tidying away clothes before undressing. 'No, leave that,' he said as she started to put on her nightdress.

'Oh right, it's like that is it?' Liam flung back the bed clothes to admit Cathy and pulled her hard into himself.

'Come here, let me have hold of you. I get so jealous watching you play music with other people. It feels so intimate, practically indecent, and it's something I can't do.'

'Well, no-one else gets to do this,' said Cathy as Liam started kissing her breasts with his hand between her thighs, 'but if you're serious, I can teach you how to read music. What do you want to play? The piano? Or maybe you'd like to sing; I reckon there's a decent voice inside there.' She ran her fingers through the rusty fuzz on Liam's chest but there was no reply. Other matters were occupying her husband's thoughts.

Liam fell asleep the instant they finished making love. Cathy studied his peaceful face, now free of the little frown lines that normally clouded his forehead. Such a dear, kind man, but still troubled in ways she couldn't seem to help. She turned over onto her front but quickly turned back saying a silent 'Ouch'. Her breasts were rather painful tonight. She didn't think Liam had been especially rough… 'Oh Christ,' she whispered to herself, the realisation hitting her that she had had no period for two months. Could it possibly be? She was flooded with hopeful excitement but she would wait another month to be extra sure. It would be awful to give Liam hope if it was just an early menopause. But maybe, just maybe.

The next morning, Cathy shouted up the stairs to raise Bridie and Bill. 'Come on you two lazy scuts, it's nearly ten o'clock, there'll be no breakfast for you soon and we have kites to fly.'

Bridie and Bill's muggy heads were rapidly rinsed out an hour later, running up and down chasing the dancing, wilful kites, in competition with Liam and Johnny.

'Come on, Mama, you have a go. It's great,' encouraged Johnny, but Cathy thought she would just take things easy for a while and sat watching from the dunes with her hand over her belly.

'Well, that's fantastic fun,' said Bridie, collapsing onto the sand next to Cathy. 'We must come back and do it again, but only when our finals are finished. Stop tempting us from now until June, OK.' She kissed her sister's cheek and stuck her arm out for Bill to pull her up. 'Come on, Bill, let's get back to Galway and get our heads down for the rest of today.'

'And you need to do some homework too, Johnny, before you go running off with that football.'

Sunday afternoon ended up being a studious time for everyone. While Johnny did his algebra and Cathy revised behavioural theories, Liam spent more time reading about beef-cattle farming. He was determined to be as clued up as possible in case Jack Brodie's land came up for sale.

Cathy, bored and fidgety, closed her book and wandered into her son's bedroom. 'How's it going, my love?'

'Fine. It's algebra. No problem.' Johnny was not just proficient at all forms of mathematics, he relished them.

'There's a proven connection between music and maths, you know.'

'Rhythm is just counting, I suppose.'

'Harmony too, believe it or not. Well, I'd better get back to my revision but I'll make tea first. Do you want a cup, Johnny?'

'Yes, please. Any chance of a biscuit as well?'

Cathy turned to leave but Johnny called her back.

'Mama! Mama, I forgot to give you that letter from school. It's there on the bed.'

Cathy gently shifted Tiny Ted from the centre of the bed onto the pillow. Cathy sat on the bed, tore open the envelope and studied the contents before exclaiming.

'Christ almighty, Johnny. Did you know? I can't believe it… Galway Grammar is closing down.'

Chapter 22 – May 22nd 1957

'*Happy birthday to you, Happy birthday to you,*
     Happy birthday, Missus Cathy, happy birthday to you.'
Brendan triumphantly finished singing and Dearbhla deposited a gigantic chocolate cake on the kitchen table.

'Thank you, Brendan, and just look at that gorgeous cake. Please thank your mother for me, Dearbhla.'

'Actually I made it myself, Cathy. I've been learning all my Mammy's tricks.'

'I suppose you've been watching her bake and cook all your life, Dearbhla.'

'Just you cut yourself a big slice of it, Missus Cathy, and you'll soon see that Dearbhla has learned all that she could possibly know from her Mammy. Mikey and me and the lads are just as happy when we find out that our supper has been cooked by Dearbhla and not by Mrs G herself, and maybe even happier.' Brendan gave Dearbhla a nudge and she blushed.

'Well, is it okay if I wait until this evening to have a piece when Liam gets home, and, of course, I must save most of it for when Johnny is home at the weekend.' Cathy detected a hint of disappointment in Brendan's face. 'But I shall cut off a third of it for you to take back to share. Is that OK? I reckon that'll make six or seven decent slices.'

'Oh, that'd be grand, missus, and we shall make sure to toast your birthday when we eat it tonight, won't we, Dearbhla? But now I must be off before himself finds out I'm not sweeping out the sheds as he instructed.'

Brendan scuttled out of the door, while Dearbhla fetched a plate to put the huge portion of cake on to take back home. 'I'll make sure Mikey gets a piece, Cathy.' Dearbhla smiled at Cathy and left.

Cathy was looking forward to enjoying a peaceful and romantic birthday evening with Liam: lobster, and white wine, topped off with chocolate cake. She made herself tea and sat at the table with her revision notes, picking at cake crumbs. Only two weeks before her finals were to begin and she had never felt more nervous. It was stupid; she had done many more brave and difficult things in her life: leaving home at fourteen, going to England alone to train, nursing through the war, giving birth, declaring her love to Liam, but, for some reason, getting her psychology degree was absurdly important. She had asked Liam to sacrifice so much so that she could devote three years to this venture and she wanted to prove that it had not been in vain and that it would lead to a new career. He really did need another boat.

But now there was this other little matter to deal with. Being pregnant was a joyful problem to have but a disruptive one and Cathy hadn't yet broken the news to Liam, even though she had been to see a doctor last week who had confirmed she was about thirteen weeks pregnant. Past the risky stage.

Another big change was being forced on them because of the imminent closure of Galway Grammar School. The future of Johnny's education had been hotly debated over the last month, not just between the boy himself and his mother but also with Liam, Seamus, Ellen and Aoife. On hearing the news, Johnny had almost instantly declared that he wanted to go and live in Dalkey and attend the Maple Academy but this horrified Cathy. She didn't want her son to go and live away for the whole of each term, and anyway, he was two years younger than the age at which most students joined the Academy. Liam was adamant that no school run by the Catholic church should be considered for even a moment but, try as she might, Cathy could find no school in the whole of the counties of Galway and Mayo that was free of the input of priests, nuns or monks. She thought about teaching her son herself at home, but the subjects he loved best, maths and science, were definitely beyond her abilities. Anyway, she would soon either be looking after a baby or pursuing a career as an occupational therapist, and Johnny needed the company of school friends.

Several long phone calls between Cathy herself or Johnny with either Seamus or Ellen examined all the options, weighing up the pros and cons. Seamus and Ellen tried hard not to let their own emotions colour their advice but they were both excited at the prospect of having Johnny back living near, or even with them in Dalkey. They also both sincerely believed that it was the right choice for Johnny.

'Hey, Mama, just think about it: I'll be with people we love whom you trust; I'll get a great education without any church stuff; I'll be able to get a better cello teacher and I can re-join Merrion Square cricket club. And I won't have to talk in Irish. I can come home every half-term and you can come and see me in Dalkey any time you like. I'd have had to board somewhere anyway.'

Johnny had no inkling that there would be a baby-shaped consideration to add into these arrangements. In the end, the logic was inescapable: it made perfect sense for Johnny to go and live with his guardian angels and join the Maple Academy, albeit with some special provisions to account for his relative youth. He would live with Aoife and Ellen in their little house in Nerano Road until he reached fifteen when he could begin to board along with the other students.

'Remember, I taught and looked after Liam when he was just a young lad, so having Johnny with us will be no different. It will also be a great privilege, macushla. We will treasure your boy, won't we, Ellen,' reassured Aoife.

So, it was settled. Seamus would come at the end of August to take Aoife and Ellen back to Dalkey from their holiday stay in Cleggan, as he normally did, only this time there would be an extra passenger returning with them.

Cathy re-read her birthday cards: three from Rowanbridge, two from Dalkey, and one from her Great-aunt Lily. Nothing from Bridie but that was hardly surprising in light of her sister's panic-stricken state with finals approaching. For the first time, Cathy had been given separate cards from Liam, his featuring red roses and ribbons, and Johnny, his patterned with abstract stripes and circles. Not only had Liam bothered to buy an extra card for Johnny to sign, he had chosen one to suit the boy's personality. How lucky she felt having this kind and considerate man to share her life with and how wonderful it would be to tell him they were going to have a child together.

Liam took a bath after work, changed into clean clothes and prepared the meal himself, grilling the lobsters he had brought home with a thermidor sauce made by Mrs G. As he worked away in the kitchen, Cathy played the piano. Liam opened the bottle of white wine, lit two candles and laid the table, bringing out two of the rarely used Waterford crystal glasses. When he thought everything was just right, he went and stood behind Cathy until she finished playing the Chopin Nocturne. Then he put his arms around her and kissed her neck.

'Dinner is served, madam,' he whispered into her ear.

It was all delicious. 'Thank you, darling man, for going to so much trouble after a hard day's work. Now you have to eat the birthday cake that Dearbhla made for me.'

'Okay, but do I have to sing at the same time?'

Cathy laughed, taking the slices out of the fridge as Liam made to refill her glass. 'No more for me, thank you, darling, I've had enough.'

'And I shouldn't drink any more either because you look just heavenly tonight and I have evil designs on you.' He took her hand and kissed it tenderly. Liam demolished his cake and finished the half that Cathy left too. 'Delicious. Pass on my congratulations to Dearbhla in the morning if I don't see her.' He went to the pantry, returning with a small package wrapped in tissue paper and blew dust off it. 'This has been hiding in the flour jar since yesterday. Happy birthday to my wonderful, amazing, beautiful wife.'

Cathy opened the package, revealing a small velvet box; inside it nestled a necklace of seed pearls with a heart-shaped pendant made of gold.

'Here let me put it on you. I thought it would match your Claddagh ring well. Do you like it?'

'I love it. I had a pearl necklace once upon a time that my grandmother gave me, but it got broken. But this is much prettier. It must have cost a fortune, Liam. You shouldn't spend your money on such things when we need so many more practical things.'

'It makes me happy to be able to buy you little yokes like this. And you deserve them, macushla. The boat can wait.'

'Well, for once, I'm going to be able to give you something in return that's worth even more than gold.' Cathy took Liam's hand and placed it on her belly. 'Our baby is in here, my love. We did it. I've waited to tell you until I was absolutely certain and until the first trimester had passed so it looks very hopeful that, come November, we will be welcoming a new little Molloy into our family.'

Liam looked into Cathy's eyes, then, quite speechless, threw his arms around her. They rocked together for several minutes, interspersed with gentle words and laughs from Cathy, but it took some time before Liam was able to let go of his wife and find the words he wanted to say.

'Macushla, I don't think I'll make a very good father, but you have made me complete and I shall work every minute of the day to be the best father I am capable of being.'

'You're a wonderful father to Johnny, so don't worry. You'll be great, I promise. But are you happy?'

'Am I happy? I'm shocked, and I'm scared! And I'm astounded and grateful, but yes, yes I am happy. Very, very happy, for you as much as for me. And I shall make sure our child never has an unhappy day if I can help it. He shall never, ever know fear or want in his life like I did.'

The couple lay for an hour in bed talking through what a future might hold for their baby. Would it be musical or love the sea or like animals?

'I'm thirty-seven, which is quite some age to be having a baby. I shall be very nervous to be out here in Cleggan when the time comes and not near a hospital.'

'We can get a midwife to be with you near the time.'

'Yes, but it would take over an hour to get to a hospital if I needed to.'

'Well then, maybe you need to be in Dublin or in Rowanbridge when your time gets near.'

'I've been thinking that but didn't want to suggest it because it would mean you wouldn't be around. Thanks for saying it for me, my love. Plenty of time to worry about all those things though.'

'Six months will go in a flash.' Liam stroked Cathy's belly. 'I shall enjoy watching this grow. Good night, my darling macushla.' Liam kissed her and turned to switch off the bedside lamp.

'Oi, I thought you had designs on me.'

'I did have - but you're pregnant. Is it safe?'

'You daft eejit. Of course, it is. I'm not going to live without you touching me for the next six months and more. And it is my birthday after all.'

Chapter 23 - Christmas 1957

'Johnny, my love, can you just go out and give Liam a hand? I'm a bit tied up here,' said Cathy as she shifted the baby over to the other breast.

Johnny sighed, threw down the length of track he was assembling, wearily got to his feet and went to the kitchen. Christmas Day was turning out to be no fun at all. Instead of being with all his relatives in a big, bustling, bedecked house in Rowanbridge, he was stuck here with just his Mama, Liam and a seven week-old baby, who cried a lot and had to be fed so often his mother seemed to be incapable of doing much apart from nurse it, burp it and wash it. Dearbhla was around on other days but today Liam was in charge and he'd had no time to help him set up the amazing Scalextric set that his Granny Ashfield and Auntie Shirley had sent over for his Christmas present.

'Thanks, Johnny. Could you just drain the carrots and the spuds and put them in bowls please,' said Liam as he wrestled with a glistening turkey. 'Stick them on the table and then get your mother.' Johnny made a space for the bowls between the plates, crackers and cutlery. The crackers were the only nod to Christmas decoration in the house apart from a jug of holly and ivy that Dearbhla had brought in and put on the sideboard next to the Christmas cards.

'Liam says it's ready, Mama,' Johnny shouted through the door.

'Ssshh. Okay. Coming.'

Cathy stood up gingerly. The Caesarean scar was still a bit tender. She walked over to the crib and laid the baby down as gently as she could and then did up her buttons. She looked at the angelic sleeping face of her child and smiled. 'I hope you're not going to be as much trouble all your life as you have been so far, Erin Máire Molloy,' she whispered before tiptoeing out of the room to join her boys.

Cathy's plans had been all set back in August. The baby's due date was November 25th, so she had arranged for Liam to drive her to Dalkey two weeks before where she would stay in Nerano Road, cossetted by Ellen and Aoife. It would be a wrench leaving Liam for a fortnight and he would miss the birth but everyone agreed it was the safest option, with Seamus only a couple of streets and a phone call away when she needed to be whisked off to hospital.

The Wednesday before she was due to leave for Dalkey, Cathy was upstairs packing her suitcase when she had felt a sharp stab in her bump. She thought little of it, knowing she should expect these fake contractions in the weeks leading up to the birth. She went downstairs. where Dearbhla had just finishing mopping the kitchen floor and was about to leave for the day.

'See you tomorrow, Cathy. Take it easy now and don't slip on the slates.'

Cathy sat at the table reading the paper. Fianna Fáil had won the election in July but they were being even more brutal in the use of internment against IRA suspects than Costello had been. Liam thoroughly approved of this policy but Cathy was not so sure. It was hardening opinions and the resolve of IRA sympathisers. The debate was raging, fanned by the four Sinn Féin TDs in the Dáil.

More twinges. She rubbed her enormous belly and then looked at the floor. Was that wetness down there from Dearbhla's mop? Cathy stood up. Her knickers were wet and there was a steady drip drip onto the floor. No, no... this mustn't happen; it was three weeks too early. Contraction pains were one thing, but Cathy knew that if the amniotic sac had ruptured there was only a certain amount of time that could be allowed to elapse before the baby must be delivered.

Cathy went out of the front door to find someone. Liam, Brendan and the other lads were off doing the deliveries. She threw her coat on, stuffed a towel between her legs and started to waddle down the road. Coming around the corner of the lane, was a wonderful and welcome sight; it was Mikey on his way back from checking the sheep.

'Mikey, Mikey, help me. I think the baby's coming. Get Dearbhla quick.' Mikey ran towards Cathy and supported her as she staggered back into the cottage. 'You just sit quietly, Cathy. I'll get Dearbhla and then I'll get on my bike and find Liam. I know what his rounds are today.'

When Dearbhla and Mikey got back, Cathy was standing, leaning on the table.

'Cathy, are you okay? Do you want to lie down?' Dearbhla rubbed Cathy's back.

'No, just get Liam, can you. Please, Mikey.'

Mikey took Dearbhla to one side. Cathy could hear his whispers telling her to fetch towels and to get as much water boiled as possible before he dashed out.

When, forty minutes later, Liam crashed through the door with Mikey trailing behind him, Cathy was lying on the kitchen floor, supported by Dearbhla kneeling behind her, her suitcase ready by the front door.

'Macushla, are you okay? What can I do? Tell us what to do.'

'Can you just check to see if I'm dilated at all. You know what to do, Liam. Humans are not that different from sheep, you know.'

Liam removed the towel between Cathy's legs and peered at her vulva. 'I can't see much. Do you mind me giving you a feel?'

'Ha! Feel away.'

Liam went to the kitchen sink and scrubbed his hands and then gently inserted a finger inside his wife. 'Not even two fingers width. You've a long time to go, macushla. Do you know what you're supposed to be doing with all the breathing and stuff? We don't have to worry much about that with the sheep, do we Mikey.'

Cathy laughed and then cried out as a contraction hit her. 'Fuck the sheep. I've done this before, you know, Liam Molloy.'

Mikey knelt down beside Liam. 'Cathy, do you mind me giving your tummy a little feel. I'll be very careful.' Cathy pulled up her dress to let Mikey place his hands directly on the tight bump, moving them around, sweeping them up and down and side to side before giving his verdict. 'I can't be sure, but I don't think the head is down in the right place. I think the baby is likely to be breach unless it decides to turn around by itself.'

Cathy shook her head. 'There's no time for that. I can't risk staying here if it's breach. Liam, you're going to have to get me to Galway hospital right now. For feck's sake man, go and get the car.'

A hair-raising car journey ensued, Cathy lying in the back seat with towels under her, moans interspersed with yelps, Liam driving as fast as he dared with Dearbhla next to him in the front seat, on hand for no particular reason other than to make them both feel safer. Mikey ended up following them on his motorbike, bringing Cathy's forgotten suitcase that the smart lad had spotted by the door.

After seven hours being palpated, prodded and poked, the midwife at Galway Hospital decided things were not progressing fast enough so referred Cathy to the duty doctor. Seventy anxious minutes later, Liam was called into the recovery room where Cathy lay, still unconscious. The midwife handed him a small bundle, 'Here's your daughter, Mr Molloy.

She's small, just five and a half pounds, but right as rain and a proper little fighter.'

Liam looked at his daughter with her reddish hair plastered to her head and her tiny pink fingernails and sobbed more tears than he had ever shed before.

Cathy and baby Erin didn't come home for two weeks which was probably just as well because, when Liam did bring them back, he would hardly let the baby out of his arms, other than to let Cathy feed her. Erin got used to being held at all hours, rocked, dandled and walked up and down. She protested loudly if anyone dared put her in her crib. Liam forced himself back onto the boats after a week at home luxuriating in his new-found fatherhood, but Dearbhla was around when Cathy needed a bath or a nap.

Erin was just four weeks old when Cathy came downstairs after her bath to find a remarkable scene: Dearbhla was making bread, Erin was lying in her crib on the kitchen table and Mikey was playing his tin whistle softly to her. Her green eyes were wide open as she listened, mesmerised by the silvery sounds.

'That's amazing, Mikey. You need to move back in sharpish.'

By mid-December, Erin had settled down somewhat. She started to sleep through the night – oh bliss - and Cathy began to feel almost human again, but Erin slept little during the day and craved constant attention. Thankfully, there was a gang of people only too happy to spend time with her. Brendan always popped in before he started deliveries to sing her a song or two, rocking her in his arms and dancing comically around the kitchen.

'Don't tell Liam I've just sung Erin a Republican song now, Missus Cathy, or he'd eat the head off me.'

Mikey always knocked gently on the door mid-afternoon, tin whistle in hand, ready to delight the baby girl. Erin seemed to recognise him and would flash him a little smile, raise her arms towards the lad and kick her legs enthusiastically. He just kept playing and never picked her up. By contrast, when Liam was in the house, Erin was always in his arms, even at mealtimes.

When term ended before Christmas, Seamus drove Johnny all the way home and brought Ellen and Aoife along too to see the new baby. Johnny ran through the front door when they arrived and immediately went to kiss his mother who was holding Erin. She offered the baby up for Johnny to take but he shook his head. After hugs and kisses, Aoife took the baby from Cathy.

'Aah, the little darling girl, would you come and see her Ellen? You hold her while I make the tea. I don't think I've ever seen you holding a baby, you know.'

'I held my brother's babies and I held Rose when she was just a wee one. But I never held you as a baby, Johnny. You were already a little boy when you came into our lives.'

Johnny looked on silently until Cathy went to him and put her arms around him. She could swear he had grown an inch or two since she had last seen him.

'So, what do you think of your new sister, my love?'

Johnny paused. 'She's very small.'

They all laughed.

'Not for long, you wait and see. She's already twice as big as she was at birth. She was so tiny, though with a huge pair of lungs on her from the off. You'll find that out soon enough.'

The three guardian angels refused to stay in the cottage and instead booked a couple of nights in a Clifden hotel. After they returned to Dublin, the cottage fell back into its baby-centric regime. When Johnny wasn't in his bedroom, he would disappear out with his football and return windswept with glowing cheeks, but it was obvious to Cathy that he didn't want to be around Erin too much and this upset her. She encouraged him to play his cello but he refused, saying that he was now used to his grandfather's bigger instrument in Dalkey and didn't want to go back. 'Play the piano then. Erin might like that. She loves listening to Mikey play the whistle to her.' But Johnny said he 'didn't fancy it'.

Two days before Christmas, Cathy told Liam that she was going to give Johnny his Christmas present early because she couldn't stand him moping around the place any longer. She was confident he would love it.

Almost as soon as he had left Cleggan in September to start at the Academy, Cathy had started thinking about when Johnny would be back home for Christmas. The baby was an exciting prospect but was still just a bump, heartburn and constipation, whereas her son was real. Cathy wanted his Christmas to be special despite the difference a new baby would make. She had already decided what to buy him: a record player. Cathy studied the models, read the leaflets, listened to the Galway shopkeeper's advice and, finally, chose a red and grey portable so that Johnny could easily take it back to Dalkey on the train. She also bought an assortment of singles and LPs: Buddy Holly, Jerry Lee Lewis, Paul Anka, Pat Boone and every Elvis Presley disc she could find.

Johnny looked quizzically at his mother when she dragged him into her bedroom on December 23rd and told hm to unwrap the present on the floor early. Had she gone mad? She was certainly not quite the same Mama he had said goodbye to at the start of term but he did as she instructed anyway. He pulled the paper slowly off the big rectangle. A grey plastic box with a handle … with red trim…and golden mesh. The appreciative wows and gasps that Johnny uttered as he realised exactly what this gift was cheered Cathy; she'd got it right. Johnny spent the next two days playing through every record, some endlessly.

'If he plays that Jerry Lee Lewis record any louder the whole cottage will be doing a 'whole lotta shakin',' remarked Liam when he got home at lunchtime on Christmas Eve. 'But it's fine. At least he's happy, and Erin seems to like it too.' Liam picked up his daughter and smothered her in kisses.

Liam's Christmas dinner turned out fine, not exactly Cordon Bleu but perfectly edible, and Mrs Gallagher's Christmas pudding was delicious. 'You go and have a sit down, Liam,' urged Cathy. 'I can wash up easily now Erin's asleep.'

'Will you race the Scalextric with me, Liam, when I've finished setting up the track?' asked Johnny.

'Of course, I will. It looks fun. Come here, fella.' Liam pulled Johnny into a tight hold. 'We've both missed you. A lot. I'm sorry the place is turned upside down with baby things but I hope your Christmas isn't turning out to be too awful.'

Johnny laughed. 'No. It's fine. Just a bit of a shock. Thanks for all my presents.'

Liam picked Erin out of her crib and settled himself in one of the armchairs. Johnny knelt on the floor concentrating on the instructions in his Scalextric set. When Cathy came into the sitting room half an hour later, she found Liam fast asleep, mouth open and gentle snores whistling from his nose with Erin asleep over his shoulder. Johnny was sitting triumphantly on the floor with the track all assembled, two race cars already in their slots. 'Come on then, Mama, you'll have to give me a car chase instead.'

After tea, Cathy made brief phone calls to all the family members to wish them a happy day. Johnny went up to his bedroom to play more music and Liam wrapped Erin up in blankets to take her down the lane to wish Mrs Gallagher, Dearbhla and all his lads a Merry Christmas, taking two bottles of whiskey with him and an envelope for each of them, containing a Christmas bonus.

Cathy was alone downstairs, a rare occurrence. A thought seized her. The timing would be fine. Why not? She picked up the telephone and rang Bernie in New York. She hadn't spoken to her friend since October when Bernie had congratulated her on her first-class psychology degree but had groaned to hear that pregnancy would now stop her pursuing a career. Cathy wanted to wish her friend a Happy Christmas – or maybe Happy Haunnukah – but also to promise Bernie that, before Christmas next year, she should expect Cathy to have begun her new life as a therapist. She was not going to let her baby, adored and desired though she was, get in the way for long.

Liam stayed out for more than an hour so no surprise that, when he returned, Erin was bawling to be fed.

'Here you go, macushla.' Liam handed over the baby to Cathy. 'I've had a drop of whiskey with the lads and I mean to have another. Can I tempt you to join me?'

'No, I'd better not. God knows this child is lively enough without alcohol-infused milk getting into her. I'd love some cocoa though. Johnny might like some too.'

Liam called up the stairs to Johnny when the drinks were ready. The boy clattered down the stairs and came into the kitchen. 'I'm sorry I didn't get Erin anything for Christmas, but I thought she'd like this.' He took Big Ted from behind his back. I know Auntie Shirley made him for me, but I never played with him. He just sits on my shelf getting dusty.'

'Oh, you darling boy, that is such a lovely thought. I'm sure she'll love him. He can sit at the end of her crib and watch over her.'

'Night night Mama. Thanks for a lovely Christmas.' Johnny kissed his mother on the cheek and then bent over to give his suckling sister a kiss on the top of her head. 'Night night, Erin.' Johnny ran upstairs with his cocoa; the sound of Pat Boone soon filtered through the floorboards.

'Don't cry, macushla. Here.' Liam used the corner of the baby's sheet to mop Cathy's tears. 'You're tired and I know you've been worried about Johnny but see, he's fine, honestly. It just takes time. He's thirteen and he's been your only baby for all that time, so he needs space to adjust.'

'I know that,' sniffled Cathy. 'I'm the bloody psychologist, thank you very much.'

'He'll be so thankful he has a sister in time. As for me, I am the happiest man alive to see my beautiful Cathy holding my baby, though I fear she has inherited my hair instead of your golden mermaid tresses.' Liam stroked Cathy's hair. 'I can hardly believe that I'm a father. I'm so blessed. Thank you for all you've been through for me. I love you, macushla.'

It didn't take long for news of the wondrous Scalextric set to spread through the tight band of Liam's lads and they were all madly envious that Brendan and Mikey got special privileges when their working day was over, and if the weather stopped them kicking a ball around on the beach. Cathy loved to see the two of them with Johnny sprawled over the sitting floor in good-natured but fierce competition, big kids the lot of them. Even Dearbhla was occasionally persuaded to have a go. She proved herself no mean racing driver, second only to Johnny himself. The giggles and whoops coming from the sitting room, as Cathy sat pinned to the kitchen table, relieved the tedium of the endless feeding sessions.

The day before Johnny's Christmas holidays ended, Cathy was upstairs packing his bags when the noise of her son's singing drifted up to her. She had left Erin asleep in her crib in his care, but she guessed the baby had woken up. Cathy crept down the staircase and listened at the sitting room door.

'Oh baby let me be, Around you every night
Run your fingers through my hair, And cuddle me real tight
Oh let me be, Your Teddy Bear.'

Cathy opened the door to find Johnny singing and dancing, holding Erin in the air clasped to Big Ted while the baby laughed and squealed at her brother's antics.

'Oh, hi Mama. Erin says she likes Elvis Presley.'

They were all up early the next morning because Liam was taking Johnny off to Galway train station. Cathy gave her son a long hug and loads of kisses. 'Have a good term, my darling boy, work hard, do lots of cello practice, don't play your records too loud and give my love to the three amigos.'

'Thanks for a great Christmas, Mama. I don't mind if Brendan and Mikey want to play with the Scalextric while I'm away. And I thought Erin might like to cuddle him,' Johnny took Tiny Ted out of his bag and into the crib next to Erin. 'Big Ted's too big for her just yet and, anyway, Tiny Ted gets lonely when I'm not here.'

Chapter 24 – March 1959

'Bye-bye now, my little chicken. Be a good girl and I'll see you in a few days.' Liam covered Erin in kisses, which made her giggle, and then he handed her over to Cathy so that he could load their cases onto the Dublin train.

'Look after yourself, my love, and don't just live off bread. Dearbhla will leave you something to warm up every day.'

'Bye macushla. Don't miss your train. I'll see you on Saturday. I love you.'

Cathy and Liam had a final hug and she climbed onto the train. 'Wave to Daddy.'

Erin knew how to wave - she did it most mornings to Dearbhla and then to Brendan and Mikey after their visits - but she had never waved her Daddy good-bye before; he was always up and out of the house before she woke. Erin waved, but her bottom lip started to wobble when she realised that Liam was not coming with them.

'Dadaaaa.' Erin stretched out her arm towards Liam as the train started moving off. She wailed solidly for the next ten minutes which hardly endeared Cathy to her fellow passengers but, eventually, Erin was placated with Tiny Ted and a bottle of milk.

'Jesus Christ Almighty,' thought Cathy to herself. 'I hope this is worth it.'

They were on their way to help celebrate her Great-aunt Lily's eightieth birthday. At the weekend, all the family would be gathering in Pembroke Street and, at Lily's request, Cathy was going play alongside Johnny, Seamus and a young violinist from the Academy.

Cathy gazed at Erin, asleep now in her arms, Tiny Ted clasped to her chest. 'Please God, let her sleep the whole way,' she thought.

It was a challenging job looking after Erin. Cathy felt guilty realising that, in reality, she had it easy in comparison to Dearbhla, who spent the day running around after this lively and mischievous toddler while trying to keep the cottage running smoothly, though Dearbhla seemed to enjoy it well enough. Why was childcare always women's work? Cathy found it much easier to go and have civilised discussions about occupational therapy strategies at the two hospitals where she had started work last summer. When Johnny had been a baby, there had always been people around. Cathy had never had her mother or sisters close by to help but she had been blessed with the Ashfield women or Ellen and Aoife at her side throughout Johnny's infancy. Funnily enough, she had never found looking after Rose and Fergus difficult when they were little but, of course, Aggie had really done all the hard work. Maybe Cathy was just too old now to be dealing with an energetic and wilful sixteen-month-old, or maybe this particular child was unusually demanding.

Cathy loved her job and worked conscientiously for the three days she was paid for and extra time on top. She got exhausted by the end of the week but, visiting the hospitals, she rarely felt the same frustrations that a day left alone with Erin aroused.

In January, she had also started a modest counselling practice, renting a small consulting room in Clifden two afternoons a week. Business was slow to start with. The people of Connemara were not familiar with the concept of seeking help for their anxieties, depressions and troubled marriages, not even from a priest; they were more likely to resort to alcohol, gambling or domestic violence to drown their miseries and numb their pain. But it was starting to pick up a little and

Cathy took great satisfaction knowing that, for every client she helped, many other people would feel some benefit.

This week was the first proper break Cathy had taken since starting her new career, and her first stay away from Cleggan since Erin's birth. She couldn't wait to see Dublin again and introduce Erin to her Great-*great*-aunt Lily. Cathy had brought her camera to record the presence of four generations of women in the same room.

Liam would drive to Dublin at the weekend for the party and then take his whole family back for Easter. It was such a relief that Liam could leave the animals and boats in Brendan's care. Now a burly twenty-four year-old man, Brendan was still as loud and cheery as ever and daft as brush when he wasn't working, but he was responsible and mature when necessary and had naturally assumed the role of Liam's deputy. The other lads accepted Brendan's authority in Liam's absence.

Liam could probably have stayed away longer but he was driven to work as much as he could, always trying to raise money for another expansion of the business. Molloy's Seafoods now boasted three delivery vans, newly painted in smart blue and green livery. He wanted to stop renting the fourth boat and buy it outright, and he planned to get ice machines down in his harbour shed so he could pack fish off to other cities by train; the demand was there. Cathy worried about how hard Liam worked but it seemed to satisfy a deeper need than a purely financial one. Compared to her own daddy, who had always prioritised his children, his music and his politics, Cathy admired Liam's industriousness but didn't want either her husband or Erin to miss out on the special bond between father and daughter that she had herself enjoyed.

Erin woke up half an hour before their arrival time in Dublin but Cathy juggled snacks and stories to keep her distracted. Sure enough, dear Uncle Seamus was there on the platform, his height making him unmissable in the throng.

'Darling Cathy. How are you? And how are you, little one?' Seamus tickled Erin's chin. She glared at him and then buried her face in Cathy's bosom.

'Don't worry, Seamus. She's a bit of a grouch and she hasn't been awake long.' Cathy set Erin down onto her feet and attached a walking rein to the little harness she was wearing. 'I have to keep her on a lead because she has a fairly strong mind of her own.'

'I wonder where she gets that from?' Seamus winked at Cathy and they laughed together.

'I know. I'm convinced that she's pure Hannah sometimes. When she wants something she just won't give up. But she doesn't look much like her, does she, with her gingery curls?'

'Oh, I'm not so sure. Your mother's hair had strong auburn highlights running through the chestnut. But I see a lot of Liam in her, too. Nothing of you, mind.'

'Well, I shouldn't be greedy. Johnny is the spit of me and Daddy, after all.'

Cathy relaxed instantly in Nerano Road while Ellen and Aoife vied to be Erin's favourite auntie with stories, games and treats. Watching Johnny rolling about on the carpets with his sister or making her giggle at Tiny Ted's acrobatics was just adorable.

The next morning, Cathy and Johnny walked to the Maple Academy for the eleven o'clock rehearsal that Seamus had organised with the young violinist.

'Is she nice, Johnny, this Julia girl?'

Johnny shrugged. 'Nice enough. She's a much better player than me.'

Seamus opened the familiar green front door of the Academy and took mother and son through to the music room.

'Dear old piano.' Cathy opened the lid. 'Still here but looking a bit the worse for wear.'

'I know. I should get a new one really,' said Seamus. 'It gets a lot of punishment, at least three or four hours being pounded every day. We could go and use the grand if you prefer but I thought this would be a bit cosier for our first attempt.'

Johnny took his cello out of its case. 'An A please, Mama.' Cathy sounded the note and turned to look at her son. The sight took her breath away. Seeing Johnny with his head of long, silky golden hair bent over her father's cello, disturbed as much as it delighted. Cathy imagined her father at the same age as Johnny, on the brink of adulthood, playing this instrument with carefree joy, ignorant of all the sadness that lay ahead of him. She hoped that Johnny would never have to experience such loss and betrayal as John Fitzgerald had suffered.

There was a knock on the music room door and Seamus opened it. 'Come in, Julia.' Into the room walked a sliver of a girl in turned-up denim jeans and an enormous baggy green jumper with frayed cuffs. Her black hair was cut close to her head and her huge brown eyes dominated her gamine face. Cathy was immediately reminded of Audrey Hepburn in the film she had taken some Ballinasloe patients to see recently.

'This is Cathy, Julia, Johnny's Mama.'

'How do you do, Mrs Ashfield.' Julia held out her hand shyly.

'It's Mrs Molloy actually, Julia. Johnny's father was killed at the end of the war.'

Julia nodded and looked over to Johnny. 'Oh. I'm sorry to hear that.'

'But please, just call me Cathy.'

The Mozart G Minor piano quartet, which Lily had specified, went fairly well for a first run-through. The young girl was an exceptional violinist, full of intensity and flair.

'That sounds pretty good, don't you think?' Seamus declared. 'I wish you could play for us more often, Cathy. My piano skills are just not good enough, though we manage to play some lovely music as a string trio. We'll play the Mozart Divertimento for you some time – I used to play it with your mother and father, do you remember? We've had a go at this beauty too, but the piano part is beyond me. Why don't you take it away to look at and next time you're here you can play it with Julia and Johnny.' Seamus handed Cathy a copy of Beethoven's *Archduke Trio* which she flicked through.

'I see what you mean. Definitely not sight-reading material.'

After talking through some finer points of tempi and dynamics with everyone, Seamus took Cathy into his sitting room for a pre-lunch drink.

'I thought you'd have changed the colour in here by now,' said Cathy looking at the crimson walls. 'You said you were going to turn it pale blue.'

'I know. It's only just been painted too but, when it came to the crunch, I just couldn't do it. This room has been dark red the whole time I've known the Academy, and that's more than forty years now. I think your grandmother would have turned in her grave to see it go sky blue. Not a colour I ever saw her have any truck with.'

'Far too frivolous for granny.' Cathy took the vodka and tonic offered. 'So, tell me more about Julia. She has amazing talent.'

'She has and that's why I thought she deserved to come to the Academy so that she'd be able to devote time to her playing, like your mother did. Her father could never have afforded the Academy fees so I thought it was the least I could do. I'm sure there are hundreds of other youngsters out there who need the same thing, but I don't know them.'

'So, how did you find her?'

'Her mother, Maggie, was my secretary for twelve years before she died last year. That evil breast cancer again. Julia's father, Christie, is a postman, and a lovely hard-working chap he is too, but without Maggie's wages the family became really strapped for cash. Julia's brother, Aidan, had a place at University College to read medicine but was going to have to turn it down and find a job. So, I'm helping him out too.'

'You're so generous, Uncle Seamus.'

'Nonsense. There's nothing my money could do that gives me greater pleasure than seeing Maggie's children benefit from it – unless it's helping any of Hannah's children.'

Cathy took a long drink and then cradled her glass, before tentatively asking the next question. 'Seamus, forgive me asking – are Aidan and Julia your children?' Her face burned with embarrassment but she was relieved she had been brave enough to ask.

'Good God, Cathy. Why on earth do you ask that?'

'I'm sorry. It's just that … I've learned that people are often hiding secrets. And that those secrets can explain mysteries. And that things are generally more complicated than they seem.'

'Well, not in this case, lovely girl. I did love Maggie but only as a good friend. No, I never had an illicit affair with her. She and Christie were very close. He's still devastated at her loss.'

Having crossed a line, Cathy felt emboldened to go further. 'Have you never been in love with anyone but my mother then?'

Seamus smiled indulgently. 'My dear Cathy, after Ellen and I broke off our engagement I did live like a monk for several years. When your father died so tragically my hopes of persuading Hannah to marry me burst into life and I dashed to Rowanbridge to ask her – too soon after your Daddy's death though.'

'I remember. I was so hopeful that you would become my step-father and I thought that in time Mammy would of course say yes to you. But then Tricky happened. I couldn't believe it.'

'Nor me, as you can imagine. Ellen and I assumed Hannah must have had some sort of nervous breakdown.'

'I think she was under huge stress at the time. But there was a reason she married Tricky.' This felt like the right time to tell Seamus.

'I assume she felt some affection for him and that he offered a solution to all her problems. There must have been some attraction there or there would be no Bridie.'

'He did offer a solution but not the one you're thinking. She was pregnant by another man, Seamus, and Tricky, God bless him, was prepared to marry her despite that.' Cathy let the revelation sink in, while Seamus took a sip of whiskey.

'I think I can guess who the father was,' he said, 'and you're going to tell me that Father Stephen is also Fergus's father, aren't you?'

Cathy nodded.

'Well, I'm shocked but not totally surprised. Ellen and I have often remarked how Fergus and Bridie look like twins and so unlike you and Rose. Your poor father. Hannah must have broken his heart, as she did mine.'

'I'm sure that's the main reason Daddy took his own life.'

Seamus nodded. 'I, on the other hand, had a broken heart but I had not been betrayed. I got my head down and devoted myself to work. If it makes you happy, you should know that I have had several discreet affairs over the years, mostly with ladies met through the Dublin Orchestral Players. All pleasant enough, but at the point they start to get serious, I always back off. My rules are never mess about with anyone married or a colleague. So, even if I had fancied Maggie Delaney, she would have been off-limits on both counts.'

The week in Dalkey passed quickly. On the Friday afternoon, Cathy and Johnny walked over for a final rehearsal. Cathy had managed to practise the first movement of *The Archduke Trio* in Nerano Road and, after they had ensured the music for Lily's party was up to scratch, she suggested they give it a go.

'Come on, let's go and use the drawing-room piano. I'm looking forward to being the audience for this one.' said Seamus.

Cathy found it thrilling to play such powerful music with the two young players and vowed to prepare the whole piece for the next time they were together.

Next afternoon, she opened the lid of Lily's piano ready for their final rehearsal. Johnny set out music stands while her great-aunt wafted around, whispering to the two housemaids who were arranging flowers around the room.

'Now then, do you have everything you need, Cathy? I need to go off to have my hair done for this evening. The staff will look after you. Just ring the bell and someone will sort you out.'

'We're just grand, Lily,' said Seamus. 'Go and get yourself beautified - not that you need it, of course.' Seamus took Lily's hand and kissed it.

'Oh, you flatterer you, Seamus,' simpered the grand old lady. Cathy could see just how Seamus's charms might have seduced all those lady musicians over the years.

'Before I go, I hope you don't mind me asking, Julia, but do you have something appropriate to wear for this evening?' Julia was wearing her turned-up denims, white socks with sneakers and a man's shirt enveloping her slight frame. 'If not, Cathy can take you up to my wardrobe and you can pick something from there. Or perhaps Bridie would have something more suitable for your age. She'll be back soon.'

'Don't worry, Mrs Murphy. I do own a dress.'

Bridie was out shopping. She had taken up residence with her Great-aunt Lily in Pembroke Street eighteen months ago when she had started studying for her barrister's exams but, even after starting her practice and earning a salary, she was still occupying Lily's largest guest bedroom. The arrangement suited her and her great-aunt just fine, so why change anything; Bridie got to live for free in a splendid central Dublin mansion, with staff to cook and clean, and Lily got the company of a spirited and a lively young woman who shared her radical ideals and was prepared to keep her company at exhibitions and concerts.

After the quartet had rehearsed the Mozart, Cathy and Seamus left Johnny and Julia to practise their other pieces just as Bridie crashed through door carrying several Brown Thomas shopping bags.

'Hey there. How the devil are you, Cathy?' Bridie gave Cathy a hug and then ran her hands down her sister's body. 'Got your figure back I see.'

'You cheeky bitch. Got your bank balance back I see, spending your cash in Grafton Street, but why the hell not when you don't have to pay rent.'

'I know. It's a gas. But I do pay for it by having to be a sort of high-grade lady's companion.' Bridie beckoned them to follow her down the hallway to the morning room. 'I get to go to all sorts of amazing events as Lily's guest, most of them interesting though there's rarely anyone there I'd want to get much closer to, if you catch my drift.' Bridie gave Cathy a nudge.

'Why are Hannah's daughters all so interested in romance at the moment?' Seamus bemoaned as he sat on the sofa. 'It must be your age. Any chance of some tea for an old man?'

Bridie disappeared and returned five minutes later with a tray. 'Every time I see Johnny he seems to have grown six inches, Cathy. It must be worse for you only seeing him every few months.'

'Yes, I'd really like to pop over to Dalkey more often to see him. Maybe when Erin is a bit more manageable…'

'Johnny'll be grown up and gone by then, Cathy,' Seamus remarked, 'and I have a suspicion that becoming 'more manageable' may never be on Erin's agenda.'

Cathy laughed. 'You're right. I must make the most of him while he's still mine.'

'Is Erin walking yet?'

'Walking and talking a bit and generally being a pain in the backside. But, as far as Liam is concerned, his little chicken can do no wrong.'

'Well, that's as it should be. Fathers and daughters have a special bond.' Bridie turned to pour the tea and Cathy exchanged a meaningful look with Seamus. 'Bridie, I need to confess something. Yesterday, I told Uncle Seamus all about Mammy and your daddy … and Father Stephen. I'm sorry. I should have asked your permission first.'

Bridie swung around, looking startled. 'Right then. What must you think, Uncle Seamus? I hope you don't think too badly of them.'

'Certainly not. If anything, I think even more highly of Tricky. And nothing could change how I feel about your mother. Love is a force that's hard to destroy. But it must have been a shock for you and Fergus.'

'No, that's the funny thing; it wasn't. I think the reality of the situation had been seeping into our brains over years, even if we couldn't have expressed it as such. It was a relief to have the truth confirmed.'

Cathy decided to change the subject. 'Have you heard from Bill recently, Bridie?'

'Yep. He's having an amazing time. It all sounds very exciting. That Senator he started working for last year has decided to run for President. He's called John Kennedy, John Fitzgerald Kennedy. He's Irish too.'

******

By half seven that evening, Lily's drawing room was heaving with guests, of whom the family made up a small percentage. At eight o'clock sharp, an actor from the Abbey delivered Yeats's poem *Easter 1916* and then it was the turn of the piano quartet. The Mozart went well enough, but Cathy was relieved when it was out of the way so that she could relax and have a drink with Liam, handsome in his wedding suit. Julia and Johnny were now chugging through various bits of light music that no-one was listening to and, frankly, no-one could hear above the chatter. Cathy stood in the corner with Rose, drinking champagne, Liam's arm around her waist as he chatted to Andrew and Paul about keeping livestock.

'Just look at how slim that girl is,' said Rose enviously, stroking her still rounded belly, which had given birth to her third child, Joanna, only last summer. She was looking at Julia. The young girl was dressed in a cute polka dot dress with a cinched waist and neat black collar, and flat black ballerina pumps on her feet.

'I think she looks a bit like Audrey Hepburn.'

'I see what you mean, Cathy. And Johnny looks just like our Daddy,' said Rose, watching her nephew. Cathy squeezed Rose's hand.

'I think Joanna is going to end up like Johnny and have our colouring. Her hair is very blonde now.'

With the exception of Johnny, Lily's great-great nieces and nephews had not been invited to the birthday party - 'Far too grown-up an occasion for little ones,' Lily had decreed - so Erin was tucked up in Nerano Road, with two Academy students baby-sitting.

The two sisters watched Bridie follow Lily around the room, introducing herself to artists, actors and politicians with ease. Cathy envied her youngest sister's confidence. Fergus had plenty too, though he was over in the corner chatting to Ellen and Aoife with Hugo at his side. Hugo was now also working my pleasure. I hope Julia makes the most of her talent, unlike Hannah who married young and went off to have babies - not that I don't love all those babies, of course, but women should not have to give up their careers for families.' More applause and a whoop from Bridie.

'When I think of Evaline and Hannah, both dying so young, I realise I should be immensely grateful for every wrinkle I try to hide. I've seen such a lot of history fly past me in eighty years. Many things have improved but there's still one bleeding wound yet to be healed. I hope that, before I die, I will see a united Ireland.' Half the room applauded wildly. 'But, if I don't, I hope I can rely on many of you here in the room to keep up the struggle. Hannah's daughter, Bridie, is a young barrister doing what she can to defend those fighting for Irish unity from persecution by the government. I'll say no more on the subject; I know not everyone here agrees with me.

What I hope everyone can agree on, though, is that old age is a blessing to be appreciated – better than the alternative at least. I am thankful for my eighty years and I hope to have many more. Who puts it better than the Bard himself:'

Lily drew herself up to her full height and adopted what Bridie called 'actress mode', used mostly for complaining to shopkeepers. Her voice was strong and steady as she recited Shakespeare's 73rd Sonnet to the packed room.

> *'That time of year thou may'st in me behold*
> *When yellow leaves, or none, or few, do hang*
> *Upon those boughs which shake against the cold,*
> *Bare ruin'd choirs, where late the sweet birds sang.*
> *In me thou see'st the twilight of such day,*
> *As after sunset fadeth in the west,*
> *Which by-and-by black night doth take away,*
> *Death's second self, that seals up all in rest.*

In me thou see'st the glowing of such fire
That on the ashes of his youth doth lie,
As the death-bed whereon it must expire
Consum'd with that which it was nourish'd by.
This thou perceivest, which makes thy love more strong,
To love that well which thou must leave ere long.

Amid the appreciative applause someone started singing *'Happy Birthday'* and afterwards *'For she's a jolly good fellow'*. Lily beamed, looking around the room, drinking in all the warm wishes.

'Can women be 'jolly good fellows?' asked Johnny in the back of the car on the way back to Nerano Road.

'Well, if anyone can be, your Great-great-aunt Lily would be at the front of the line,' Cathy answered.

'Nah – Bridie, Bridie would beat Lily to first place, no question,' laughed Liam.

Chapter 25 - May 1961

'Just hold his head like this. Gentle now.' Mikey was helping Erin feed the orphaned lamb by bottle. She was sitting on the kitchen floor, an old blanket over her knees, concentrating fiercely on the frail creature she was cradling, her cinnamon curls falling over her eyes.

Liam rarely had to bring lambs into the cottage. They lost few animals overall, with Mikey's expert hands guiding most tricky births, and they hardly ever lost a ewe. Liam suspected the lamb's mother had already been sickly. They tried to get another ewe to adopt the little scrap of life but with no luck. Mikey was not going to give up on it however and was feeding it by hand, helped by Dearbhla during the day and Liam through the night. The whole time, Erin had been nagging to be allowed to take a turn feeding 'Curly', as she had named him.

'Okay, Erin, he's taken enough. Leave him to rest a while. Do you want to come and help me feed Rocky?'

If Erin had been allowed to, she would have followed Mikey around all day long, not just to feed the pony. But Cathy had instructed Dearbhla not to let her get in Mikey's way too much and, anyway, Cathy wanted Erin to get ahead with her reading before starting at the local school in the autumn.

Today was one of Cathy's two weekly sessions at Ballinasloe hospital, recently renamed St Brigid's, thankfully losing the 'lunatic asylum' tag. She loved coming to St Brigid's compared to her other hospital even though the journey was longer. It wasn't just that she felt the benign presence of Ada English as she walked along the corridors but she had created something she had dreamed of doing: she had established an actual orchestra in the hospital. Well, maybe not quite an orchestra, but definitely a decent enough band with a couple of professional musicians among the patients and a number of other talented amateurs including the addition of a few members of staff.

It was an unusual ensemble: only three violins, one cello, one bass and no violas at all at the moment. People came and left all the time. Right now, the band also boasted two clarinets, three flutes, a trumpet, a bassoon, a saxophone, an accordion and a harmonica, with several people competing to play the drum kit. She soon stopped looking for published repertoire for her eclectic ensemble and got used to writing out her own arrangements from a wide range of music: Baroque classics, Thomas Moore ballads, Irish folk songs and even some recent chart hits.

At both of her hospitals, Cathy had also developed burgeoning choirs. She believed that everyone can learn to sing and feel the benefit, emotionally and physically. Who cared if there were a few low grumbling noises in the background; it didn't spoil anyone's enjoyment and they weren't trying to win any prizes - although, wouldn't it be amazing if she could get one of these groups good enough to enter for the Feis Ceoil one year? she mused.

Johnny had entered the music festival on his cello for the first time that year and come second. He'd been a bit disappointed but, as Seamus had told him, he needed to spend a bit more time practising and not playing so much cricket if he was serious about his cello. Julia Delaney had, of course, won her category 'by miles', Seamus reported.

Cathy was proud of the occupational therapy teams she managed at her two hospitals. Few of them had formal qualifications but most were anxious to learn and it was amazing how many activities they were able to offer their patients, from gardening, cooking and painting to gymnastics and soccer. Not hurling though – the sticks might have been too tempting to use as weapons - and all the sewing patterns were already cut out, leaving just tiny clippers for the patients to use. Both hospitals put on plays twice a year to which patients' families and local residents were invited.

Cathy finished her working days feeling hugely fulfilled. By the time she had driven all the way home to Cleggan it was usually gone seven o'clock and Liam was waiting to eat supper with his wife while trying to amuse a tired and irritable four-year-old who refused to go to bed until she had seen her Mammy.

That Friday night, Cathy arrived home to find Liam snoozing on the sitting room sofa with Erin fast asleep on his lap, the orphan lamb wrapped in a blanket in her arms. Cathy smiled to herself; she wished she had her camera to hand. She gently shook Liam's shoulder and he woke with a start.

'Ah, it's you macushla. Give us a kiss.' Cathy lent over, her blonde hair swinging down over his face. 'Mmm, you smell nice. Careful now, do you think you can get the lamb out of Erin's arms without waking her?' he whispered.

Cathy gently moved Erin's floppy arms and picked up the lamb allowing Liam to stand up carrying Erin.

'I'll take her up to bed. Just pray she doesn't wake.' He crept out of the room and mounted the stairs, avoiding the loudest creaks.

When he came back down Cathy was standing over Curly by the kitchen fire.

'Fingers crossed, I think we might have the evening to ourselves,' he said holding Cathy and kissing her neck.

'Darling, just take a look at the poor creature. I'm pretty sure it's dead - or as good as.' Liam bent down and felt for a heartbeat. He shook his head. 'You're right. We've lost it. Mikey will be heartbroken, not to mention our little chicken.' Liam wrapped up the limp body in the blanket and they sat down to a sombre supper.

About three o'clock in the morning, Cathy jumped awake. She had heard a strange noise. She shook Liam.

'Wake up. There's someone down there. Did you lock the door?' They didn't always bother.

Liam got out of bed, put on his trousers and unplugged the bedside lamp. 'What's that for?' hissed Cathy.

'For whacking people.'

Cathy sighed. 'You eejit. Take Johnny's hurley.'

Liam went to the top of the stairs and listened hard while Cathy crept into Johnny's room and took the stick from the corner. Cathy followed a few steps behind down to the kitchen. They looked around; nothing to see. Liam put the light on. Nothing. They were about to take themselves back to bed, having agreed it must have been a fox rummaging in the bins when Liam glanced at the basket they had used for the poorly lamb.

'It's gone. Where's the fecking lamb gone?' They checked the sitting room too and the scullery out the back but there was no sign.

'It's a mystery.'

Defeated, they took themselves back upstairs. They would have to solve it in the morning. As Liam passed Erin's open bedroom door, he paused, gently pushed against it and stepped inside. He beckoned to Cathy and dragged her into the bedroom to share what was making him smile. Erin was fast asleep, her arm over the lamb in the bed with her. Curly was very much alive, chewing Tiny Ted's ear.

******

Erin was eating her boiled egg, the lamb asleep on the floor behind her.

'So, chicken, how did the lamb get into your bed? Did he climb the stairs to find you?' Liam wiped a drip of yolk off his daughter's chin.

'She said that Dearbhla kisses Mikey on the mouth every morning when they're alone.'

'Oh, Jeezus Christ Almighty.'

'I think it's lovely.'

'No, it's not lovely, macushla. Dearbhla is Brendan's sweetheart. He's on the verge of asking her to marry him. He's even bought a ring. And Dearbhla has behaved like she's Brendan's girlfriend for years, hasn't she – she holds his hand and rides on his bike not Mikey's. I've no idea what goes on upstairs at Mrs Gallagher's though it can't be much. Brendan and Mikey share a bedroom over there.'

'Well, if Brendan is like most of the Irish men I've known, he won't have actually told Dearbhla how he feels, even though he will have told her every other bloody thought in his head.'

Liam chuckled. 'You're right. I'll have a talk with Brendan on Monday before things get out of hand and tell him to get on with it. But, right now, I have other things on my mind …,' and Liam took the book out of Cathy's hands.

By the end of the month, Curly was out of the cottage and in a pen in a field. Erin wasn't too happy about this but she put some straw bedding down for him and she could still give him a milk feed twice a day to supplement the solid food.

'That's enough, Erin,' Mikey cautioned as she tipped grain into the little trough. 'He'll soon start eating grass and then he can come out of the pen.'

'Will the other sheep be nice to him.'

'Of course, they will. He's one of them. Part of their family.'

'Will he miss us?'

'I don't think so, not really. But you can come and visit Curly any time if you're missing him.'

They set off back to the cottage, the lanky lad hand in hand with the determined little girl skipping by his side, trying to keep up.

'Mikey, why doesn't Dearbhla kiss you goodbye anymore?'

Mikey gave a rueful laugh. 'I don't think Brendan would like it too much. She has his ring on her hand now, you know.'

'I know. I'm going to be a maid at their wedding next year.'

'A bridesmaid, not a maid. I can't see you ever being a maid to anyone, Erin.'

'But we can still kiss people even if we aren't married to them, can't we? I kiss Dearbhla all the time - and all my aunties and uncles, as well as Johnny and Daddy and Mama.'

'It's not quite the same thing. You'll find out one day.'

'I think we should be able to kiss anyone we want because it makes them happy. Dearbhla used to make you smile when she kissed you, didn't she?' It took a while for Mikey to answer.

'She did. But now I have to be happy that Dearbhla gives Brendan all those kisses instead.'

Chapter 26 – Christmas 1961

It was more chaotic than usual at Auntie Stasia's Boxing Day tea. All the Hughes boys were there, of course: Peter and Maureen with two-year old Cathleen, Mattie and Lucy with their three kids, and Paul, newly engaged to Siobhan, a reality that Auntie Stasia was learning to accept. Sam and Rose's kids were running around, madly chasing their squealing young cousins, but Erin could outrun them all.

At one end of the room, the younger men, plus Bridie and Siobhan, were standing drinking and swapping jokes, while, at the other end, Stasia sat with Cathy, Rose and her daughters-in law talking about the trials of pregnancy; Maureen was due to give birth to her and Peter's second child in March. In the corner, Uncle Edmund and Tricky sat silently, side by side in armchairs, puffing on their Christmas cigars, and looking on as Fergus and Hugo started to arrange a line of dining chairs down the centre of the room.

'It's lovely to see all the children having fun together, isn't it, Cathy? Even little Cathleen is managing to keep up.' said Stasia.

'I can't believe she's two already,' said Cathy. 'And she looks just like you, Maureen.'

'Even though she's named after you.' Maureen had let Peter name their first child after his favourite cousin.

'That's one of the downsides of us living so far away in the west, not getting to see the kids grow up.'

'It *is* a shame that Erin hardly gets to see all her McCarthy and Hughes cousins,' added Stasia. 'She must get lonely in Cleggan with no other children her own age nearby. Would you and Liam not think about having another?'

'I'm forty-one, Auntie Stasia. It's not going to happen. Anyway, it would cause a stink at work, now that I'm in charge.'

'It's not as if Johnny's at home very often either, is it, him spending all his time in Dalkey, and not even here with us this Christmas.'

Auntie Stasia still knew how to stick in the needle of disapproval. Cathy was sad enough to be spending her first Christmas without her son and didn't need Aunt Stasia to rub salt into the cut.

Last autumn, Shirley Ashfield had written to tell Cathy that Mam was not at all well. She was being sent into a sanitorium for a while but Shirley wasn't sure Mam would even make it through to Christmas. When Cathy shared the bad news with Johnny, he had wanted to set off immediately for England but had been persuaded to wait until his grandmother had recovered enough to leave the sanitorium. Seamus gallantly offered to take Johnny to Ollerton over the Christmas break and this seemed like a good solution, despite it taking Johnny away from an Irish Christmas for the first time.

Bridie was standing by the piano and beckoned to Cathy to come and join her. 'Hugo thinks we should get the kids organised in a game of *Musical Chairs*. We could get the radio going but it'd be nicer if you'd play.'

'Course I will. Clever old Hugo. He's very much part of the family now, isn't he? You thinking what I'm thinking?'

'I don't know. What *are* you thinking?'

Before Cathy could reply, Fergus clapped his hands. 'Now then kids, who wants to play *Musical Chairs*? Your Auntie Cathy is going to play the piano for us. This is what you have to do.' Fergus, Hugo and Bridie proceeded to demonstrate how the children should walk around the chairs until the music stopped and then find a chair to sit on. 'The only thing is, kids, there will be one chair missing, so the person who can't find a chair fast will be out. Now then, you bigger lads, just be kind and take care of the smaller ones.'

Cathy struck up *The Teddy Bears' Picnic* and the eight children began walking around the line of chairs, little Joanna and Cathleen holding hands with Hugo and Bridie. There was a bit of a scramble when the music stopped and Fintan was the one left without a chair, having made sure that his sister Anastasia was safely seated and, anyway, thinking that this was all a bit babyish for him.

'Such a gentleman,' said Stasia, 'just like Matthew.'

Cathy started playing again. Eventually, there was just nine-year old Elizabeth, five-year old Thomas and Erin left, circling the two remaining chairs like hungry wolves. Cathy played *Here we go round the Mulberry Bush* with averted eyes. She didn't want to be tempted to favour Erin, however subconsciously. When she stopped, she turned round to see her chairless daughter standing in front of a seated Thomas.

Erin gave her cousin a sharp kick and pushed him off the chair, making Thomas howl. Cathy ran over, dragged Erin off the chair, picked up the sobbing boy, rubbed his bruised shin and ensconced him back in his rightful place. Erin ran off, screaming, with Liam in pursuit.

'That child needs a good slap on the legs,' Cathy heard Stasia say to Maureen.

'No, we don't hit children in our house,' retorted Cathy.

'Well, that's only too obvious. You're going to have trouble on your hands if you don't discipline the girl. Such a temper on her. She reminds me of your mother.'

'Thank you for the advice, Auntie Stasia, but you can leave Erin to us.' Cathy followed her husband and daughter to the kitchen where Erin was bawling her eyes out in Liam's arms.

'I've told Erin that she was very naughty and that she must go and say sorry to Thomas or she will be put straight to bed.'

Erin bawled a little louder.

'Your Daddy's right, Erin. Come along. That was a very selfish and cruel thing to do to Thomas. You really hurt him. How would you like him to do that to you?'

Liam set Erin down and Cathy dragged her back into the drawing room, where Thomas was sitting on Rose's knee being comforted and eating a chocolate biscuit.

'Erin has something to say to you, Thomas.'

Cathy let go of her daughter's hand and stepped back. Erin drew her sleeve across her runny nose and looked up at her mother and back to her cousin.

'Sorry Thomas.'

Erin put her arms around the boy for a brief hug, and then ran back to Liam who picked her up. She snuggled into his arms and whispered into his ear: 'Can *I* have a chocolate biscuit now?'

******

'Ah, kids forget these things in an instant and bruises heal. Don't trouble yourself, Cathy. Erin is just a child with spirit – like your Mammy.' Aggie brought the platter of sandwiches over to the table.

'Yeah, his own brother gives him worse than that most days. He has to stand up for himself, doesn't he, Rose?' Sam said, as his wife came into the kitchen after seeing all the children to bed.

'The boy shouldn't expect to be attacked at a family party by his four-year old cousin that he only sees once or twice a year. We have to face facts – we've let Erin become a spoilt brat, and that's mostly my fault, isn't it.' Liam took Cathy's hand.

'It's both of us. It's understandable that you find it hard when you saw children thrashed at Letterfrack. I don't have that excuse; Johnny was always so easy.'

'Stop beating yourselves up,' said Rose. 'Thomas is fine and they're the best of friends now, splashing in the bath together and holding hands as I read to them all.'

'Well, that's a relief. Sit down now, Aggie, and you Rose. I'm making the tea.'

They were half-way through their second cups when the kitchen door opened and in strolled Bridie and Fergus, followed by Hugo a little way behind them.

'I knew it. That eejit can smell a ham sandwich two miles away,' said Aggie as Fergus immediately stuffed one into his mouth.

'Do you want tea? We need a new pot, anyway.' Cathy filled the kettle and emptied the leaves into the sink.

'Tea would be grand, but I reckon a nip of something stronger wouldn't go amiss. Can I go and get a bottle or two from the bar, Sam?' Fergus hovered by the door.

'Help yourself, man.'

'Make sure you bring the Tullamore for me,' shouted Aggie.

Half an hour later, everyone was glowing with food and their favourite tipple, laughing at the family gossip and in-jokes.

'Did you see Auntie Stasia's look when Siobhan gave Paul that massive snog?' said Sam.

Rose laughed. 'Let's be honest, Siobhan *is* a bit forward, which is why she's so popular in the bar. But good on them, I say. Whatever makes them happy.'

'I reckon Lucy disapproves just as much as Auntie Stasia but she hides it better. She's a proper headmistress that one, isn't she,' said Bridie.

'Which is probably why her children are all so well-behaved, unlike our monster.'

'Now, that was our fault, Cathy,' said Fergus. 'Stupid bloody game which makes all the kids losers except one. It was your daft idea, you know.' Fergus whacked Hugo on the arm, who looked momentarily abashed.

The clock in the hall struck eleven.

'Well, it's been a long day, and I have to be up at dawn just like any other day so I think I'll say goodnight to you all,' said Aggie, collecting the dirty pots.

Fergus came over and took the crockery out of her hands. 'No, just sit down for a minute or two, Aggie. I promise to clear up later, but I want to say something now we're all here together. It doesn't happen very often, does it.' Fergus stood at the head of the table. 'Bridie has nagged me to come to talk to you. To confess, I suppose, although I don't think I've done anything wrong.'

'Neither do I,' Bridie protested. 'It's just – I hate secrets.'

'She's right,' continued Fergus. 'We've seen how secrets eat away at people. Mammy and Father Stephen had little choice I suppose, but look what it did to them, and to your father too, Rose and Cathy.'

Fergus sat down next to Hugo. 'You all know Hugo and I have been best friends for years now. Team-mates in the hurling club, business partners in the farm...' Fergus took Hugo's hand. '...but we also love each other. I mean like lovers love each other. I mean... like we sleep together. You know, in the same bed.'

Cathy laughed. 'We know exactly what you mean, Fergus. I'll be honest, I had an inkling. And, for my part, I couldn't be happier for you both.' Cathy came over, put her arms around Fergus and kissed his cheek and she was swiftly joined by Rose.

'See, I told you no-one would give a damn.' Bridie linked arms with Hugo. 'I'm just furious that this lovely fella is off the market. I fancied him for years until I sussed out what was what.' Hugo blushed scarlet, laughed and put his arm around Bridie. 'Just promise me, Hugo, that I'll always be your favourite of Fergus's three beautiful sisters.'

Sam filled up everyone's glasses again and they raised a toast to Fergus and Hugo's happiness.

'Well, this is as close to a wedding as we're gonna get, I suppose.' Fergus threw back his whiskey but then spotted Aggie with her pinny to her eyes. 'Aggie? Aggie, are you okay?' Fergus went over and knelt down beside her. 'I'm sorry, have I upset you? I hope you can forgive me and accept me and Hugo as we are.'

'You great donkey. Now, why would I need to forgive you, for Christ's sake? I've known since you were fifteen how things were. I'm very, very happy you've found your special one and that you've told us all yourself.'

'Not sure I knew myself at fifteen. I've always suspected you're a witch, Aggie Carroll. Why didn't you tell me instead of watching me take all those poor girls out. Mind you, I was always happy enough to get my leg over. I don't hate women - or their bodies. Quite the reverse.'

'I could tell your heart wasn't in it.'

'It's not about bodies though, is it,' said Hugo. 'It's about who you fall in love with.' He looked over to Fergus and gave him a shy smile. 'But thank you all for being so understanding. Bridie and Fergus said you would be, but there's no way I can tell my parents. It'd kill my Pa.'

'Are you sure?' asked Cathy. 'Parents often know a lot more than they let on, but it's the Irish way to turn a blind eye.'

'What do you think our Mammy would have made of me, Aggie? Would she have thrown me out? And Father Stephen too?'

'Your mother always followed her heart even when it got her in a load of trouble. Your father too, obviously.'

'I'm sure Mammy and Father Stephen would have understood and blessed you both, whatever the church might say,' Cathy reassured Fergus.

'I tell you one thing that'll make you sad though,' said Fergus. 'There'll be no Fitzgerald babies. I'm the end of the line. Although, if it would make you both happy, I suppose I could find a willing woman and get her up the pole.'

Cathy thumped her brother on the chest. 'Given there's not a drop of Fitzgerald blood in you, what'd be the point of that, you ludder?'

'It's just a name, Fergus. But it will be sad not to see you be a father.' Rose stroked Fergus's cheek. 'So, more reason for you to be a devoted and generous uncle to our lot, and to Johnny and Erin.'

'And to mine - when they get born,' added Bridie. 'Hugo might be off the market, but I have every intention of capturing some boyo one day soon and having exactly two babies.' She laughed. 'That'll make Daddy happy too.'

'Does Tricky know about you and Hugo?' Aggie asked. 'I think he deserves to know, don't you? sharing a house with you and all. And he can keep a secret like no-one else.'

'Oh God. I'm not sure I can start that conversation with him. He must have his suspicions, although we do keep separate bedrooms, for Mrs Nolan's eyes.'

'Let me tell him then,' Aggie offered. 'There's very little Tricky and I haven't shared over the years. But, right now, I must be away to my bed.' Aggie rose slowly, stretching her back before giving Fergus and Hugo each a fierce hug and kiss. 'There'll be proper cooked breakfasts here tomorrow at eight if you three can get your arses out of bed in time.'

'Excuse me, Aggie Carroll, I will have milked sixty cows by then, but I can't answer for their ladyship and lordship here.'

'And I must get off to bed too.' Liam followed Aggie towards the hallway. 'I setting off home early, but don't let me

their Christmas trip to England, Seamus had allowed Johnny to drive the Jaguar for a short while along the empty, wintery roads near Ollerton. Seamus had advised Cathy that Johnny should not be allowed to have his own car until he was at least seventeen and Cathy had turned the advice into an edict. But that date was now only two weeks away and Cathy felt that Johnny was still too young.

'Don't fret, Cathy. He's an excellent driver and he'll only have the clapped-out Morris; it barely goes above fifty. You have to stop thinking of him as a little boy; he's a very capable young man now,' Seamus had said in answer to Cathy's anxieties.

It was undeniable. In the space of a year, Johnny had turned from an introverted adolescent into a self-assured teenager, still quiet but happy to speak when he had something to say. There was no doubt that the Academy had done this for him. Living a quasi-independent life away from his mother and mixing daily with forty other students his own age had forced him out of himself. Playing his cello regularly in public and playing cricket for his club had also built his confidence.

Cathy was looking forward to the afternoon ahead. She only had a week in Dublin before she needed to get back to work but she had come to the Academy every afternoon to play music with Seamus, Julia and Johnny. The day before, they had played the Mozart piano quartet again and, afterwards, Seamus introduced them to the Schubert *Piano Quartet in F Major*. Julia and Johnny were shocked to hear that Schubert had written it when he was even younger than they were. Cathy loved to play the piano back home in Cleggan but there was nothing to beat playing with other musicians. The week of music-making was a huge treat and Cathy was grateful to Liam for understanding that it was something she needed.

That particular afternoon they were planning to play without Seamus, and Beethoven's *Archduke Trio* was at the top of the list. Cathy had put hours of practice into it and she was confident she wouldn't embarrass Johnny. Nevertheless, after lunch, she took herself off to the music room and put in another half-hour, working methodically through the cascading runs in the last movement. Cathy stopped when she heard loud laughter and animated conversation outside the music room door, which then burst open and a giggling Julia ran inside chased by Johnny, flushed in the face but laughing too.

'Hey, give it back, you thief. It's not for you to see. Oh … hello Mama.' Johnny spotted his mother hidden behind the piano.

'Oh, I'm sorry Mrs Molloy. Didn't know you were in here already.'

'Hand it over, Julia.' Julia looked over at Cathy and then begrudgingly produced a sheet of paper from her violin case and stuffed it down Johnny's jumper.

'Hello, you two. Remember, it's just Cathy, Julia.'

'Sorry. We're so used to calling the teachers here Mr this and Miss that.'

Johnny retrieved the sheet of paper and hurriedly stuck it into his music case; he set up chairs and music stands and then took his cello out to tune up.

'That's a very striking skirt, Julia.' What Cathy really meant was 'That's a very short skirt, Julia'. The hem was at least six inches above her knees and the chequerboard pattern would make anyone's eyes go a bit funny. 'I hope you don't catch your death of cold in this weather.'

'That's why I'm wearing these as well, Mrs Moll… Cathy.' Julia pulled the very long, very thick black socks over her knees and up onto her thighs. Just as well you're not playing the cello, thought Cathy. 'I wouldn't go outside wearing it mind you - not until the spring anyway – but they're all the rage over in London you know,' Julia added.

'Wow, that is one great piece,' Johnny exclaimed when they finished. 'I don't understand how it can be so … you know… positive, when you think about all the crap that was going in Beethoven's life, his deafness and stuff.'

'You can hear the anguish underneath it all,' said Julia. 'I mean, it's not like his early violin and cello duet, is it, which is genuinely carefree.'

'Do you two play that? I'd love to hear it if so,' said Cathy. '…if you don't mind me listening.'

'Sure, we'd love to, wouldn't we Johnny. But I think we have better duets that we've practised like the Kodaly, or maybe the Ravel.'

'I don't know either of those, so you choose. I'll sit over here by the window.'

'Shall we do the Ravel then, Johnny? That's my favourite, but I'll have to go and get the music from my room.'

'Okay.' Johnny turned his back to look for his music in his case as Julia dashed off to retrieve her part.

Cathy watched him take out the sheet of paper that Julia had stolen, stroke it flat and return it between pieces of music. 'What's that paper that you and Julia were fighting over?'

'It's nothing. Just some stupid poetry I've been trying to write but it's for no-one's eyes but my own. I'd be embarrassed for anyone to read it – it's not even finished.'

'Do you read much poetry, Johnny?

'If I'm in the mood. I prefer to write my own though.'

'Your grandfather John loved his Yeats. I have all his volumes back in Cleggan if you ever want to borrow them.'

'We have them here in the library, thanks all the same, Mama.'

'Here we go,' Julia was back and brandishing her sheet music.

Cathy listened to Julia and Johnny play the four movements of the Ravel sonata. It was quite challenging, atonal at times, the second movement spiky and jagged, the third filled with grief but the fourth offering an energetic and upbeat conclusion.

'Bravo, you two,' Cathy said applauding the pair when they put down their bows. 'I can see you've put in a lot of practice. It reminds me of his string quartet at times but it's less lyrical.'

'We play all sorts of duets together, Mama, some a bit more up to date than Ravel, and some that we arrange for ourselves. Like this one.' Johnny began to play a slow waltz from memory and almost immediately Julia overlaid it with some harmonising flourishes.

'I recognise that from *Breakfast at Tiffany's*.'

'That's the one. *Moon River* it's called.'

'Lovely, very romantic,' said Cathy.

'Anyway, we'd better get on, hadn't we?' said Julia. 'We need to practice the Elgar for Saturday night.'

******

Cathy woke up on Saturday morning in the luxurious guest bedroom at her Aunt Lily's. She could remember jumping onto this bed when she was a little and her Mammy and Daddy were inside this 'magic ship'. They had seemed so full of love for each other at that moment. She sighed. She was missing the smell and warmth of Liam beside her. She had spent too many years sleeping alone in a double bed and hoped those times would never return and she was looking forward to getting home. But she would miss the wonderful music-making that had filled the past week. It had gone too quickly. Tonight would be a last hurrah, playing for Lily and the family.

'You simply cannot deny this old lady the joy of seeing Hannah's daughter and grandson play music in my drawing room as she did herself so many years ago. After all, I might not be here much longer to hear you.'

Cathy laughed inwardly at that remark: Lily would outlive them all. But it would be a treat to play for her. Maybe not so much for Johnny, but he and Julia had agreed to be part of it all with good grace, bribed with the promise of caviar and champagne.

Cathy hauled herself out of bed, wondering why Erin hadn't woken her already. She went along the landing to Erin's little bedroom but the bed was empty. Where was the rascal?

As she walked back towards the staircase, she heard Erin's chirpy voice and giggles coming from behind Aunt Lily's door. Oh no, please, Holy Mother of God, let her not have woken Lily. Cathy knocked gently on the door.

'Come in,' declared Lily. The room looked like a chorus girls' dressing room. Lily was sitting up in bed, wrapped in her silk dressing gown and sipping tea genteelly from a china cup. All around her were strewn scarves and gloves, bags and hats. And, in the middle of it all, was Erin, swathed in a black lace camisole trailing on the ground, a blue feather boa around her neck and a massive scarlet straw hat which completely obscured her eyes.

'Oh my God, I'm so sorry, Aunt Lily. How on earth did she get herself in here. I hope she didn't wake you.'

'Certainly not. I would have sent her away if she had. But I was already awake with my tea tray here, so I let Erin have some milk and we read *Irish Fairy Tales* for a while. Utter nonsense, but Erin likes them. When she got bored, I let her open my wardrobe and dress herself up. All children love dressing up.'

'That's kind of you, Aunt Lily, but she could damage your stuff.'

'The last time I wore that hat was the day you were born, on Stasia's wedding day, so it's almost as ancient as me. I'll never wear it again.'

'Mama, look at me. I'm being the Morrigan.' Erin growled and adopted a menacing pose.

How appropriate, thought Cathy: the goddess of war and unrest. 'You're a cheeky girl, Erin. Pick up all those scarves and bring them to me to fold away.'

'No, Cathy. Erin is not in the least bit cheeky. She just has a lot of energy and a vast imagination. We're the very best of friends, and the maid will tidy all the clothes away when I come downstairs later.'

Cathy and Erin were finishing their breakfasts when Bridie dragged herself down, still in her pyjamas.

'You'll never guess where I found Erin this morning,' Cathy greeted Bridie.

'I know. I sent her in there. She came into my room, looking for you and there was no way I was getting out of bed. If I'd thought she could switch on Lily's television set by herself I would have suggested that. For a bit of devilment, I sent her next door to Lily. She's always awake by eight even though she doesn't totter downstairs until midday.'

'You're a wicked cow, Bridie,' Cathy whispered, so that Erin wouldn't hear. 'She's eighty-four.'

'Ah, stop giving out at me and eat your rasher. I have to have a bit of fun, don't I, living here with the ancient one? or I'd go mad.'

'I don't believe you can't have plenty of fun with your own friends.'

'Oh, I make sure I do. Bill is a fantastic source of swanky parties. He's coming tonight you know.'

'Grand. It'll be lovely to see him again.'

After returning to the United States to work for two years on Senator John Kennedy's Presidential campaign team, Bill had been rewarded by the victorious President with a role on his inner team. And then, last summer, he had been given the position of attaché to the US Embassy in Dublin on account of his Irish heritage and his reasonable mastery of the Irish language, more, at least, than the Irish-American President himself. Bill and Bridie had immediately rekindled their friendship and accompanied each other to all manner of formal law dinners and Embassy receptions. They made a handsome couple. The sight of a black man in Dublin was relatively rare and this one was extremely well-dressed and good-looking. Most people assumed they were romantically linked, which provided convenient camouflage for Bill's sexuality and kept unwanted suitors off Bridie's case. Bill had become a very welcome guest at Pembroke Street and Lily revelled in her occasional invitations to the Embassy.

Cathy sat at the dressing table in her bedroom getting ready for the dinner. Colm O'Brian would also be joining the gang to play in the Elgar Quintet. Erin would *not* be joining them; she was already asleep next door. Bliss. It would be just a small intimate dinner but even so, Cathy took special care over her appearance. She put on the pearl and golden heart necklace that Liam had bought for her, remembering the gentleness with which it had first been laid around her neck. When she came downstairs, she found Bill alone in the drawing room, studying one of Lily's portraits.

'Hey Cathy, it's wonderful to see you again, and looking so well.' Bill opened his arms wide to give Cathy a hug. 'A lot has happened for both of us since I was last with you in Cleggan, you with a new baby and a new career, I hear.'

'Yes, but not exactly the world-changing stuff you've been involved with.'

'I've just been a tiny cog in a very impressive machine.' Bill handed Cathy a glass of champagne from the tray a waiter was holding. 'But it's certainly been a privilege to watch that machine in action.'

'Is President Kennedy really the demi-god he appears to be?'

'He's very much a mortal himself, Cathy, if you know what I mean…,' Bill winked. '…but one of the best, no doubt about that. He's giving all of America hope for a better future. And, thanks to him, I'm back in Ireland in a great job at the Embassy. My parents are so goddam proud. How is Liam?'

'Working too hard as usual. The fishing business is going great guns but he's desperate to get more land. He's obsessed with owning beef cattle for some crazy reason. Some sort of primal urge.'

'Oi you, sister. Keep your hands off my man.' Bridie had appeared and slipped her arm through Bill's. 'We make a fine couple don't you think?'

'Very handsome. When's the wedding?'

'Did I hear someone mention a wedding?' Aunt Lily had entered the room, her hearing as sharp as a pin.

'Just a joke, Auntie.'

'Well, I sincerely hope I live long enough to see you married, Bridie, and you make a bigger splash than Cathy did. I didn't even get to buy a new hat.'

'Sorry about that, Aunt Lily, but you did wear a very nice new outfit I remember.'

'And I see you're wearing the dress you wore that day, Cathy. It's lovely, but a little out of date now; I suppose it's only family tonight. Now, there's the door – that'll be the rest of the party.'

In fact, it was Colm O'Brian arriving alone. 'What's your guess, Cathy? I reckon it must be nearly thirty years since we were last in this room together. I hear you've been busy since I last saw you at the Dublin Orchestral Players, with a new husband and a little girl. Is she as musical as Johnny?'

'I'm not sure Erin will ever have the patience to sit still long enough to play an instrument or to practise, but I'm trying.'

'Johnny is turning into a fine cellist. I hope he'll join the Players when he's old enough. But that Julia is something else.

She is destined for great things and Seamus will make sure she gets every opportunity.'

It wasn't long before Julia and Johnny, with Ellen, Aoife and Seamus walked into the room. Lily stepped forward to greet Julia.

'How lovely to welcome you to my home again, Julia. I'm very much looking forward to all the music planned for later. I haven't had any musicians at Pembroke Street since the last time you played for me at my eightieth birthday. I must say, Julia, that is a very 'jazzy' skirt you're wearing. Is that the right word? Cathy, come and see – this is what all the fashionable young people are into.'

Julia was wearing the psychedelic mini-skirt again but this time with black tights and a white lacy blouse.

'Yes, very trendy isn't it? But I don't think a skirt that short would suit me, Aunt Lily. You need Julia's slim legs to do it justice.'

'Like mine you mean?' said Bridie. 'Though even I wouldn't dare wear anything like that.'

'I wear whatever I like. You all should too,' said Julia helping herself to a caviar canapé and a glass of champagne.'

'Come and meet my friend Bill, Julia.' Bridie took the teenager's arm. 'We did our law degrees together and then he went home to the States but now he's back and working at the American Embassy.' Bridie guided Julia over to where Bill was chatting to Ellen and Johnny.

'Ah, the confidence of youth. I remember,' said Lily looking wistfully at Julia's retreating backside.

After a fairly simple dinner by Lily's standards, they moved back into the drawing room to start the music-making. The *Archduke Trio* was first on the programme and it went better than ever. Then they added Colm and Seamus for the Elgar quintet, with Colm taking the first violin part. Five players and five spectators. This piece had not had quite as much rehearsal as it warranted but they reached the end in one piece. Cathy stood up from the piano and turned to look at the audience. The five had magically become six over the course of the quintet. Erin was there, sitting on Aoife's knee, sucking her thumb with Tiny Ted in her arms.

'Now then, madam, who said you could come downstairs?'

'Don't worry, Cathy,' reassured Aoife. 'She's been as good as gold, haven't you, macushla?'

Erin nodded solemnly. She knew she was pushing her luck being down with the grown-ups and she had crept into the room on tip-toe to avoid her Mama's attention.

'Back to bed now though, poppet,' said Cathy, holding her hand out to Erin while around her everyone helped themselves to drinks.

Johnny ran to pick Erin out of Aoife's arms and swung her into the air making her giggle. 'No, she can stay, can't she Mama? I'm sure she'll be quiet as a little lamb, won't you, monster? And I know for a fact that Tiny Ted loves a spot of Beethoven,' said Johnny giving Erin a kiss and a tickle.

'It's true, Cathy,' said Ellen. 'She's been totally hypnotised by the music, sitting very still with Aoife.'

'So, now I get to meet Erin,' Bill came over to Johnny and kissed Erin's hand which made her bury her head into Johnny's shoulder.'

Seamus handed Lily a brandy and sat himself down next to her. 'What did you make of the Elgar, Lily? I adore it.'

'I can see why. That wonderful viola part in the second movement is a gift. It's an odd piece. It feels quite modern at times, at least it did back in 1920, but then it lapses back into full-blown Edwardian romanticism.'

'I wouldn't call that a lapse though...'

'Now, if you want to play a truly modern piece you should give the new quartet from Shostokovich a go. The 8th I think it is.

Chapter 28 – August 1962

'**D**amn you child, stand still.'

'Cathy!' Liam didn't like his wife chastising his daughter, even when Erin tested the patience of a saint. Cathy was struggling to pin a little spray of flowers into Erin's unruly hair and the little girl was not happy about it. Erin also hated the blue organza bridesmaid's dress, cut down from the one Bridie had worn for Rose's wedding. She said it felt 'crackly and sticky'.

'Most little girls would be excited to be a bridesmaid and to wear such a pretty frock, chicken. You look sweet enough to eat,' Liam said, pulling Erin onto his knee. 'Is it a bit uncomfortable? I hate wearing this suit and tie too, but it's what we have to do for Dearbhla and Brendan's big day. Okay?'

Liam had agreed to walk Dearbhla down the aisle, which he was happy enough to do. Brendan had asked Mikey to be his best man but Mikey had declined; he told Brendan that it just wasn't in him to do it. Brendan tried to reassure him that he didn't need to make a speech – Brendan would be doing all the talking – but Mikey had shaken his head sadly, so Brendan had asked Frank, another co-worker, to do the honours.

Mikey had, however, agreed to play his whistle for the wedding alongside Cathy and Johnny. Brendan had requested Cathy's arrangement of '*Sheep may Safely Graze*' which he considered the 'music of the angels'. Mrs Gallagher asked for Gounod's *Ave Maria*, played at her own wedding many years before; Dearbhla seemed happy to go along with others' suggestions.

Cathy was looking forward to seeing Mrs Gallagher wearing something other than her pinny and slippers. At eleven-fifteen precisely, Liam knocked on the Gallaghers' door, while Johnny waited in the car to drive Mrs G and Erin to the church. Cathy had gone ahead to play music while the congregation assembled. Liam and Dearbhla were arriving on a pony and cart, all bedecked with flowers and ribbons.

'I'm gonna look a total eejit sitting up there on a flowery cart,' Liam complained to Cathy that morning.

'Stop giving out. No-one's even going to see you. It's for the married couple's benefit when they come out of the church and drive back.'

The front door opened and Mrs Gallagher stepped out; she was wearing a borrowed fur stole, despite the August heat, and the way she was walking suggested that her shiny high heels were a size too small.

'You look very glamorous, Mrs Gallagher,' said Liam gallantly.

'Thank you, Liam. I've done my best but I'm sweating like a pig.'

Liam helped her into the car and waved them off before entering the house where Dearbhla was sitting at the kitchen table, her posy of roses beside her and her hands screwing her handkerchief around and around.

'You look a picture, Dearbhla. Brendan's a very lucky man. Are you fit because it'll take a while to get there in the cart?'

The young girl stood up and arranged her fluffy white skirts around herself. It was obvious she had been crying. Liam made no remark, just kissed her on the cheek and lifted her veil over her face. Their journey to church in the cart took place in silence, Dearbhla holding Liam's free hand the whole way. When they arrived, the welcoming party of Aoife and Mrs Gallagher took over, holding Dearbhla's bouquet as she was lifted down from the cart, fussing over her dress, and smoothing her train so that Erin could hold it properly. Then they were ready and Cathy got the signal to start playing the *Wedding March*.

Dearbhla looked a great deal more relaxed after the ceremony, up on the cart with Brendan's arm around her, the pair speckled in pastel confetti. Erin thought confetti-throwing was ace. She climbed onto the little wall by the church gate with her Daddy's help so that she could scatter it over anyone who walked through. When her box was empty, she jumped off the wall, tripping over in the process, covering her knees and her dress with fresh mud, but she picked herself up quickly and laughed it off. Cathy captured it all on her camera.

The wedding reception in the village hall started off sedately enough. The combination of a mountain of Molloy's prime seafood and Mrs Gallagher's superb baking meant people's mouths were occupied for quite a time.

Aoife sat between Ellen and Cathy, shelling a prawn. 'I've known Dearbhla since the day she was born so it makes me very happy to see her married in the sight of God to a good man.'

'She'll never have a quiet life, will she,' Ellen added, '...but she could do a lot worse than Brendan Sullivan.' Cathy looked across the table to where Mikey was sitting with Erin on his knee. Speech-giving was not something that came naturally to Liam, but he had prepared well. He gave an affectionate tribute to Dearbhla, whom he had watched grow up; he said what a kind girl she had always been, how much Erin looked forward to her arriving every day, how much the family relied on her and how she had blossomed into a very pretty, young woman. Mrs Gallagher burst into tears when he talked about Dearbhla losing her daddy when she was only twelve, drowned at sea in a freak storm. Liam toasted all absent loved ones and sat down again.

'Here we go then. Hold tight,' said Ellen as Brendan got to his feet, took off his jacket, loosened his tie and cleared his throat.

'Thank you, Liam, for those lovely words. Yes, I'm the luckiest man alive to have this beauty as my wife. I can hardly believe I'm saying those words, and I wouldn't be saying them if your man there, Liam, had not taken me in, a crazy, snot-nosed sixteen-year-old straight from St Joseph's who knew feck all about fishing - or anything else for that matter. They don't teach you much at St Joseph's – only how to grab the biggest slice of bread and how to dodge a beating. I only had four years there but, Jeezus, that's enough for anyone. I'd lost my Dublin family and never thought I'd get another one, but Liam gave me not just a job, but a home, and then Missus Cathy came along and she gave me lots of love and care too and treated me to everything she gave her boy, Johnny. No difference at all. And then I went to live at Mrs Gallagher's and she became like a mother to me, and no, not just because of the pies, you smart-arse, Dermot,' Brendan shouted over to one of the lads.

'I remember my own mother very well with her red hair and Mrs G looks nothing like her but she gives great hugs like my real Mammy. And all the while Dearbhla was there growing up into this absolute beauty and she's always been so kind to me and Mikey and has come with us to all our gigs at the pubs over the years, and never complained once being on the back of the bike in the wind and rain. That makes her one in a million. I can't believe that I'm now married to her but I'll try every day to be worthy of her and to work hard and not drink too much and to get a car soon so she can stay dry. I'm part of her family now and I'm allowed to call Mrs G "Mammy". And one day I hope we'll have a family of our own and I'll never, ever take for granted that I have a proper family again and I'll love Dearbhla so hard that I'm thinking I'll probably annoy her sometimes but she won't let on because she's an angel.' Brendan took out his handkerchief and wiped his eyes but he wasn't the only one with wet cheeks.

'I've nothing to give her but my heart and the ring now on her finger, apart from one thing – and that's my voice. Instead of singing you a shanty or a drinking song, I dedicate this to you, my darling wife.' Brendan nodded at Frank who picked up his guitar and started playing gentle arpeggios.

'Bloody hell, he's going to sing her that Elvis number,' hissed Johnny to Cathy. 'You know, from last year: *Can't Help Falling in Love.*'

Brendan began to sing in his rich, baritone. Where he would normally have a rollicking, cheeky sway to him as he sang, he was now deadly serious, looking directly into Dearbhla's eyes. Halfway through he took her hand and urged her to stand up so that he could put his arm around her waist.

'Like a river flows, surely to the sea
Darling, so it goes, some things are meant to be
Take my hand, take my whole life too
For I can't help falling in love with you'

The hall burst into applause and cheers when the song ended and Brendan gave Dearbhla a long kiss.

'Thank you everyone, from us both. Thank you for coming, for being our friends. Thank you to all the people who have made it a special day: Liam for giving Dearbhla away; little Erin for being a perfect bridesmaid; Cathy, Johnny and Mikey for the music; and my amazing mother-in-law for the grub. It's such a great day for us and I'm thankful to be able to share it with you all. Now I have pleasure in passing you over to my best man, Frank, who's kept me calm, played his guitar and managed not to lose the ring.'

Three days later, they were still eating the potato salad from the wedding, so generous had the catering been, especially as there was no Brendan around to eat his share. He and Dearbhla had taken themselves off for a week to a Galway hotel, courtesy of Liam and Cathy. But life in the village settled down instantly. There were still fish to be caught and sheep to be tended.

'I've a mind to give Brendan a share in the seafood business, you know,' Liam mused to Cathy over supper the day before the newly-weds were due back home. 'He's done so much to help me build it. He was my first employee and now he's my deputy. I'd be lost without the man.'

'That would be a lovely thing to do.'

"All wealth is created by the workers so maybe you should give them all a share,' Johnny commented. He had just read the *Communist Manifesto* at Julia's suggestion which had reawakened his *Robin Hood* tendencies.

Johnny would soon be reconnecting with Sherwood Forest. Seamus was driving him over to Ollerton the following week to start out on a French adventure with Mam Ashfield and Shirley. Despite being frail, Mam had a fervent wish to visit Joe's grave before she died but Shirley had no idea how to make this happen, neither how to find the grave nor how to get themselves over there. Johnny, however, knew exactly who would help them make Mam's wish come true. Between them, Johnny and Seamus traced Joe's grave to the cemetery at Bayeux, where nearly 4,000 British military personnel were buried along with a few from other countries.

Ten days after the wedding, Cathy dropped Johnny off at Galway station. 'Give Mam and Shirley my love and tell them I hope to be over early next year. And would you put some flowers on your father's grave please? – from me.'

'Will do, Mama.'

'I have very happy memories, you know, despite the war keeping us apart. Your father was a real gentleman, solid gold, one of the best.'

Johnny kissed his Mama, got out of the car and ran into the station. Cathy watched him go then continued on to

Ballinasloe to start her working week. As she drove through the leafy lanes, lined with ragwort and centaury, she imagined how different her life would have turned out if Joe hadn't been killed, if she had stayed in England and kept working as a nurse. Johnny would talk with an English accent and maybe have several more English siblings. And what would have become of Liam? Would he be living alone still, a lost soul, or would he be married to some Clifden girl?

A week-and-a-half later, Cathy was preparing supper with Aoife, waiting for Seamus's and Johnny's return. Johnny had hummed and haahed about whether it might be more sensible to stay up in Dublin until the start of term but had finally decided that he would like to spend the last fortnight of his summer holidays in Cleggan after all, and Seamus was driving there anyway to bring Aoife and Ellen back home. Cathy was happy to see Johnny home but it occurred to her that perhaps Julia was away at the moment.

They arrived at just gone five o'clock. Cathy got a shock watching Johnny get out of the Jaguar's driving seat. He looked totally grown-up and assured.

'You're a brave man aren't you, Seamus, letting Johnny drive the Jag,' commented Liam as he came out to help carry in bags.

'Oh, it's been a godsend having someone to share all the driving with. We've been on the road from Ollerton since four this morning to make it to Holyhead in time.'

Erin ran out of the cottage and was swept up by Johnny.

'How's Tiny Ted? I hope you're looking after him properly,' said Johnny.

'He's asleep – in your bed. He said he wanted to be there for when you got home.'

'Come on, come in and have some tea now,' said Cathy but Aoife had already filled the teapot and was sitting with Ellen at the kitchen table.'

'Here. Mama. Take this, it's gingerbread from Granny.'

'Christ, we're drowning in cake. Dearbhla's made a chocolate cake just for you and we still have a big chunk of wedding cake to get through.'

'You can't drown in cake, silly Mama,' said Erin.

'And you can never have too much cake as far as I'm concerned,' said Seamus helping himself to a chunk of Mam's Ashfield's sticky deliciousness.

'Well, I'm pleased to hear Mam is able to make cake still – not completely incapacitated then. How did she cope with the trip to Bayeux?'

'It was tough in all sorts of ways, as you can imagine. Thank God we took a wheelchair with us, and I'm not sure what she made of the French food. What was it she said, Johnny, about the soup?' 'She said there's was enough oil floating on the top to fry a sack of chips in. She ate it all though.'

'She did. And she said that the bread was delicious,' Seamus smiled, 'but going to the cemetery was very emotional, for her and for Shirley. They got through a fair few hankies between them.'

'How did you find it, my love?' Cathy stretched out a hand to take Johnny's but he pulled his away.

'Oh, you know. Impossible not to be shocked at white graves as far as you could see.'

'Mrs Ashfield was outraged that there were some Nazi graves in there, wasn't she, Johnny? She didn't think it was right.'

'There were French graves, Italian graves, Czech graves, Canadian graves, Russian graves – you name it. Loads of other nations, but not a single Irish grave. I was embarrassed.' Johnny stood up and paced up and down the kitchen.

'Nothing to be embarrassed about, Johnny,' said Ellen. 'Ireland was in no position to be fighting any wars back in

1939. We could barely feed the nation and there was every chance of it starting up the Civil War again.'

'So, do you just sit back and let tyrants rampage around Europe and slaughter millions of Jews and others. You can't be neutral in the face of fascism. It's disgusting. I was ashamed to be Irish standing there at my father's grave.'

'Johnny, macushla, listen now,' Aoife's gentle voice intervened. 'The Irish government did what it could behind the scenes to help the Allies without breaking neutrality. Their hearts were in the right place – and thousands and thousands of Irish people joined the British Armed Forces, even men from the Irish Defence Force.'

'Fat lot of good it did them. They all lost their Irish pensions when they got back, didn't they, and were vilified?' Johnny's cheeks were blazing and he kept pushing back his long fair hair from his eyes as he shook his head in anger.

'And don't forget what Irish people like your mother did for the war effort in the medical services,' Liam said.

'You don't need to tell me what my own mother did, thank you.' Johnny stormed up the stairs to his bedroom.

'Jesus Christ Almighty. The trip was a big success then,' said Cathy.

'Don't worry about him,' Seamus said. 'We've talked about it a lot since. Seeing his father's grave meant as much to him as to Mam and Shirley, I could tell. But it's stirred up all sorts of thoughts and feelings that he'll have to work through. Give him time.'

Erin had listened intently to all this from the safety of her Daddy's knee but now she slid off and picked up a piece of gingerbread. 'This is for Johnny, to make him feel better.' And off she stomped up the creaky stairs, dropping crumbs as she went.

After they had waved off Seamus, Ellen and Aoife on Saturday morning, Cathy, Liam, Johnny and Erin went to the beach, to swim and fly kites in the warm August sunshine. Then Brendan, Dearbhla and Mikey appeared and they started a makeshift game of cricket. This is more like it, Cathy thought to herself; happy family times by the sea will soon make Johnny forget all the turmoil in his chest.

'Come back for tea, you three, and help us eat all the cake, will you,' shouted Cathy above the noise of the waves. They didn't need a second invitation.

'And how about we have a go on the Scalextric afterwards, Johnny?' Although he was now a married man, the child in Brendan was never far below the surface.

After she had cleared away the tea things, Cathy looked into the sitting room. The four supposed grown-ups were sprawled on the floor, each with a control for a little car, while Erin directed the competition, stepping over the track precariously, sometimes kicking a section out of alignment or picking up a car from its slot. But Johnny or Mikey would patiently restore them to their original positions and the car chases would resume. Brendan kept distracting Dearbhla with kisses which ruined her concentration and ensured that neither of them ever won a race but they didn't seem to care.

It was the Saturday before Johnny was due back at the Academy and Cathy was helping him speed through his packing. They were done by midday even with some 'help' from Erin.

'Will you come down and play for me? I never get to do that with just you, but you have your big cello here for a change. Erin will be happy playing upstairs, won't you, poppet?'

Erin ignored her mother and carried on building with her wooden blocks.

'Try this with me, will you Johnny. It looks very short and easy. I bought it because I thought it might be fun to play at the wedding. It's Beethoven's variations for cello and piano on Papageno's song from *The Magic Flute*, you know, the one where he sings about being desperate for a wife: *'Ein Mädchen oder Weibchen'*. Brendan reminds me of Papageno; a simple, hard-working, good-hearted man with a big voice, looking for love and happiness and his own Papagena.'

'Except instead of catching birds he catches fish.'

When they were halfway through, Erin appeared at the door and began to dance around the sitting room, Tiny Ted dangling merrily from her hand.

'I like that music, Mama, and so does Tiny Ted.'

'Wouldn't you like to be able to play an instrument, poppet, like Johnny or me? Maybe a violin, like Julia?'

They heard the kitchen door bang shut and then Liam opened the sitting room door, his face anguished and drawn. Erin ran to her Daddy but he didn't pick her up.

'What is it, love?' Cathy took his hand.

'Johnny, would you take your sister out to the beach for a bit. Please.'

'Swim, swim, Johnny. Let's go swimming.'

Johnny sensed that he needed to get Erin out of the cottage fast and took her hand. 'Come on then, trouble. Let's get you into your costume.'

Cathy put the kettle on and, when her children had left, she sat down at the kitchen table with Liam who was pale with shock.

'Come on then. Tell me what's wrong.'

'Here. Read this.' Liam shoved an opened envelope across the table and put his head in his hands. Cathy picked it up. She didn't recognise the uneven and naïve handwriting saying *'Cathy and Liam Molloy'* but, as soon as she unfolded the sheet of paper, her eyes darted to the bottom of the page. It was from Mikey.

'Dear Cathy and Liam,

This is a letter to say goodbye and thanks for everything. I have gone to join the corse of a free and united Ireland. I know you don't approve of the IRA, Liam, but sometimes you have to fight for what you beleive in. I shall miss you all something terrible – truely – but I hope to come back one day when we have won our freedom and then we shall all sing and dance and have our fill of scoops together.

I shall miss watching Erin growing up for the next few years. But it wont be for ever. Tell her that I am doing this for her, and for Dervla and Brendan's babbies when they come along – and for Johnny too. Please give Erin my whistle which is on my bedside table and tell her I expect her to be able to play me a tune or two when I get back.

Keep yourselves well now. I should say so much more about how greatful I am for what you have done for me but I hope you know.

May God bless you all,

Mikey

Ps Liam, I ment to tell you that the sneck on the gate to the field by the brook is hangin half off. It just needs a screw.'

Cathy lowered the letter. 'Oh, that poor dear boy. What must be in his head to go off to live with thugs and murderers?'

'He thinks they're heroes. Bigger heroes than me anyway, macushla.'

'No, it's nothing to do with you, so stop feeling guilty right now. It's because he can't bear to see Dearbhla married to Brendan, I'm sure of it.'

'It might be a factor, but there's more to it. He's a man with no-one in the world except all of us, and we aren't enough.'

'Erin will be heartbroken. She idolises Mikey.'

'Well, I'm going to find him. Brendan went off first thing, Dearbhla says, as soon as he found the letter to her and himself this morning. He reckons he knows where the men live who they give the singing money to – they're up in Mayo. She was waiting at the pier for me when we brought the catch in. She said she couldn't face you so waited to give me the letter.'

'Should you really go after him, my love? He's a grown man and must make his own decisions.'

Liam grabbed Cathy's hands and put them on his chest. 'Feel that. My heart pounding and my chest heaving. For as long as I take breath, I shall look for him. He's *me*, macushla; he's what I would have become if you had not saved my soul. And he has only gone because he thinks we won't really miss him, all of us wrapped up in our own little happy families. He doesn't think we care enough and that breaks my heart.'

Liam spent until late night on Saturday and all of Sunday crossing Galway and Mayo counties, visiting every pub Brendan and Mikey had ever played in, to ask questions and to get more leads. After Cathy dropped Johnny off at Galway station on the Sunday morning, she drove up and down every street in the city, hoping to spot Mikey's lanky frame outside some pub or by the riverside.

'Where are we going Mama?' asked Erin eventually. 'Are you lost?'

'No, poppet. We'll go home now.' Cathy knew she wouldn't be able to defer breaking the news to Erin for much longer and she felt sick at the thought. Mikey had gone and didn't want to be found.

Chapter 29 – June 1963

The barman placed the Manhattan cocktail down in front of the elegant woman sitting on a stool at the Horseshoe Bar in the Shelbourne hotel. Bernie O'Rourke took a sip, checked her watch, fixed another cigarette into its holder and lit up. She surveyed the clientele with an acute eye; this must be the best that Dublin could offer by way of fashionable society. Everyone was a little drably dressed but there was an air of anticipation nevertheless. She smiled at the red, blue and white bunting over the bar, which must have caused a frisson of anti-colonialism until it had been supplemented by Stars and Stripes flags. Dublin was getting ready for the arrival of John Fitzgerald Kennedy, President of the United States of America.

Bernie was nervous and excited too, but not because of the Presidential tour she had been sent to cover; that was all in a day's work. It was annoying that the First Lady had cancelled the trip, fearing for her pregnancy, but she had secured interviews with the President's sisters, Eunice and Jean, who would be accompanying him. No, she was nervous and excited because, at any moment, the schoolfriend she hadn't seen for over thirty years would appear.

The schoolfriend was feeling much the same trepidation. Cathy checked her hair in the car mirror, got out and crossed the street before walking into the Shelbourne Hotel. She'd been here before – it was one of Lily's preferred lunch venues – so she knew where to go, and, thanks to exchanged photos, she knew how Bernie looked.

A squeal of delight greeted Cathy and she was soon enfolded in her friend's arms. The two women laughed and looked each

'No longer a honeymoon, it's true, but we're very happy together.' Cathy smiled at the thought of their last evening together. 'Considering what he went through at that evil school, it's amazing Liam's as happy as he is and Erin is a big part of that. He is a driven man, Bernie, never satisfied until he has another boat or another field, but he'll always carry the scar around, and not just because of the bastards at Letterfrack School. His mother sent him away, albeit in good faith, but she sent him back after he ran away. That's hard to bear.'

'Does he not want to check whether she's still alive? Cork did you say he was from?'

'He absolutely refuses to entertain the possibility if I mention it.'

'But he might have family there.'

'Well, there they must stay. Come on, let's go and eat. I'm starving.'

******

Lily's breakfast table, two days later, was livelier than usual, mainly thanks to Fergus who, between stuffing his mouth full of sausages, was doing some excellent impersonations of Cathy and Bridie on seeing President Kennedy in the flesh at Dublin airport.

'Oh, he's so handsome isn't he. Yes, and so young and with such lovely hands.'

Bridie threw a piece of toast across the table at her brother which landed on the sideboard.

'Oh dear, oh no, Aunt Lily won't like that at all, Bridie.'

'Shut the feck up.'

'My sister is not at her best first thing in the morning, Hugo, as you might have noticed.'

'Anyway, there's plenty I don't like about JFK, like his attitude to socialists and Cubans in particular. But I'm not about to say that to Bill or I might get my invitation withdrawn.' Bridie was Bill's guest at the diplomatic dinner that evening. 'But I suppose he did the decent thing by laying a wreath to the 1916 martyrs. That'll have pissed off the Brits big time.'

Bridie wasn't the only member of the family hoping to meet the President. Before the dinner there would be a garden party in de Valera's official residence, and, thanks to Bill, Julia and Johnny would be two of the musicians there, along with Irish dancers and pipe players. Bill had also wangled an invitation for Cathy and Bridie so that they could witness Johnny and Julia's performance.

Julia and Johnny were totally caught up in the Presidential fervour. They had joined the welcoming party at Dublin airport, along with hundreds of Dubliners, all madly waving Stars and Stripes. Lily had opted to stay at home and watch the spectacle on her television, inviting Seamus, Aoife and Ellen to join her saying that it was the first time her new television had been of any value whatsoever. When the airport welcoming party arrived back at Pembroke Street there was much discussion about the President and his entourage and what the visit meant for Ireland.

'It was mortally embarrassing to see De Valera greet him,' pronounced Lily. 'The man should just retire and let someone younger with more energy be President.' Cathy caught Seamus's eye and the pair exchanged amused looks.

'Well, of course, I have a connection to the President,' said Fergus, filling up Lily's glass and then his own. 'I'm a Fitzgerald, the only one left in the family, aren't I?' He winked at Bridie.

'Mama was a Fitzgerald too before she married my father, and Auntie Rose too,' said Johnny coming to his mother's defence. 'President Kennedy only has that name from his mother's side of the family. I could claim it too – *and* I'm called John.'

'That's very true, young Johnny, but your mother forgot to give you that name, didn't she. So, I still win.' Fergus emptied his glass.

'No, I could just claim it for myself – that would be legal wouldn't it, Uncle Seamus?' Seamus nodded and Johnny gave Fergus a triumphant smirk. 'There you have it, people. Please refer to me from now on as John Fitzgerald Ashfield.'

'I couldn't believe the cheek of you, Fergus Fitzgerald, claiming to be the only one sharing JFK's heritage when you know perfectly well that you have not a single Fitzgerald cell in your great lumbering body,' declared Bridie, recalling the previous night's conversation.

'Yes, but they don't know that, do they. It's just us, isn't it? And Rose.'

'And Sam - and Aggie. And Tricky. Oh, and Uncle Seamus,' said Cathy. 'I'm sorry, I had to tell him.'

Fergus and Hugo set off back to Rowanbridge straight after breakfast. The weather looked rather threatening, not ideal for the garden party. Before then, President Kennedy would hold meetings at the Embassy before dashing to the Kennedy family home in Wexford by helicopter. Cathy knew that Bernie had gone to Wexford first thing with the rest of the press pack but she hoped her friend would be back in time for the garden party; she wanted to show off her talented son.

Walking into the grounds of the Áras an Uachtaráin that afternoon was intimidating but Cathy was with Bridie, and Bridie was intimidated by nothing. Cathy took courage from her sister as they pushed through the crowds of attendees. She spotted the little group of musicians on a stage some distance away and waved but she doubted that Johnny could see her. The band was already playing but it was impossible to hear above the noise of expectant Dubliners awaiting JFK's return.

The rain started up and the rush of air from the landing helicopter amplified the prevailing wind. People held back while Kennedy stepped down but in moments he was surrounded by swarms of well-wishers. Poor man, thought Cathy, how many hands must he have shaken today.

'Do you not want to try and meet him?' asked Bridie.

'No, I'm fine. Let others get to him.'

'That's your trouble, Cathy. You're too ready to let others push in front of you.'

'You go on over then.'

'Nah, it's okay. I'll get to meet him properly at the dinner. Let's have another cake and then I need to get back to change into my evening finery.'

The President made his way through the throng towards the group of schoolchildren who had performed some Irish dancing and the band of musicians. Before Bridie pulled her away, Cathy glimpsed John Fitzgerald Kennedy shaking the hand of John Fitzgerald Ashfield and she knew that it would be a special memory for him.

The following morning, Cathy received a phone call from Bernie.

'I'm sorry Cathy, but there wasn't much point me driving back to Dublin when I need to get to Cork today for JFK's visit there.'

'No worries, Bernie. I'm heading back home today so I'll be gone by the time the President's trip is over, but it was such a gas to see you. So much better than talking on the phone.'

'No, listen Cathy. Tomorrow, he's going to Galway and then he's flying back to the States from Shannon, so then I'll be free – and Galway is not far from you, is it? Why don't you get yourself and your family to Galway and maybe I can come back to yours for a night if I can change my plane ticket. What do you reckon?'

'I'll try. But even if I don't make it to Galway, there's nothing to stop you coming to Cleggan, though you'll be shocked at how rough and ready we are out west.'

'Don't be daft, Cathy, you know I grew up in a hovel until I was eleven. As long as you have an indoor toilet and hot water, I'll be fine.'

It took some persuasion to get Liam to give up a day's work to see the President in Galway, but Cathy told him that Erin would never again get the chance to be part of such a historic occasion. This was a ruse that Cathy tried not to overuse but she knew that Erin was the surest button to press when she wanted Liam to do something.

They were up good and early to secure a prime position in Eyre Square. Dominick Street was streaming with cheerful people heading over the bridge to get to the leafy Square, flags and bunting flapping above their heads. Erin was getting jostled so Liam lifted her onto his shoulders. He was glad of the warmth of her sturdy legs around his neck on this chilly June day. Erin was just starting to get fidgety when they heard the helicopters overhead coming down to land at Salthill. They didn't have to wait too much longer before the procession arrived in Eyre Square, President Kennedy accompanied by Patrick Ryan, the Mayor of Galway and by the Taoiseach, Seán Lemass.

'You see that man there, Erin, that's the President of America and the man next to him is our own Taoiseach, who leads the government.'

'Who is the man in the red coat and the big necklace. He looks the most important.'

'That's the Mayor of Galway, chicken, and he's just given the President a scroll which is the Freedom of the City, which means he's entitled to come to Galway any time as if he were a Galwegian himself.'

'Could you be the Mayor of Galway, Daddy?'

'I suppose so, chicken, but your Mama would be the one gagging for it.' Liam kissed his wife and Cathy slapped his backside behind Erin's gaze.

Cathy took dozens of photos of Liam and Erin with the backdrop of the stage and then asked the woman next to her if she would take a few photos of all three of them. Schoolchildren started some Irish dancing on the stage and Erin clapped along as enthusiastically as the President tapped his feet. More music and more speeches followed before frantic shushings when JFK approached the lectern.

'If the day was clear enough, and if you went down to the bay, and you looked west, and your sight was good enough, you would see Boston, Massachusetts. And if you did, you would see down working on the docks there some Doughertys and Flahertys and Ryans and cousins of yours who have gone to Boston and made good.'

Around them, conversations sprang up as to who could lay claim to a Ryan or a Flaherty or any other relation in America.

'It is strange that so many years could pass and so many generations pass and still some of us who came on this trip could come home and – here to Ireland – and feel ourselves at home and not feel ourselves in a strange country, but feel ourselves among neighbours, even though we are separated by generations, by time, and by thousands of miles.'

'You send us home covered with gifts which we can barely carry, but most of all you send us home with the warmest memories of you and of your country. So I must say that though other days may not be so bright as we look toward the future, the brightest days will continue to be those in which we visited you here in Ireland. If you ever come to America, come to Washington and tell them, if they wonder who you are at the gate, that you come from Galway. The word will be out and when you do, it will be "Cead Mile Failte," which means "one hundred thousand welcomes!" Thank you and goodbye.'

After all the excitement, it took no more than a minute before Erin fell asleep in her bed that evening, Tiny Ted in one hand and her Stars and Stripes flag in the other.

Cathy was up early the next morning, primping the cottage for Bernie. She made up the guest bed with the best linen sheets and cleaned the bathroom again, finally laying out fresh towels. She prepared that evening's dinner and cut some of the roses that climbed over the back of the cottage to put by Bernie's bedside. It would have to do.

Bernie arrived just before lunch, laden with gifts of wine and chocolates, marvelling at the beauty of Connemara which had taken her breath away.

'I had no idea Ireland was so gorgeous. Bit different from Rowanbridge, eh, Cathy?'

Erin ran straight up to Bernie. 'Are you American like the President and Bill? We like them very much. Can we come and visit you there? Do you have any animals?'

Bernie laughed and ruffled Erin's curls. 'Well, I'm both American and Irish – I have two passports – and yes, of course you can come and visit me in New York any time you like, though I'm afraid I don't have any animals, unless the occasional cockroach counts. I'd love your Mammy to come over. And you and your Daddy - and your brother too.'

Liam came forward to shake Bernie's hand.

'How do you do, Liam,' she said. 'I'm the terrible woman that costs you so much in phone bills.'

'You're Cathy's best friend who she loves very much so you're good with me.'

'Can I get you a glass of wine, Bernie – or a whiskey maybe?'

'What I'd really love is a cup of proper Irish tea, Cathy. I can't get enough of it. American tea is shite. I bought a load of Barry's tea in Cork to take home. My suitcase is rammed.'

Cathy busied herself making tea while Liam showed Bernie into the sitting room. 'You were born in Cork, I believe, Liam.'

'I was, but I only lived there for six years.'

'Until you were sent to that dreadful school.'

'That's it.'

'You might still have family down there in Cork. I could do some digging for you. That's what journalists do…'

'If I have, I don't care, so please don't trouble yourself.'

They spent the day showing Bernie the delights of Cleggan and took a picnic over to Inishboffin island. Cathy lent her friend some casual clothes but Bernie's footwear proved quite unsuitable for clambering over rocks so they ended up on a little sandy beach where Erin was in her element dancing on the sand. The little girl even persuaded Bernie to take off her shoes and stockings to paddle at the water's edge.

'Jesus Christ Almighty that is feckin' freezing, pardon my language.'

'Can you feel the waves tickling your toes?' asked Erin.

'I can hardly feel my toes at all, my sweet. I think that's enough of the Atlantic for me.' Bernie went to sit on the dunes with Cathy and lit a cigarette.

'It's all very beautiful here but I'll be honest: I think the view from the restaurant at the Empire State building is more to my taste. You can have too much nature although I see the little one loves it.'

'She's a wild child, in all senses of the word.'

'But is it enough for you, Cathy? Do you not get lonely?'

'I love it, Bernie. And I work with scores of people in the hospitals. But even when it becomes just me and Liam and the sea, I'll be ecstatic. You'll see.'

'Cathy, listen. I tried to talk to Liam about his Cork family but he clearly doesn't want to know. When I was there, I got talking to a journalist from The Echo. I asked him about their archives and whether it would be possible to trace the family of a lad who was sent away to Letterfrack School when his father died. He wanted to know the name of the father, his age and the year he died, plus Liam's year of birth.'

'Well, I know that of course. Liam was born in 1918 and I assume his father died when he was six because that's why he was sent away. His mother couldn't cope.'

'So there might have been siblings?'

'He's never talked about any. I don't know his father's first name either and I'm not inclined to ask.'

'Is there no birth certificate?'

'He has nothing. He doesn't even know his precise birth date, though Aoife and the de Bhailises always celebrated it on July 10th, the date they finally got him away.'

'They're a shocking shame for the country, these schools, aren't they? Who's fighting for the poor children?'

'There's Bridie for one. I think there are plenty of lawyers and judges starting to take testimonies. Senator Sheehy-Skeffington told Bridie that a man living in England, an ex-pupil, is writing his autobiography so that'll cause a stink when it comes out.'

'Ah, they're bomb-proof, the feckin' church. This stuff is known already but nothing happens. Let's hope the new Pope will tackle it. Perhaps you need fewer lawyers and politicians and more journalists to get these poor kids the compensation they deserve.'

'Liam's not bothered about compensation. He just wants the schools shut down so that no more children have to suffer what he did.'

Chapter 30 – November 1963

Johnny parked the car and walked up the street. God, that Morris Minor was an embarrassment but it would be his birthday in two months. His Mama was making him wait until he hit nineteen before allowing him something snazzier. He patted his breast pocket to make sure the tickets were still safely there, the hottest tickets in town, acquired thanks to Bill and his 'connections'. When his Great-great-aunt Lily heard that he was desperate to see the Beatles play on their visit to Dublin she commented that if he was really interested in contemporary music he should have come with her to see Stravinsky conduct his own music at an RTÉ concert earlier in the year. Johnny did rate Stravinsky, in fact, but just not quite as much as The Beatles. He wasn't sure what it was that was so intoxicating. Their music was rather crude harmonically , but he couldn't get enough of those raw fourths and fifths and the occasional modal flattening of the sevenths. He had bought every record that had been released since *Love Me Do*. His mother said it was 'his raging hormones' and in revenge he had played *Twist and Shout* very loudly every day through the summer holidays. Erin could now perform a mean twist with her brother. Johnny wasn't sure that Julia was as crazy about the Beatles as he was but she had jumped at the offer of going with him to the Adelphi that night.

Johnny was missing seeing Julia every day. She had left the Maple Academy and had just started studying at the Royal Irish Academy of Music, thanks to a scholarship and some ongoing financial support from Seamus. They had met up a couple of times at weekends to play chamber music with Seamus and some students on her course which had been wonderful. Johnny was anxious that his playing might not be good enough to keep at bay any other cellist Julia might befriend and had upped his practising regime.

Johnny located No 18, walked up the path and took a deep breath before knocking on the battered front door. He ran his fingers through his long fair hair and adjusted his collar. He hadn't known what to wear and had settled for jeans with an open-necked shirt, pullover and casual jacket. This was, after all, a first date. At least, it was in Johnny's head.

The door was flung open. 'Come in, come in,' said Julia hopping on one foot as she tried to get on her second boot. 'I'm nearly ready. Come on. Get in. Da, look after Johnny, will you?' And she slammed the door shut before dashing up the narrow staircase.

Christie Delaney ambled out of the little back room, puffing on his pipe. 'So, this is the famous John Fitzgerald Ashfield, as I believe you are now to be called. Pleased to meet you.' They shook hands. 'I trust you'll look after my daughter, treat her like a lady and get her home in one piece. I hear there might be a bit of a stramash down at the Adelphi tonight. Gardai all over the place.'

'Don't worry, Mr Delaney. I'll make sure she's safe and she'll be back here before midnight – at the latest,' Johnny added, seeing Christie Delaney's raised eyebrows.

Julia clattered down the stairs and presented herself to Johnny and her father. 'New dress. What do you think?' It was a short A-line dress in an orange silky fabric with a long golden chain around her neck.

'Very nice,' said Johnny.

'Looks expensive. Enjoy yourselves now - but not too much.' Christie sauntered out of the hallway.

'You'll need a coat, Julia. I'll try to park close but it's chilly out there.'

Julia grabbed a denim jacket and pulled Johnny out of the house.

'Your mother would disapprove of how short this dress is.'

'No, she wouldn't. Mama doesn't do disapproval; she'd just be worried about you getting cold legs.'

'Ha! Well, my mother would certainly have disapproved, but I guess that's one small plus about her being dead. Only joking.' Julia added seeing Johnny's shocked look.

'My Mama worrying about me is just as annoying as her disapproval. That's why I'm still driving this shitty car.' Johnny opened the passenger door for Julia.

'Still, it's a car, which is more than I've got, so stop complaining and let's go, baby!' They laughed and drove off.

When they arrived at the Adelphi they were practically swept inside on a tide of fans, all the way to their seats. They tried to chat but the noise level was so extreme they just surrendered to the experience. It was a bit different from going to hear the Dublin Orchestral Players. There were some warm-up acts but they could hardly be heard above the hubbub. When the Beatles finally appeared, Johnny thought his eardrums might split, so loud were the hysterical screams, but they subsided a little when they started up. They played most of his favourite tracks and he and Julia started dancing on the spot.

'She was just seventeen, you know what I mean,
And the way she looked was way beyond compare.
How could I dance with another
When I saw her standing there?'

Julia was eighteen, but the sentiments were a perfect match. When Paul started to sing the quieter *'Till there was You'*; Johnny slid his arm around Julia's shoulders and she didn't object. Song after song echoed his feelings: *From Me To You; All My Loving; Love Me Do.* Did *She Loves You* echo Julia's?

The audience went wild when the band tried to leave the stage and kept demanding encores but eventually it was all over and time to leave the theatre. That was easier said than done because the same size crowd trying to leave the Adelphi was now waiting to get in. It was total pandemonium. Johnny grabbed Julia's hand and she grabbed his arm as they forced an escape route through the throng, past harassed Gardai trying to keep control. Eventually they got themselves far enough away to feel safe. Johnny let go of Julia's hand.

'Bloody hell. That was mental, wasn't it.'

'I thought we mightn't make it out alive. But definitely worth it. I wonder what your mother and Uncle Seamus would make of *Roll Over Beethoven*?' laughed Julia.

'Ha! I don't think it was meant to insult Beethoven. Just getting Ludwig to make room for others.'

'Yeah, I'd be lost without Beethoven. Wouldn't you, Johnny?

'I would. I love lots of music but he gets into my heart and soul.'

'Whereas the Beatles just get into your pants, yeah?' Julia started dancing down the pavement, singing *Twist and Shout*.'

'What's your favourite song?' Johnny shouted after her.

Julia stopped dancing. 'I'm not sure. I like them all really. *Please, Please Me* maybe... what about you?'

'No, I can't choose. It's different every day.'

They got into the car and drove back to Finglas.

'Thanks for giving me the ticket, Johnny and for picking me up and dropping me home. It's way out of your way. I'm very grateful. I never would have got in without you and your fancy friends. First the President of America and now the Beatles. I'm not sure which I preferred. But we're very lucky, aren't we?'

'We're living in amazing times. The world can only get better, don't you think?'

Julia was silent for a few moments. 'I would say yes, if my Mammy was here to see it all with me.'

Johnny wanted to take Julia's hand but he couldn't find the courage.

They arrived at the Delaney home before half past ten. 'There you go. I think your father will be pleased that you're home safe and sound if he's been listening to the news tonight. I hope no-one's been hurt in the scrum.'

'Goodnight then, Johnny. I'll see you next weekend at the Academy, right, yeah? We're doing Janáček's 2nd string quartet, Uncle Seamus's latest purchase. I tell you what, the Maple Academy is way ahead of the Royal Academy. We just do standard repertoire: Haydn, then Mozart, then Haydn again, then, if we're lucky, maybe some Schubert.' Julia sat, not talking but not getting out of the car, just looking at Johnny.

'Are you missing something, Julia?'

'Nope, I have everything I came out with. I'll be off then.' Julia got out but, no sooner had she slammed the door shut, she opened it again. 'I've changed my mind. I think *All my Loving* is my favourite song.' Julia knelt on the passenger seat and stretched over to kiss Johnny full on the lips.

Julia got out of the car again, ran up the garden path and waved before going inside.

'Close your eyes and I'll kiss you
Tomorrow I'll miss you
Remember I'll always be true'

'Damn and blast,' Johnny groaned inwardly, as he drove back south through the city. 'I should have been the one kissing her.' Then a wide smile crept over his face.

******

Saturday afternoon, only two weeks later, Johnny was sitting in the music room at the Academy, playing a melancholy Bach *Sarabande*, waiting for Julia to arrive with another violinist from the Royal Academy to play string quartets with Seamus. He didn't think he could bear to play the Debussy they had lined up for today but the *Sarabande* fitted his mood. Last night, Seamus had come to his bedroom to deliver Bridie's dreadful news: President Kennedy was dead, shot by a lone madman, while being driven through Dallas. Johnny had phoned Bridie straight back but she was not at Pembroke Street, according to the maid, and Mrs Murphy had gone off to bed early after seeing the terrible news on the television. Johnny phoned his mother; Cathy knew nothing as she neither listened to the radio nor owned a television, but she had cried down the phone to him.

'That gracious man, dead? I can't believe it. Why must some people destroy what is noble and good? What is it that they cannot allow to exist?' She had asked between her tears.

Johnny had no answers but told his mother that he loved them all to bits, that he would see them soon and to remember that the world was still mostly full of good people. But his eyes were full of tears too when he put the phone, leaving his Mama to call Bernie in New York.

The door opened silently behind him. Julia stood listening to the *Sarabande* until Johnny had finished.

'That was beautiful. Can I have a hug now please.'

Johnny put down his cello and threw his arms around Julia. They held each other for a long time, swaying gently together and reminiscing about the time they had shaken hands with the inspiring man who had just been assassinated.

'I wanted to see you but I don't want to play. I've told Uncle Seamus. The pictures on TV would break your heart, Johnny – Mrs Kennedy there trying to hold his head together, her suit all covered in blood. My Da is sad about it, of course, but he really doesn't get it, the crushing of dreams, but I knew you'd understand, Johnny.'

'Come on. Let's go and make a drink. Then we can listen to some music.'

Johnny searched through his record collection while Julia lay on his bed drinking coffee. 'I don't have much American music, just this record of Copland.' They listened first to *Fanfare for a Common Man* and then *Appalachian Spring*.

'Such optimism in that music. That's what comes to me when I think of America: energy and hope, not hatred,' Julia said, draining her cup.

'Let's hope the American people don't let the dream die. There's a poem I think that sums it up.' Johnny rifled through the books on his shelf. 'Yes, here you go; Longfellow's *A Psalm of Life* it's called.' He passed the book over to Julia. She studied it intently and then read out a passage:

> *'Lives of great men all remind us*
> *We can make our lives sublime,*
> *And, departing, leave behind us*
>
> *Footprints on the sands of time;*
>
> *Footprints, that perhaps another,*
> *Sailing o'er life's solemn main,*
> *A forlorn and shipwrecked brother,*
> *Seeing, shall take heart again.'*

'Do you see? President Kennedy has left his footprints on the sands of time and it's up to all of us left behind to keep going and to make his hopes for the world a reality.' Johnny took the book back from Julia.

'Maybe, but there's no way I feel like that today, Johnny. Today, I just need to be sad. I need to listen to the Bach *Chaconne* and have a good blub. Have you got any clean hankies? Mine is sopping.'

Johnny found Julia a freshly ironed handkerchief and unearthed his record of Bach *Partitas*. Once it was playing, he agonised whether to sit at his desk or on the floor, but, in the end, he braved the bed, wrapping his arms around Julia as she wept her way through to lunchtime.

Looking at all the coverage in the papers, in particular the photographs of a devastated Jacqueline Kennedy with her young family, Cathy relived the moment she had heard that Joe had been shot, leaving her a widow with a baby to protect. Cathy rang Bernie every day for the next week as all the shocking repercussions unfolded. Kennedy's assassin, caught soon after the Dallas shooting, was himself shot two days later, live on the television, despite being in police custody. Bernie shared all the fears and theories that were springing up privately and in public across America: was there a second gunman maybe who had fired a fourth shot? was Jack Ruby acting on the orders of the CIA when he shot Lee Harvey Oswald? Conspiracy stories, whether blaming Russia, Cuba, the Mafia or right-wing groups within the USA itself, grew like mould on bread.

'Nature abhors a vacuum, Cathy,' Bernie had said. 'It's a challenge for journalists. Should we air the theories or suppress them? Should we follow every crazy idea down a rabbit-hole until we can rule it out? Anyway, it's keeping Harry very busy and selling a shedload of newspapers.'

In Ireland, a national day of mourning was declared. JFK had called himself an Irishman and his compatriots grieved for him as one. Aoife attended mass every day for a week and Ellen even accompanied her on the first Sunday. 'Why the hell do I feel the need to do this?' she had complained, but Aoife understood. Aoife lit more than two dozen candles over the week and paid for a mass to be dedicated to JFK's memory.

Bill Kenny was inconsolable; he came to dinner with Lily and Bridie most nights to talk and talk through the nightmare.

Bill had worked so hard, for so long, to get this talented man into the White House, only to see him wiped out after less than three years. Bill had little time for Lyndon Johnson and was not hopeful for the future of the Democratic Party.

In Rowanbridge, they paid respects to the dead President in their own ways: the Hughes family all attended special masses and Stasia wore black for a week; Sam put up a framed photograph of President Kennedy in the bar; Rose indulged the kids in small ways; Aggie drank a little more Tullamore Dew than usual up in her bedroom, humming *'Unforgettable'* to Nat King Cole on the radio; Fergus and Hugo, who had been part of that joyful welcoming crowd at Dublin airport a mere five months before, held each other closer at night, realising that death can come out of nowhere, even to fine young men like them.

The first few days after the assassination, Johnny turned to music – more Bach *Cello Suites* – and poetry – lots of Yeats, Dickinson and Shelley. But the Wednesday after the day of mourning, he got out of bed full of energy and decided he needed to do something, something to make things better. As soon as Academy lessons finished, he went for a run along Killiney beach, then he tidied his room before supper, sorting through his books and rearranging his shelves accompanied by the Beatles blaring out from his record player.

Just as Seamus was making his way to bed, Johnny stopped him in the corridor and asked permission to use the phone in Seamus's private sitting room. 'I promised to ring Mama,' he lied.

Thankfully, Julia was still awake and picked up the phone instantly.

'Hey you.'

'Hey you too. What's wrong, apart from the obvious?'

'Nothing's wrong. I just wanted to hear your voice.'

'Well, here I am. What do you want me to say?'

'Just answer this question please: do you remember when we went to hear The Beatles back in June and, when I dropped you home, you kissed me – on the lips?'

There was a pause. 'Sure. I remember.'

'Were you kissing me as a friend, or maybe as someone who might be your boyfriend?'

'I think that's for you to work out for yourself, Johnny. Night, night now.'

'Wait, wait. What are you doing this Saturday? Do you want to go to the pictures?'

'What's on?'

'I dunno. There'll be something. But I think we should have more fun, don't you? I love playing chamber music with you but that's quite serious. We could just go for a walk maybe if the weather is okay here in Dalkey – or I could drive us into the Wicklow mountains or something.'

'I'm busy in the day, Johnny. I have to do the housework here you know, and then in the afternoon I've got orchestra rehearsals. But maybe Sunday afternoon…'

'Okay, it's a date. I mean literally, Julia. It's a date date.'

Julia laughed down the phone. 'You eejit. Go on, get yourself to bed and I'll see you Sunday afternoon. Three o'clock, yeah.' And she put down the phone.

Johnny was up early on Saturday. He had to get into central Dublin to make a very important purchase and then he needed to get all his homework finished before tomorrow. Maths, physics and chemistry, plus literature and Irish for his leaving cert all of which Uncle Seamus said he would sail through. But he wanted to get the best grades he could so that he could have the pick of universities. Johnny was fairly certain he would choose to stay in Dublin and go to Trinity if he got the right grades but Seamus and Ellen were nagging him to try for Oxford or Cambridge. They urged him to visit Cambridge to have a look around because they had an old Maple Academy schoolfriend there, Daniel Brookman, who was now a Professor of Maths. Johnny realised that this Professor Brookman would also have studied with his grandmother, Hannah. Johnny was certainly tempted by the thought of Cambridge, but Julia would be in Dublin and the Royal Academy of Music was just around the corner from Trinity.

Julia was wearing jeans, boots, and duffle coat when she ran out of the house on Sunday.

'Where are you taking me to, then? I thought I'd put on plenty of clothes just in case.'

'We've only got a couple of hours before the light goes so I thought a walk along Dollymount Strand would be fun. I can drive the car right onto the sand. It's not as beautiful as the beaches around Cleggan but it's the best I can do.'

They drove over the narrow wooden bridge onto Bull Island and then over to the strand itself.

'How about we just sit in the car and watch the birds,' said Julia. 'It looks feckin' cold out there.'

'No, come on. Move your arse for a while.'

'Okay. As long as you don't expect me to paddle.'

They walked a mile along the shore, sharing Johnny's bar of chocolate, laughing about stupid things: teachers and students at the Maple Academy mainly, how Johnny's hair was twice as long and twice as feminine as Julia's, and then more serious discussion about the aftermath of JFK's assassination. The sky was a deep smoky blue when they turned to walk back to the car. Julia put her arm through Johnny's and slipped her hand into his coat pocket. 'Forgot my gloves like a complete dope.' When they came within sight of the car, Julia stopped and turned to Johnny. 'So, what makes this a date then?'

'Was the chocolate not enough? Here, have a nip of this.' Johnny took the hip flask that he had pinched from his Uncle Seamus's desk that morning out of his other pocket. 'It's brandy, so go easy.' Julia took a long draught and then ran away from Johnny, teasing him by holding the flask in the air. They were both laughing hysterically when they got inside the car and Julia passed over the brandy for Johnny to take a swig. The sky was now inky blue and, when Johnny switched on the engine, his headlights shone out across the water to infinity.

'Well, I reckon it's a date because I am going to ask if I may kiss you… like this.' Their brandy-tinged mouths found each other in the dusk and stayed together for some time. 'Pretty good kissing, Johnny Fitzgerald Ashfield. Who've you been practising on?'

'You know damn well you're first girl I've ever kissed. I've been imagining what it would be like.'

'Well, did it live up to your expectations?'

'Way exceeded them,' and Johnny kissed Julia again, this time stroking her cheek, her neck and nearly down to her breasts.

'It's okay, you can touch them. And can I touch you … here?' Julia placed her icy hand over Johnny's swelling crotch; he moaned. Eventually, Julia pulled away.

'This is all great fun – happy to do this any time with you Johnny – but, I have to tell you, I don't want a boyfriend.'

'That's okay,' said Johnny sliding his hand under the duffle coat and squeezing her left breast as he kissed her again.

'No, I mean it. I'm not going to get serious with anyone. I have to study hard now I've got into the Royal Academy.'

'I know. Me too. But isn't it nice to have a friend you can play Beethoven with *and* have a snog with?'

'Yeah, I suppose so.'

They arrived back in Finglas not much later than six o'clock but with an empty hip flask and sore lips.

'Here, I got you this.' Johnny reached into the glove compartment and took out a small disc in a paper bag. 'I was first in the queue at Tara Records yesterday and I spent all day listening to it. I want you to listen to the words now and imagine it's me singing them to you.'

Julia slipped the disc out of the bag; it was a copy of The Beatles new single, *I Wanna Hold Your Hand*, released only the day before.

'Great. I heard it on the radio yesterday while I was mopping the kitchen floor. But I'll listen properly, I promise.'

Johnny took Julia's hand and kissed it before she hopped out of the car and waved him off. All the way back to Dalkey he sang to himself, a big fat smile playing over his face.

'And when I touch you I feel happy inside.
It's such a feeling that my love I can't hide.'

Chapter 31 - February 1964

'Oh God, I love this. Have you heard it?' Johnny turned up the car radio and started singing along to Bob Dylan.

'Your sons and your daughters
Are beyond your command
Your old road is rapidly agin'
Please get out of the new one
If you can't lend your hand
For the times they are a-changin''

'It's so true, don't you think?' Johnny looked questioningly at Julia. 'If the old guard can't make the world a better place, they just need to feck off and leave it to us. Dylan is such a great poet. I've decided I'm going to buy a guitar so I can sing his songs. It can't be that hard to learn.'

'Just listen to yourself John Fitzgerald Ashfield, peaching revolution while sitting here in your new car bought for you with your mother's money, talking about buying yourself a guitar like it was a pack of chewing gum, educated privately at a fancy school, with enough free time to play music and cricket at the weekend rather than have to get a Saturday job. And I bet you've already bought the new Dylan album.'

'You went to the same school as me.'

'Yes, but only thanks to the patronage of Uncle Seamus. It shouldn't have to be that way. You have no idea what it's like to be from the real working class like my Dada: up at five and in bed by nine every day and paid such a pittance that he couldn't dream of getting a car, or even a guitar. When was the last time you did any manual work, eh? At least I wash and iron my own clothes and clean my own shit off the lav.'

Johnny laughed and bent over to kiss Julia. 'Fair point, Comrade, but unless the middle classes join in the struggle we'll never change the system.'

'I agree, but it's only when they make a real sacrifice, give up some right or thing that they own or are entitled to that it'll be more than hot air.'

'Well, I'm prepared to give up my slice of pork pie if you'd like it.'

'Eejit!' Julia gently punched Johnny on the chin and then kissed him.

They had driven out to the Wicklow Mountains on this frosty February Sunday. Johnny had been waiting at the church to pick up Julia from early mass in his new – well, new to him – Ford Corsair. When his nineteenth birthday had come around last month, Cathy had said there was no way she was buying him an Alfa Romeo; he'd have to wait and do that with money he had earned himself. But Johnny was thrilled to be rid of the Morris Minor and to be the owner of a scarlet machine that could actually reach seventy in less than ten seconds. They were now parked on a road with a breath-taking view of Glendalough beneath them, eating a makeshift picnic that Johnny had filched from the Academy's fridge that morning.

'Are we going to have this walk then? I'd be quite happy to stay in the car.' Julia turned up the heater and brushed crumbs off her jumper.

'Come on. It's stunning down there and we have the place almost to ourselves.'

'That's because most people are not insane enough to let themselves freeze to death by an isolated lake.'

'I won't let you freeze.'

They walked for two hours, down the slippery hill path towards the water and along the lakeside towards the monastery buildings and ruins, Julia clinging onto Johnny to save herself from falling and Johnny holding Julia's hand or putting his arm around her shoulders or waist at any opportunity. The orange sun was just about to disappear behind a mountain when they began the trek back up to the car.

'It's sad to think that the goodness and optimism of those early monks has been so corrupted by today's church,' said Johnny, thinking of Liam, Brendan and Mikey.

'That's a bit harsh. I know your stepfather had a rough time but our parish priest is a lovely old soul.'

'Do you believe all that God nonsense?'

'If I say yes, you'll think I'm stupid, but if I say no, you'll see I'm a hypocrite.' Julia took Johnny's hand as she jumped over a brook. 'I go to mass because I want to be with my Da and it makes me feel closer to my Mammy. I don't want to pick at the threads too much, you know, in case it all unravels and I have to confront the fact that I'll probably never see her again. Come on, race you back.'

Julia charged up the hill towards the road but, seeing a more direct route over a field, she veered off only to find herself knee-deep in a reedy bog with two bemused sheep looking on. If she'd asked them, they'd have warned her not to go near anywhere with reeds in it. Johnny hooted with laughter but when he went over to help Julia scramble out, he had a clod of mud hurled at him for his pains.

'Do you want to stay in there all night then?'

'Fuck off, Johnny. Just get me out. I'm soaked through.'

Perched on the edge of the passenger seat, with the engine running and the heater on at full blast, Julia pulled off her boots, peeled off her socks and then her jeans. 'I'm sorry but if I don't take them off I'll get mud all over your smart new seats.'

'It's fine by me. There's a rug in the back.' Julia wrapped the rug around her lower half while Johnny stuffed the muddy clothes into the picnic bag and threw it into the boot.

'Oh, Jesus Christ, my feet are like blocks of ice.'

'Give them here. Come on.' Julia lifted her legs over the steering wheel onto Johnny's lap so that he could massage some life back into them. He blew on her toes and rubbed her feet and then pulled his jumper and shirt over them so they were next to his skin.

'Oooh… that's fabulous. Just let me stay there for a while.' Johnny squeezed Julia's feet affectionately and then dug out the hip flask from his jacket pocket; it was Seamus's whiskey today. Johnny could feel Julia's feet draining heat from his body and it felt curiously intimate. He took one foot out from beneath his clothes and kissed it.

'Yuk. Doesn't it stink?'

'No, not really. And anyway, I like how you smell.'

Julia moved her other foot down onto Johnny's crutch and began rubbing until he was hard. Then she unwrapped the rug and pushed Johnny's hand inside her knickers. Johnny was shocked at how wet and warm she was there and his penis jerked further into life. Julia held Johnny's hand, showing him how to give her pleasure and, when she had reached her orgasm, she lifted her legs off his lap.

'Here, let me touch you too.' They had never gone as far as this before on their Sunday excursions. Johnny let himself be unzipped and stroked by Julia. Just as she had done with him, he placed his hand over hers, instructing her through subtle pressures. When she took him in her mouth he thought his head would explode. It took a little time before he ejaculated, thankfully not into her mouth but only avoiding what he thought would have been a disaster by a couple of seconds. He sat back in the car seat and breathed out heavily for several seconds before leaning over to embrace her and kiss her deeply.

'That was lovely, thank you,' he said and took his handkerchief out to wipe up the semen on his underpants.

'Bit too close for comfort though, don't you think, fella.'

'I was just following your lead. I thought it was okay with you.'

'I know. I'm not blaming you. I've been wanting you to get inside my pants for a very, very long time, and to get inside yours. But it's dangerous. We need to stop.'

'I'll stop wherever and whenever you say but you won't be able to stop me dreaming about kissing your bosoms or being inside you.'

Julia unbuttoned her blouse and slipped her bra straps down. 'Fill your boots, Johnny.' She cradled his head as he kissed and licked her small breasts. Johnny could feel himself getting hard again and so stopped, kissing her on the lips before zipping himself up and starting up the engine.

'Right, I think we should make for home and stop all this funny business, delightful though it is.'

When they arrived back to the Delaney home, Johnny got all of Julia's wet and muddy clothes out of the boot so that she could greet her father fully dressed.

'Yuk. Putting on sopping wet socks is revolting. Thanks for the trip, Johnny. Have a good week and I'll see you next Sunday. Same time, same place.' Julia got out of the car and threw the car rug into the back seat. 'But, can I just say it again – I'm really not looking for a boyfriend.'

******

Cathy was listening to Erin's enthusiastic practice on Mikey's tin whistle. Even though he had been gone a year and a half now, they still missed the lad, painfully so in Liam's case. Her husband went out of his way after daily fish deliveries to call in at a few new pubs to ask after him and he would share with Cathy where he was planning to search next. Erin had cried a lot after Mikey had first gone, but she then told Cathy that she was sure Mikey would come back as soon as he had 'made Ireland free again'. That's why she urgently needed to learn how to play the whistle because he had asked her to learn some tunes for him.

'That sounds very nice, poppet. You're a clever girl. Would you like to play a real flute if I bought one for you? It would sound a lot nicer.' Cathy found the tin whistle just a little too penetrating. She always felt a headache developing after Erin had been playing for more than ten minutes, though she never said a word. From her work at the hospitals, she knew that relentless encouragement and positivity were essential and that little fires could be easily extinguished. It was like nurturing a seedling: lots of sunshine and water and no pruning.

'No, thank you, Mama. I like Mikey's whistle best.'

St Joseph's was still casting a shadow over the lives of people whom Cathy saw in her counselling sessions. She had moved her clinic to an office in Galway where the demand was much higher. In fact, she could probably have filled three days with her own patients, but she found the work she did at the hospitals satisfying in a different way. It was a good balance. Although the hospital patients were suffering from a range of mental disorders, the occupational therapy work she oversaw generally brought them happiness. In contrast, her counselling often unearthed deep trauma and pain, and Letterfrack School was at the root of much of it.

One young woman who had started consulting Cathy was in despair at what her new husband, an ex-pupil of St Joseph's expected of her in bed. Cathy explained that anal intercourse was something that could bring pleasure to both partners but that the woman should only do what she was happy to consent to, and her husband should respect that. It turned out that some of the issue was the husband not wanting to get his new wife pregnant and what he had experienced at the hands of a Christian Brother had seemed a sensible solution. It took only a few sessions with Cathy for the young woman to feel able to confront and resolve her marital problems.

Cathy found the cases of child abuse harder to hear but, as long as the conclusion meant that some child somewhere could start living without fear, she felt that her work was worthwhile. She had encountered at least five cases where a father would be in the habit of administering severe beatings to his child, having experienced the same himself repeatedly at St Joseph's. These cases usually came to Cathy by way of the mother, but, in one instance, the grown-up son himself came to see her but only after his father had died. So much betrayal, confusion, guilt and rage all mixed up together in one unhappy soul.

The worst case had required Cathy to involve the Garda: a mother had refused to leave the family home despite the fact that the father, an ex-Letterfrack inmate, was raping his own eleven-year-old daughter. Cathy had agonised about the matter: what if the authorities removed the child from the mother and she ended up in an institution like St Joseph's, out of the frying pan into the fire? But, thankfully, the father was arrested, charged and sent to prison, albeit only for a couple years, but long enough for the mother and her family to move away. Some justice, although, in truth, the man was a victim too. Would the guilty Brothers at Letterfrack ever face justice? Hopefully, all the efforts of legislators and lawyers that Bridie updated her on would lead somewhere. Until it did, Cathy would do her best to heal the wounds.

When she lay in bed at night, looking at her beloved husband sleeping fitfully next to her, his lean muscular frame and rough hands the outcome of self-punishing work, Cathy pondered how deep his pain went and whether he would ever be free of it.

******

Valentine's Day fell on a Friday. Johnny agonised over what to do. He would see Julia on Sunday as usual but he wanted to mark the day itself somehow. He'd be in lessons until four, so he couldn't easily get to a shop for flowers, but the day before he managed to get to the corner shop in Dalkey, hoping to buy the biggest box of chocolates they had. They had no boxes at all so he had to make do with two bars of chocolate instead. Then he took his precious LP *With the Beatles* and wrote a message on it.

"It Won't Be Long" until Sunday and then you can "Hold Me Tight" because "I Wanna Be Your Man". "All My Loving", Johnny. xx'

He waited until ten o'clock on the Friday evening, by which time he knew Christie Delaney would be in bed, and then drove to Finglas. He left the gifts on the doorstep in a plastic bag and gently knocked on the front door before running back to the Corsair. He watched Julia come to the door and pick up the bag, looking around before she closed the door again.

Two days later, Johnny was waiting in the car park outside St Canice's. He was feeling rather pleased with himself having assembled the best picnic yet, he thought, with chicken legs and some cheese and bread rolls, plus apples and biscuits. And he had sneaked a bottle of red wine from Seamus's wine rack under the stairs, not forgetting a corkscrew. It was fairly sunny and another trip over to Dollymount Strand would be fun. Or maybe a walk in Phoenix Park. Whatever Julia fancied was fine with him.

'Hey you,' said Julia, getting into the car and throwing her bag onto the back seat.

'Hey you, yourself.' Johnny gave her a kiss on the cheek but Julia didn't respond. 'Do you fancy Dollymount or Phoenix Park – or anywhere else you can think of?'

'Wherever you like, yeah?'

Julia seemed in a bad mood. Maybe she was on her period, thought Johnny. She could get a bit irritable then. He didn't mind.

Johnny drove over the wooden bridge and across the island to the beach, parking just beyond the high tide mark. 'Are you fit then?'

'No. I don't want to go for a walk today Johnny. I just need to talk to you.' She refused to look at him and stared straight ahead at the two gulls wheeling over the water. 'You know I said I don't want a boyfriend. I know that my behaviour hasn't exactly stacked up with that but I have to stop it now – I really can't get involved with anyone, Johnny. I hope you'll understand. If I don't put all my energies - and my emotions - into my playing, I'll never make anything of my life. I'll never escape Finglas. I'll end up behind a counter in a shop or in an office, typing and filing like my Mammy, and I don't want that. I have to make the most of my time at the Royal Academy.' She turned to look at Johnny but he was now the one staring out to sea. 'You're still my friend, my pal. My best friend even. I'll still come to Dalkey and play with you and Uncle Seamus some Saturday afternoons but these times, the kissing and – the other stuff – has to stop now.'

Johnny took Julia's hand. 'I understand, I think. I don't want this to end but I know that your music means the world to you. And it won't be forever. I'll still be here when you're ready, Julia.'

'Could you take me home now, please Johnny. And thank you for understanding.'

Before she got out of the car Julia leant over to the bag in the backseat. 'Here. I've brought your LP back. I know how much it means to you and I don't deserve it. Bye now, Johnny. Look after yourself and I'll see you soon.' Johnny tried to kiss her but she was already out of the car.

Chapter 32 - August 1964

C athy and Liam were reading in bed after some gentle sex – it was usually only on a Saturday night when Liam could find the energy to make love to his wife. The rest of the week, he was either too exhausted in the evenings or out of the house before anyone was awake. All spontaneous sex had ended when Erin arrived. Cathy was perfectly content with the familiar routine of their love life. It was reassuring and kind and considerate, just like Liam himself, and she hoped it satisfied him in the same way. She was forty-four now and sex was just one element of their deep and trusting intimacy.

It must be different for Johnny, thought Cathy. He should have a girlfriend, but, since Julia had, in his words, 'dumped him', he had refused to even consider finding another candidate for his youthful lust, even when, last April, Seamus broke the news to him, quietly and gently, that Julia had acquired another boyfriend. From that moment on, Johnny had thrown himself into his academic work for his leaving cert rather than look for anyone to take Julia's place. He asked Seamus to take him over to England to meet Professor Daniel Brookman and, when an offer to read Maths at Cambridge had followed, he had accepted it instantly, turning down the offer from Trinity. Johnny didn't want to risk bumping into Julia around Merrion Square, with someone else's arms around her. As soon as his exams were over at the end of June, he had driven - much too fast – home to Cleggan rather than stick around for a while to play chamber music or cricket.

Remembering Julia's barbs about his privileged middle-class existence, Johnny asked Liam to give him a proper job over the summer months. He was now grafting away on the boats as hard as any of Liam's other men, getting up at dawn and going to bed at nine o'clock, covering for other men's summer holidays.

'You should be very proud of that young man, Missus Cathy,' Brendan said. 'He's always the first to volunteer to do the shittiest jobs and you'd think he had some batteries up his arse the way he never sits down to take a rest and even eats his sandwiches standing up. I'll be honest and say that I never thought he'd stick at it what with his big brain and his head in all the books and then there's his cello playing and his delicate hands so all credit to the lad.'

And there was always a fresh chocolate cake in the larder for Johnny, courtesy of Dearbhla.

Liam didn't expect Johnny to work after three o'clock or at weekends so Johnny had enough free time to devote to his new obsession, his guitar. He had bought it at Easter in a Galway music shop along with sheet music from his favourite bands and had quickly mastered the basic skills. Erin was fascinated by it and Johnny was happy to entertain her and accompany her simple tin-whistle tunes. When Cathy looked her two children, making music together or laughing and playing with the Scalextric, with a big age gap but a real loving bond, she counted her blessings.

Cathy accepted that Johnny was now a man. Physically, he was acquiring muscles and strength and could apply himself solidly to hard work; emotionally, he now knew what it was to love someone and to lose them. Yes, it had brought pain, but also maturity, reflection and a realisation that he couldn't have everything he desired.

Johnny had also become very considerate, anticipating things that might help his mother or Liam before he was asked to do them. One reason he'd given for choosing King's College over Trinity was that he'd be able to drive from Cambridge to Ollerton to see his Granny in only two hours, whether for a weekend break or an emergency dash. The bond with the father he had never known was as strong as ever and the two Ashfield women were grateful for it.

At the start of August, Seamus drove Ellen and Aoife to Cleggan. Ellen was increasingly immobile and talked about her plan to retire soon as principal of the Maple Academy, though she and Aoife would still go in to teach their respective languages a couple of afternoons a week.

'What do you think, Cathy? Should we advertise for a new principal or should we promote one of the staff?'

'Only you and Seamus can decide that. You two own the school. I should have no say at all – I'm just your landlord and I don't know any of the teachers well.'

'We like Anthony Kelly very much, don't we Aoife?'

'We do. He's a great history scholar himself and he knows how to inspire the students. But he's also a good disciplinarian when he needs to be.'

'Damn sight better than me.' Ellen had never been any good at punishing the rare instances of bad behaviour at the Academy. Aoife said it was because Ellen preferred to be part of any shenanigans rather than the authority figure.

Cathy loved having Ellen and Aoife in the cottage, just for the delight of their company, but it also gave her freedom to go to work or to go pleasure shopping in Galway, because there was always someone there for Erin. Aoife insisted that Ellen come swimming every morning with her and Erin, good exercise for someone who could no longer walk much and good therapy for Ellen's bad leg. It was great fun too. Despite lots of grumbling, Ellen soon looked forward to their daily sessions in the sea.

The cottage was hosting additional visitors this weekend.

'Careful, Bill, you eejit. You're getting all tangled up with me,' shouted Bridie across the beach. The pair of lawyers were each attempting to steer a kite, trying not to trip over Erin who was running around at their feet, laughing and catching the sails when they dipped towards the ground.

'Our turn now,' Fergus shouted over to his sister and he pulled Hugo up from the sand. Sitting on rugs over on the dunes sat all three of Cathy's wise old birds: Aoife, Ellen and, on her first trip to Cleggan, Aggie. They were deep in some juicy gossip. They'd make a good trio of witches for *Macbeth*, thought Cathy. Aoife and Ellen were bare-legged but Aggie refused to take off her shoes and stockings. Fergus had had to carry her off the boat onto dry sand. She was sitting smoking a cigarette, with her cardigan clutched tight around her - 'It's terrible breezy out here' - despite the sunshine.

What a glorious summer day this was turning out to be. Liam had brought them round the headland for a picnic on Mermaid beach. Johnny was sitting cross-legged playing his guitar; he had been practising one of the latest Beatles tracks for the last two weeks non-stop and even Liam had picked up the lyrics. Cathy could hear him now, singing along to *And I Love Her* as he tended the small driftwood fire on which he was grilling some freshly caught mackerel. Liam had asked Johnny to show him a few chords on the guitar yesterday. There was music in the man somewhere, Cathy reckoned, and she resolved to buy him a guitar for his next Christmas present. She wandered up and down the beach taking snaps of all these darling people. If only Rose and Sam and their kids could have come up too. Maybe next year.

Cathy put her camera away and went to sit with Bridie and Bill, both stretched out on towels.

'Don't let yourself get burnt. It's not often we have to worry about that in Connemara but the breeze is deceptive.'

'I don't think you need worry about me, Cathy,' said Bill, opening one eye. 'There are many things about Georgia that I don't miss but the sunshine is definitely one I do.'

'Do you think you'll ever go back to America, Bill?'

'Some day but if a Republican President follows Johnson, all political appointees like me will lose our jobs, and I've been thinking about maybe doing something different anyway. I don't like this regime much – we're getting too embroiled in Indochina for one thing – but deciding what else to do is tricky. I'm thinking the Civil Rights Movement could use a lawyer. Plus, my parents aren't getting any younger and I should be nearby for them. So, I guess I'll be going back home soon.'

'But you'll miss me something terrible, won't you?' Bridie gave Bill a sandy kick. 'Though, now I come to think about it, Bill does too a good a job of deterring any suitors by hanging around me all the time. I'm thinking I need to find a man, sister. Not just any man, 'the one'. Someone's got to replenish the human race with all you gay fellas around.' Bridie kicked Bill again.

'I don't think there's any chance of the human race dying out any time soon, Bridie,' said Cathy.

'No, not if the feckin' Pope has anything to do with it. But if I managed to squeeze out a baby, I'd want my career to keep going, like you manage, Cathy. Hey, did you hear that Ireland is getting its first female judge? Justice Eileen Kennedy, who is a very good egg. I fancy being a judge one day myself – there's a lot of revenge I need to take on some of my fellow barristers.'

'Have you told Cathy and Liam about *Hibernia*?' said Bill.

'Christ yes - I mean, no – but yes I must tell you. Listen up, Cathy. One of my partners brought in a magazine he'd been sent called *Hibernia*. In it, a couple of women wrote about this man who had been in Letterfrack Industrial himself – Peter Tyrell I think his name is – and Aunt Lily says it's the same man who's been writing to Senator Sheehy-Skeffington. It's all starting to come out. We just need to keep up the pressure.'

Cathy looked over at Erin, Johnny, Fergus and Hugo, running in and out of the sea, dementedly splashing each other and then scampering away. Then she watched Liam take the fish off the rack and put them neatly on plates; the man couldn't help but find jobs to do. Erin was so confident and carefree, skipping through the waves. Maybe Liam would have been the same had he not had his childhood stolen from him, like all the boys from St Joseph's. The sooner it was closed down the better and maybe this man writing for this magazine was the beginning of the end.

After they had eaten, Liam and Cathy walked off the beach with Fergus into the adjacent fields. This was part of the land that they hoped to buy whenever Jack Brodie decided to sell or kicked the bucket.

'What do you think, Fergus? Is it good enough for beef?'

'It's perfect. Very rich for around here. How many acres does he have?'

'Not sure, I guess about fifty. Enough. I'm not trying to make a fortune from beef. It's just something I've been wanting to do for a while. I just love the heft of those creatures.'

'You'll be able to fit maybe eighty head on it. Beef's not something I've ever thought about for Rowanbridge. We're happy with the dairy and arable mix we have.'

They wandered back onto the beach. 'I tell you what I've been talking to Bridie about though,' Fergus said in a hushed voice to Liam and Cathy, '– the Byrne farmhouse is far too big for me and Hugo, and far too much work for Aggie. It's a house for a big family. When Tricky goes, we're gonna sell the house, maybe to Peter and Maureen, and then I am going to build us a lovely bungalow so that Aggie doesn't have to slog up and down stairs, and I'm thinking of putting it in Cromwell's Tower field. It's only a short walk then along Mill Lane to Main Street so Aggie can pop in to see Rose any time she likes. And Bridie would get half the money so that she could buy herself a place in Dublin. It's driving her a bit mental living with Aunt Lily.'

'Does Aggie know?' asked Cathy.

'No. Because I don't know when we could do it. We wouldn't dream of uprooting Daddy. But he's doing less and less, fading away fast. He just sits in his chair all day watching TV, apart from going to look at the cows or the milking sheds once a day. He's a bit younger than Aggie but he looks twenty years older.'

'It's a hard life working on the land.'

'Does that mean I'm going to lose my gorgeous, youthful looks soon?'

'No, you'll always be my beautiful baby brother.' Cathy reached up to give Fergus a big kiss.

The weekend was over too soon. A week later Seamus arrived to transport Ellen and Aoife back to Dalkey. Life in the cottage settled down, or as much as any home with a bouncy seven-year-old could settle down. It was never totally quiet; there was always music, either Erin's tin whistle or Johnny's guitar, cello playing or record player.

Cathy found a little time to play the piano, sometimes preparing for her work at the hospitals and occasionally purely for her own pleasure. She was working her way through Beethoven's piano sonatas and Liam enjoyed listening to them in the evening as he read the paper and drank his tea.

'I wish we had the room for a decent piano for you. You deserve something classier than that battered old thing.'

'I love this battered old thing. I love it because you bought it for me before we ever knew that we loved each other.'

'I've always known I loved you, even when I was eleven. I just never thought you'd love me back and be here with me. That you'd be mine.'

Cathy went to sit on her husband's lap. 'Just as long as you don't want to exchange this battered old thing for a classier model.' Cathy kissed Liam so vigorously that he was forced to put his cup of tea down and concentrate on the task in hand.

It was the last Sunday in August; the four of them were sitting finishing a rare leisurely breakfast . Erin was eating her second boiled egg while Liam and Johnny had split up the Sunday paper to read a few pages each.

'Oh, wow, do you hear this now, Mama? Apparently the Beatles met up with Bob Dylan a couple of days ago in New York. Imagine being a fly on that wall.'

'Are they going to play together?'

'Who knows but it would be awesome if they did. It all happens in the States doesn't it and bugger all happens in Ireland.'

'Be careful what you wish for, Johnny,' counselled Liam. 'Be grateful for a quiet life. Let's hope the IRA stay underground.'

'Thank God there's no fighting that Mikey could be getting involved with. I wonder whether he'll lose interest and just give up, leave the IRA and come home.'

'Is Mikey coming back, Mama?' squealed Erin excitedly. 'I hope so because I can play him lots of tunes now.' She ran into the sitting room and picked up the tin whistle. Johnny followed her in and started accompanying his little sister's surprisingly good efforts with some simple strumming.

Cathy knew that she needed to make the most of these times. Only a month to go before she'd be packing Johnny off to Cambridge and who knew when he'd be home again.

Chapter 33 – August 1965

In the end, it was another whole year before Johnny made it home to Cleggan, a year full of loss.

Mam Ashfield was the first to go. She was taken into hospital in November and Shirley was told that it was unlikely she would be coming out ever again, given the state of her lungs. Mam was hooked up to oxygen most of the time. Johnny drove from Cambridge to see his Granny every weekend, visiting the hospital for a couple of hours, taking grapes and reading magazine love stories to her, leaving behind the wild social life he'd been enjoying in college. He could see that it gave Shirley a much-needed break. He wished he could stay longer so that he'd be there to drive her to the hospital rather than her have to stand at bitterly cold bus-stops. When autumn term finished, he moved entirely to Ollerton and was able to ferry Shirley anywhere she needed to be. He even started cooking for them both and when she got back from the hospital they would sit watching television, eating supper from their laps.

On December the 19th, Johnny rang his mother to tell her the doctors had said Mrs Ashfield would not see Christmas so Cathy got herself over as soon as possible. Mam Ashfield was thrilled to see Cathy. She realised what the visit presaged but it didn't stop her smiles. Two days before Christmas, Cathy was sitting by Mam's bedside in a busy geriatric ward festooned with paper chains and balloons. Despite the proximity of death, Christmas jollities must be observed. Mam was sleeping while Cathy held her hand, thinking back to her own mother's death bed fourteen years before. This time, it was some other nurse's responsibility to administer the pain-relieving, death-hastening morphine. Mam suddenly opened her eyes and squeezed Cathy's hand. She lifted her oxygen mask with a trembling hand.

'Cathy duck, can I tell you something? First of all, I'm sorry I've nothing to leave you, no jewels or anything. This old ring will be Shirley's.' The old lady touched her thin wedding band. 'But take any old photographs you and Johnny would like and take my recipe book. It's got the gingerbread you love in there. Shirley never bakes. Now, I've told Shirley this but I don't know whether she'll do it – I want to be cremated and I'd like Handel's *I Know That My Redeemer Liveth* sung at the service, you know, from *The Messiah*. I did so love to sing that every year when I had some puff in me. Then, I'd like my ashes scattered at Joe's grave over in France, where we visited. Johnny'll take them, I know he will. What a blessing that boy is to you. Fancy him coming up here to sit with his old granny when he could be having fun. He looks very like you, Cathy, of course, but he has Joe's nose, don't you think? and he's a proper gentleman just like Joe. I wish Shirley had got herself married and had some kids but at least I can die knowing that Joe lives on through Johnny. And will you look after Shirley when I'm gone, Cathy, duck?'

'Of course, Mam. But she has Kazik, you know.'

'I know, but he's a foreigner, isn't he. I can't understand a word he says.'

Cathy smiled. 'Lucky you've always understood my Irish accent, Mam.' But the old lady had closed her eyes and was asleep again.

Cathy and Johnny were alone at breakfast on Christmas Eve, enjoying Mam's delicious Seville orange marmalade, when they heard the front door open and close. Shirley walked in with Kazik close behind her. She looked utterly empty, a grey face with red, puffy eyes. She walked over to Johnny and put her arms around him. 'It's all over now, duck. She's at peace, thank God.'

She collapsed into the armchair.

Cathy phoned Liam to tell him the news and to talk to Erin, who was most concerned that Father Christmas might not know where to bring the presents with the family split in two but Cathy reassured her that Santa had been properly informed.

'God, I'll miss you something fierce, macushla, but it makes sense for you to stay there until the funeral is done,' said Liam. 'Don't worry about us. We'll go down the road and join Brendan and Dearbhla at Mrs G's. They won't turn us away.'

It was hardly the Christmas Day Cathy had been planning but Kazik generously made room for them at his family's table and they enjoyed some interesting Polish delicacies. Cathy watched Kazik's eldest daughter making eyes at Johnny across the poppyseed cakes, who was utterly oblivious of the effect he was causing in her seventeen-year-old breast. Her son was a heartbreaker for sure.

They had to wait until the New Year for Mam's funeral. Cathy tried to use the time productively and she helped Shirley clear out Mam's clothes. They laughed together at Mam's corsets and at various hats that couldn't have been worn since the thirties and packed up any useful stuff for an old people's home nearby. And Cathy made the most of her time alone with Johnny. They had a few walks out to see the Major Oak that Johnny had played in and out of on his first trip to his Ashfield family.

'It looks so much smaller now,' he commented, looking up into the bare branches. 'I thought it was as big as a planet when I first saw it.'

'Well, that's the price you pay for growing into such a great tall monster yourself.'

After some gentle nudging, Johnny revealed a modest amount about his first term at Cambridge. Yes, his room was warm enough and, yes, he was playing his cello in the college orchestra and, yes, he was playing his guitar in a sort of folk club and, yes, he had had a girlfriend.'

'Have had?'

'Yes, Mama: "have had", past perfect tense.'

Cathy smiled. 'Plenty more fish in the sea, son.'

Cathy and Johnny left Ollerton in their separate cars the day after the funeral. Cathy took away some photographs, mainly to keep safely for Johnny, and Mam's recipe book, encrusted with grease, flour and sugar. Those recipes had seen them through wartime. Cathy didn't think she'd ever cook from it but it would go in her wooden box of memories.

'I'll see you soon, Auntie Shirley, maybe even before Easter. We need to organise taking Granny's ashes over to France.'

'You'll always be welcome here, Johnny duck, you know that. And Trent Bridge is always waiting. You too Cathy,' said Shirley giving her sister-in-law a hug.

'And you would be more than welcome to visit us in Connemara. It's a beautiful spot for a holiday. Plenty of Catholic churches for Kazik.'

The next death was as quiet and unassuming as the victim himself. Tricky simply walked a herd of cows back to Cromwell's Tower field one afternoon in early March, sat down against a stone wall and didn't stand up again. When he failed to come home for supper, Fergus went searching and found Tricky sitting peacefully, eyes closed and his willow switch in hand.

The day after Tricky died, Cathy got a second phone call from Rose. Rose had been allotted the task of talking to her sister about a sensitive matter.

'Cathy, the three of us are just thinking about where Daddy should be buried.'

Cathy's back stiffened. 'Daddy' was it, indeed. 'He never made his wishes known. That wouldn't have been his way; he never asked for anything much. It might be the right thing to bury him on the Byrne family plot with his parents and Nicholas and Louisa, and there's room there. But the three of us know that in his heart he would want to be buried with Mammy somehow, or near to her at least. He was her husband for nearly twenty years after all and he worshipped the ground she walked on.'

'But … but she's buried in a grave with *our* Daddy. Tricky wasn't even the father of any of you.'

'Oh, he was, Cathy, not in a physical way, of course. But he was a father to me for longer than my real daddy. He wasn't very demonstrative but he really loved us all and always made sure we were okay. I'm not saying our real daddy didn't love us, but he did leave us all to cope alone, didn't he?'

'He wasn't in his right mind, Rosie.'

'I know he wasn't well, Cathy. I'm not criticising him in the slightest and I have some lovely memories of him. The three of us have said that we wouldn't bury Daddy – Tricky – in with Hannah and John unless you were completely fine with it. But it would be a lovely thing to give him, a parting gift.'

Cathy took a deep breath. 'Okay, Rosie. That's fine. He *was* a good man and our daddy would be very grateful to Tricky for all that he did for Mammy and us after he'd gone.'

'Thank you so much, Cathy, you darling. You've no idea how much that means to the three of us.'

Of course, she did. Tricky was her stepfather too.

Cathy went to Rowanbridge for the funeral and, when she saw how grief-stricken her siblings were, she was shocked. Although Cathy had long since realised that Tricky was far from the ogre he had seemed to her in her childhood and that, thinking rationally, he had been her mother's saviour in many ways, she had never been able to throw off her resentment and suspicion of him completely. She knew he was generous and indulgent, otherwise some distant Byrne cousin or other would now be inheriting the vast farm. Maybe he'd been able to moderate her Mammy's quick temper and sharp tongue in defence of the children – Cathy hadn't been around much to see that. There was no denying that Rose, Fergus and Bridie were as distraught at Tricky's passing as she had been at her own father's funeral.

Everyone stood at the graveside as Tricky's coffin was lowered. At the bottom of the deep hole it was possible to make out the side of Hannah's oak coffin – it was a tight fit. Tricky would be on one side of his wife and John Fitzgerald on the other side. Was it really fourteen years since they had stood here to say goodbye to their mother? So many births, deaths and marriages had happened since. Life went on and death was just a part of it.

When Johnny's Easter holidays came round, he was busy for the first week with various social commitments: playing his cello for a wedding, going to an opera in London with friends; taking part in some early cricket fixtures. But the Wednesday before Good Friday, Cathy and Erin drove to join him for the trip to France. Cathy hadn't been able to persuade Liam to accompany them even though they'd only be gone a week. 'Too many lambs waiting to be born, macushla,' but she knew he would have found a reason to stay at home and work whatever time of year they had gone. Shirley and Kazik would arrive on Easter Monday, carrying the precious cargo of Mam's ashes.

Erin was excited to be going to another country where they spoke another language and ate snails – yuk! - and, not only that, with her brother Johnny, whom she hadn't seen since the previous September and had been missing badly. Erin had been most insistent on bringing just two things; Tiny Ted and her tin whistle. She didn't care what she wore.

'No kicking the back of my seat and no whistle playing in the car, okay?' Johnny laid down the rules – it was his car after all – but whatever Johnny decreed was fine with Erin.

The three of them enjoyed the Easter weekend, driving around Normandy, visiting the famous tapestry, walking along the beaches which had witnessed so much conflict and eating vast amounts of charcuteries, patisseries and confiseries.

On Easter Sunday, seized by a sudden compulsion, Cathy dragged Johnny and Erin to mass with her. Neither of her children had been brought up within a religion but the stone, the oak pews, the incense and the candles all evoked strong childhood memories for her; the Latin mass still resonated. The Gothic cathedral was full of vibrant coloured light and white lilies, the smell almost overpowering. After the mass, she lit several candles for Joe, for her father and mother, her grandmother Fitzgerald, her grandfather McDermott – and one each for Mam Ashfield and Tricky. It was a silly superstitious thing to do, she knew, but it was meaningful nevertheless.

The three tourists met up with Shirley and Kazik at the gates to Bayeux cemetery on Easter Monday afternoon. Shirley had hidden the urn of ashes in a shopping bag because she wasn't sure whether they were allowed to scatter them around the war graves and didn't want to ask in case the answer was no. Cathy brought two white roses. It only took half an hour before they were out of the cemetery and in a café. Erin had been perfectly behaved throughout, almost reverential, taking her cue from her brother, but also uncharacteristically shy with these two people she had never met before.

'Right then, I need some grub. We haven't eaten since breakfast on the ferry. Can you translate the menu for me, Johnny? We need to toast Mam and Joe. What would you like to drink, duck?' Shirley asked Erin, stroking her cheek. Erin shook her head and stood closer to her mother.

'Don't be shy little one. Is that Tiny Ted you've got there? I remember him. He looks even thinner than when I made him.'

'You made Tiny Ted?' Erin's eyes widened.

'Well, I sewed him together but Johnny brought him to life. That's what happens to teddies when you love them.'

Erin put Tiny Ted on the table and fed him some bread. 'He likes this bread, like me, and that will make him fatter.'

'She lovely little girl,' said Kazik to Cathy. 'So like my girls when her age. But fast, fast they grow up.'

Too fast, thought Cathy, but then again, sometimes not fast enough.

Cathy didn't go back to Rowanbridge until July, for the christening of Maureen and Peter's baby, a brother for Cathleen. She knew that by now the headstone would bear Tricky's name along with her mother's and father's. As the family flooded out of the church in a happy gaggle, godfather Sam holding baby Rory under the wary eye of his Granny Stasia, Cathy slipped away to the graveyard. She thought she was prepared but the sight stopped her in her tracks.

John Fitzgerald 1888-1931

Johannah Fitzgerald Byrne 1900 -1951
Beloved wife of John Fitzgerald and Patrick Byrne
Sacred mother to Cathleen, Rose, Fergus and Bridget
'At one with the angels'

Patrick Aloysius Byrne 1891 – 1965
A wonderful husband and father, rest in peace

There they were then, the three of them, their strange relationship immortalised in marble while their flesh and bones dissolved into the earth.

******

At the end of the summer term, Johnny stayed in Cambridge to play more cricket. He'd just finished with his latest girlfriend, Emma. She'd been nice enough but when he'd visited her parents in Weybridge for a weekend after his exams finished, her father had ranted about the 'blacks' everywhere, driving the buses and in the hospitals, and Emma had nodded along. So that was that. But he had no trouble getting girlfriends even though female students were rather thin on the ground in Cambridge. Cricket was a hopeless hobby for meeting women but playing in the university orchestra and the folk club was extremely fertile ground. Girls didn't exactly throw themselves at Johnny but he didn't have to resort to any embarrassing pick-up routines. He was tall, good-looking with long blonde hair and a very seductive Irish accent. He was also good company, witty and kind. But he hadn't kept any girlfriend longer than six weeks or so; it was practically a policy.

The ferry bringing him home docked at Dún Laoghaire just after five o'clock on a beautiful sunny August evening. He could have driven the Corsair hard back to Cleggan that night, but he had arranged to spend a couple of nights in Dalkey to catch up with Uncle Seamus, Aoife and Ellen and he had something to deliver to them.

When Johnny arrived at Nerano Road he found the three friends out in the small back garden, drinking wine amid the roses, awaiting his arrival. After warm and happy embraces and a quick supper, they sat outside again until all the blue drained from the sky and the stars and moon grew brighter. Johnny answered their well-meaning questions about his first year at Cambridge, honestly but cautiously. Whatever he said would get back to his mother, as he well knew. They asked gently all about losing his Granny Ashfield at Christmas, the funeral and then the Easter trip to France to scatter her ashes at Joe's grave.

'None of us ever met Joe, Johnny, but Aggie tells us that you definitely have your father's nose and I'm sure he was a wonderful man or Cathy would never have fallen for him,' said Ellen.

'There's only Mama and Shirley left now who knew him, I mean, of people that I know too. And I think Shirley will now marry her Polish bloke so I'll be the only Ashfield left.'

'Only until you have children of your own, Johnny,' prompted Aoife.

'That's all crap though, isn't it, when you think about it,' Johnny replied. 'Why should it matter about my father's name when my mother's name, and my grandmother's and great-grandmother's names, were all lost through marriage.

'Well said, Johnny.' Ellen clapped her hands. 'Aoife and I still have our names but no children to pass them on to. Mind you, there's no shortage of McPartlins - I have a dozen cousins at least - but I reckon de Bhailises might be in shorter supply.'

'It's quite a rare name even in Connemara,' said Aoife thinking of her own family, long gone.

'I suppose I should get back and let you all get to bed,' said Seamus getting up slowly and stretching.

'I can run you round in the car, Uncle Seamus. I haven't drunk much – well, not as much as all of you. 'No, no. It's just a short stroll and God knows I need the exercise. Looking forward to our round of golf tomorrow, Johnny.

'Wait, before you go, I have something for you all.' Johnny ran to the hall and opened his case; he took out a package wrapped in brown paper which he brought into the sitting room. 'Come inside and see.' Johnny unwrapped the package carefully, the three others watching on with mounting curiosity. Revealed before them were several sketches. Johnny spread them all out on the table. There were nine in all.

'Oh, Jesus Christ!' Ellen picked up one of the drawings. It was of herself aged seventeen. 'And look, here's you, Seamus.' Ellen pointed to a drawing of a very youthful lad playing the viola.

'And these are of your grandmother, Hannah, as you must know.' Seamus picked up one of the sketches reverentially.

'Yes, Professor Brookman explained who everyone was. He said he's kept them safe since he left the Academy in 1918. Aren't they marvellous?'

'I remember now that Daniel was a very talented artist. He could draw anything from memory and he could really capture their essence. Don't you think I was a pretty young thing once upon a time, Aoife.' Ellen laughed and handed the sketch over.

'You were and you're still very beautiful, my love.' Aoife kissed Ellen on the cheek. 'And of course, I remember Hannah looking like this because John brought her to Cleggan on their honeymoon when she was just eighteen.'

Seamus was silent. Four of the drawings were just of Hannah. The last one was of the pair of them playing their instruments at the concert Aunt Lily had organised at the Gaiety Theatre. He gazed at the sketch in silence.

'Professor Brookman wanted you each to have your own portrait and I'll take the ones of my grandmother back to Mama. There's a couple there of people I don't know.'

'Oh look, Seamus, here's Maisie and Eamonn together and one of Visha with her brother Sourja. What memories they bring back. How wonderful of Daniel to give them to you for us, Johnny. No problem getting this to Maisie and Eamonn Driscoll but I've lost touch with Visha completely. But she shouldn't be too hard to find: a female Indian Doctor Bhose in the East End of London. How many of those could there be? It's a good nudge to make me go hunting.'

The next day, Seamus was delighted to thrash Johnny at golf. The young man was learning fast but Seamus had decades on him and golf was a game that was kind to older folk. They came back to the Academy for a bachelor supper and afterwards played a little music together, each playing the piano for the other. Then they went into Seamus's private sitting room and sat drinking brandy.

'It's very curious. My brandy and whiskey seem to be lasting a lot longer since you left for Cambridge.' Seamus winked at Johnny who had the grace to blush a little. Johnny asked after teachers and students he had known, and they talked some politics.

'I realise what a privileged education I had here – am still having. The majority of boys at Cambridge have been through the English public-school education. They all think I'm a peasant, of course, because that's how they think of everyone from Ireland. Arrogant feckers most of them but some are okay, even if they were born with a silver spoon up their arse.'

'Yes, I was privileged to come here too, like your mother and granny before you; it never occurred to me to question it, at least, not until I got to know Julia.' He had said it, said Julia's name. Johnny tried to ignore it and turned the conversation back to the Academy.

'What do you think'll happen to the Academy when… well… when you and Ellen want to retire.'

'When we're dead, you mean?' Seamus laughed. 'Say what you mean, Johnny. The honest answer is I haven't a goddam clue. Your mother still owns the house and land you know. Maybe you'd like to come back and be part of it.'

'No way. I wouldn't touch a bastion of privilege like this with a barge-pole.'

They sat for a while in silence, sipping their brandy.

'Well, I'd best get back to Nerano Road before they lock me out and I want to get on the road early.'

'Just wait, Johnny.' Seamus laid his hand and the boy's arm. 'Sit down again, will you? Two things I need to say: first of all, could I ask a big favour of you and ask you to sell me one of Daniel's drawings, the one with your grandmother Hannah and me together, playing our instruments?'

'Don't be daft. It's yours. I think Mama will have quite enough drawings of her mother with the other four. I'll leave it with Ellen and Aoife.'

'Thank you. You don't know how much that means to me. The other thing I need to tell you is about Julia. I think you should know … that she has got herself engaged.' There was a long silence. 'I've met the man. He seems a decent enough fella. He's an insurance agent. Enough money to see her through the rest of college … if that's what she decides to do.'

'If that's what she decides to do? Of course, she will. It's all she cares about. She lives to play and she is going to be a professional violinist.'

'Yes, let's hope so. But the thing is, she's getting married because she's having a baby. I'm sorry to be the one to tell you but I hope you'll be happy for her.'

Johnny said nothing for several minutes, then he gathered his things, thanked Seamus for supper and bade him a terse good night.

Cathy had been pre-warned by Seamus that Johnny might return home in a distressed state on account of the news about Julia. Seamus told Cathy he wasn't happy about it himself and thought Julia's fiancé was 'a bit of a gombeen – and a pompous one at that' but Julia was unshakeable in her decision, apparently. When Johnny arrived and walked into the cottage, he gave his mother and Erin hugs as usual but then went up to his room and was very quiet for the next week. He didn't mention Julia and Cathy didn't think it was her place to mention her.

The first day back, Johnny handed over the four sketches of his grandmother to Cathy. She was enraptured by them. When he saw how much they meant to her, he apologised that he had let Uncle Seamus keep one where he and Hannah was playing together. 'That's fine, love. My mother meant a lot to Uncle Seamus and I can always see it in Dalkey.'

When she saw the drawings, Erin asked endless questions about the grandmother that she and Johnny had never known; Cathy was thrilled that her daughter was so interested and the more she watched her daughter studying her mother's portraits the more Cathy could see the likeness. It explained a lot.

'I shall have them all framed and then give Rose, Bridie and Fergus one each.'

Johnny threw himself into working on Liam's boats again over the summer. He volunteered to do more afternoon deliveries so he was up at 5am and out for ten long hours, six days a week. Any time he had for the family was spent eating or entertaining Erin and the rest of the time he'd be up in his room playing his guitar, reading or listening to music.

In the middle of August, a package arrived for Johnny from Tara Records in Dublin and for the next fortnight, Cathy was aware of one track being played a lot more than any other. She could normally just make out what was being sung if she stood on the landing. One song had the word 'Help' repeatedly, but this other song was much too quiet. Eventually, her curiosity got the better of her one Sunday afternoon when Liam was out swimming with Erin. When she heard the track start-up she went and knocked on Johnny's door.

'Sorry to disturb you, love, but I'm desperate to know what this song is. Can I come in and listen?'

The music stopped. Eventually the door opened and Johnny ushered his mother inside. Cathy could see he had been crying, but he tried to keep his back to her as he restarted the track and then went to stand looking out of his window. Cathy sat down on his bed.

'*Yesterday,*

All my troubles seemed so far away…'

Cathy could see that it was from a new Beatles album called '*Help!*' – the cover was lying on the floor - but this song was unlike anything she had heard the band sing before. It had a string quartet in it, for heaven's sake, over which there was a simple acoustic guitar accompaniment. It was obvious why this song carried particular meaning for Johnny: *'There's a shadow hanging over me'* and *'Now I need a place to hide away'*.

When it ended, Johnny lifted the needle and slipped the disc back into the cover.

'Well, that is very beautiful. Poignant. And so unusual – I'd never have thought you could use a string quartet in a pop song. Maybe you could try and...' But Cathy stopped when Johnny flung himself onto the bed next to her and wept onto her shoulder. She stroked his hair.

'I'm so sorry, Johnny, that you've had this ... this hurt on top of everything else. It's been a terrible hard year for you.' She wanted to comfort her son and tell him that this too would pass and that he would get over the loss of a first love, but she didn't want to insult his feelings by making light of what he was going through. They sat together until Johnny blew his nose and stood up.

'I understand now what you must have gone through when my father was killed.'

'That's sweet of you to think of me. But time passes - and pain with it.'

Johnny nodded solemnly and picked up the LP. 'But you should listen to all the tracks. It's an amazing album.'

Over the next weeks, Johnny shared his favourite music with the family, bringing his record player downstairs and playing his guitar to them. He even managed to learn *'Yesterday'* and could play and sing it while keeping his tears inside, though it made Cathy sniff hard to hear him. At the end of the month, Cathy fetched the framed portraits home and Liam hung the one Cathy liked best on the sitting room wall.

'She must have been an amazing woman,' said Liam.

'Oh, she was. For all her faults, she was truly a wonder and I'm very happy to think of Erin carrying her spirit inside her.'

'I'm like my granny, am I?'

'Like your Granny Hannah mixed in with your darling daddy and I couldn't love you more.'

Later that evening, Johnny and Cathy were sitting alone together at the kitchen table drinking cocoa.

'You need to get yourself off to bed, darling, if you're to be up at five o'clock.'

'I know.' Johnny drained his cup and made for the stairs but turned back. 'I've been thinking about Hannah and Seamus, Mama. You said that time passes and pain too. But love doesn't always pass, does it. I think Uncle Seamus is as much in love with Hannah today as he was fifty years ago. He's never got over it and I think it's blighted his life.'

He walked slowly up to his bedroom.

Chapter 34 – September 1966

Seamus rang the front doorbell and was instantly confronted by a very irritable Lily who had been sitting waiting on the hall chair for the last fifteen minutes.

'You're very late, Seamus. You know how I hate to be late. I rang the Academy but there was no reply.' Lily shut the door behind herself and marched down the steps to the pavement, where the green Jag was parked.

'Apologies, Lily, but it took longer to get Ellen into the car than I expected.'

Ellen and Aoife were seated in the back to allow Lily to take her rightful place in the front. Seamus helped Lily into the car and tucked her skirts under her legs before closing the passenger door.

'Evening, Lily,' said Ellen.

'We're late. Seamus knows I hate to be late.'

'We'll be fine Lily. It doesn't start until seven thirty and it's not even seven yet. That's a beautiful dress you have on there,' said Aoife doing her best to sweeten the mood.

'Seriously, Lily, don't fret. I'll drop you three ladies off at the door of the Abbey and then park. You'll be in your seat in ten minutes, I promise.'

'But I like to pay a visit to the bathroom and buy a programme. And, anyway, I enjoy having a word with all my friends.'

Of course, thought Seamus; this wasn't just a theatrical trip but an important social engagement when Lily would be able to greet her literary, political and artistic coterie while swanning around the foyer of the newly re-built Abbey Theatre in crimson silk. It was exactly fifteen years from that terrible day when the old Abbey Theatre was destroyed by fire to its re-opening recently on July 18th. Lily had, of course, been in the audience for the opening night.

'Considering how much money I threw into it, I was very surprised I didn't get introduced to De Valera on the stage afterwards with the other VIPs,' She had complained to Bridie. 'Though he made a shocking mess of his speech, and what a frightful hotch-potch of a programme that Walter Macken had put together.'

But a month before, Lily had been delighted when O'Casey's *The Plough and The Stars* returned to the Abbey and she took Bridie with her for its opening night. 'A play from Ireland's golden age, Bridie. I saw the first production at the Abbey in 1926 you know and, although political progress has been made, I cannot believe that we still do not have a united and independent Ireland.' Bridie agreed whole-heartedly. Lily had enjoyed the new production so much, she bought tickets to take Ellen, Aoife and Seamus a month later.

Aoife found Ellen a seat in the foyer and then went to buy programmes while Lily promenaded, waving at people and shaking hands with dozens of them. Seamus made it to the theatre with five minutes to spare and Lily glared at him as he shuffled along the row to the seat at her side. When the interval came, Elle and Aoife chose to stay in their seats while Seamus accompanied Lily to the bar.

'I need to stretch my legs, ladies. I find these seats a little uncomfortable and my back is playing up.'

'"Stretch my legs" my arse,' pronounced Ellen when Lily and Seamus were out of earshot. 'Stretch my ego, more like.'

The second half began and then it seemed no time at all before the curtains closed and the applause burst forth.

'That was terrific, don't you think?' Seamus said, turning to Ellen.

'Yes, it's a classic. Required reading for all our students. We should try and bring them to more live theatre.'

Seamus was hardly listening to Ellen because he had become aware that Lily, in the seat to his right, was not applauding. Maybe she hadn't rated this evening's performance. He whispered in her ear. 'Not up to your high standards, Lily?'

But she didn't reply. In fact, she did nothing at all. She didn't turn or speak or applaud.

She was dead.

******

'You have to hand it to her, Cathy, she couldn't have organised her death any better if she'd been planning it for years,' Bridie said on the phone to Cathy the morning after Lily had suffered what was subsequently diagnosed as an aortic aneurysm. 'Instant death and likely no pain but maximum drama and notoriety. Can you imagine? Seamus shouting for a doctor and five of them legging it over, but she was already very, very dead. She'll have to go to the coroner of course...'

'Oh Christ, it's so sad. Poor Aunt Lily. I thought she was going to live forever.'

'Yes, it *is* sad, but maybe more shocking, coming out of the blue like that. Just think about it, Cathy: she died in her best frock, in a theatre, with her make-up and hair all perfect; that must be how all actresses dream of being taken. She'd not been ill or suffered or even declined. And she was eighty-seven. She'd had a great life.'

'I know, but even so I feel it's yet another person who knew our Mammy and Daddy we've now lost. Not many left.'

The need for a post-mortem meant that Lily's funeral couldn't take place for three weeks but, considering how elaborate the funeral arrangements were, that was just as well. Seamus, as executor of Lily's will, needed plenty of time to deliver Mrs Lily Murphy's very precise instructions as to how she wished to depart the world. She had obtained prior approval for the service to take place in the Newman University church, despite rarely appearing at mass and regularly declaring that she was an agnostic to her social circle. But there was no stage quite like a gilded church and the archbishop was perfectly happy to accept that Mrs Murphy must have 'come to God' as death approached. The church was heady with what looked like Dublin's entire supply of Madonna lilies as specified in the will. Seamus hired several professional singers and string players to supplement the church choir in a full requiem mass and the readings were all exquisitely delivered by actors from the Abbey Theatre itself, scene of her dramatic demise.

The funeral reception took place back at Pembroke Square where Stasia automatically assumed the role of hostess, directing the younger family members to fetch this or that while she greeted mourners and nodded her head gravely, graciously accepting their solemn words of condolence, Uncle Edmund standing silently at her side.

'Stasia's been waiting all this time to become the materfamilias, hasn't she?' Bridie whispered to Cathy as they cleared plates into the kitchen, 'but I'm now mistress of this house.'

'Not for long, Bridie. I assume Stasia will inherit everything.'

'We shall see.' Bridie tapped the side of her nose in conspiratorial fashion.

Two days later, about half of Lily's relatives squeezed into Colm O'Brian's small office for the reading of the will. The delay of the funeral had allowed all legal processes to be completed. Sam had stayed up in Dublin with Rose and, of course, Stasia had insisted that Uncle Edmund be by her side, but most of the other men had gone home – too many animals and children to care for.

'I suppose none of this is going to surprise *you*, Seamus,' said Stasia taking the seat directly in front of Colm's desk. Seamus gave a non-committal smile.

'Are you all sitting comfortably?' Colm unlocked his top drawer, removing a long brown envelope tied around with red ribbon. 'Righty-ho then.' Colm put on his half-moon spectacles and began to read:

'I, Liliana Assumpta Murphy, known as Lily, born the 21st of March 1879, presently residing at 117, Upper Pembroke Street, Dublin, and, being of sound mind, hereby revoke all former testamentary dispositions made by me and declare this to be my last Will and Testament.'

Cathy could tell Bridie was getting impatient; she was tapping her foot while Colm O'Brian waded through lots of verbiage about the appointment of two executors, their duties and permissions, and Lily's funeral requests which were already in the past.

Colm O'Brian looked up and lowered his spectacles. 'We come now to the bequests which are fairly detailed but don't worry you will be able to read a copy of this will at a later date:

'I hereby request that two scholarships in my name be established each academic year at the Maple Academy in Dalkey, each to last for four years. These scholarships will be awarded to young people of exceptional musical talent who do not have the pecuniary means to extend their studies. The executors of my will shall determine how much money from my estate should be directed into the scholarship trust fund.'

Stasia shuffled a little.

'I hereby bequeath my Steinway grand piano to my great-niece, Cathleen Molloy, previously Ashfield and Fitzgerald, so that she can play on an instrument worthy of her musical prowess.'

'I hereby bequeath all my jewellery, personal items and all other household goods including paintings and wine cellar to my niece, Anastasia Hughes, previously McDermott, with the proviso that she offer one item of jewellery of moderate value to all the women who have looked after me and Pembroke Street in recent years. I also bequeath the sum of one thousand pounds to each of them in addition.' Colm read out the six names of Lily's faithful retainers.

'I hereby bequeath five thousand pounds to William Slattery, my faithful driver, recently retired after forty-seven years' service, and the elephant foot umbrella stand that he so admired.'

'All remaining assets, including but not limited to: bank accounts; stocks; shares; gold reserves, and the proceeds of the sale of 117 Upper Pembroke Street, shall be divided equally between the eight grandchildren of my beloved sister Evaline, namely, the children of my two nieces, Anastasia and Johannah. My three great-nieces and five great-nephews have given me endless joy over the years and I thank them all for everything they have done for me.'

Behind Stasia's back, Cathy, Rose and Bridie exchanged guilty grins.

When the will-reading was over, Stasia and Edmund set off for Rowanbridge immediately after exchanging strained goodbyes with everyone. Then everyone else legged it to the pub around the corner.

'What'll you all have? I'm buying now that I'm in the money.' Mattie had made it to the bar first and waved a ten-pound note at the barman. He was the only one of the Hughes boys to have attended the will-reading, the others all content to be represented by their mother and father. When everyone was armed with a drink, Mattie raised his glass. 'I'd like to propose a toast to Great-aunt Lily. What an amazing woman she was in so many ways but what I most admire is that she has been able to get one over on my mother even from beyond the grave.'

They stayed drinking until late afternoon and then got themselves back to Pembroke Street for dinner.

'Be honest, did you know what the will contained, Uncle Seamus?' asked Cathy.

'I did not. I'm an executor not a witness. But I did have an inkling about the scholarships because Lily had been talking about how many other talented musicians there must be in Ireland like Julia Delaney who never get a chance and she wanted to know what it would cost to pay for a student for three or four years at the Academy.'

'I had more than an inkling,' said Bridie. 'But she swore me to secrecy. She said I didn't need to worry about where I'd live when she died because she'd make sure I had enough money to buy my own flat.'

'I think Lily did absolutely the right thing.' said Seamus. 'Stasia and Edmund have no need for money. They should be happy that their children are well-provided for now and I'm sure that, once the shock has worn off, they'll realise that too.'

'We can refurbish the bar again,' said Sam.

'And expand the shop,' added Rose, 'and Fergus will be able to build the bungalow he's been planning without needing to sell the farmhouse first.'

'I am going to get myself a flat right on St Stephen's Green – or maybe Merrion Square - so that I can look at a tree or two and just stroll to work. And a new car. And a holiday to the States to see Bill. And a Chanel suit.' Bridie's wishlist kept growing.

'What about you, Cathy?' asked Mattie.

'Oh, there's not much to spend money on in Cleggan, but Liam is always looking to buy extra boats or vans or new fishing yokes. There's Jack Brodie's farmland, I suppose, if he could ever be persuaded to sell up. Mind you, it'll probably take all the money to hump the piano back to Cleggan – but, I must say, I feel very honoured and very happy to be given it. When you think what it has witnessed over the years. But it'll entirely fill our sitting room, so maybe we'll have to extend the cottage again.'

'Good old Lily. Or, should I say, Liliana?' Rose laughed.

'To Liliana Assumpta Murphy.' Bridie stood on a chair and raised her glass. 'You are a legend and a total one-off. We all thank you and we will never forget you.'

'To Liliana Assumpta Murphy,' they all echoed.

Chapter 35 – June 1967

When Cathy got home from her day at Ballinasloe Hospital, she found Liam sitting at the kitchen table drinking whiskey; this never happened.

'What's with the dram?' Cathy dumped her bags and got herself a glass. 'Are we celebrating something?'

'We certainly are, macushla. Come and join me. We're now the proud owners of fifty-eight acres of prime farmland with direct access to Mermaid beach.' Liam winked at her and ran his hand up her thigh. 'And a very ramshackle old farmhouse of course.'

'He's signed then – finally!'

'He has. It's a great relief to his daughter and it certainly is to me.'

Jack Brodie had not farmed his land for a decade and he had retired to his daughter's in Limerick three years before. But, despite Liam's regular approaches and offers, Brodie had not, to date, been minded to sell, clinging to the hope that one of his two children, or maybe one of their children, would come and take over the farm that had been the Brodies' for three generations. But Jack's son was a successful dentist in Waterford and his daughter and her husband were both teachers and none of them had the slightest interest in some remote and windswept fields on the coast of Connemara; they were much more interested in the money.

'I won't get any cattle in until spring because all the fences need repair and I need to build some housing for the beasts. I'm going to need a couple more lads from St Joseph's. I hope we can get someone good with animals. There's been no-one since Mikey really.'

Erin asked after Mikey occasionally but less and less frequently, though she still said she was practising the tin whistle for when he came back. They could hear her now, up in her bedroom. Cathy had bought her a classical flute last Christmas and Erin had agreed to go to lessons but she was much more attached to the whistle. When Brendan sang the old songs along with Erin's tin whistle, sometimes with the addition of Liam's tentative guitar playing, it made Cathy's heart ache.

St Joseph's had been in the news. In April, Bridie had phoned Cathy with the shocking news that Peter Tyrrell, the ex-pupil of St Joseph's who had been writing to Senator Sheehy-Skeffington for years about the abuse he had suffered there, had killed himself. He had walked onto Hampstead Heath in London one day and set fire to himself. Bridie said she could hardly believe that anyone could be so traumatised that they would do such a desperate thing, but Cathy understood how terrifying experiences in childhood can haunt people forever and end in tragedy.

'But look, Cathy, don't despair. Eileen Kennedy is now on the case and these industrial schools can't last much longer.'

The Minister of Education had recently appointed Judge Eileen Kennedy to chair a committee tasked with surveying and reporting back on the whole reformatory school system in Ireland.

'I'm sending her all the testimonies we took from your lads in Cleggan, and all the letters Peter Tyrrell wrote to people and the articles written about him will be part of the evidence.'

'Bit late for that poor man. And how many years will it take? We took on a new lad last month and he talked about another monster in Letterfrack, a Brother Maurice who's in charge of the kitchens. I had to take him to Galway Hospital because he arrived with an anal fissure. I'm sure you can imagine how he acquired it.'

But there was happy news too. Johnny was in the middle of his finals and was predicted to get a first. He had already been encouraged to stay on at Cambridge to do a PhD which he said he would probably do.

'I don't think I'll ever get him back.' Cathy needed a hug from Liam after Johnny had told her about his plans over the phone. 'He'll be the complete Englishman soon, which I suspect he's always wanted to be – like his father.'

'Don't worry, macushla. As long as he's happy.'

'Of course, I'm thrilled for him. I am. Forgive my self-pity.'

Then, the news that Dearbhla was pregnant had sent the whole village into ecstasy. It had been several years since her and Brendan's marriage and people were starting to whisper that it was obviously a barren union. They were a popular couple. Brendan was a generous foreman to all of Liam's workers and Dearbhla was a kind young woman, happy to help out any of the older people in the village who needed a hand. The prospect of a baby Sullivan made everyone smile.

The acquisition of the Brodie farm produced a surge of energy in Liam. He was tireless, patrolling all the fields after a long day on the boats, making notes of where walls, gates and fences needed repair. He took Cathy to visit the farmhouse.

'What do you reckon, macushla? It's a little way out of the village and it's in a shocking state – needs a whole new roof and most of the window frames are rotten – so maybe I should just knock it down and build you a new house. But can you see yourself living here?'

Cathy wandered through the downstairs rooms. There were three in addition to the large kitchen and a scullery, only the smallest of which appeared to have been used for the last twenty years. She pushed open the double doors from the hall and found herself in a large room, with high ceilings and elegant cornices, which ran along the entire back of the farmhouse. It had three French windows opening out onto a wilderness of garden. Two of the glass window-panes were cracked and another was missing entirely. In the fireplace were two dead gulls. And yet… She turned to Liam and kissed him hard.

'I think Aunt Lily's piano would look wonderful in that corner over there, don't you?'

A week later, she was playing some Bach Preludes while Liam sat and made sketches and plans for the farmhouse. Erin was finally asleep upstairs having amused them greatly with her impersonation of Mrs Gallagher kneading bread. Some sort of performance gene had definitely been passed onto her. There was a soft knock at the cottage door and Liam went to answer it.

It was Brendan.

'Come in, man. Is everything all right?' The usually cheery man was looking troubled.

'Is the little one in bed?' he whispered.

Cathy joined them in the kitchen. 'She is, after having us in stitches doing a savage impression of your mother-in-law,' Cathy laughed. But Brendan was not even smiling. He sat himself down at the table.

'I've waited to come and tell you because I didn't want your girl to overhear though she will have to know I suppose at some point but that will be up to you when you think it's right. Today, on my way back from the Galway deliveries, I was driving past the pub in Oughterard - you know the one where Mikey and I used to sing and where you and your sister and her negro gentleman friend came one Saturday night to hear us – and I thought I could just murder a pint what with the weather being so warm and I hadn't had a drink since morning. So, I stopped and went inside and got myself a pint of Guinness and the landlord was out the back at first but when he came out front he hailed me like a long-lost brother and asked how was I doing and was I still singing and he got me another pint on the house when he heard I was married and expecting a babby.' Brendan paused and took a deep breath. 'Then he said, "that was a bad business that happened to your friend who played the whistle, wasn't it?", so I told him I didn't know what he meant and then he said that last year one of the IRA men who we used to give the singing money to had dropped into the pub and told him that there had been an accident ... and that Mikey had shot himself. He's dead.'

Brendan stopped speaking to let the news sink in and to wipe his eyes.

'He said Mikey had been loading a gun and it had gone off in his hands. He's buried in a little churchyard just up the coast from Sligo. I've written it down here.' Brendan reached into his trouser pocket and fished out a crumpled piece of paper that he smoothed out on the table in front of Cathy and Liam, who were frozen in horror. 'The landlord said he was buried with full military honours...'

'Full military honours?' Liam leapt up, snatched the scrap of paper and screwed it into a tight ball of anger which he threw at the wall. 'There's no honour in the IRA.' He paced around the kitchen, running his hand through his hair, almost demented with grief.

Cathy took Brendan's hand, her eyes swimming with tears. 'I'm so sorry you've lost your friend. We've all lost our friend. Does Dearbhla know?'

'She does Missus Cathy and she is inconsolable and she's been up on the bed ever since I broke the news and weeping and screaming so much that I'm fearful for the baby's life to be honest.'

'Don't worry, Brendan. The trauma is not ideal but... but you can help each other through this. Lots of hugs and lots of tea and ...' Cathy's attempts to sound calm and sensible deserted her and she let loose a raw groan that came from deep in her belly. 'Noooo. Oh no. Mikey, Mikey.'

Liam ran over and grabbed her until the worst of her howls were finished and her body stopped shaking.

'I'm sorry you had to be the one to hear this news and have to come and tell us, Brendan. You're a good man and you were always the best friend Mikey could have wished for.'

'Not good enough.' Brendan gave a weary nod and walked out of the cottage with a heavy tread.

******

Three days later, Cathy walked through the tall gate and up the long path to St Joseph's Industrial School in Letterfrack. She had cancelled her afternoon appointments to come and do this and she was terrified. The building loomed in front of her. It felt as if she was walking into Bluebeard's castle, or the Witch's gingerbread house or the Sheriff of Nottingham's dungeon or any other place of dread from myth and legend, so monstrous were the stories she had heard about this institution throughout her life. Yet she felt compelled to come.

The door was opened to her by a teenage boy. The smell nearly knocked her over: old dishcloths, cabbage, sweat, toilets – and fear. It smelled of fear.

'I have an appointment with the Head Brother.'

The boy turned and she followed him in silence down the bare corridor to a side door, which he knocked on.

'Yes?' The boy opened the door and said quietly 'Your appointment is here.' Then he gestured for her to enter.

The grey-haired Brother sitting at the desk didn't look up for several moments. If this was designed to intimidate people it had quite the opposite effect on Cathy. 'How rude and ignorant,' she thought. She walked right up to the desk and asked, 'Shall I sit here then?' and took the chair before any answer came.

'Erm, yes, okay. It's ...' the Brother glanced at his diary,'... Mrs Molloy, I believe. How can I help?'

'Thank you for seeing me. I've come to talk about some aspects of St Joseph's. You might know of my husband, Liam Molloy, of Molloy's Seafoods. He employs probably three or four lads from St Joseph's every year so his workforce is almost entirely made up of your ex-students.'

'Yes, he's an excellent employer and we're pleased that St Joseph's can supply him with such well-trained young men.'

'You might not know that he himself was a student here from the age of six.'

'I'm not sure that I did, but it's a great tribute to our school that one of its pupils has become such a successful businessman.'

'You certainly wouldn't know that my own father was once a teacher here, way before your time of course. John Fitzgerald was his name. Only for a year mind, back before the Great War.'

'Well, well, how very interesting. Things must have changed a lot since then.' The Head Brother was smiling now and sat back in his chair. He looked quite kind.

'No, not really. At least, not from what the lads tell us. My father worked here and was very shocked to see the boys treated so harshly, beaten for small transgressions and practically starved. He complained to whoever was in charge back then but he was not only not listened to, he was dismissed from his position. Just before Christmas. He had a wife and young disabled child who both died subsequently.'

'I am sorry to hear that. Times were very different back then when...'

But Cathy cut him off. 'Then, when my father first brought me, aged just ten, to Cleggan, we met a young lad who had run away from St Joseph's because of the horrors he had had to endure. He could barely read or write and he wouldn't even sit at the table with us, so beaten down and crushed was he. He thought he was no better than an animal because that's how he'd been treated here. My father took him to the Garda to give testimony but they ignored it and he was sent back to St Joseph's. The guilt that my father felt, because of making the guards aware of where that lad was, stayed with him all his short life - until he committed suicide.'

'Mrs Molloy, I really don't think...'

'Just listen to me. That young lad grew up to become my husband. Yes, despite all that he suffered at the hands of the Christian Brothers, Liam Molloy has risen above it but he's still deeply damaged because not only was he beaten and starved, some Brother used his young body to satisfy his sexual urges. You might think that he was unlucky, that his experience was a rarity, but I can tell you that he's far from the exception. Maybe you read that, back in April, a man called Peter Tyrrell killed himself in London by setting himself on fire? Imagine that. How much despair must a man feel to do that? He'd been writing to politicians, trying to get people to listen to his story about what he had been subjected to at St Joseph's, trying to get people to believe him - but mostly trying to get something done about this disgusting place.'

'Mrs Molloy, I must ask you to leave imm...'

'I'll go when I've finished. I'm a psychologist and I have a counselling practice in Galway. I must have encountered twenty cases at least where a man from St Joseph's has been implicated in some terrible family situation that my patients come to seek help for. Maybe he's a gambler, or an alcoholic, or a wife-beater or, tragically, even a child molester. None of it their fault. And there have been a couple of patients in Ballinasloe Hospital who were unlucky enough to have been sent to this school, one with profound clinical depression and another a habitual self-harmer who tears at his own flesh.

Then, this week, we got the news about Mikey Flynn. Mikey Flynn was only the second lad that Liam employed from St Joseph's. When he arrived, he suffered from frequent night terrors and he would sometimes wet the bed. You see, at St Joseph's, from the age of six, he'd been beaten every time he wet the bed, which, unsurprisingly, just made the problem worse. Eventually, with lots of love and support from Liam and me and his friends he conquered it. He was a wonderful shepherd and played the tin whistle like an angel, but he was always searching for something to believe in – and I can assure you he was never going to turn to the church.'

Cathy was still speaking with angry resolve but now she was shaking and some tears accompanied her words. 'So, he went off and joined the IRA and we've just heard that he managed to shoot himself. Maybe it was an accident, but I doubt it. That gentle soul is yet another tragic victim of this evil place. A small vulnerable child was sent here and should have received nothing but kindness and gentleness but instead he was used by vicious men who abused their positions of power.'

She stood up. 'I'm here to tell you that my family and I will keep doing whatever we can to stop you all, to get you shut down. My sister is a lawyer in Dublin and she's taken dozens of witness statements over the years and has now handed them over to Judge Eileen Kennedy who is currently conducting a review of the whole reformatory school system. Surely, you know that? I hope you're quaking in your boots. Before her report comes out, you might like to do what you can to clean up this cesspit. You have a Brother right now working here in your kitchens who is abusing boys sexually. Liam has three lads who can testify to that. Brother Maurice he's called.'

She slapped her hand onto the desk. 'Stop turning a blind eye. You must know. Like all the people over the years, you've all known and yet you've let this evil flourish. Men of God? Don't make me laugh. You all disgust me. But your days are coming to an end.' She paused and took a deep breath. 'Thank you for your time.'

Trembling from shock and with a racing heart, she turned on her heels and marched out of the room, out of the school, and back to her car where she sat and sobbed for ten minutes before driving home.

'I must say, macushla, for someone so kind and gentle, you can be a brave and ferocious fighter when you want to be.' Liam was stroking Cathy's hair as she lay in his arms in their bed that night.

'I was terrified and shaking like a leaf but - Jesus Christ - it felt so good to say it straight to his smug face. How many years have we spent bellyaching to each other about that feckin' place, love? Must be twenty at least. And so many others before us. Decades of futile whingeing. You have to take the fight to them.'

Liam kissed Cathy gently. 'Well, I'm very proud of you. And Mikey would've been too.'

'Can we go and visit his grave some time?'

'Of course. It's not that far and Erin has been asking. It'll be a nice drive up there. And, guess what, Dearbhla and Brendan are going to call the baby Michael in Mikey's memory.'

'Ah, that's so lovely. Let's just hope it's a boy.' And they chuckled together in a sleepy embrace.

Chapter 36 - Christmas 1969

It was going to be a big day for Cathy; she was about to welcome all her most beloved people into her new home. For the first time, all three siblings plus families would be spending Christmas with Cathy and Liam now they had the space to accommodate them all in the huge, restored farmhouse, which had taken two years of work and a heap of cash to transform.

They had moved in across the summer when Johnny was home from Cambridge to help and to choose his new bedroom. Erin had already claimed the bedroom with the best views of the cattle and the sheep and was happy to leave the sea views to her parents and brother. Soon after the Molloy move, Aoife and Ellen moved out of Dalkey and into the Cleggan cottage – a homecoming for Aoife - following their complete retirement from the Maple Academy. Meanwhile, Seamus had taken over their house, leaving his apartment in the Academy to the new principal, Dr Anthony Kelly.

In all the chaos of the triple-house move, the disturbing news from Belfast of escalating clashes between the Royal Ulster Constabulary and Catholic, nationalist groups, culminating in the deployment of British troops, had rather passed them by. As the months went on and the troops failed to go home, the situation was looking increasingly ugly.

Events certainly hadn't passed Bridie by. Arriving the afternoon before Christmas Eve, she had barely taken her coat off before she launched into a lengthy analysis of the political situation that had been brewing in Ulster since the previous autumn. She took a swig from her large gin and tonic.

'This is oppressive colonialism, pure and simple. And you see how they are bending the truth for their own agenda, blaming the IRA for inciting violence which is utter shite, but the papers all go along with it.'

Cathy could see Liam's jaw tightening and took her sister's arm.

'Yes, I'm sure there's been plenty of dirty business on all sides but can we just try and have a peaceful Christmas. Come and have a look upstairs, Bridie.'

Pandemonium descended the next day when the cars arrived from Rowanbridge, the McCarthy brood in one, Fergus, Hugo and Aggie in the other, but it was a close call as to who was more noisy and over-excited, Kevin, Thomas, Joanna - or Fergus. Erin was soon part of the gang and she and her cousins took themselves off upstairs to listen to Johnny's records, coming down later to play on the old piano in the living room. Thomas was a good pianist and he and Erin, on her flute, entertained everyone with carols.

'Now, this is a house and a half, Liam,' said Fergus, slapping the walls and sliding his hand over the architraves of the doors. 'Where did you get all your labour from? I'm guessing it's cheaper than in county Kilkenny. Our little bungalow would fit into half your downstairs but I bet it's cost almost as much to build. But, come the spring, Aggie will be the Queen of Mill Lane and Peter and Maureen are welcome to that dusty old Georgian pile.'

'I reckon we'll all have moved house by next spring,' said Bridie. 'Even Aoife and Ellen and Seamus have upped sticks.'

'Don't forget us, Bridie,' Rose reminded her sister. 'We're still there in Main Street and we always will be, won't we Sam? Rooted to the spot.'

Cathy smiled. It was true; it was sometimes easy to overlook her sister; her other two siblings were so loud and energetic. But Rose was quietly strong and stable in the family home.

Seamus was staying with Aoife and Ellen for Christmas week. He had said he would be fine in Dublin with a few friends but the women had insisted and he had acquiesced very quickly. It always gave him a warm glow to be in the company of Hannah's children and their families. He saw rather less of them these days and he was particularly anxious to talk to Johnny about a few things.

Ellen and Aoife offered to provide Christmas Eve supper for everyone, considering the next day would be a big effort for Cathy and Liam. But, realistically, they had conceded that they could hardly fit sixteen people around the cottage's kitchen table so they had agreed to come over for supper on the proviso that they were allowed to contribute a cooked ham and some desserts.

'And anyway, you can bet that Aggie will really be the one in charge in the kitchen tomorrow, giving us all our instructions though I've told her she's not allowed to so much as sniff a sprout,' Cathy reassured Aoife. 'She's brought three of her famous Christmas puddings so everything will be just great. I'm really excited to see my all my very favourite people around our new dining table.'

After supper, Johnny set up the Scalextric for the teenage boys plus Erin, Bridie and Fergus at one end of the enormous drawing room, while the boring grown-ups sat at the other end around the fire. Joanna was sitting on Hugo's lap with the cat on hers.

'I think I will have company at Midnight Mass this year, won't I?' commented a delighted Aoife.

'Poor old Aoife is usually surrounded only by us heathens at Christmas but all credit to her that we have never dented her faith a jot over the years,' said Ellen.

'I actually think that we God-fearing folk might be the majority this year,' ventured Aoife. 'Rose and Sam and the children, Aggie, Fergus and Hugo - and even Bridie maybe - will all be coming to mass with me.'

'Not me,' said Aggie. I'm okay with the God part but these days it's just too late for me. I shall go to early mass in the morning with Joanna.'

'Actually, can I come tonight?' said Cathy. 'Is that allowed, even if I don't believe?'

'Of course it is, macushla. God will be overjoyed to see you in his house, whatever your feelings.' Cathy couldn't bear the thought of her three siblings going off into the night without her when she had missed out on so many Christmases with them in the past.

'Is that okay, Liam, leaving you here with Erin and Joanna?'

'Of course, my love. I shall have Johnny, Ellen and Seamus to keep me company. We should be able to manage the pair between us. You go and sing your heart out.'

'There's Aggie upstairs too, Liam, don't forget, and she can be a shocking handful, especially on Christmas Eve,' quipped Fergus.

When the midnight mass party had left, Liam excused himself. 'I need to draw the turkey and bring in some logs and then I'll be off to bed. But stay and chat as long as you like. Johnny'll keep your glasses full.'

Seamus put another log on the fire.

'It's good to have a little time with you, Johnny. There are a couple of things I'd like to chat to you about. First of all, Ellen and I want to ask your opinion about the plans we've been making for the Academy. We know you've always disliked the privilege the school represents.'

Johnny laughed and swigged some brandy. 'Yeah, well, I was probably at the height of my Marxist phase. And I'm a shocking hypocrite because I probably wouldn't be doing a PhD at Cambridge right now if I hadn't had that step up. But I do still think it's fundamentally wrong that money can buy a better education and that millions of cleverer, more talented but poorer people miss out.'

'Well, it might surprise you to hear that Ellen and I agree. We were both students at the Maple Academy ourselves – we just took it for granted that it was a good thing back then. But you've made us think and now we're not so sure.'

'Does that mean you'll close it down then?'

'Not necessarily. All the work we had to do to set up the two scholarships that your Great-great Aunt Lily provided for in her will really opened our eyes, didn't it Ellen.'

'We were shocked, Johnny. That's the truth. When we first sent notification to high schools that these two places were up for grabs we were inundated with letters from head teachers telling us about all these wonderful fiddle, clarinet or trumpet players who would have to leave school, give up their instruments and get a job. We didn't how the feck we were to choose just two students. It nearly broke our hearts.' Ellen looked at Seamus and they nodded to each other.

'But two places are better than none, aren't they?'

'Yes, Johnny, they are. But it started us thinking. We can accommodate forty students now at the Maple Academy; that's an intake of ten places each year for a four year stay. So, we wondered whether there was any way we could get enough extra money into a trust or a charitable foundation - on top of Lily's bequest - to make all forty students at the Academy free places; ten scholarships every year for talented kids who don't have the financial means to keep studying their instruments. I mean it's far from perfect but we really want to make it a reality.'

Ellen took up the story. 'Seamus has done wonders building up a pot of money talking to all the corporations he's ever worked with and we've put a bit of our own money into it too. He's not taking a salary anymore and of course neither am I, but we still have to pay teachers and feed the students and keep the building going. And that's where your mother comes in – maybe. Cathy has always owned the building for which the school pays her rent, and she now owns half the school itself again, along with Seamus, because we've reversed the deal where she got Aoife's cottage in exchange for her share.'

'So, we're going to ask your mother if she would forgo the rent and any profits in future for the sake of the charitable trust. But we'll only do that if you think it's a good idea, Johnny. We think she won't hesitate if she knows it's what you want too.'

Johnny looked from Ellen to Seamus and back and then gave them a big grin. 'What are we waiting for?'

'Well, we should wait until after Christmas Day. She's probably got quite enough to think about until after tomorrow. We'll get off back to the cottage now.'

'Leaving the door unlocked for that dirty stop-out Aoife de Bhailis,' added Ellen with a chuckle.

'What was the other thing you wanted to talk to me about?' asked Johnny as he showed them to the door.'

Seamus hesitated. 'It'll wait. See you tomorrow.' He waved Johnny goodnight.

The midnight-mass gang got back at close to one in the morning. Sam dragged Kevin and Thomas upstairs immediately, whispering to Rose, 'Don't be too long.'

'I won't,' Rose replied but she couldn't resist Cathy's invitation for a night cap with her brother and sisters. 'At least they don't get up at dawn any longer on Christmas Day. Something to be said for teenagers.'

'There's still some life in the fire,' said Fergus kneeling in front of the hearth and giving the smouldering logs a jab with the poker before putting on a couple of fresh ones. 'They can't be long gone off to bed.'

'Well, this is lovely isn't it, just the four of us – and Hugo. I think of you as a sort of faithful dog, Hugo,' said Bridie ruffling his hair. 'Tagging along for the treats. Is that very rude?

'Not in the slightest. I know how much Fergus loves his hounds and they get fed better than me.'

Bridie laughed. 'While we've got you all to ourselves, Cathy and Rose, without your husbands interfering, we three want to talk to you about an idea we've had. It's a bit wild but listen up.' Bridie threw back some whiskey and then stretched out on the hearth rug. 'So, you see this…' she patted her belly. '… well, it's empty, but it's been yearning for a baby for a few years now. I have all these boyfriends but I don't want to marry any of them. They're good for a few dinner dates or even a ride or two but the thought of having to live with them forever appals me. On the other hand, I'm nearly thirty-eight so I'm probably already down to the last egg in the box in there.' She sat up and shuffled over to lean against Fergus's legs. 'If Bill was still over here I'd have asked him but he's not. So, I've asked Hugo.'

'Asked Hugo what?' Rose asked. But Cathy had already guessed what Bridie was inching her way towards explaining.

'Of course, giving birth to a brown baby would have caused extra earthquakes on top of giving birth as an unmarried woman, but it wouldn't have bothered me.'

'And what does Hugo think about it all?' said Cathy.

'Stop. I don't know what you're all talking about,' wailed Rose.

'Now then Rosie, you know how we inseminate the cows sometimes rather than let the bull in with them. Well, that's all Bridie is suggesting she does. With Hugo's sperm.'

Rose shrieked and covered her mouth with her hand and looked very shocked.

'Don't look like that Rosie. If it works for a cow why can't it work for a barrister?' Bridie laughed. 'Do you think it's immoral or something?'

'Will Hugo have to have that thing shoved up his arse that they use to milk the bull's sperm?' Rose asked. Fergus roared.

'No, Rosie, I think we can manage that bit all by ourselves. But what do you think of the idea? I mean - why not?'

'You're very quiet, Hugo,' Cathy said looking at the modest man on the sofa. 'I know that you would say yes to anything that Bridie or Fergus asked of you. But it's not a small thing is it, to become the father of a child that you wouldn't be able to acknowledge.'

'You're right, Cathy. But I have thought hard about it since Bridie asked me. The truth is that it would make me madly happy to see a child built out of my blood and Bridie's, the nearest thing to Fergus's blood - even if the child could never call me father. Fergus had to exist without his real father's name or knowing who his father was for most of his life.'

'But he did know who his father was supposed to be – the same father as Rose as me – and he carries the Fitzgerald name. And he had a stepfather who was there to look after him. This child would have none of those things. And how would this go down in Dublin legal circles, Bridie? How would your clients feel about an unmarried mother representing them? Even your IRA defendants are very traditional when it comes to things like marriage, you know.'

'Aww, stop being so feckin' sensible, Cathy. I can get round all of those things.'

'And we would do lots to help bring up the child, Cathy,' Fergus took Hugo's hand. 'The very best pair of uncles that money can buy. It would be so loved. Seriously, why not? What do you say, Rose?'

'I don't know what to think, to be honest.'

'Well, you know what they say about the best way to keep a secret: hide it in plain sight.' Cathy came to sit on the arm of the sofa. 'What's to stop Bridie and Hugo actually getting married and then any baby that followed could know its father, and you, Bridie, would not have to be labelled a Dublin floozy at all. In your profession, you can just tell them that you go home to your husband in the country at weekends because he's a farmer. It would be nothing more than the truth after all.'

'There's a thought. I like it. I mean, why not? It might even put Auntie Stasia off the scent,' Fergus added, warming to the idea.

'It's a bloody genius idea, Cathy,' said Bridie leaping off the rug and running to embrace her sister. 'You've always been such a clever mot.' Bridie stopped short. 'But it does rather depend on Hugo being prepared to marry me.'

Bridie turned anxiously to look at Hugo. He had immediately slipped down from the sofa and was on his knees at her feet. He took her hand. 'Bridget Carmel Byrne, would you do me the great honour of becoming my wife.'

******

The Christmas morning mayhem wasn't allowed to start until Aggie returned from early mass with Joanna and Erin, who had decided to tag along. When the three of them walked back into the farmhouse they were accompanied by two big people and a little one.

'Look who was at mass with us,' shouted Erin along the hall. 'Brendan wants to see Bridie and to wish us all Happy Christmas.'

'Come in, you two. Will you have a drink?'

'No, no, no, Missus Cathy, thank you all the same, not with me driving the little one in the car, but I might have a scoop or two later on.'

'Brendaaaan!' Bridie hurled herself into his arms. 'And happy Christmas, Dearbhla, and ... who is this?' Bridie knelt down to take the shy two-year old's hand.

'This is Michelle ... ma belle.' Brendan grinned at his own wit. 'We were all set to call the baby Mikey, you know, in honour of our sadly departed friend,' he crossed himself, '...

and then this cheeky girl popped out, but she's such a blessing and the sweetest little chiseler Dearbhla and I could have wished for so it all turned out okay in the end.' He picked up the little girl and walked to the door of the drawing room where the chaos of paper and presents had begun. He waved at everyone. 'A very happy Christmas to you all and God bless you. I'm off home to stuff a turkey.'

Dearbhla turned to Cathy and whispered, 'He's such a gobshite. All the work is done. He'll just be on the floor playing with Michelle – but he's still a love.'

As they were about to drive off, Bridie ran to the Sullivans' car and opened the passenger door. 'I just meant to say that I was utterly devastated when I heard about Mikey and I can imagine how bereft you must all have been. But you should know that the fight is still on. Judge Eileen's report will come out soon. We will beat those Brothers in the end, for Mikey's sake and for all the Letterfrack boys. Michelle is gorgeous, so have a lovely day and I'll see you next time.' She waved them off and ran back into the farmhouse.

The Rowanbridge contingent departed on the 27th and the farmhouse regained some order. Between them, Johnny and Erin kept the place full of music. Cathy recognised the LP that Johnny seemed to play up in his room endlessly; *St Pepper's Lonely Hearts Club Band* was famous even in Cleggan. It was more than two years old now but certain tracks seemed to be played every day, *She's Leaving Home* in particular. Cathy could guess why the melancholy song, with just strings and harp for accompaniment, would speak to Johnny so deeply. It made her think of Julia and Mikey ... and Johnny. Maybe it worked like that on him too.

Johnny was back to Cambridge soon after New Year so Cathy wanted to make the most of the time with him. When Liam and Erin had gone off one afternoon to check all the animals she managed to persuade Johnny to play some cello sonatas with her.

'It's good to see Aunt Lily's piano here, isn't it,' Cathy said.

'Yeah. Some great memories. Do you remember when Uncle Seamus played on it for your wedding and I made an eejit of myself singing and dancing?'

'Of course, I do. You were so adorable.'

'Were?'

Cathy planted a kiss on Johnny's cheek. 'You'll always be adorable, my beautiful golden son. I miss you, you know, but I understand that you're making a life in England. Will you stay when you finish your PhD?'

Johnny hugged his mother. 'I think so, Mama. They're offering me a teaching post in the department and it's a wonderful life, living in venerable buildings, surrounded by ancient stone and endless opportunities for music and cricket - and drinking! You must know that there's no way on earth I would ever come back and live in Cleggan. I mean, you haven't even got a TV yet.'

Cathy laughed. 'And not likely to either. But I have to accept that you've left home for good, and I'm happy to see you do so well and be so independent. I can even tolerate you becoming an English gentleman. I'd just like to see a bit more of you; Cambridge seems such a long way away.'

They were all going over to the cottage for supper that evening, Seamus's last before his return to Dalkey. They could just about fit seven around the old kitchen table and Aoife had conjured up a hearty lamb stew which was soon demolished.

'Before you go back, Seamus, let me tell you what Liam and I have discussed about your proposal for the Academy,' said Cathy. 'He and I agree that we can well afford to give up any income from rent or a share in any profits from the school to enable the place to change into what is a wonderful vision to help less privileged children than our own.'

Ellen clapped her hands enthusiastically, but Cathy hadn't finished. 'There's just one request I'd like to make: can we please change its name? That would make it clear that it's now a very different sort of school from the one we all attended. And, if it isn't too vain, can we please call it the Fitzgerald Academy? I'd like to pay tribute to my grandmother Letitia who founded the school in the first place and who gave me a home twice when I needed one, and also to my father who lived and taught there.'

'And, of course, to Hannah who became a Fitzgerald and to you who was born one.' Seamus took Cathy's hand and squeezed it. 'I think it's a wonderful idea and it makes a clean break. And I can't tell you how grateful we are for your generosity. I hope many generations of music students will have reason to bless you in time.'

Liam and Cathy excused themselves soon after nine. They left with many hugs and promises to come up to Dublin soon to see the changes to the Academy. But Johnny hung back. While Aoife and Ellen cleared up, the two men took themselves into the sitting room with their glasses of red wine.

'So, what was the second thing you had to tell me?'

'Second what?'

'You were going to talk to me about two things on Christmas Eve but you only managed to talk about the Academy,' Johnny reminded Seamus.

'Ah yes. I'm clearly going senile. I just thought you might like to hear some news that was passed on to me. Julia Delaney is now living in England. She's joined the City of Birmingham Symphony Orchestra and she's teaching too. She moved there in the spring with her daughter Imogen.'

'Why would I want to hear that?'

'Well, I just thought that she can't have many friends in England and you can't be that far away, and you might like to see her. For old times' sake.'

'She won't be short of friends for long and, anyway, she has a husband.'

'Well, she's still married, it's true, but she walked out on the insurance man a year ago now.' Seamus paused and watched Johnny's face but it betrayed no emotion of any sort. 'Christie Delaney told me that it's never been much of a marriage and that she's never been happy with him. That's why she's left home - to get far away from him.'

'Well, I hope she makes a new life for herself and her child, and I hope she's happy. But I doubt she'd want to see me after all this time.'

'Well, I just thought you might like to know.'

Chapter 37 – September 1971

Cathy was sitting on Mermaid Beach, theoretically reading her book. In the field behind, Liam and Erin were assessing two of the beef herd as potential entrants to the Ballinasloe Fair next month. For years, Cathy had watched preparations for this annual agricultural shindig and two years ago, she suggested the family go and have a day out there. Erin had immediately become obsessed by entering some of their own animals into the competition. Last year, she had shown two sheep and come away with a third-prize rosette for the ewe but, this year, she had persuaded Liam that they should be showing their beef and that a prize would help him sell the beast for a higher price. She was very canny for a fourteen-year-old.

Cathy stared out to sea. She could make out some dolphins arching over the waves and the gulls swooped over the scene. Such tranquillity. And yet, not that many miles north-east of Cleggan, dreadful violence was raging over the border. The British Army, with their armoured vehicles and enforced curfews, had turned Ulster into a war zone. Pubs and police stations were being bombed and people were dying, civilians as well as soldiers, police and paramilitary forces. Cathy could hardly bear to read about it and Liam refused to discuss it at all. All violence sickened him. Her father had wanted a united Ireland but would he have wanted to see such carnage? She doubted it. And yet it had all started with people trying to march peacefully for their civil rights, honourable protests all, but exploited by those who wanted to see conflict. It was the same in America. The Civil Rights Movement there, that Bill was working so hard for, had been met with violence too – Dr Martin Luther King himself had been assassinated a couple of years before. Despite this, African Americans had mostly maintained a peaceful stance and had been rewarded with the passing of the Civil Rights Act. The Official IRA preached peaceful resistance too but the Provos were intent on a fight. It was all keeping Bridie extremely busy, though even she would have to slow down for a few weeks when her baby was due.

Cathy glanced at her watch. Time to make her way back up to the farmhouse, Bernie would be phoning in half an hour. As she passed by her husband and daughter half a field away, she waved and gesticulated where she was going. Liam and Erin would be happy out there for hours yet.

The phone rang at dead on three o'clock; Bernie never let her down.

'How are you, Cathy, love? Getting ready for autumn?'

'It's lovely here today. Just hanging onto the coat-tails of summer, touch wood.'

'Well, I'm already into my autumn wardrobe which is much chicer than summer dresses. Nothing fashionable about sweating, is there?'

Cathy laughed. The idea of having separate wardrobes of clothes for each season was hilarious. She either took off a cardigan or added a second.

'Listen Cathy, I finally have some news for you about Liam's family.'

Bernie had stopped talking about getting to the bottom of Liam Molloy's origins ages ago and Cathy had assumed the trail had gone dead.

'I'll leave it up to you whether you tell him, or how much to tell him,' said Bernie, 'but I now understand why we found it so hard to trace any Molloys in Cork, or the right Molloys. My man, Conor, from *The Echo* found the record of Liam's father's death very easily, in 1924 as you said, but then his mother seems to disappear. There's no death recorded in Cork or any second marriage. He trawled through all the archives for about ten years after Liam was sent to Letterfrack. Nothing. Complete blank. But then a couple of years ago, someone else at *The Echo* was covering a story about an eighty-three year old man who had died in Cork jail. This man had murdered his wife and been sent down in 1928 and had never been released. Are you still with me, Cathy?'

'I think so. But what does an old convict have to do with Liam?'

'Hang on. I'll get there. This other Echo reporter came over to Conor and said 'weren't you looking for a Molloy story for years?' and Conor said yes and the guy said 'Is this of any interest?' It was a copy of *The Echo* from 1928, with the original story about the murder that this old prisoner Donegan had committed. It told how he had murdered his wife, Colleen, by throwing her down the stairs and that the neighbours had heard the argument. They'd rushed in to find Donegan, blind drunk, standing over his wife's body and boasting about how he'd given her what she had been asking for. A confession effectively. But at the very bottom of the article was this one sentence: 'Mrs Colleen Donegan was also known by the name Mrs Colleen Molloy.''

'What does that mean?' Cathy wasn't sure she was following it all properly.

'Well, it's just a theory, but was Liam's mother called Colleen? Conor thinks that this Colleen didn't actually marry Donegan but she got buried under his name which is why we can't find a female Molloy death of the right age to be Liam's mother.'

'Well, maybe he'll remember his mother's name... if I think it's a good idea to ask him at all. He's never mentioned it. But what good would it do, Bernie? Surely it would just break his heart to think that his mother ended up getting murdered by a drunken sot she'd shacked up with after his father died when he'd been sent off to Letterfrack.'

'Two reasons, I think. Firstly, you told me he was devastated that his mother sent him back to St Joseph's after he escaped, even though she must have known how desperate he was to run away. But if she was dead she couldn't have.'

Cathy pondered this. 'Okay. I see that it might help. But who did send him back then? They told him his mother had ordered it.'

'Oh Christ, Cathy, they just make it all up to suit themselves. I doubt the Gardai even bothered to try and find his mother to ask her, but, if he had, I'm sure he would've found that she was already dead, murdered by this Donegan bastard.' Bernie sounded triumphant.

'I'll have a think, Bernie. Liam has always been very much against digging up his past, even when it comes to exposing St Joseph's, you know.'

'Well, there's another reason. When the Garda came and arrested Donegan, they found a new baby in a crib upstairs. They took this baby and gave it to the nuns at Bessborough convent. This convent is famous for arranging adoptions for the children of unmarried mothers so it makes sense that they would have found a home for a totally motherless baby with a murderer for a father.'

'I guess so.'

'Conor tried to get hold of records for a baby Donegan born in 1928 from the convent but has met with great resistance. But if Liam made a case for why he should be granted access to those records it might mean he could trace his half-sister.'

'A sister? Oh heavens, Bernie, I can hardly take all this in.'

'I know. But his sister should still be alive. She's ten years younger than Liam. She might be living in Cork or Galway, who knows? She might even be over here in America because I know the nuns sent a load of babies over to the States to good Catholic families. She could be living here in New York as we speak, mother of a good Irish family, or she might be in Boston cooking spaghetti with an Italian family. As long as the adopters were Catholic, the nuns didn't care. But we'll never know unless Liam says he wants to dig deeper.'

There was silence on the other end of the line before Cathy spoke again. 'Well, I'm really grateful to your contact, Conor, for putting so much effort in for so long. And thank you to you too, Bernie, for keeping the flame alive. But I'll have to have a serious think about what it all means before I raise it with Liam.'

'I understand, Cathy. But you know that secrets are usually better out than in. It'll cause Liam some anguish for a short time - no question - but then I think it will ease the worries that have been gnawing away at him for years.'

'You're probably right, Bernie. But the only thing that would really bring him peace is to see St Joseph's shut down.'

'How can that not have happened yet? I thought the Kennedy Report last year had advocated that the whole system be binned.'

'It did, and two schools closed immediately. But St Joseph's is still spewing out its evil.'

'Jesus Christ. Come on, Ireland. Get your skates on.'

******

Cathy took a week to think things through after Bernie's phone call, imagining all the scenarios that Bernie's collection of facts might support. Mostly, she agonised over how this revelation would affect Liam. Cathy woke in the middle of the night; the full moon was shining strongly through the curtains onto Liam's dear face, deep in sleep. It was increasingly rare that he would wake to tell her he had had a disturbed night of lurid nightmares about St Joseph's, but the poison was still inside him. Would this news heal or open up old wounds? That consideration aside, surely, he was owed whatever facts were out there. He was entitled to know about his mother and keeping it a secret would only insert a tiny wedge between them, which was the last thing Cathy wanted or Liam needed.

The next Sunday, Erin was with Aoife and Ellen, helping out in the cottage's garden.

'Will you come for a walk with me to the beach?' Cathy asked Liam as he sat reading the Sunday papers.

'Are you asking me out on a date?'

'If you like. Let's have a swim.' Cathy couldn't remember the last time they had swum together without Erin splashing around them.

The sea in September was as warm as it ever got. The two of them dived and floated and held each other above the waves before collapsing onto the sand, wrapped in towels.

'Do you remember the first time I brought you here, for your first swimming lesson?'

'How could I forget? Isn't that how it got its name? You called me your mermaid.'

'I did. And I made love to you, not thinking for one second that you loved me back, just that you were giving me a bit more of your magic 'therapy' that I was so grateful for.'

'That's because I was keeping how much I loved you a secret. I was hiding the truth, from myself as much as from you.'

Liam grabbed Cathy and kissed her. 'Well, I'm not going to make love to you on the sand today, not when we have a comfy bed two fields away. Outdoor sex is for young people.'

'And animals.'

Liam laughed. 'Humans are just animals, though I've never seen any animal be as violent or as cruel as I've seen humans be.'

They sat in a close embrace watching the infinite waves shush onto the glittering sand for several minutes before Cathy spoke.

'You know Bernie rang last Sunday? Well, she gave me some news to pass on to you. I've been worrying about telling you but, in the end, I think you have a right to know, and I hate keeping anything from you.' She calmly related all that Bernie had told her, including the fact that there had been a baby, a half-sister, who might still be alive somewhere in the world. Liam was silent the whole time she was speaking and his hold on her shifted not an inch. When she had finished, Cathy turned to look at him. He was looking out to sea but there were tears in the corner of his eyes ready to roll.

'So, what do you think? Can you remember your mother's name? And if you think this Colleen woman was her, do you want Bernie and her Cork man to keep looking for your sister?'

Liam kissed Cathy's cheek. 'My darling macushla, thank you for telling me. Yes, my mother was called Colleen, so it's likely this person is indeed her. It's a sort of relief to hear that it was not my mammy who sent me back to that hellhole, but it hurts more that the reason she didn't was that she had been killed. Why do men kill women? It makes me so ashamed to be a man.'

'You've nothing to be ashamed of, my love. You've suffered so much at men's hands yourself that you could be forgiven for lashing out, but you've never lifted your hand to anyone. What do you think about tracing a possible sister?'

Liam hugged his wife tighter. 'Cathy Molloy, when you married me you were all the family I ever hoped for. Johnny was an extra gift and I tried to be the father that he deserved. Then you gave me Erin. You and our children give me more happiness than I could ever have imagined possible when I was back, shivering in a bed in Letterfrack, waiting for some Brother to make use of my scrawny body. More happiness than I have a right to. I bless every day that I wake up and find you still next to me in my bed.' He stood and helped her up. 'Come on, let's get back home. I want to make love to you in our big comfy bed before our little chicken gets back and causes mayhem.'

They didn't quite run, but they went upstairs the instant the back door was shut behind them, dropping their wet towels as they went. Liam peeled off Cathy's swimming costume, ran his hands over her cool, damp curves and urged her to sit on the edge of the bed so that he could sling her legs over his shoulders, as he knelt in front of her. 'You're as salty as a real mermaid, macushla. Is that you or is it the sea? Either way, I love the way you taste.'

Cathy cried out freely in ecstasy. She normally tried to contain herself when other people were in the house but, today, they were blissfully alone. And, in turn, Cathy, gave Liam's body just as much loving attention until he asked to enter her.

Afterwards, they lay stroking each other's bodies, with the sun streaming through the window.

'Your hands are much less rough than they used to be, you know.' Cathy fondled Liam's right hand while his other played with her long, wet hair.

'That's because I'm now a gentleman farmer and a seafood-business manager, not a fisherman. I can't remember the last time I hauled in a catch myself.'

'I think there's some way to go before you become a complete dilettante – and I would hate your hands to be completely smooth.'

'Your scar is almost invisible, you know.' Liam ran his finger along where Erin's caesarean birth had left its silvery line. 'I would hate that to disappear too. It's your battle scar, a battle you fought and won. It's how our child entered the world so it's precious to me.' He bent to kiss her belly.

'I reckon there are some benefits to getting a bit older, aren't there,' she whispered. 'No periods, no stupid rubber yokes and no worrying about a child walking in on us.'

'Whatever age we're blessed to reach together, I'll always worship you and your body.' He kissed her tenderly.

The back door crashed shut. 'I'm back,' came a cheerful voice from downstairs.

'Well, it was lovely while it lasted.' Liam got out of bed and got dressed. 'You have a nap while I go and make our chicken some tea.'

Chapter 38 - July 1972

Johnny carefully strapped his cello into the passenger seat of his red Alfa Romeo Spider and turned back to say goodbye to the porter. This was the last farewell he needed to say to anyone in Cambridge – the week had been packed with valedictory lunches, dinners and pub crawls. He had arrived there in 1964 as Johnny Ashfield and had enjoyed eight years of brilliant, intellectual stimulation, not to mention many affairs and huge fun, but he would arrive back in Ireland as Dr John Fitzgerald.

It had taken him two years of questioning and inner debate before he had made the decision to change his name. The notion had entered his mind as soon as the British Army had taken up residence in Northern Ireland after the 1969 riots. He could see there was violence coming from both sides but the only people who had a genuine grievance were the Catholics who were so discriminated against in the corrupt electoral system. If the British government really wanted to stop the fighting and weaken the Provos they just needed to move faster on the issue of civil rights.

Then, in 1970, his Auntie Shirley had finally married Kazik to become Mrs Dabrowski, which left Johnny the only Ashfield in his family. He wondered what significance the name held any more. What family did he belong to?

The previous August, eleven civilians had been shot in Ballymurphy as the Parachute Regiment started an operation to arrest suspected members of the Provisional IRA. Its excuse was that they had just been 'returning fire'. In December, the loyalist UVF had bombed the McGurk Bar in the Catholic area of Belfast, killing fifteen people, including two children, and injuring dozens more. The subsequent mendacious behaviour of the RUC and the British Army had been a disgrace in Johnny's opinion, blaming the IRA for detonating a bomb by accident for which there was no evidence whatsoever.

The final outrage that had crystallised Johnny's decision had come at the end of January. It had started as a peaceful civil rights march in Derry, protesting against internment without trial, but had ended up a bloodbath. The same British Parachute Regiment fired on unarmed marchers, killing thirteen people and injuring the same number again. They had shot at people fleeing and people tending the wounded. None of them had been armed. The tribunal that followed investigating the Bloody Sunday massacre had as good as whitewashed the British Army.

Johnny liked to think that his father, a man he had never known but whose memory he had always tried to honour, would forgive him for wanting to abandon his English surname and reclaim an Irish one. Everything Johnny had been told about Joe Ashfield spoke of a man who was a champion of the underdog. Well, the Irish were the underdogs right now – maybe always had been – and Johnny wanted to be part of them.

It would be a wrench leaving Cambridge. It was such an idyllic place, but it wasn't real and Johnny was ready for a spot of reality back home. In the spring, he had started applying for Irish university teaching jobs under his new name. It felt good. It wasn't just a rejection of his Englishness but a conscious embrace of all that the Fitzgerald name meant to him: his great-grandmother, his mother, the grandfather that he was named after, that he looked so like and whose cello he played. Maybe a dash of his Uncle Fergus and President Kennedy too. And the Fitzgerald Academy, of course. Johnny was extremely proud that his agitations had resulted in that admirable endeavour, now two years into its new identity enabling talented young musicians.

He had received job offers from Galway and Cork universities but had finally plumped for a position at University College, Dublin. Dublin was Irish enough for him and there were people there ready to welcome him and give him a home.

'Johnny! Welcome back. Get yourself inside and pour yourself a drink.' Bridie opened wide the door of her Merrion Square flat; she was holding her five-month old baby on her hip.

'This is your cousin Johnny, baby. Shake his hand. Go on. Ah, he'll get used to you, Johnny, in no time at all. He's a very placid child, very sweet-tempered like his Daddy. Thank God. I'm not sure I could have coped with a baby like me or Fergus, or your sister for that matter.'

Bridie deposited her baby on the rug where he proceeded to calmly chew his own foot. 'Isn't he gorgeous. I could eat him up.'

'So, it's all working out fine,' Johnny observed.

'Falling off a log, Johnny. I get a few funny looks and a few sneaky comments, more in Rowanbridge than here. But fuck 'em all. Me and baby Michael are just grand.'

'Who chose the name?'

'Just me. Hugo didn't care, he said. He's such a love. I wanted to call the babe Michael in memory of lovely Mikey Flynn as it seems Brendan and Dearbhla can only make girl babies.'

'So ... Michael Moran.'

'Michael Stephen Patrick Moran, to be precise. In memory of Father Stephen and Daddy.'

'And another member of the alliteration gang: Bridie Byrne, Fergus Fitzgerald and now Michael Moran.'

'It's cute isn't it. Actually, I now go by the name of Mrs Bridget Moran a lot of the time, except professionally. It gets me better service in shops and it saves me having to explain why I have a different name from my baby. Basically, I use whichever name suits the occasion best. Which is what you've done too, I guess.'

'Do you think I'm weird, changing my name like this.'

'Johnny, if you'd lived my life and done my job you would hardy think what you've chosen is odd in the slightest. I know your mama is half thrilled and half sad. But it's your choice in the end. It's who you want to be.'

'Thanks for letting me live here, Bridie, until I get myself fixed up. I'll be off to Cleggan in a week or so and not back until September to get ready for the term.'

'You can stay as long as you like, Johnny. It'll be nice to have someone else to hold baby Michael when I'm trying to cook. His nanny leaves as soon as I get in at night. We drive down to Rowanbridge pretty much every weekend to see his daddy and his Uncle Fergus so you'd have the place to yourself then. The pair of them dote on him, as you can imagine, and they've even taken him off my hands for a whole week when I had to go to Belfast for a case. If I wanted it, there's endless work up in the north, so many injustices are being committed. It's just horrifying and I get so blind with rage. Not the best frame of mind for a barrister really. But if I did get tempted to do more up in Belfast or Derry, I could leave Michael in Rowanbridge any time because the boys always have Aggie on hand to tell them what to do. She brought up all of us, just about.'

'Thanks. I won't rush into anywhere then, if that's okay. I'll not be able to look around properly until I'm back from Cleggan. You're in a great spot here.'

'Thanks to Aunt Lily. I wouldn't be living in Merrion Square without all the money she left me.' Bridie picked up Michael and plonked him on Johnny's lap. 'Here, best you two get to know each other properly.'

Johnny spent a rather tense week in Merrion Square with Bridie and baby Michael. He got himself out of the flat every morning soon after the nanny arrived and didn't return until he was sure Bridie was back home. But he made good use of his time, trudging through all of Dublin's sights like a tourist. He spent some time in Trinity Library. If he'd managed to get a job offer from there, Bridie's flat would be perfectly positioned, but University College was located in Belfield, to the south of the city. He went twice to familiarise himself with the UCD campus and the Mathematics Faculty buildings. Soon they would feel as much like home as Cambridge had done. The rest of his week he spent with his Uncle Seamus.

Seamus delighted in showing him around the newly configured Fitzgerald Academy – six new music rooms had been created - and introducing him to many of the students as someone who belonged to the Fitzgerald family whose name was now above the green front door. Seamus even persuaded Johnny to bring his cello one day to take part in the *Mendelssohn Octet* as they only had one cellist at the moment though two more would arrive as part of the next year's intake.

'You know, Johnny, you would be more than welcome to come and live in Nerano Road with me when you get back from Cleggan. A bit quieter, I'm guessing, than Bridie's household. You'd be a lot nearer UCD. I'd love it, of course. We could live the life of two crusty old bachelors, listen to music, play chess and golf, and drink whiskey before bedtime. Only until you find yourself a proper home, of course.'

'Thanks Uncle Seamus. I might just take you up on that offer.'

Chapter 39 - April 1973

It had been a very attractive flat near Belfield he'd looked over yesterday. Pretty much perfect for what he needed, thought Johnny: two bedrooms, small garden, no adjoining wall to the living room so he could play his instruments without worry, close enough to UCD to walk to work and a good price. But maybe he could do better. And he loved driving anyway. And it was rather nice to come home to find supper cooked and his Uncle Seamus there to share it with. But he would keep looking because it was crazy for a man of twenty-eight to be living with an old man.

Not that living with Seamus had stopped him having a girlfriend. That chemistry tutor he had spent the first three months of the year with, on and off, had her own house whenever they wanted to get into bed together, which turned out to be not often enough on Johnny's part, according to her. Ah well, the cricket season would start soon and that would keep him busy, in addition to weekly rehearsals of the Dublin Orchestral Players.

Seamus had roped Johnny into the Players as soon as he had returned to Dublin last September. Johnny hadn't expected to create a musical life as rich as the one in Cambridge but the fine amateur band turned out to be rather better than any group he had been part of in England. The previous December, his mama and sister had come to Dublin just to hear him in the Players' Christmas concert, a delightful mixture of Brahms' *Academic Festival Overture*, Bach's 5th *Brandenburg* and a Franck symphony. This Easter, the orchestra would be performing alongside two local choral societies in Mozart's Requiem and, afterwards, Beethoven's *Pastoral Symphony*. What a contrast, thought Johnny: from despair and death to light, life and nature, and all within two short hours. Only two more rehearsals until the concert which Cathy, Erin *and* Liam were coming over to Dublin for, before they all went back to Cleggan for Easter itself.

Johnny adored both pieces of music. The popular view of Mozart was that he had been an upbeat, witty, pleasure-seeking kind of guy, frivolous even at times, but his *Requiem* proved there was no profundity he had not experienced or could not express. Beethoven, on the other hand, was usually depicted as an irritable, anguished, misanthrope, raging against his encroaching deafness and angry at the world – with good reason - but his sixth symphony betrayed no sign of that. A thunderstorm was depicted in it, sure, but only one which gave way to sunshine. There was nothing trivial about joy. Johnny marvelled that a man with every excuse to be depressed could write such an uplifting symphony and weave pure happiness out of his tribulations. He found that very moving. But he also found that the *Pastoral* made him think of his home in Cleggan: the streams, the breezes, the rain, the bird-song. And the people too: Brendan and his daft dancing, Erin on her shepherd's pipe, his mama with her open and generous heart and Liam who had battled against terrible times and triumphed. He took his cello out of its case, tuned up along with the other strings, applied rosin to his bow and waited for the conductor to begin.

His desk partner arrived a little late and Johnny made more space for her. Something caught his eye on the other side of the stage. He looked over to the violins and saw someone take up a seat at the back of the firsts. A slim woman in jeans and T-shirt with dark hair cut close to her head. She wasn't a regular member of the Players and she was now hidden behind other players, but Johnny's pulse raced. Surely it couldn't be? Could it be Julia Delaney? He dismissed the thought - his mind was playing tricks on him – and tried to concentrate on the Beethoven.

When the rehearsal ended, he hardly dare stand up. He did not know whether he wanted the interloper to be Julia or not. Easier to leave it as a mystery maybe, but of course that was not possible with Seamus over in the front desk of violas. If it was Julia, she would hardly run away without speaking to her erstwhile benefactor.

Johnny watched as the woman packed away her violin and then walked over to Seamus to give him a big hug. No doubt about it now – it *was* Julia. Seamus must have said something to her about Johnny because she turned round to stare straight at him and then she slowly walked over to the cello section where everyone else was preoccupied collecting music or folding stands.

'Hello stranger. This is a bit of a shock.'

'I know. For me too. I thought you were in Birmingham.'

'And I thought you were in Cambridge.'

'Well, I was until last summer.'

'I've only just come back home. My daddy is getting on a bit and needs me here. And, frankly, I got a bit sick of all the jibes about blowing people up.'

'I know, so tedious isn't it.'

They both started to speak over each other, then laughed.

'You go first,' said Johnny.

'I was just going to say that I'm only here as a last-minute dep. The conductor was one of my tutors at the Academy. Just doing him a favour. Even Seamus didn't know I'd be here. But he did know I was coming back to Dublin – did he not tell you?'

'He never said a thing. Though he had told me you and your husband had separated.'

'Ah, that's a long story. I'll tell you some time, Johnny. But I have to dash now. My little girl is with her granddad and God knows what havoc they'll have wreaked.'

'Are you still in Finglas?'

'Oh yeah, same old shitty house.'

'Well, maybe you'd like to go for a drink sometime, for old time's sake.'

'That'd be nice. Give me your number.'

'I'm living with Seamus in Dalkey, so you'll have it.'

Julia laughed. 'Good God, that's … that's amazing. He didn't tell me that either. I'll call you. Soon. I promise.'

And then she ran out of the Concert Hall.

Johnny waited for a phone call on Monday, and on Tuesday and on Wednesday. On Thursday, he casually asked Seamus if he had Julia's phone number and Seamus handed it over without a comment, but with a searching look that made Johnny uncomfortable. Why had not Seamus told him Julia was coming back to Dublin? He desperately wanted to know but there was no way he was going to ask directly.

Christie Delaney picked up the phone. 'Hello, Delaney here.'

'Hello, Mr Delaney. How are you? It's Johnny Fitzgerald – Johnny Ashfield as was. Do you remember me?'

'Oh yes. How can I help you?'

'Is Julia there?'

'She's upstairs, putting Imogen to bed.'

'Sorry, don't disturb her then. But could you ask her to ring me please? She knows where to find me.'

'Right you are. Goodnight now.' The phone went dead.

Seamus took himself off to bed at ten. Johnny sat by the phone, trying to read a book, checking from time to time that the receiver was firmly on the cradle. He nearly jumped out of the chair when the phone eventually rang at twenty-to-eleven.

He let it ring twice before picking it up; he didn't want to sound too desperate.

'Hello.'

'It's Julia. Sorry not to ring until now, Johnny. There's a lot happening what with the move. I'm settling into the new job at the RTÉ orchestra, and doing some teaching, and Imogen had to go and look at some new schools. You know how it is.'

'I can imagine.' There was a pause. 'Actually, that's bullshit. I've no idea how hard it must be to be a single parent and look after your father and do two jobs like you do, Julia.'

Julia laughed. 'You've always had the easy life, Johnny, but that's not your fault. Anyway, when are we going for this drink? I'd like to stay and chat now but I need to get to bed to be honest.'

'Name your day.'

'Tomorrow, yeah?'

'Marvellous. I'll pick you up in Finglas. Say ... eight o'clock?'

'Fine. Johnny ... is this a date date?'

Johnny swallowed hard. 'If you want it to be.'

'Night night.'

The car instantly filled up with the smell of roses when Julia got in it on the Thursday evening. She was wearing a denim skirt, thick black tights and a leather jacket and she had definitely put on some make-up.

'Hi there. This is fun. Such a lot to catch up on. You actually look quite grown up, Johnny, with your hair short. I think it's ten years since we talked to each other, you know.'

'It's nine. Almost to the day. You look exactly the same.'

'Ha! I found a grey hair the other day, and my tits are a bit droopy. Babies, you know.'

Johnny smiled in the gloom of dusk. 'Where do you want to go? There's a nice pub I know down near Blackrock. Or I've brought a bottle of wine and a bag of crisps so we could go out to Dollymount - like old times.'

'Yes, let's do that. That'll be grand.'

They drove in silence until they had crossed the rickety bridge and were driving on the strand itself.

As soon as Johnny put the handbrake on, Julia opened the door and leapt out of the car. 'Come on out. It's a fine evening.' Johnny suspected that Julia didn't want to sit in the car alone with him.

They linked arms and started to stroll along the sand. The sky was cool and clear and the starry dots were prominent alongside a scant sliver of moon.

'You go first, yeah?' said Julia.

'Go first? At what?'

'Whatever it is you might want to say to me. If that's nothing, that's cool.'

'Okay.'

They walked on in silence for minute or two before Johnny had arranged his thoughts. He didn't want to sound in any way aggrieved or accusatory, even if he had felt like that over the years.

'It's wonderful to see you, Julia. I've really missed you and I thought about you often, even though I never got in touch when Uncle Seamus told me you'd left your husband. Because... because I thought that if you wanted that you would have contacted me. You were the one who sent me away all those years ago, remember? so I didn't think you cared that much about me.'

Julia said nothing but squeezed his arm harder.

'I've had loads of girlfriends over the last nine years,' he continued. 'Some of them were very nice and there was one I thought maybe I could make a life with. But, every time, I could only think of you and how far short they fell of what you were, what you are. I don't know exactly how to describe that, mind you. But it's special, special to me, anyway.'

'Oh, Johnny. I'm so, so sorry. I never thought that you would take so long to get over me.'

'Yeah, well. You seemed to get over me damn fast. You kept saying to me that you didn't want a boyfriend - because you wanted to devote yourself to your playing - and I took you at your word. But, within a month of sending me away, you had yourself a proper fella, I heard. So, you can't blame me for thinking it wasn't that you didn't want a boyfriend at all, more that you didn't want that boyfriend to be me. But whatever you did - when you fell pregnant and got married - it didn't change how I felt about you one jot. It's been a sort of curse but also like ... like a warm, glowing jewel that I've kept inside me. Jesus, I wrote so many poems about you. Whenever I played music, I would imagine you playing opposite me and you looking over and giving me one of your wicked smiles. I know this must all sound pathetic.'

'No, it doesn't. It sounds amazing. I wish I deserved all of your devotion.' Julia stopped walking, removed her arm from Johnny's and stood staring out to sea. The waves heaved and sighed in front of them.

'My turn. I did send you away, and I'm sorry about that, Johnny. It wasn't because I didn't want a boyfriend ... it was because I didn't want to fall in love. And I was falling madly in love with you, Johnny, and I could see that you were falling in love with me, but that was going to be a nightmare. Studying was the only way I was going to escape a dreary life that someone like me could expect. The life my mother had. I couldn't let love get in the way, but if I'd kept seeing you I wouldn't have been able to stop it.' She turned to look at him. 'Getting pregnant was just a stupid cock-up, pun intended. The Pope's methods of contraception are far from infallible, even if he is. Anyway, Dom agreed to marry me because there was no way I was getting rid of a baby. I'm still a good Catholic girl underneath, you know.' She laughed. 'And he's not a bad man and we tried to be happy together and when Imogen came along we managed to convince ourselves it would all work out. But it couldn't … because I've always been in love with someone else.'

Julia put her arms around Johnny and he encircled her in his and they kissed. Nine years of soft and sweet and hard and urgent kisses exchanged under the stars. They walked back to the car in passionate silence, the air around them taut with unspoken words. Once inside, Johnny opened the bottle of wine which they swigged, passing it from one to the other.

'So, there you have it,' Julia finally said. 'There's no way I'd expect you to be interested in me any longer, saddled with an eight year-old daughter and a rapidly aging father. But if we could be friends again and play music together that would be wond…' Johnny stopped Julia's mouth with a kiss.

'You can be such a stupid eejit, Julia Delaney.'

******

Seamus flung open the front door of the Nerano Road house and held his arms wide for Erin to run into them. She hugged him and then skipped down to the end of the hall to do the same to her brother which left Seamus's arms free for Cathy. Liam smiled and carried in their bags from the car. It was the weekend before Easter and the Molloys had arrived en masse to attend the concert of the Dublin Orchestral Players that evening.

'Come in, come in. Johnny and I have made lots of sandwiches and there's cake too. We'll get you all a cup of scald.' Seamus gesticulated to Johnny to go and make the tea.

'Well, it's nice to be entertaining you all for a change. Only for the one night I know, but it's a start. Erin, you will really love the Beethoven because there's a very important section for the flutes. See if you can spot it.'

'She's getting on really well now she's put her mind to it, aren't you, poppet?' said Cathy.

'It's fine. I like it. But I'm not giving up the whistle. Me and Brendan do lots of the songs together that he and Mikey used to do and we sometimes let Daddy play his guitar with us. He's not that good but he's trying.'

'You cheeky monkey,' laughed Liam. 'Aoife and Ellen are thrilled that you're coming to Cleggan for Easter, Seamus,' said Liam, pouring himself some tea. 'You don't usually brave the west until the summer. Maybe you're getting a taste for the Atlantic after all.'

'I have a taste for all the dear souls there. That's what it is. And the golf is more than adequate too, I suppose. Listen up, there will be someone there tonight playing in the orchestra whom you haven't seen for quite a while: Julia Delaney. So, don't look surprised to see her or she'll think I've forgotten to tell you.'

Cathy looked over at Johnny but he was preoccupied cutting up a fruit cake. 'I thought she'd moved to England after she separated from her man.'

'She did but she's decided to come back home. Christie needs a bit of looking after and she managed to get herself into the RTÉ orchestra so that's all grand, isn't it? She's only playing tonight as a favour; we must be way below her standard. She turned up to rehearsal two Sundays back, quite out of the blue. We were both rather shocked, weren't we Johnny? But in a good way.'

The chat turned to the Academy and how things were progressing and a discussion of which were the most promising students. Cathy kept looking at her son. Now she understood. He had rung her yesterday to say that he wouldn't be driving over to Cleggan until Good Friday; he needed to attend to some department matters, but that Seamus was asking to come for a couple of weeks straight after this weekend and was that all okay. Sly bugger, she thought. She knew why now. She was his mother after all.

'Right then, make yourselves at home. Johnny and I need to get changed and over to the Concert Hall for a brief rehearsal before tonight. You know where to come to, don't you, Cathy, and the tickets are there on the mantelpiece.'

The three Molloys were in their seats fifteen minutes before the concert was due to begin. Cathy enjoyed watching the Dublin bourgeoisie walk in and fill up the hall; she thought she recognised a few people. She didn't get to go to many sophisticated concerts like this one anymore, though last week they had put on a really fun evening at Ballinasloe Hospital where she had conducted the choir and mixed ability band in a variety of songs. Johnny would have been delighted that they had included *Yellow Submarine* and *Hey Jude* and the whole audience had joined in. But they had ended the evening with her own arrangement of the *Ode to Joy*. She reckoned that Beethoven would have been astonished to hear his music played by a hospital band that included a saxophone, a harmonica and a drum kit but she thought he would have been pleased. It was certainly joyful.

'Now, you two, don't clap until I do,' she whispered to Erin and Liam, both totally ignorant of the etiquette of concert-going. 'The first piece is like a mass, with different movements, but we don't clap until the very end. You can follow it in the programme here.'

The chorus filed into the back of the stage and the players started to take their seats. Impossible not to see Johnny with his golden head sticking above all the other cellists. And there was, Julia, looking as slim and waif-like as when Cathy had last seen her, dressed in a skimpy satin top, still with her dark, cropped hair. She scrutinised the pair of them as the orchestra tuned up. There were the glances back and forth. Oh yes, she knew all right.

Cathy had attended few masses since she had abandoned her faith forty years before, and those mostly at funerals, but the familiar texts in the Mozart *Requiem* were weirdly comforting, though she found the swaying *Lachrymosa* an almost overwhelming dance of grief.

'Can I have an ice cream now?' asked Erin when the interval came.

'No, poppet. It's not like the cinema. Read all about the *Pastoral Symphony* in the programme so that you can spot all the themes when they're played.'

After the darkness of the Mozart, Cathy let herself be filled with light by Beethoven. How unusual it was to have the composers this way round. When she played the piano, she was far more likely to turn to Mozart for a delightful lift and to Beethoven for some deep reflection. Cathy studied all the players, united in this wonderful performance. She looked at dear Seamus, her rock, on the front desk of the violas, and at Johnny, her beautiful boy, and at Julia, still a mystery to her in most ways but maybe not forever. Time would tell.

The applause was warm and lengthy at the end. The orchestra took several bows before leaving the stage.

'I heard the peasants dancing and the thunderstorm obviously, but I loved the birdsong on the flutes best. I'm definitely gonna practice hard so I can get to play this one day,' said Erin.

The three of them waited in the lobby for the orchestra members to appear and Seamus arrived first.

'I heard them, Uncle Seamus, I heard the birds on the flutes.'

Seamus laughed at Erin's excitement. It took several more minutes for Johnny to come out carrying his cello and a violin case. Trailing behind him was Julia, holding the hand of a young girl with a long, black plait of hair.

'Hello, Julia, how lovely to see you again.' Cathy gave Julia a kiss on the cheek.

'Nice to see you too, Mrs Molloy - Cathy. You haven't changed a bit.'

'Nor have you – apart from your daughter. I'm guessing this is her because she's the image of you.'

'She is.'

'Hello Imogen. I'm Erin. Wasn't the concert fun.'

******

'You didn't fool anyone you know, saying you had to stay in Dublin because you had work to do.' Julia and Johnny were sitting in the back garden at Nerano Road, the Tuesday before Easter, wrapped up warmly against the cool April air and staring up at the full moon as they drank their red wine.

Johnny laughed. 'I don't care to be honest. They'll all know soon enough because I am not letting you out of my sight from now on, but it was sweet of Seamus to leave the house for us this week so we can have a bit of time alone together.'

'You're full of shit, Johnny Fitzgerald, because I shall be out of your sight when you go off to Cleggan on Friday.'

'Come with me.'

'Erm … I don't think so. Unless you want me to bring Imogen and Daddy too. And for that you'll need to get a different car. You'll need a bigger one instead of that little tin can.'

'Tin can? The cheek! My beautiful Spider, I'll have you know, is my trusty bachelor-mobile.'

Tonight was the first time they'd been able to make use of the house. Imogen was staying over with Julia's brother and his family.

'Shall we go in? It's getting a bit chilly out here.'

'We should go in, I guess, but I'm scared.' Julia took Johnny's hand as they left their seats.

'Scared? What are you scared of?' Johnny gave Julia a peck on the cheek before locking the French windows behind them.

'Because now we're inside, we'll go upstairs and then we'll take our clothes off and get into bed and have sex.'

'You're scared of that? I thought that's what you wanted, love. But look, if you don't want to do it – if you're not ready - we don't have to.' He took her in his arms. 'I've waited nine years to see more than your feet totally naked and to kiss every part of you – not just your feet - and to make love to you. I can wait as long as you need. How about I just read you some of my poems? That should make you beg for sex.'

Julia laughed and kissed him. 'I'm desperate to do it, you know I am, but what if you hate the look of me or our bodies don't work together or you wish you'd stuck with one of those other women.'

'Well, we'll never know until we try, will we? But if something doesn't work quite right we can fix it. We know that the bits that really matter, the bits inside us, *do* fit together. Your sharp and spiky bits fit into my soft and squashy parts – perfectly.'

Julia took Johnny's hand and led him to the bottom of the stairs, 'Come on then, mister. Let's do it.'

Chapter 40 - July 1974

Cathy and Liam stood outside the tall wrought-iron gates, now bound up with a chain and padlock, staring at the empty building at the end of the path.

'That's it, love. It's gone. No more St Joseph's. Time to celebrate.' Cathy turned to look at Liam.

Liam couldn't answer; he started to pace up and down the road outside the school, glaring over the low wall.

'It took long enough,' he said. 'Four years since the Kennedy Report. How many more boys were beaten in those four years - or worse?' Suddenly, he did a handspring over the wall into the empty field and held out his hand to Cathy. 'Come on over, macushla.'

Cathy sat on the wall and swung her legs over. 'What are you doing?'

Liam didn't answer. He took Cathy's hand and marched up to the front door, gave it two angry kicks and then led her round to the back of the empty school, then through to the overgrown garden until they came to a thicket of bushes.

'Here. I think it was here.' He pointed to a slight mound in the scrubby grass. 'Little Bernard's grave, I mean. I can't be sure but I came here so often back then that I think it was here, under this tree.' He searched around in the hedge and found two sticks. Then he used some couch grass to bind them into a cross which he stuck in the ground. 'I must have made twenty or more of these, all removed by a bastard Brother. But this one's going nowhere.'

She took his arm. He was looking intently at the patch of ground. Was he praying maybe?

'You've chosen to mark it with a cross, even though his death was the fault of the Brothers?'

'Just habit. To be honest, even if I believed in God, I wouldn't blame him. This was human depravity.'

'We could find some stones instead to mark the spot. Or some shells maybe? Maybe they'll discover other bodies here and bury them all properly in time.'

He moved from Bernard's presumed resting place and searched under the hedge, returning with a fallen tree branch; then he marched through the garden and up to the back of the school. Cathy followed behind. There was a loud crash followed by another one and then another as Liam smashed three lower windows with the branch.

'Stop, Liam!' She ran to him and grabbed his arm but he shook her off.

'Leave me be! That's for Bernard, and that's for Mikey, and one for Brendan too. And this…' he heaved the branch right through a fourth window, '… is for me.'

Cathy was alarmed. She had seen him angry before but she had never seen him express it in such a violent and visceral way.

'I'd like to burn it to the ground, and all the evil with it,' he shouted. Then he stepped back from the school, wiped his face with his sleeve and sank to the ground.

Cathy knelt down and put her arms around him. 'I know, I know. But it's over now, my love. It's finished. Let's go home.'

******

A week later, Cathy was in the drawing room playing the piano, the French windows open to the sunny afternoon breezes coming off the Atlantic. Liam and Erin were out doing their daily inspections of all the animals out in fields. It took them more than an hour to walk the round and that was if all was well. Sometimes she would go with them but it was also good to have a little time to herself. The house would be bursting with all her siblings and their families taking their annual break in Cleggan soon enough. She couldn't wait to meet the latest baby, Lily Moran, just two months old. Bridie reported that it was almost impossible to wrench baby Lily out of someone's arms – Hugo's, Aggie's or Fergus's – in order to get back up to Dublin at the end of the weekend so Cathy would have to fight to get a cuddle. Fergus and Hugo doted on their family. They had already bought the smallest available hurley for toddler Michael.

Rose and Sam's kids were all grown-up now and Kevin even had a serious girlfriend so this was probably the last time he'd come with the family for a holiday. He was busy working with his parents in the pub and shop, whereas eighteen-year-old Thomas was much more academic and would be off to Galway university in the autumn to study geography. Cathy hoped that they would get to see plenty of Thomas then. And delicate, dreamy Joanna, just a year younger than Erin, was great mates with her cousin, despite being so different. They shared a passion for lambs and kittens.

Cathy picked up her volume of Beethoven Sonatas. She had mastered all of them but there were two that she returned to again and again. She couldn't resist the gentle swaying opening of No 15, the *Pastorale Sonata*, and the third variation movement of No 30 was so exquisitely intimate it felt right to play it only when she was alone. She loved the dramatic changes of mood in Beethoven. Like the sky over the farmhouse, the music could change from sunny to stormy and back again in a moment. It was all very well playing for her own pleasure but she needed to brush up the *Archduke Trio*; Julia, Johnny and Imogen were arriving tomorrow.

When Cathy had seen Johnny and Julia playing together in the *Pastoral Symphony*, she had known that they were still in love after so many years apart but, if she had needed more proof, the fact that Johnny would be driving them to Cleggan tomorrow in a roomy BMW, having dumped his Alfa Romeo, was proof enough. Johnny had also bought a sensible Victorian semi in Dalkey, not that far from Seamus, and Julia, Imogen and Christie had moved out of the Finglas house in February to join him. It was convenient for the two afternoons a week that Julia spent teaching at the Fitzgerald Academy and Christie had retired from An Post, so he could live anywhere, dividing his time between his daughter's and his son's homes.

The chances of Julia getting a divorce were very slim but she seemed happy to live with Johnny as man and wife, despite being 'a good Catholic girl' as she still called herself. She kept her old wedding ring on and she had always kept the name Julia Delaney for professional purposes so it wasn't too hard to bluff her way with anyone who needed it.

Cathy suspected that Auntie Stasia was a teeny bit scandalised about the situation with Julia and Johnny though, in fairness, Auntie Stasia had coped with all the unconventional family relationships over the years; she had learned to turn a blind eye. What would Stasia make of the latest news? Julia was four months pregnant. Johnny had phoned his mother two weeks ago but sworn her to secrecy. They weren't going to tell Imogen just yet, not until the bump showed. Cathy had, of course, wept joyfully down the phone to an equally ecstatic Johnny. Only later did she wonder what surname they would give the baby, but she knew better than to annoy her son with such a bourgeois concern. Cathy was sure that Erin would be happy to pass on Tiny Ted to the baby.

What sort of father would Johnny be? He had spent the first seven years of his life with no father at all and then he had been forced to accept a stepfather – but what a stepfather. At Easter, Cathy had overheard Liam and Johnny discussing what was appropriate for Johnny to do and say to Imogen as her quasi-stepfather. Liam had never put a step wrong. He was a man so attuned to a child's needs and desires that Johnny couldn't have had a better role model.

Cathy couldn't quite believe that she would be a grandmother soon. The word evoked her own grandmother, the straight-backed, unsentimental and strict Letitia Fitzgerald who had melted in her grand-daughter's company, although Cathy was nothing like her granny. She had the merest dusting of silver in her hair and she could still do a hand-stand.

That would have to do, thought Cathy, closing the piano lid. There was something she wanted to sort out upstairs before tomorrow. She wandered up to her bedroom and took her box of memories from the floor of the wardrobe. She hadn't opened it for years and the last thing she had put in it was Mam Ashfield's recipe book. The piece of cream wool that had been tied around Máire's lock of hair glittered with sand that had spilled out of a whelk shell collected on her first visit to Cleggan. There it was, the thing she had come for: the ring box holding her mother's emerald ring. She wanted Julia to have it. She hoped Julia would accept it but she would give it to Johnny first and it would be his decision to offer it or not, not quite an engagement ring but a token of something real and deep.

Cathy had also decided to offer Julia her mother's violin, which had sat unused for decades on top of their wardrobe. She didn't think she needed to ask Johnny's permission to do this. She had always been told that it was a very special and expensive instrument and Julia would know either way. Cathy wanted to hear Hannah's violin and her father's cello being played together again. That would be really special but, if the violin turned out not to be high quality, maybe Imogen could use it or an Academy student. Cathy reached up, took the violin case from the top of the wardrobe and blew the dust off. She couldn't resist opening it to gaze at the instrument her mother had been able to coax magic from. She gently ran her fingers along the strings and picked up the bow. The little rosin box revealed a strange piece of barnacle shell hiding inside. It was worn down to a thin white ring. It must have meant something important to Hannah, so Cathy picked it out before closing the violin case.

Then she slipped the ring into her pocket and was about to close the memory box's lid when she spied the folded paper at the bottom of the box. She knew exactly what it was. She took out the page of poetry and unfolded it: *A Prayer for My Daughter* with her father's heart-breaking farewell note to her written around the edges. Her daddy's own words were burnt into her. She didn't need to read the note to recall them, but she re-read the Yeats poem with care. John surely had not meant every line of the poem to apply to her directly. No, he would have been only too happy to see that she had grown into a woman with opinions. It was true that she had '*been granted beauty*' and '*not overmuch*' and that she was '*chiefly learned*'. Her bridegroom, whom her father had loved too, had indeed brought her '*to a house Where all's accustomed*' but maybe not very ceremonious. She hoped she did display '*natural kindness and … heart-revealing intimacy*'; she certainly always tried hard to.

Cathy was drawn to one passage in particular:

> '*May she become a flourishing hidden tree,*
> *That all her thoughts may like the linnet be,*
> *And have no business but dispensing round,*
> *Their magnanimities of sound…*
> *If there's no hatred in a mind,*
> *Assault and battery of the wind,*
> *Can never tear the linnet from the leaf.*'

The magnanimities of sound, through all the music she had heard and played, had certainly blessed her life. Music brought love, joy, inspiration, solace and healing to everyone it touched, as it had done for her mother and father. But there had been hatred, no question – impossible not to hate Letterfrack School and the Christian Brothers who had inflicted such pain. Her Daddy had hated them too and he would have been as overjoyed as Liam to see it closed down.

She folded the page, kissed it and placed it in the box, which she returned to the bottom of the wardrobe. Could her mother and father have ever foreseen what their children would make of their lives? that there were seven beautiful grand-children and now a great grand-child on the way? that there was now a Fitzgerald Academy nurturing young musicians? They would have rejoiced that Ireland had confronted the shocking state of their reformatory schools but they would have been saddened by a still divided and troubled island.

She went to the bedroom window and opened it wide to let in the summer air. It faced due west where the sun was just beginning to dip in the sky and would eventually bathe the farmhouse in golden light before sinking into the sea. She hoped her parents would approve of what she had done with her life. Nothing as glamorous as Bernie over the Atlantic or as dramatic as Bridie in the courtroom but many small achievements: a shell saved; a sonata mastered; a stone skimmed; a wound stitched; a baby fed; a poem taught; a loaf baked; a lad comforted; a graze bathed; a rose planted; a patient healed; a kite flown; a man kissed. What was life but the accumulation of these small triumphs.

Cathy watched Liam and Erin open the gate out of the field, heading for the farmhouse, laughing together as they strode across the grass. She thought to call out to them but stopped herself.

They would come home to her soon enough.

The End

Post-script

While the main characters and storyline of *The Pastoral Symphony* are entirely fictional, they are set against a backdrop of real historical events in Ireland between 1951 and 1974. St Joseph's Industrial School in Letterfrack and the fate of its pupils is, shockingly, one of the factual elements, including the tragic life of Peter Tyrrell. You can read his own account of life at Letterfrack School in his book, *Founded on Fear*. In 2003, the 71 year-old Brother Maurice Tobin was sentenced to 12 years in prison for his behaviour at Letterfrack School, some of which he had pleaded guilty to. The school buildings today, more happily, house the National Centre of Excellence for Furniture Design and Wood Technology, one campus of the Galway-Mayo Institute of Technology.

BV - #0012 - 050821 - C0 - 216/140/24 - PB - 9781914424090 - Matt Lamination